The Emerald Orchid

by Harold Koopowitz
© 2017

Cover art by Deborah Shaw and Steve Gollis. Image of Thai sword by kind permission of Michael Backman Ltd, London, UK. Image of *Paphiopedilum rothschildianum* by author.

ISBN 9780991276134

Orchid Digest Corporation 2017

This book is dedicated to all the good people of the world who fight the tough fight for the survival of wild orchid species and face increasingly difficult odds as the world's climate changes.

These many people include:

Peter Tobias of the Orchid Conservation Alliance and its Membership

Michael Fay who leads the Orchid Committee of the Species Survival Commission for the IUCN

and

Alejandra (Alex) Quinones Allen only now starting off on her brave journey for saving species for the American Orchid Society

Table of Contents

Cast of Characters

George – Biology Professor

Matilda – George's loving wife

William – George's laboratory assistant and long time friend

Jake Seemore – Security Agent for Tylo and Associates, and William's boyfriend

Great-aunt Bertha – Matilda's adoptive relative

Wie Wee – one of Bertha's many men

Paul Tylo – CEO of Tylo and Associates

Vicknes bin Osman – A really nasty type

Max Fiercely – Nerd at Microbotics

Jennifer Pandit – Security Agent for Tylo and Associates who works at Microbotics

Brian Kim – Engineer at Microbotics

Beryl White – Tylo's former office administrator.

Grace Mposa – Security Agent for Tylo and Associates, Penang

SCORE Members

Charles Guildenhuis – CEO of Swansdown Cosmetics, President of SCORE

Phillipa Madison – CEO of *Fashion Digest Magazine*

Morris Quicker – Hedge Fund Manager

Hillary Herschel – Wife of an Automobile Manufacturer

Boris Prokov – Russian Entrepreneur

Willis Formby – Successful Clothing Designer

Happy Forrester – Famous Romance Novelist

Melinde Berser – Movie Producer

Horace Terkhamian – Plastic Surgeon

Southeast Asia Characters

Soh Fat – Manages a Safe House

Jimmy Blakely – Would be spy

Rosalie Hernandez – Jimmy's girlfriend

Carlos di Sorrento – all round bad guy

Dr. Raymond Wong – Academician

Peter Wang – T & A Security Agent, Singapore

Kevin Ahmed – T & A Security Agent, Singapore

Charlotte – Kani's (Channarong Bunyasagaboon's) wife

Bunyarup (Buni) Sutakuliapoon – chief security officer at the Golden Lotus Hotel

Channarong Bunyasagaboon – known as Kani, he is also a Thai nursery proprietor

Several very bad Buddhist monks

Prologue

I really don't like Paul Tylo. I suppose he stands for everything for which I have little patience. He is a manipulator, driven by success in a way that levels or destroys anyone and everyone who stands in his path. The man is fabulously wealthy. His business, Tylo and Associates, is a multinational octopus with strangleholds in many countries. I can only think of one time when he met his match in another man. That incident was related to me, by the way, by Matilda's Great-aunt Bertha. She was, much to my disgust, an intimate confidant of Mr. Tylo.

Tylo's first wife Ester was, as to be expected, an exquisite beauty. Their marriage was the stuff that made the society pages hot reading for most of the nation. That is why after a few years, when Ester was seduced and ran away with a Thai warlord with the unlikely name of Vicknes bin Osman, it made major headlines around the world. Tylo eventually sued for divorce on the grounds of desertion. According to Bertha, however, his love for Ester never diminished, despite the fact that he did not waste any time finding a new bedmate for himself. Ester, apparently, disappeared into the harem of the warlord where she became desperately unhappy. It was reported that she tragically ended her own life. The warlord seemed unfazed by the loss of one of his beautiful women. He could afford to buy a replacement. Of course the papers made a hay of that as well.

Tylo swore revenge. He set out to learn all that he could about the warlord and promised himself that he would destroy whatever the man held most dear.

It turned out that there was little that this Vicknes bin Osman really treasured. There was, however, one thing and one thing only. Surprisingly it was a plant, a literally priceless, one of a kind, emerald green orchid…

Chapter 1 - A Family Meal

"Have you ever been to the island of Borneo?" Great-aunt Bertha asked.

We were seated around the dining room table on a sunny mid-afternoon enjoying our traditional Christmas dinner. Despite this being Great-aunt Bertha's home, I sat at the head of the table with Matilda, my beautiful wife, on my right. Great-aunt Bertha was on my left. William, our long-time, young friend sat next to Matilda and opposite him, but next to Bertha was Jake Seemore. Jake was young William's new fiancé. William worked with me at the University of California as my lab tech and was pretty good at his job. On the weekends he went up to Los Angeles where Jake was stationed. Jake worked in the security department for Tylo and Associates, a private multinational conglomerate. Security was very loosely defined. Many of his assignments seemed somewhat iffy to me, but for the sake of peace with William, I did not inquire too deeply about Jake's job. After all, Jake had saved Matilda and me several times on a recent trip to Africa. At the far end of the table was Matilda's cousin, Ernie. Ernie was in law enforcement but worked for the FBI. Jake and Ernie could talk with each other on certain levels. Bertha figured they might have something in common and had seated them next to each other. It was a small cozy group.

Matilda is the love of my life. I think she is absolutely gorgeous with blonde hair and a curvaceous figure. It does not hurt that she is stacked like the proverbial sex goddess. One of my associates looked at Matilda when I introduced them and turned around to me and said that obviously I was a breast man. I saw no sense in denying it. And it is a feature of Matilda's of which I am particularly fond. Today her silky hair was parted in the middle and hung straight to her shoulders. Her hair was spun gold with amber highlights. I could barely refrain from stroking it and I wanted to feel it floating against my face. But that is not all that Matilda is about. She is much more than my favorite sex object. She is my best friend and has a superior mind that I admire as much as I do her body. On top of that she is an accomplished athlete with a black belt in taekwondo and Olympic pretensions for skeet.

We all considered this a family dinner but there are no blood ties in our particular family. Sometimes the best families are not tied together by genes but by mutual love and understanding. Matilda is an orphan. She was adopted by Great-aunt Bertha after Bertha had gone through several husbands, had made a fortune in her own right and was still looking for meaning in her life. Bertha is quite elderly but no-one, not even Matilda, knows her true age. She could have been in her seventies or even her eighties. However, she is very spry and her narrow face is still unlined. Her mind is as sharp as the proverbial tack. She was wearing her hair dyed black and drawn into a tight bun at the nape of her neck. She sometimes reminded me of a famous lady who sat on the United States Supreme Court. She was dressed in a simple beige ensemble that showed off her slim figure. My guess was that the dress had been designed specifically for her and probably cost the equivalent of several months of my salary.

Bertha decided to honor Jake Seemore with the task of carving the large goose that Matilda had carefully stuffed and roasted. At first Jake tried to get out of the job claiming incompetence at meat carving, but Bertha would not hear of it. So, Jake stood up and walked over to the sideboard where the meat was laid out for carving. Jake tops six feet tall, about the same as me, but his shoulders are probably a little wider. He still spends a lot of his time in the gym pushing weights around. In the past his fitness had stood us in good stead. He has regular features, a small nose and a square chin, almost Hollywood facial features. I must admit that I like him. He is a good man, almost too good for William, who sometimes demands a lot of patience with his curious sense of humor and boyish enthusiasm. We had known William as a young teenager who eventually wriggled into our family and became Matilda's other best friend. He looks up to me as an older brother and I regard him as my younger sibling. However, I am also his boss. He works in my laboratory but our relationship there is strictly professional.

This was Jake's first meeting with Great-aunt Bertha and he was desperate to make a good impression. I must admit that I took an almost perverse delight in watching this normally very competent young man, looking at the goose in dismay. Matilda, who always seems to know what I am thinking, kicked me on the shins and I wiped the grin off my face.

As you no doubt know, even large geese have relatively little flesh on their bones. The large carcass is deceptive. Jake was obviously unsure of himself as he pondered the creature on the platter in front of him. Where to start? The bird was large and vaguely similar to a turkey. He had carved a Thanksgiving turkey before but the goose differed in that it was flat-breasted. With a turkey he knew how to cut slices off the breast.

Besides the goose there was also an enormous ham that the two men had contributed to the meal. William volunteered to deal with the ham and joined Jake at the sideboard. Standing alongside Jake, William looked like a slender teenager although he was close in age to Jake. His tousled curls are a sandy brown. He seems to change his hair all the time. At least it was not peacock blue this time and he no longer paints his nails black. I think he has finished with his Goth phase. William had the easier task because the ham had already been spirally cut by the butcher, and taking off slices was easy. The goose on the other hand was a challenge. How to deal with it?

"How do I handle this?" Jake whispered to William.

"Dunno. Just be grateful it's not a large roasted Easter bunny sprawled across the plate. They always look like a small dog that's been butchered."

Matilda, who has exceptionally sharp hearing, picked this up and took pity on Jake. He held the carving knife over the bird wondering where to cut first.

"Take the stuffing out first and pile it onto that empty platter next to it. Then it is easier if you cut the wings off the goose first," Matilda suggested. Matilda always takes food very seriously and knows how to do everything properly. "Use the poultry shears to dismember the wings," she said and then continued, "Instead of slicing into the breast right away, cut each breast off as one big lump, and then slice that cross ways into medallions. Then you can deal with the legs and thighs."

"Thanks," Jake replied and set about following her instructions. He transferred the sliced meat to a serving platter and William added the ham to one side of the same plate.

"George," Bertha turned to me. "Make yourself useful and pour the wine. The bottle has been opened long enough so it should be good to drink. It's a robust claret and should complement the goose. Ernie looks as if he is ready for something alcoholic." Ernie grinned in reply and held his glass out to me. I went around the table filling the glasses. Now I need to point out that there has always been a little tension between Bertha and me. Despite the fact that I am a tenured professor at a very respectable university, Bertha has made no bones that Matilda could have done much better for herself in the husband line. So I took the opportunity to point out to the Great-aunt. "You know there really is no such thing as a claret wine. It's really a red Bordeaux." I peered at the label. The wine came from Medoc, a famous wine producing area near Bordeaux situated on a piece of land jutting between Gironde River and the Atlantic.

"Of course George, everyone knows that the term 'claret' is used by the Brits to refer to red wines from the Bordeaux area. This particular one is an excellent blend of Cabernet and Merlot as most of these claret wines are."

Matilda was scowling at me.

Fortunately, before the Claret war could go any further, the two men brought the meat over to the table and we served ourselves, taking turns in passing the meat around, followed by stuffing, gravy and vegetables.

"You did a good job with the goose." Great-aunt Bertha complimented Jake who smiled in turn.

"Jake, you did a really creditable job on the goose. They are not easy to carve." Matilda agreed.

"Thanks, that was a first for me. Actually I have never eaten goose before. It looks quite good though perhaps a little more greasy than what I am used to."

"First time for me too," Ernie added. "Thanks for inviting me Bertha. This is a great meal."

"Well thank Matilda, she did most of the work."

12

"Matilda is an excellent cook," Jake added. "I know. She did all the cooking for us on our recent trip to Africa."

"Yes, I heard all about that from George and Matilda," Ernie said.

We all referred to him as cousin Ernie but he was not a blood relative to anyone at the table. Somehow Matilda had ensnared him into the group as well. Ernie had dark hair, bushy eyebrows and spoke with a Brooklyn twang. His large beak of a nose could have been described as Roman but he probably had no Italian genes in his makeup. We did not see him very often, but Matilda was always only too happy to greet cousin Ernie.

As the meal progressed everyone made small talk until Matilda turned to Great-aunt and asked, "What was your question about Borneo and why?"

We turned and focused on her.

"I am thinking of going there and wondered if any of you had travelled there before."

"Why do you want to go there?" Matilda queried. "Are you after some special orchid, again?"

"Not really. I received an invitation from SCORE, the Southern Californian Orchid Resource Exchange, to join them on a tour."

"Who are these people? I have never heard of them," William said, "and I thought I knew all the major local orchid organizations."

"I have heard of them," I said, "but don't know much about them."

Bertha looked at me as if my comment was what she expected from me.

"Tell us about the group," Matilda asked.

"It is a small group of very wealthy orchid enthusiasts dedicated to collecting and growing only the very best orchids in the world. It is an elite group and only twenty members are allowed at any one time – a play on words – SCORE also equals twenty."

"Ah, elitists, I can see why that appeals to you, but what does Borneo have to offer? You know it is illegal to collect orchids over there." I could not resist.

"Well for starters that is where *Paphiopedilum rothschildianum* is found. It is *the* tropical slipper orchid and everyone

13

agrees that it is one of the most spectacular species in the world." Great-aunt Bertha waxed enthusiastic. She spelled the name out. I suspect that was to impress Jake and Ernie who were not really interested in orchids. For most enthusiasts the abbreviation 'roth' was sufficient.

"Have you ever seen a good roth with flowers each over a foot wide and five to six blooms on a four foot long stem?" she asked. "So magnificent!"

I countered with, "Yes, there are lots of good ones around in cultivation, but the wild ones only grow on Mount Kinabalu and that is a nature reserve. No collecting is allowed. Anyway, people have been breeding them for decades. Man-made plants are probably far better than any of the wild ones."

William interrupted at this point. "Sorry I must contradict you George. There are already rumors on the internet of some fantastic forms of the roths that have been seen in a new population recently discovered in Kinabalu Park."

"And that is where they should remain, in the wild and safe in the reserve," I pontificated.

"But George, you know that is not the way the world works," William argued. "If there is anything special in that new population it will find its way into private hands very easily. Money talks and palms are always ready to be greased."

"Whatever," Bertha said. "I want the opportunity to see a roth flowering in the wild even if it is only a second rate one."

"So, you are going to go with SCORE to Borneo then?" Matilda asked, and she looked at me. "When is the tour?"

"Probably next March or April. That is when the roths should be in flower."

"Do you need a travelling companion?" William volunteered. "I have always wanted to go to Borneo and meet the wild men of the woods."

Jake looked at him quizzically. "Wild men of the woods?"

"He means orangutans," I explained.

"Not what I thought he meant," Ernie added "Never can tell with William."

Matilda was not listening and I saw a wistful expression growing on her face.

"Don't give me that look, Matilda. We are not going to Borneo, not even for some spectacular orchid plant. And that is final."

"But Great-aunt Bertha probably needs a companion with her."

"Nonsense, she will have an entire tour group to act as companions for her. Anyway, I cannot travel as I have to finish my chapters for the introductory biology textbook that the department wants to be able to use next year." If truth be told, I was dreading my assignment but most of the book had already been written and it now just needed my chapters. A good introductory text book is a very lucrative proposition especially if it gets adopted by some of the top universities.

Nothing more was said about Borneo and we adjourned to the living room for dessert.

Bertha had furnished the living room with modern light-wood Nordic style furniture. The large picture windows opened onto an immaculate garden with a lawn bordered by roses. Being California, the roses were still in bloom and would remain so for most of the year. In one corner of the lawn one could just see the glass of an ornate greenhouse. It must have furnished some of the orchids carefully posed on small tables around the lounge. I recognized a large plant of *Paph.* Annette 'Golden Age' with three superb, deep yellow, rounded flowers. It was one of the most sought after hybrid slipper orchids in the country; the sort of plant members of SCORE would probably select for themselves if they could. Another container held an enormous plant of *Cattleya* Bob Betts 'White Lightning,' covered with snowy flowers. It normally flowers in the autumn so how Bertha had persuaded the plant to bloom in the winter was beyond me. It was magnificent with ten large crystalline white flowers and a contrasting yellow botch on the lip. To my mind this is one of the best white cattleyas ever produced, even though it is well over fifty years old. Great-aunt Bertha would have a piece of the original plant and not some mass produced, cheaper meristem. On one wall were exquisite French impressionist paintings. The entire room exuded an aura of great wealth. This was not surprising as Bertha had at one time married great wealth but had also made her own fortune on the stock market.

A tea cart had been brought into the room. On a lace cloth was a large deep-dish apple pie and a bowl of *crème fraiche*. Matilda served the pie with generous dollops of the cream while William took orders for either tea or coffee.

"This pie is delish. I suppose you baked it Matilda," Ernie said. "If I ever get married, Matilda you will have to give my wife your recipe."

"Oh, are wedding bells in the offing?"

Ernie blushed and only mumbled, "Well maybe – if Irene ever makes up her mind." We knew that Ernie shared an apartment with Irene but were unsure of their exact relationship.

"You don't have to be married to get my recipe," Matilda pointed out. "Men are fully capable of baking apple pies too. Why don't you make one for Irene?"

"If you show her you can bake great pies it might help her make up her mind." That was from William, for whom food was a very, if not the, most important part of life. He would bake a pie everyday if he thought Jake wanted one. It always surprised me that William was as slender as he was. I used to tease him about hosting the world's most voracious tapeworm.

The conversation devolved into small talk and the idea of Borneo and orchids faded into the background. The sun was low in the sky when we said goodbye and drove home. In fact, I forgot all about Great-aunt Bertha wanting to join SCORE to look for *Paphiopedilum rothschildianum* for the next several weeks, until I got an invitation from Paul Tylo to come and visit him at Tylo and Associates in Denver. Paul Tylo and Bertha go back a long way and I tend to associate the two.

Chapter 2 – Tylo Suggests a Deal

It was a slow day at the office. I was there on a Saturday morning working on a recalcitrant chapter of the damn text book. It was on conservation genetics, a topic that I considered important, but I was not sure of the best way to deal with the subject at the introductory level. Originally I had been an ecologist and did research on how plants adapted to various environments, but in recent times I had been drawn to the problems of global climate change and species conservation. My classes on conservation biology attracted large numbers of students.

The building was quiet because, except for a handful of graduate students hidden away in various laboratories, no-one else was around. William was in Las Vegas spending the weekend with Jake. He had been bubbling about having bought tickets to two different Cirque du Soleil shows.

I had hoped that the peace and quiet of the empty building would be conducive to writing but that was not the case. My writing was not going well and I procrastinated by looking for other things to do. On one corner of my desk sat an unopened FedEx envelope that had arrived on Friday afternoon. After one look at the return address, I had put it aside. What did Paul Tylo want of me now? I really did not want to deal with him anymore. A year ago he had inveigled us into going to Africa, against my better judgment. He had wanted us to collect a rare *Disa* species that possessed great commercial potential for the orchid pot plant market, and we had done so. I thought after that he would leave me alone. But it seemed not to be. It did not help either that William was entangled romantically with Jake and unfortunately Jake appeared to be very loyal to Tylo. William had reported that Tylo often asked Jake after Matilda and me when he reported back in Denver.

I tapped away at the computer for a while, but I kept getting drawn to the envelope. I supposed it might be a progress report on the *Disa* project. Or did he have some question on disas? In the past he seemed to regard me as the expert on the subject.

"I suppose I had better open the bloody envelope and see what the bastard wants," I mumbled to myself and reached for the envelope. I pulled it open and inside was a folded piece of note paper and an airline itinerary. The itinerary was for both Matilda and me; a pair of first class tickets to Denver for the following Friday. I was free that day – no lectures, which Tylo must have had researched. I glanced at the short handwritten note and I recognized Tylo's handwriting. Like everything in his life it was a well-controlled hand.

Dear Professor George:

I hope to see you in Denver on Friday. I have a proposal that I know will tickle your fancy.

Best
P.T.

As usual there was minimal information. Well, I was damned if I would sit up or roll over on his command. I tore up the itinerary and threw it in the circular file.

The next week went by as usual and I forgot all about Paul Tylo and his invitation. It was just after lunch time on Friday when the phone rang. It was Matilda. I could tell from the tone of her voice that something was troubling her.

"I just got a phone call from Great-aunt Bertha. She was in Denver with Paul Tylo. Apparently they were expecting both of us for lunch today. Did you know anything about this? How come you never said anything?"

"An invitation came a week ago and I wasn't interested in partaking of any of his schemes. I just ignored it."

"Was that wise?"

"I simply do not care. I don't like the man."

"Yes, but…"

"No buts. I don't want to have anything more to do with the man," I said as firmly as I could.

"Sometimes, you are too pig-headed. I think they had a special surprise planned for us."

"I don't need any of Paul Tylo's surprises. It always means trouble."

"Well, according to Bertha, Tylo was going to fund the entire purchase of that orchid conservation reserve in Ecuador that you wanted to set up. I always thought you said you would sleep with the devil if you thought it might save an orchid species from extinction. My dear, I think you just blew it and in a big way." I could sense the annoyance in her voice as she hung up on me.

Damn and double damn. Let me go back and explain.

Three years ago, William and I were working on the pollination biology of phragmipediums in Ecuador. We were walking along the edge of a small stream looking for a suspected population of *Phrag. besseae*, the famous scarlet slipper orchid. To one side was a steep cliff festooned with red begonias, fuschias and passion flowers. We thought that all the red flowers were part of the same pollinator's guild. Red flowers are usually pollinated by butterflies or hummingbirds but it never made sense that the red slipper orchids were pollinated by either of those two agents. (Later an enterprising observer found a very different insect pollinating *Phrag. besseae*.) We were hoping to find a convenient group of the red slippers to observe. Most of the slippers were high up on steep cliffs and too difficult to approach. We hoped for some clumps lower down along the edge of the stream. The stream turned a corner between two hills as we followed its banks. Unexpectedly, the hills there, were covered with old growth forest. We forgot about the red slippers as we started to explore the woods. I was amazed by the orchid diversity and richness of those forests. The forest contained all sorts of orchids. I was particularly taken with the diversity of *Dracula* species. Dracula orchids are so named because the flowers can resemble bats in flight. The plants perch on tree branches and produce numerous threadlike flower stems from which the flowers are suspended. They can be the size of an outstretched hand and are in shades of brown and black. They do look like bats in flight. There were numerous species of these peculiar flowers that occurred nowhere else in the country. Some were so new they had not even been described. This area had to be protected from "development."

The forest would make an exceptional conservation preserve. Later we investigated the ownership of the hills. The area was part of a private farm. We met with the land owner and I was delighted that he was anxious to sell. But the price he mentioned was astronomical and way beyond my means. He understood the need for a preserve but he had planned on retiring in two years and wanted to move to Quito, the capital of Ecuador. I explained it would take time to raise so much money and was given the two years to try and raise enough cash. That time was running out and I had already been told that a timber company had shown interest in purchasing the land. I had three months left and had only raised half the needed money. And now here was my nemesis with an offer that would be difficult to refuse. Sleep with the devil, indeed.

Whatever Paul Tylo was offering, I was quite sure that it would be no free gift. He would demand payment in blood. I just hoped that it would not literally lead to bloodletting. He was perhaps the most coldblooded, egocentric individual one could ever expect to meet. He literally did not care if some of his "trusted" employees got hurt carrying out his schemes. He figured he paid so much compensation in wages that it was up to his people to make sure they earned it no matter what.

The following week, I was still wrestling with myself and had not contacted Denver. I tried to put him out of my mind and almost succeeded.

It was a pleasant Tuesday mid-morning. I had just delivered a satisfactory lecture to my upper division class on the nature of tropical forests and they appeared engrossed to the point that I felt they really understood why these forests were important to the economy of the earth. So I was feeling pretty smug. I was walking down the corridor to my office. I usually leave the door open so students can pop in, without making formal appointments. Someone was standing in my office looking at the book titles in one of the bookcases. I recognized it was Paul Tylo before he turned around to greet me.

"What are you doing here?" I said rather brusquely.

"As the old saying goes. If the mountain will not go to Mohammed, then Mohammed must go to the mountain." And he extended his hand towards me.

I glared at him and ignored the proffered hand.

"Come, come professor. This is no way to treat an old friend."

"I am not sure that friend is the operative word."

He shrugged and sat down in one of the chairs facing my desk. He looked relaxed despite focusing those piercing, dark grey eyes on me. "You may as well sit down. I am not leaving until I have had my say." He smiled as if we were long time friends coming together after a lengthy absence.

"How is Matilda getting along? Pity she is so attached to you. She would make a splendid operative for Tylo and Associates."

I sat down, "Leave my wife out of this, please!"

"Let me tell you a story," he said.

"Oh, by all means. I don't think I can stop you. Go ahead, and let us get this over with." I was angry and it showed.

"George, don't get your tidy whities in a snit. This is not going to take very long and I think in the end you will agree with me and appreciate my coming to see you."

"Get on with it," I growled.

"Have you travelled much in Thailand or the Malaysian peninsula?"

"No," I answered. "Does this have anything to do with SCORE and Great-aunt Bertha?"

"Only indirectly... I assume from what you just asked, that you know about the new locality for *Paphiopedilum rothschildianum*. Well you don't have to worry about that any longer. There is no point in Bertha or any of the other members of SCORE visiting Borneo now. Last month the locality was deliberately and totally destroyed."

I think my jaw must have dropped.

"Why would anyone do that? You might ask," Tylo continued.

"How did that happen?" I asked instead.

"It seems the area was first sprayed with Agent Orange. A crop duster plane was used. Then after a month that portion of the forest was set on fire. A clear case of arson. In the blink of an eye an endangered species' population was exterminated."

"This seems pointless to me. Roths are quite common in cultivation. It does not make sense and an operation such as you describe must have been quite expensive. If the locality is within the boundaries of Kinabalu National Park, then someone is deliberately flouting the law. Won't the government go after him or them?"

"Maybe, or maybe not. Do you remember back in 1996 there was an attempt at reintroducing roths into Kinabalu? Several hundred plants from artificial propagation were planted out. The timber industry was upset because that part of the park was declared off limits to logging, so they set that portion of the forest on fire and destroyed all of the young plants out of spite. No one was arrested and no one was brought to justice."

I finally took the hook, "So tell me why were the roths destroyed this time?"

"When the population was discovered, a few of the plants were in flower. Among them was a rare albino form of *P. rothschildianum.*"

Albino forms of slipper orchids are those very rare mutants that cannot make pink or purple pigments in their flowers. Consequently, the flowers are white, yellow or green. Sometimes among the millions of individuals in the wild there is only one, or at most two, of these rare mutations. Sometimes there are none. While albinos are known for most *Paphiopedilum* species there are a few species for which albinos have never been recorded. *Paphiopedilum rothschildianum* was one of these where until now albino forms were unknown. About twenty years previously, there had been rumors of an albino roth and seedlings purporting to be those color forms were sold in Taiwan at high prices. That turned out to be a fraudulent scheme, a scam, and when those plants eventually flowered they were proven to be an uninteresting hybrid. None of the money spent on those plants was ever recovered. A truly albino roth could be worth a great fortune.

Tylo continued, "As you are no doubt aware, there has never been a confirmed sighting of an albino roth before. The plant was collected and smuggled out of the park. As long as the plant is a one-of-a-kind, its value is priceless. I suppose that as long as other members of that population remained, there was the chance that additional albino clones might be present in the park..."

"So, in order to insure this plant's immense value, any other potential detractors were destroyed," I completed his statement.

22

"Yes. That is it in a nutshell."

"So what does this all have to do with me? What makes it worth your while to fly out and visit me?"

"I need your expertise to teach this fellow a lesson. I want to make the albino roth valueless."

"You want me to destroy this…this living jewel?" I exploded. "No way! Goodbye, sir! You know the way out. Don't bother to close the door." I stood up and pointed to the open door.

I challenged him, staring directly at those gun-metal eyes of his. He did not look away. I knew he would not but I was not going to blink first. I stared at his eyes. The irises were blue-grey around the large black central pupil. The outer edge of the iris was darker making the entire eye look like a target. They say that large pupils are a stimulus for sexual attraction. But I could only feel repulsion. He reminded me of a snake trying to hypnotize its prey. I wanted to look away but fought against that impulse. I had to stand up to him. In my mind I pictured him as a demon and just let the hatred build. It was always a battle of wills between us.

"Wait a minute George, and get off you high horse, and stop your silly self-righteousness," staring back at me "Give me a chance to explain. I don't want you to destroy this plant. There is a better way to stop that bastard from enjoying his ill-gotten gains."

"I will not help you steal it, either."

"I have no plans to destroy the plant or have anyone steal it. There is a better way. My scheme will make for fantastic poetic justice and you stand to benefit, too."

"And how is that?"

He made himself more comfortable in the chair while never taking his eyes off of me, and gestured to me to sit down again. I settled back in the chair on the other side of my desk, never taking my eyes off of him. I suppose I must have blinked several times. But he did, too. Yet we did not take our eyes off each other.

"Tylo and Associates will buy your *Dracula* reserve for you and get you full title to it. You know you cannot raise the money on your own."

I sat down, "I will not be involved in any illegal scheme of yours. I have a reputation to maintain."

"Yes, I know. You are a world leader in orchid species conservation, an important member of the international community trying to save tropical forests and their endangered species. What I have in mind will stop poaching of endangered species by clearly showing that this sort of crime does not pay. And the criminal will have no clue about how and why his precious plant will suddenly become valueless."

"And how do you propose to do this?"

"This is what I have in mind..."

Tylo left an hour later. He did not bother to shake hands, for which I was grateful, for I was still not in the mood to be pleasant or grateful. I must admit, however, that the scheme he proposed was intriguing but I was not sure that it would work. I would have to discuss it with the family. There were several potential problems, not the least of which was the fact that if we were discovered, I doubted that we would be allowed to return to the States alive. Capture would be life threatening. This had all of the makings of a *Mission Impossible* plot. I had not agreed to anything and Tylo gave me a ten day period to mull it over. He sweetened the pot by offering not only to purchase the Dracula reserve, but to also endow the reserve with enough money to hire guards and conservation officers for a ten year period. It would be very difficult to turn the offer aside. It was worth many millions of dollars. Tylo knew every man has his price and as he agreed to fund the Dracula project, even if the mission failed, it seemed like a no-brainer. But the entire project was fraught with danger and it would take intense organization and work before we could embark on it. Tylo offered the entire resources of his company; men, money and whatever I might need. All I had to offer was my life, that of my loved ones and to sell my soul and self-respect. Does the end really justify the means?

Chapter 3 – Sleeping with the Devil?

Although Paul Tylo had told me what he wanted me to do, he did not tell me exactly how I could accomplish those goals. He showed me several possibilities. I spent the hours after he left in turmoil. Establishing the precious *Dracula* reserve in Ecuador was very high on my ambitious list of worthwhile projects for my life. But earning the enormous amount of revenue that was asked to cover the purchase price also seemed an impossible goal. And additional resources would be necessary to monitor and guard the reserve. But along comes Paul Tylo with a proposal that would let me accomplish my dream. The cost, however, necessitated placing myself and possibly those I loved, in the way of harm. I always try to avoid dangerous situations. I am no hero but this scheme that he so boldly put forward would place me in grave jeopardy, and that of my family. I did not think I could do it on my own, but I had no right to drag them into perilous adventures.

I was still wrestling with the problem as I drove home to our suburban Orange County home.

"Okay, what's happened?" Matilda took one look at my face when I walked in the door. She was always ultrasensitive to my moods.

"I had a visitor in my office today."

"Paul Tylo flew in just to talk to you." I swear she can read my mind. "What was it all about this time? What scheme is he trying to inveigle you into now? Did he make you an offer that you just cannot refuse?"

"Enough with the questions. I need a drink."

"Now you have me worried. What did you agree to this time?"

"I have not agreed to anything, but you are right. He made me a very tempting offer to purchase the reserve and even endow some jobs for it."

"But you have to do something extraordinary in return. Is it very dangerous?"

"Yes, it could be."

"I suppose he gave you a deadline to make up your mind?"

"Ten days."

"That is a long time – what are you going to do? You had better tell me all about it." She strode over to the small bar we had built into the family room and selected two Waterford cut crystal whiskey tumblers, added several ice cubes to each and asked, "Two jiggers tonight?" She reached for a bottle of Glenlivet 21 Year Old Archive single malt whiskey, a birthday present to me from Great-aunt Bertha. The whiskey was advertised as having "notes of oily walnuts and winter fruitcake…" For the price it fetched, per bottle, it was allowed to be as pretentious as it wished. We normally could not afford such a luxury for ourselves. Without my replying, Matilda added a generous double jigger to each glass and a few splashes of water. She knew how I liked my Scotch.

We sat in our favorite recliners and I recounted my conversation with Paul Tylo, giving a verbatim account. She did not interrupt and after I had finished she sat slowly rotating the glass in her hand, her eyes focused in the distance as she considered Tylo's offer and what she thought I should do about it.

Eventually she looked over her glass at me and said, "You have to admit that this could be a pretty difficult assignment. Can one pull it off? In a funny way it delivers justice to a man who has a very nasty reputation and deserves all the bad Karma coming to him."

"Are you thinking that I should accept Tylo's proposal?"

"Well. The rewards are very great."

"Yes, but, the problem is that it might require the coordination of a whole team of operatives. I don't see how a single person can carry it through. And the more people the greater the chance that something will go wrong."

"But he promised the full support and cooperation of Tylo and Associates."

"Also, it isn't clear to me how we are to carry out the assignment. The main objectives and goals are clear, but there are so many potential obstacles in the way of achieving them. And it involves stealing something from a thief to teach him a lesson. But how are we going to do it?"

"What motivates Tylo? I am sure it is not the goodness of his heart. I doubt that he even has a heart. What does he have to gain from all of this?"

"I am sure that this project will cost an enormous amount of money."

"As I understand it, the wealth of Tylo and Associates is astronomical and what seems like a fortune to us is probably piddling to him."

"I think we need to call a war counsel of our small family. Invite Great-aunt as well as William. I suppose we had better invite Jake also. He understands Paul Tylo's brain better than any of us and he also knows what resources might be available. Do you think we should invite Ernie as well?"

"No. Ernie knows nothing about orchids."

"But he does understand law enforcement. And I am sure that what Tylo wants us to do is not strictly Kosher."

"But Ernie is FBI. This operation will have to take place overseas."

"True. I suppose it will; but it will not hurt to invite Ernie as well. His insight may be valuable."

"Whose lab is William working in these days? Did you say you were lending him to Marcie? Is he still with her?"

"Yes, she is at a critical stage in some of her experiments. Her own tech was in an auto accident and broke her arm. Until that mends she is useless in the lab. I don't need William at the moment because I am just writing grant proposals and working on that damn book. So he is helping Marcie until that tech's arm mends."

"Do Marcie and William get along now? I thought she was mad at William after he broke up with her when Jake came along."

"Naw, Marcie forgave William. Anyway, now she is having an affair with one of the other postdoctoral researchers."

"I swear your department is a regular Peyton Place."

"Maybe."

"Well we had better get together as soon as possible. I will try for tomorrow night. Your ten days will run out faster than you realize."

Matilda and I have been in many scrapes before, but luckily, we always seem to emerge from those adventures unscathed, although I must admit that in our recent expedition to Southern Africa it was touch and go. There were moments when I was sure that it was all

27

over for us. And here we were now contemplating jumping into another dicey situation. Could I really do this and put my loved ones into another set of precarious situations?

Matilda looked me up and down, "You are over-thinking this. What can I do to make you relax and forget about your conundrum for a while?"

"That's easy." And I stepped forward and gathered her in my arms. We hugged for a while and I buried my head in her breasts before leading her to the bedroom.

As is Matilda's wont, she invited the other four over for a meal the next evening.

"What's for dinner?" William had asked, "I am not coming over just for hamburgers. I want something special."

"Doesn't matter what's for dinner. George needs you."

"Oh, why didn't you say so? What time is this meal?"

"Come right after work. Is Jake in town?"

"Yep."

"Good, bring him too."

"Of course. Do we need to dress up?"

"No, wear your work clothes."

"Well for me that's a pair of Levis and a tee shirt. For Jake it is a suit. Why don't we let him change into something casual?"

"Okay, but try and get here before seven."

"Are you going to tell me what this is all about?"

"No. I will let George do it."

"See you then."

Great-aunt Bertha was not so easy to contact. Matilda eventually ran her down at one of the local Irvine Senior Citizen clubs. She was playing bridge. She confessed to Matilda that she was going out of her mind with boredom and was delighted to come to dinner even if it was just to discuss one of George's current problems. She seemed to feel that trouble looked for me all the time and it was poor Matilda's job to keep me safe and sound. It's funny, because I pride myself on being self-reliant, but in Great-aunt Bertha's estimation I am just a second-class nerd and she is sure Matilda could have done much better in finding a mate. Actually, Matilda has never looked at another man since she met me and likewise, I am completely smitten with her and there is no one else like her in the world.

Our dining table easily accommodates six people and we sat around enjoying some hearty braised lamb shanks with roasted potatoes and steamed asparagus. Matilda knows how to season the shanks in red wine with just the right amount of rosemary and a hint of garlic the way I like them. The potatoes had been peeled and basted with duck fat until they were crisp and light brown on the outside and white and fluffy on the inside. The plump asparagus spears were tender but not overly cooked to mush and they had a smooth Hollandaise sauce on them.

Despite William's earlier hesitation I could tell that he was enjoying the meal. It was far better than he had hoped for. As usual we did not discuss business during the meal and everyone had to wait until after desert when the table was cleared. Instead of removing ourselves to the living room we all sat around the table. Everyone looked at me expectantly, waiting for me to speak. We each had a small glass with a sweet ice-wine to sip. I lifted the glass to my lips and looked at everyone over its rim.

"Well, get on with it George," Great-aunt Bertha almost exploded.

"As you all know, I have had a tough time trying to raise enough money so that we can buy the land for that orchid preserve in Ecuador. In fact my option on the land will run out at the end of the current month. I had already resigned myself to the fact that the reserve was a lost cause when I had a visit a few days ago from Paul Tylo. He is prepared to finance the entire project on one condition."

"Wow, that's great." Bertha's face broke into a grin.

"But what is the condition?" William asked cautiously. He had the same reaction to Tylo as did I.

"He wants me to steal some pollen for him," I blurted out.

"What? How? Why?" Ernie's eyebrows had lifted halfway up his forehead with the word "Steal."

"He is rich enough to buy anything he wants. This does not make any sense." That was Jake.

"Let me start at the beginning," I said. "Do you remember a man called Vicknes bin Osman?"

"Wasn't he that Thai warlord who ran off with Ester Tylo? Made all the scandal sheets for a few months. But that was a number of years ago," Great-aunt Bertha reminisced.

"Yes," Matilda replied, "I always wondered whatever happened to her. She just seemed to drop off the scandal sheets after a few years."

"There was a rumor that Ester was so unhappy after the elopement and she could not admit to having made such an egregious mistake, that in the end she simply committed suicide," Great-aunt added.

"How sad," Matilda commented.

"Of course," Great-aunt continued, "there was also the suggestion in the fake news tabloids that she was murdered by a cult of devil worshipping monks. But that seems so ridiculous."

"Why do you think Tylo wants that pollen?" Ernie asked, changing the subject. "What is so special about it?"

"It is always hard to second guess Paul Tylo. I should know. I work for him." Jake offered.

"I bet it is somehow linked to getting revenge for having lost Ester." William was always ready with some hypothesis or other.

"Again, what is so special about this pollen that it can only be stolen and not bought?" Ernie asked.

"Let me tell you about the plant," I said. "On Kinabalu mountain on the Western tip of the island of Borneo is a nature preserve. In this preserve there are a few plants of a species of slipper orchid, *Paphiopedilum rothschildianum*…"

"Easy for you to say," William interrupted snidely, as the long scientific name tripped off my tongue, and then he thought better of it. "Sorry, continue."

But Bertha interrupted as well. "You remember at Christmas, I said that SCORE was thinking of mounting an expedition to go and see that new population of the roths that had been discovered somewhere on the mountain."

"Let me finish what I need to tell you and then everyone can have their say." They looked at me expectantly, "*Paphiopedilum rothschildianum* was named for the ultra-rich financial family of

30

Rothschild because this was thought to be the most spectacular orchid species in a popular genus of strange and curious flowers; only the very best could carry the name of one of the wealthiest families in the British Empire. And the roths are quite fantastic. I would say this is one of the most magnificent orchid flowers in a family known for wonderful plants and flowers. For many decades the plants commanded such high prices that only the wealthiest enthusiasts could possess one. I heard of a medical doctor who lived in Southern California who threw a fantastic dinner party whenever his plant flowered. It only flowered on rare occasions. A friend who was fortunate enough to be invited to one party said that the plant occupied the place of honor at the table and the guests drank a champagne toast to it. A good *rothschildianum* flower can measure over a foot across and carry five or six flowers spaced along a vertical three to four foot stem. The petals are held horizontally like a long, thin mustache. The other parts of the flower have strong, dark brown to black vertical stripes and there is a reddish brown, slipper-shaped pouch suspended in front of the flower."

"Doesn't sound very beautiful to me," Ernie volunteered.

"No it is not beautiful. It is handsome, a very masculine flower," Bertha added.

"Get back to telling us what makes Vicknes bin Osman's orchid exceptional because surely these days many other people also possess this species."

"Let me finish setting the scene first," I continued. "The species was really never very common in cultivation until an enterprising couple managed to get their hands on two different plants. They bred the two together and made hundreds and hundreds of seedlings. They grew them all until they flowered. It took about a dozen years for a plant to mature to flowering size. From these, they selected the very best and took them into an orchid show in downtown Los Angeles. The plants created a sensation. They then invited the public to visit their nursery for a showing. I read accounts of it. There were over five hundred plants all in flower at the same time. It must have been incredible. The plants were sold and priced according to the lengths of the two longest opposite leaves. The lengths were added together and charged at ten dollars an inch. A mature plant might have cost a thousand dollars, but this was considered cheap at the time.

31

Many plants were sold and they appeared in collections around the world."

"So there are lots of them in the world now. Why would Tylo want some pollen? It just does not make sense." This was from Ernie, again.

"Well bin Osman's plant is something different and special," I answered. "There is a very rare mutation found in nature where a plant is unable to make red pigments in its flowers. Such plants are called albinos and their flowers are green and white, or sometimes yellow, rather than reddish-brown. These plants are very desirable and can command enormous prices."

"Are you saying that bin Osman has an albino roth?" William whistled through his teeth, "Why, that would be priceless. Now I think I see what Tylo is after."

"Wasn't there a scam about albino roths in Taiwan some years ago?" Great-aunt Bertha asked.

"Yes there was this woman from Sumatra who claimed to be selling flasks of albino roth seedlings at a thousand dollars a flask. Each bottle contained ten seedlings. She even had a doctored photo of the supposed parent plant. Apparently she made a lot of money, but when the plants eventually flowered, they turned out to be some misbegotten dreadful hybrid and of course not albino roths. By that time the woman had vanished."

"So if this actually is an albino *rothschildianum*, where did bin Osman get his plant?"

I recounted how the plant had been found in the newly discovered population and then poached from the preserve and how the rest of the plants had been destroyed on the off chance that there might be another as yet to be discovered albino flower in that population.

This drew gasps of dismay from the family, as they contemplated that another endangered species' population had been deliberately driven to extinction to bolster the value of the albino plant.

"The bastards!" William declared, tossing his curly locks in the air. He had no time for those who felt they could destroy nature on a whim.

"So what is Tylo going to do with the pollen?"

"The plan is to pollinate normally colored roths with the albino pollen and gather and grow the seeds. All of the offspring when they flower will have normally colored flowers because albinism is a recessive gene. Then in the next generation if those plants are bred to their siblings about a quarter of the offspring will show the albino genes and have emerald green flowers. The plants can be mass produced and distributed cheaply. Then the original plant will drop in value to almost nothing."

"What do you think it is worth now?"

"We calculate it is probably about a quarter of a million, but really, if there is only one albino roth, it is priceless."

"But at twelve years a generation that is going to take twenty-four years," Ernie calculated. "Will bin Osman still be alive."

"Probably, he is only in his early fifties now. But it will take much less time to get the second generation."

"How do you recon that?"

"In Japan they have been breeding roths that mature much faster than before. We also know, today, how to cultivate and grow them faster. There are now strains of *rothschildianum* where the seedlings will flower in as little as three or four years from flask. Six years to mass produce albino roths is not a long time."

"So we have to get into this warlord's greenhouse and steal the pollen out of a flower or two. It will have to be a ninja operation." William's eyes were glowing at the idea.

"Where does bin Osman's money come from? Does anyone know?" I asked.

"He inherited it, "Great-aunt answered, "His father was one of the prime drug lords in the Golden Triangle."

"What or where is the Golden Triangle?" William wanted to know.

"It is or was an opium poppy growing area in Northern Thailand." Ernie seemed to know about it. "Northern Thailand borders on both Myanmar and Laos. All three countries seem to be ideal for growing the poppies."

33

"I thought Afghanistan was where most of the poppies are grown."

"Yes, that is the Golden Crescent, but before Afghanistan took the lead most opium came from the Golden Triangle."

"So this man is a very rich drug-warlord and Tylo wants us to go traipsing in there and steal the pollen from some dictator, gangster, godfather or whatever's favorite orchid. He may as well ask us to go and challenge a dragon in its den."

"It's worse than that," Matilda butted in, "bin Osman's estate will be well guarded and we do not know exactly where he keeps the plant."

"We do not need to know where he grows his plant. I think I know where and when the plant will be put on display. We can get access to it then," Great-aunt said.

"How do you know that?" I asked.

"Vicknes bin Osman is a corresponding member of SCORE. He has been alluding to having a special orchid that is one of a kind and he wants to show it off to people who can appreciate it. He is going to make a big production of unveiling the plant to a few select individuals the next time it flowers."

"Are you sure it is the albino roth that he is touting?"

"He has not said what the plant is, but with what you have just told us, what else can it be? All that we know is that it is a spectacular slipper orchid. He has not said where he got the plant but then he cannot say that it was poached from Kinabalu Park. Of course he would never admit to that."

"I wonder then how he will explain where or how he got the plant," William wanted to know.

"I guess he will simply claim that it was a lucky mutation that occurred in a group of seedlings that he bought. No one would be the wiser anyway. It would be hard to disprove." Matilda ventured the guess.

"Are all members of SCORE invited to attend?"

"According to Mercedes Grilling, the current SCORE secretary, she has been asked to invite no more than five or six members and their spouses to accompany the president, Mr. Charles Guildenhuis. She invited me to go along but I have not accepted yet."

34

"You turned this down? Now what are we going to do?" I felt a flush of exasperation building.

"Hold your horses. I have not turned it down. I just said I would think about it."

"Does Tylo know about this?" Jake asked. "Is he going to go? Isn't he also a member of SCORE?"

"Yes he is a member, but for obvious reasons, he cannot show up at bin Osman's." Bertha answered.

"It seems to me George – that you need to be a member of SCORE. Why don't you join the group and then you have your admission to the plant?" Ernie suggested.

"It's not that simple," Bertha said. "Not just anyone can join SCORE. One has to be invited."

"Well invite him, then."

"It would have to be voted on by the group. Members have to have standing. Not just anyone qualifies for membership. George is only a professor, I am not sure that would be enough."

"Not qualify! Only a professor? This man is world famous for his work on orchids and he does not qualify? What is this SCORE anyway, the KKK of the orchid world? This is total bullshit!" Once William got riled up it was hard to get him to calm down again. His eyebrows were pinched tightly together and his cheeks inflamed. "Why, why…" William spluttered, he was so angry he was at a loss for words. William was always ready to guard my back. Bertha's subtle insult had loosed his trigger.

"Now, now William, easy now. Great-aunt is not denigrating George. It's just that SCORE is a club for the ultra-rich. It does not mean George in unworthy but you have to admit he is only a professor and not a billionaire. I am sure Great-aunt appreciates George's true worth." Matilda tried to calm him down rubbing his shoulder and using her most soothing voice.

"William! Calm down!" Bertha said sternly, "I am just being practical. SCORE is not interested in academicians. We have to find another way to work this and I am sure we will. It's not just George we need; it will be you and Jake as well. And you guys would have no claim on membership either. I need to find another way."

35

"How well do you know the anatomy of *Paph. rothschildianum* flowers?" Matilda changed the subject.

"Pretty well. We see them frequently in shows but I have never dissected one," I answered. "I assume they are just like other paphiopedilums."

"Well we had better assume nothing. We need to know exactly. We don't want to be facing the flower and discover some funny little fact like the exact position of the anthers isn't where we thought it should be. That might screw up everything. We need to get some flowers that we can tear apart and make sure that we know where all the parts are in relation to each other." Matilda sometimes acts like she has an engineer's mind. She wants all her 'i's' dotted and her 't's' crossed.

"There are several other problems that we will need to solve too," I continued. "How do we get the pollen if the plant is on public display and probably only available for a very short time? Also Tylo wants it done in such a way that bin Osman will be totally unaware that he has lost any of the pollen."

"Sounds as if you need a magician or someone trained at slight of hand," Matilda said.

"Can you not simply touch the flower and get some pollen on a finger tip?" Ernie asked.

"It's not that simple," I replied, "the anthers that bear the pollen are tucked away near the base of the pouch. The pollen is in a gooey sticky mass. Looks like soft ear wax. Fingers are too big and clumsy to get to the pollen without damaging the flower in an obvious way. Anyway, my guess is that no person is going to be able to come within touching distance of the plant. I'm sure bin Osman will post guards to make sure of that too. I would if I were him."

"Well, how else are you going to get the pollen?"

"Pity one cannot train a pollinator to get it for you," Matilda mused.

"What do you mean?" Ernie asked.

"*Paph. rothschildianum* is pollinated by a species of fly that crawls through the pouch and as it emerges through a small opening near the base of the pouch, it rubs its back against one of the anthers and the pollen, which is sticky, gets stuck on the insect's back. If it flies off and crawls through the pouch of another flower, some of the pollen gets scraped off its back by the stigma and the orchid ends up being pollinated."

Jake piped up at this point. "There may be a way." We all looked at him and he continued. "Tylo and Associates has a special research division that works on microrobotics. They are making robots about the size of small insects that carry tiny cameras and can be guided to crawl though small crevices and cracks. I wonder if there is a microbot we can use to secure some pollen?"

"Are there any that fly through the air or do they all crawl?" I asked. "Do you think they can be made small enough to crawl through the pouch and get out the exit holes at the base or the pouch?"

"Only way to find out is to go and ask," Matilda said. "I am sure Paul Tylo will be only too happy to give us clearance to visit. Jake do you know where the research division is located?"

"No, I have only heard rumors of it. We will need to ask Mr. Tylo. Do you want me to make inquiries?"

"Yes please."

"So where does this leave us?" Great-aunt Bertha asked. "Let me see if I can sum it all up. One, Vicknes bin Osman has or maybe has a priceless albino *Paph. rothschildianum*. Two, he will invite the members of SCORE to visit for the unveiling of some special plant in flower late this spring. Three, this plant is probably the albino roth. Four, we need to get George and Matilda invited to join the SCORE group. This might be difficult. Don't scowl William, what if your face freezes in that position. Jake won't like it. Five, we need to find a guidable microbot to steal the pollen. Six, we need to ask Paul Tylo for the microbot. Seven, if we can get a suitable microbot we need to be able to practice stealing (or borrowing) pollen from roths. And finally, eight, where do we find a number of roths in flower so we can get familiar with the anatomy of the flowers? I think that is all."

"You left out something important," William declared.

"And what is that?"

"Jake and I are not going to let George and Matilda go gallivanting to some tropical country in Southeast Asia and get into dangerous situations without us to back them up. And that is that!" He glared at Great-aunt, daring her to challenge his assertion.

Matilda returned to the meat of the subject, "Does this mean we are going to accept Tylo's offer to purchase and fund the orchid reserve? With its obligation to go and steal the pollen for him."

I looked around at the faces of my family. "Shall we take a straw poll?"

"You make the decision George, whatever you want. We will back you up." William and Jake said this in unison and the others nodded.

The die was cast. I had said that I would sleep with the devil if necessary to save an orchid species from extinction. I had to hope that it would not result in my own extinction or that of any of my loved ones.

Chapter 4 – Playing with Spyders

Conveniently, the Tylo and Associates Microbotics Division was situated in the City of Irvine only a few blocks from the campus of the University of California where William and I both worked. Paul Tylo had arranged security clearances for Jake and the two of us to visit and talk with some of the technicians who worked at Microbotics. Matilda's clearance had not come through yet so we decided to go ahead without her. This was not totally satisfactory but I needed to get a clear idea of what the microbots were like and if I thought we could use them. Tylo had set an appointment for ten-thirty the morning after our security clearances came through. This was a top secret facility working on a military contract to engineer small spy robots that could be remotely operated. I had proposed the possibility of using microbots to collect the pollen and he thought that there might be some merit to it but he had no idea if any of the bots currently under constructions even approached the dimensions we needed.

Jake picked us up at the loading dock of our building at the university. I texted William when Jake let me know that he had arrived. For once, William had exchanged his jeans in favor of some khaki chinos and instead of a tee he had on a casual open neck short sleeved shirt. I had asked William if he could find a slipper orchid flower for us to take along. Unfortunately, there were no roths available and William had found a hybrid slipper in flower in the University greenhouse. It was not exactly the same as a roth but it would give the technicians at Microbotics some appreciation for what we needed to accomplish. Jake was at the wheel of a large black sedan, a new model luxury Lincoln. He was wearing a dark suit with sunglasses and a tie. I wondered if this was standard uniform for security guys but decided not to ask. The Lincoln must have been a work car, belonging to Tylo and Associates. I knew that even with his generous salary, Jake could not afford that kind of auto. It was way beyond his means.

Jake drove down MacArthur Boulevard towards John Wayne Airport, turned onto Campus Avenue and into a section of the city reserved for light industry. There were many high tech research facilities here. A quick turn down a side street brought us to a block surrounded by a berm densely covered in shrubs and trees. A sharp eye could just pick out the tall security fence with razor wire, on the other side of the berm. A sharper eye would have noted the insulators on vertical supports indicating that the fence was electrified. A modest sign near the driveway merely announced T & A Robotics.

"I thought it was Microbotics, not Robotics," I said to Jake.

"It is Microbotics but the sign was changed for security reasons," he answered.

There was a small guardhouse in front of an imposing gate that had a sign on it. *Entrance prohibited except by special permission.*

Jake pulled up at the window of the guardhouse and lowered all of the car windows. The guard on duty came out of the building and walked over to the car and looked at Jake. He wore what appeared to be a military uniform but I could not place which division of the armed forces it belonged to. He asked Jake for identification. Jake handed over a small wallet containing his Tylo and Associates ID and the guard took it and scanned it with some sort of device. He then peered intensely at the screen.

"Thank you Mr. Seemore, I must ask you to hand over your Beretta. It will be returned when you leave." Jake obliged. I had not known that Jake was packing heat at the moment and wondered why, but did not ask. And then the guard turned to William and myself, "And who are these other two gentlemen?"

William and I fished out the security clearance and identity badges that had been issued to us and handed them over. He looked at our faces and compared them to the photos on the badges, then scanned them and waited for an okay.

I turned to Jake, "How did he know you had a gun and its make?"

"The make, model and T & A's permission to carry are encoded in my ID."

Finally, when satisfied, the guard returned the badges to us. "Please wear these badges at all times." We pinned them onto our shirt pockets.

Then he noticed the orchid that William placed on the car seat as he put on his badge.

"Sorry, you cannot bring that in here. It is not on your permit."

"That is ridiculous. This is just a flower."

"How do I know that it is only a flower and not some sort of weapon in disguise?"

"Oh please." And William rolled his eyes.

"I will contact headquarters and get clearance for the flower," and Jake dialed a number on his cell phone. He talked quickly into the phone and then handed it over to the guard. Who placed it to his ear, mumbled several 'yeses,' a few 'sirs' and one, 'of course, sir.' He returned the phone with a curt, "You may proceed."

The guard pressed a series of numbers on a small tablet and the gate slowly slid open. Jake rolled up the windows and the car glided through. He drove to a sign that indicated visitor parking and brought the car to a halt. We climbed out.

"Wow, talk of paranoia. He thought the orchid might be dangerous," William exclaimed cradling the flower in his hand.

Jake answered somberly and in a low voice, "This is a secret military weapons research unit. You'd be surprised how paranoid they can get and with justification, too. Actually, you really don't want to know. Also, it's wise to keep your voice down and don't get all jumpy."

I looked around. The building was an unprepossessing single story warehouse with a flat roof. A door was labeled 'Office Entrance.' None of the walls I could see had windows. I supposed there were entrances and exits on other sides of the structure. The door was locked with a speaker console next to it and a digital key pad with a swipe strip. Above that was a small scanner about the size of our security badges. I saw a camera fixed above the doorframe in one corner.

"Hold your badge against the scanner and then stand back and look at the camera," Jake told us. We did it in turn. Then Jake pressed some sort of numerical code and ended up by swiping his ID card. The door swung open silently and we went inside. We were in a small room with a few chairs. Jake sat down and gestured to us to join him. "Someone will be along to fetch us momentarily." It was a very sterile little room with a closed door across from the entrance. In front of the second door, what I had been told to expect, was a very sensitive metal scanner. I noticed another camera high up in one corner near the ceiling scanning us. Paranoia indeed.

No one said a word as we waited but within a few minutes the door opened and a woman stepped through. I heard a sharp intake of breath from William and she stepped forward and extended a hand.

"Hello. My name is Jennifer Pandit. I am a security agent for Tylo & Associates and will be your guide during the visit." (Apparently she was unaware that Jake also worked for T & A.) "I will take you to meet with Dr. Fiercely." She looked at us expectantly waiting for introductions.

"I am Professor George from down the road." And I shook her hand. "And these are my associates, Jake Seemore and…"

"I am William and you are gorgeous." He stood up and took her hand, a broad smile on his face. She was indeed quite beautiful. I estimated she was in her late twenties, with black, lustrous hair and big, dark brown eyes. She possessed high cheekbones on an oval face above a slender neck. My eyes took in the rest of her body. She also wore a military type uniform similar to the man at the guardhouse but this did nothing to hide a narrow waist and generous curves. Her breasts were nothing to be ashamed of but I thought not quite up to the standard of Matilda's. I guessed from her name and honey-colored skin that somewhere in her background was a mix of Indian and North European ancestry.

Jennifer seemed unfazed by the compliment but I noticed a quick scowl slip across Jake's face. "William, control yourself," Jake muttered to William who just continued to smile radiantly at her, totally unaware of everyone else. I was sure he would get an earful from Jake after we left the place. Everyone likes eye candy but one needs to control for it, especially in the presence of one's lover.

She stared at the flower in William's hand.

"What is that?"

"It is a slipper orchid."

"Quite unusual, isn't it. I always thought orchids were beautiful. But that is kind of weird."

"You are correct," I butted in. "There are thousands of different kinds of orchids and some are rather unusual."

"Why are you carrying it around with you?" She asked.

"It's our reason for coming to see Dr. Fiercely."

"Oh. If you follow me now, I will take you to him, but first I must ask you to remove any metal objects from your pockets and leave them in those little plastic dishes on the table. They will be quite safe until you return."

"We were warned not to bring any such objects with us and I don't think anyone has done so," I said and the others nodded.

"Well then, follow me though the detectors." And she opened the door and led the way into a narrow corridor that ended abruptly at what looked like an elevator door. This was interesting because the building appeared, on the outside, to be one story. It was an elevator with a shaft that dropped us down to the lower of two basement levels, and when the door opened it revealed another long corridor with several doors. All were closed. Jennifer stopped in front of a door and punched in some sort of code. A light above the door blinked green and it slid open. We followed her into what appeared to be an ordinary office, albeit windowless. A man, facing away from us, peered at a computer screen. He turned and looked up at us upon our entrance. A slight frown was replaced by a shallow smile.

"Hello. I am Max Fiercely. Please take seats. I will be with you in a moment." He turned back to the computer and switched it off.

Fiercely was casually dressed. I would have put his age at about forty-three and when he stood up to greet us, measured about five feet nine inches and with what might charitably be called a scrawny build. His ginger hair set off green eyes and a pleasant freckled face, but I could not help thinking that he was the total stereotype of a nerd. A narrow mustache completed his face.

We introduced ourselves.

"I had a conversation with Paul Tylo yesterday. He explained some of your mission and he told me to give you all the help you require. However, some of the devices that we have or are developing are top secret and are promised to the military, so even if Tylo is my ultimate boss, I am afraid that I cannot give carte blanche access to all of our devises. Nevertheless, we do have a few bots that have not yet been classified and may work for the project that you have in mind. Now, tell me exactly what you want the robot to be able to do."

We had our secrets too and Paul had warned me not to give out personalities, locations or the exact reasons behind our mission so I merely said, "We need a remotely controlled tiny robot that can collect pollen out of an orchid flower."

"Why do you need a robot that can do that? Surely you can simply open the flower and extract the pollen by hand?"

"It is not that easy. The plants are situated in an almost inaccessible location."

"You mean they are growing on something like a vertical cliff or are they epiphytes at the top of a tree?" Fiercely obviously knew a little about orchids.

"Something like that."

"So what are the dimensions of these flowers?"

"I brought you a flower that approximates the size of the plant we need to extract the pollen from," and William held out the flower.

Fiercely took it and turned it over in his hand. It was immediately obvious that while he might have had an inkling where orchids could grow he had absolutely no ideas about the anatomy of the flower. He handed it over to me and said, "You had better show me exactly where the pollen is in this flower. Better yet, can you explain how whatever pollinates the flower is enticed to get to the correct position to receive the pollen?"

"Most lady slipper orchids are pollinated by female syrphid flies. They are carnivores and normally feed on aphids, which themselves are small insects that feed on plant sap. This flower has little bumps on the surface at the base of the petals and on the pouch, that are thought to be aphid mimics. She flies around looking for a colony of aphids where she can lay her eggs. Sometimes the flies fall into the pouch." I pointed to the opening in the front of the one petal rolled into a slipper shape or pouch. The opening to the pouch has a waxy inner lining that is slippery. The only way that the fly can escape is to crawl through the tunnel and out one of two small openings on each side at the base of the pouch." And I pointed these out.

Then I extracted a small plastic knife blade from my pocket. I had sharpened it carefully the day before because I needed to be able to cut into the flower. I turned the flower over and sliced down the midline of the pouch, carefully removing one half of the structure and laying the severed portion aside. Fiercely picked up the half pouch and

44

inspected it carefully. Then I showed him on what was left of the rest of the flower, where the half dome of the stigma and the stamen with its pollen was positioned. On the intact side I pointed to the small hole that the pollinator would have to climb through.

"I can see several problems already," Dr. Fiercely said. "The exit hole is much narrower than the diameter of any of the bots we have manufactured. Another problem has to do with how you would get the microbot into the front opening of the pouch. Do you envisage it flying into the front opening of the pouch? How will it be guided? It cannot fly through the pouch. You will have to change from a flying mode to a crawling mode. We do have small flying bots, but again, they are much too large to get out of the pouch through those exit holes."

"What is the range of the bots?" I asked. "How long does their power last?"

"Several hundred feet. Power is no problem. They can keep moving for five or six hours."

"Are they rechargeable?" Jake asked. He had been quiet until now.

"Yes. There is a special recharging unit."

"How much noise does a bot make?" William figured he needed to get into the act and he tore his eyes off Jennifer for a moment. He had been ogling her like an adolescent. I noted that Jake was deliberately ignoring him and avoiding making eye contact with William. He had tried to warn Jennifer off by glaring at her but she seemed totally unaware of him. All her attention was focused, in turns, on William and the flower.

"Flying bots make quite a bit of sound almost like the buzz of a very large bumblebee, but crawling bots are normally quite silent. Does it matter?"

"Yes, actually," but I did not explain why. I had been told in no uncertain terms by Paul Tylo that the exact mission was to be kept secret from the nerds at Microbotics.

He look at me quizzically but did not ask why. Maybe he was used to secrets.

"How easy are these things to steer and can one see where they are going?" It was Jake being practical.

"Any kid used to video games can master it and there is a tiny video camera mounted in the front that can relay back to you what the bot sees. It takes a touch screen on a pad or smart phone to nudge the bot along. But it will take practice. How long do you have before you need to use it?"

"Long enough to master the skills."

"That is great!"

"What if one is not a kid brought up on video games?"

"Are you talking about yourself? Well, if you have enough time we can teach you and let you practice until you get the hang of it. But you still have the problem of that narrow exit aperture."

"How about.....is it possible…. to get a bot to cut its way into or out of the pouch?" William's question meant that some small part of his brain had stayed focused on our problem and not Jennifer's panties.

"Actually we now have some microscopic lasers inside some of the bots so you can burn a hole in the side of the pouch," Fiercely suggested.

"Well we don't want to cook the pollen."

"Ah. Hmm… a small sharp microscalpel mounted on the head of the bot in front of the eye. That might do it."

"Do we have to worry about noise?"

"Sometimes there is a soft clicking noise when they crawl but that is not discernible, unless the bot is crawling near your ear," and a shiver ran down Dr. Fiercely's back. Was there something about these bots that Fiercely found disturbing and that he was not telling us?

"So instead of crawling through the pouch, we can simply cut through the side, make an opening and go straight into the pouch until the probe brushes against the stamen and gets the pollen?" William was still thinking about the problem.

"That sounds feasible and then we don't need a flying bot," I said.

"The flying bots are not a hundred percent reliable. You will need a fair number of them in case some fail," Fiercely suggested. "The crawling bots are more reliable."

"Maybe we should get a couple of flying bots as well," Jake wondered. "Especially if we can mount cutting blades on them as well."

"Why would we need those?" William asked.

"It might be easier or faster to fly to the plant than crawl to it."

"Oh."

But I thought a flying bot would probably be easily seen by the guards that I felt sure would be stationed near the plant. I could not say that in front of Fiercely. He thought we were after inaccessible jungle plants. I would talk to Jake about it later.

"Again, how long will it take to master driving these bots?" I asked.

"Probably about a week."

"We will set up a laboratory for you to learn how to control them. I would like to start next Monday. But first I think we need to introduce you to these little monsters. If you follow Jennifer, she will take you to a conference room where I will show you what these things are like and how we control them. I will follow as soon as I get a control tablet."

Jennifer took us down towards the end of the corridor, William chatting amiably at her, laughing now and then. She merely nodded from time to time. Jake had a grim expression. He looked at the way that William was chuckling and his face clouded over. I was surprised that William was so unaware of Jake's resentment to his behavior.

She opened the door, again by using a series of codes on the door's keypad. This time she also peered into a scanner. I suppose it was matching her retina. Once the door unlocked she kept it open and we trooped inside. When we were in the room, Jennifer closed the door and we could hear it locking. Security was tight. This was a medium sized room, rather like a business conference chamber, with a large bare central table surrounded by a ring of chairs. Jennifer motioned to us to be seated and we chose the chairs we wanted. William waited until Jennifer sat down before selecting a seat next to her. Jake sat down across from William. He was still glaring at his fiancé, but William again seemed to be unaware. He was so totally focused on Jennifer.

47

At a buzzing sound, the door opened and Fiercely walked in. He was carrying a small metal box which he placed on the table in front of where he had selected his chair. He took the lid off the box and reached inside. First, he retrieved a small touch screen tablet that he placed on the table near his seat and then, he took out what I assumed were several microbots. They were oval in shape, rather like small shallow domes with flat bottoms. One might have mistaken them for some sort of lozenge. The long diameter of the oval was barely an inch and the smaller diameter, less than three-quarters of an inch. On what we assumed was the front was mounted a small camera eye on a short stalk.

There were three of these objects and he laid them out in the center of the table. The top of each dome was scarcely a third of an inch tall. They did not move but merely sat there. Fiercely fiddled with the touch screen on the tablet and small legs unfolded from the bottom of each robot lifting their bases off the table. I could barely discern the eight small legs. Soon they were scurrying around on the table top.

"Ah cute. They look like large sow bugs," William exclaimed.

"We call them spyders because they have eight legs and with their cameras, they can spy for us," Fiercely said.

William stretched out a finger towards the one nearest him.

"Don't do that!" Fiercely said sternly, but he was too late. As William touched the bot it turned on him and dug its front claws into his finger.

"Ouch!" And he shook the thing off, sending it spinning across the table top. "Look, its drawn blood!" He held out a bleeding finger. There was a deep gash.

"Lucky the bot was not primed with a toxin. You might be writhing on the floor dying already. Remember these are not toys. They are designed to be weapons of war, albeit very small ones. There is self-defense AI installed in their circuitry."

"AI?"

"Artificial Intelligence. These are very sophisticated little machines."

Meanwhile the bot had righted itself and went on crawling back towards William. When it got close to William it stopped, as if looking up at him and warning him.

Jennifer cooed at William's bleeding finger and gave him a tissue that he wrapped around it. This did not help Jake's mood.

We all looked soberly and warily now at the little bots as they crawled around in circles. They seemed to be avoiding each other. Whether this was because of the way Fiercely was piloting them or because of their own innate abilities I did not know, but expected that as we went through training, it would all eventually become clear.

Jake drove us back to the University. He was grim faced and did not say a word. Questions were answered with either a terse yes or equally terse no. William sat in the back seat. I considered staying out of it as I knew Matilda would tell me to, but hell, I have known William most of his life and have never neglected to tell him when he was being an ass. It is a big brother privilege, so I said quietly and with an even keel, "Hey William."

"Yea?"

"You were really acting like a horn dog this morning."

"What do you mean?"

"Looked like you were hitting on Jennifer."

"I was just being friendly."

"Well you could have fooled me; looked to me like you were really trying to get into her panties."

"That's ridiculous." He voice was a little raised. "I'm not interested in her."

"I think you must have fooled your friend here, too. Am I right Jake? Or am I right?"

Jake did not answer, but I could see his knuckles white on the steering wheel.

"Oh shit, Jake. I'm sorry." It was his little boy voice.

Jake said nothing, he just looked at the traffic ahead on the road.

"I think," with my big brother voice, "Jake should drop me off at school and then you ask him to take you home and you show him how really sorry you truly are. And next time, when we are at our training sessions I expect you to act professional. Am I getting through to you?"

"Yes sir!" I half expected William to tell me to mind my own business but he reached forward and gripped Jake's shoulder. "Jake, I

49

did not mean anything serious. You are the only one for me. You know that. Sometimes I can't help being an ass. Forgive me, please."

I heard a grunt from Jake. Fortunately, we were already driving into the department's parking lot.

"Let me off here," I said and he pulled over to the curb. I got out. William's door opened and he climbed out and then slipped into the front seat that I had vacated. I waved goodbye and saw William trying to snuggle next to Jake. Hopefully another sticky situation had been averted.

Chapter 5 – At Microbotics

Great-aunt was at the house that evening when I got home from work.

"I need a drink," was the first thing I said as I walked into the kitchen where they were seated at the island in the middle of the room.

"It was that bad?" Bertha asked. So I pulled a stool towards the table as Matilda poured my Scotch. And as I sipped and rolled the liquid gold round my tongue, I recounted the entire day to them, including William's fiasco.

"You know," Great-aunt said, "William just gets exuberant. Sometimes he is just like a kid with ADD. He means well, but he does get into these situations. He has trouble recognizing limits. Surely Jake has figured him out by now?"

"Jake did not say anything but I could see that he was really exasperated."

"Well hopefully, they have kissed and made up by now," she said.

"I will know tomorrow." And then I changed the subject. "So tell, me Great-aunt – what brings you to our neck of the woods today?"

"Matilda had some concerns and she invited me over to discuss them."

"Did the two of you get everything sorted out then?"

"Not really. Matilda is worried, and I agree with her, that perhaps Paul Tylo has not been playing straight with you."

"What do you mean? You think he will not fund the conservation project?"

"No, I am sure that he will fund that. Once he makes a promise he usually follows through. It's simply that for such a complicated man it is hard to believe that he will be satisfied with merely having you steal some pollen to devalue a plant belonging to bin Osman, who he hates so vehemently. I think he would prefer a more spectacular revenge. I am scared he has planned something more elaborate and we are simply unsuspecting dupes. Cogs in some master plan he has developed."

"And you know him well enough to agree with Matilda?" I asked Great-aunt Bertha.

"Paul Tylo and I go back a long way. Yes, I think that Matilda may have some legitimate concerns."

"What are you suggesting that we do about this? Should we back out of the project?"

"NO! I understand how important setting up this reserve is to you. We must be ultra-aware and super careful about everything. And we need to keep looking for Tylo's real motive for getting you involved in his plot. What is it he wants and what does he really stand to gain? It cannot be simple revenge. He does not work that way."

"Any ideas who might help us understand that?"

"No, not really. However, I wonder if he had any business deals with Vicknes bin Osman before bin Osman seduced his wife."

"You know I was quite friendly with Beryl White, one of his former Girl-Fridays. She was his Chief Operations Officer before she retired. I don't think anything at Tylo and Associates missed her eye. I am sure she would never reveal any of Tylo's trade secrets but she might drop a clue or two about his early history with bin Osman and that might give us some insight. Perhaps I should go and visit her for the weekend. She lives in Vegas now and she likes to play the machines. We could do a girl's night out on the Strip. Have not done that for a long time."

"That is a good idea. Please tell us if you turn anything up," Matilda said and then she turned to me. "So back to our roles in this drama or whatever it might be. What do you think about the microbots – can we use them to get the pollen?"

"I think so but it will take quite a bit of training to learn how to steer them and get them to climb up a flower stalk and get to the pollen in the flowers."

"I thought you wanted to fly them to the flowers and then crawl through the pouch."

"Will not work – they are too big and even if they were small enough, microbots flying through the air will attract attention. They make a loud buzzing sound. Imagine a giant mosquito. And I suspect we are going to have to do this surreptitiously and probably in front of an audience."

"When does training start?"

52

"Soon as we can – in the next few days. I need to get clearance for you, too. It should not take too long to get clearance but I don't know how long it will take us to learn how to control the little blighters. And just in case one of us has a problem, we will need as much back-up as possible."

"Well I had better come along and get trained as well, then." That was Great-aunt.

"I don't feel comfortable having any more of my family involved."

"Listen George, I probably know more about my smart phone than you do, and I can use a touch screen as easily as any eighteen year old."

"I have no doubt of that, but I don't want to put you into any dangerous situations. I can't help feeling that we will be marching blindly into a real messy situation."

"Well, I will be present anyway. I am your passport to getting an invitation from SCORE, and just in case something unpredictable happens, it will be useful to have a back-up operator," she argued.

"Great-aunt has a point." Matilda took her side and I gave in.

"Speaking of SCORE, how is that going along?" I asked.

"Main problem in getting you membership is the fact that while you are a recognized authority on orchids, you do not grow any. But I do believe that I can get you temporary membership because Gen. Alistair Sloan passed away unexpectedly and we are currently down to nineteen members. SCORE is going to hold its annual Julian meeting next weekend. Are you and Matilda free to come to it?" She looked at Matilda and me. "It will be a bit expensive."

"How expensive?" Matilda was not shy to ask. "And how many days is the meeting?"

"Meeting will be a day and a half and will cost about two and a half thousand dollars. It is held at an exclusive spa hidden away in the mountains near Julian."

Julian is a small touristy town set high in the Cuyamaca Mountains, some 60 miles north east of the city of San Diego. It is at a high enough altitude to get some snow in winter and gets part of its reputation from the apples and lilacs that flourish in that environment. Most of southern California is too warm for those plants. It has become a weekend destination for city folk who want to get away from their urban environment. It also has a reputation for excellent apple pies.

"That amount of cash is mere tiddlywinks to Tylo. I will charge it to him," and I grinned at Matilda. "We may as well get some benefit out of being blackmailed into doing this." Normally we could not afford that type of getaway.

Great-aunt Bertha continued. "There is a rumor that bin Osman's plant may be showing a sheath and it is expected to be in peak bloom in a few months time. He told Mr. Guildenhuis of the Swansdown Group (neither name rang a bell) that he might put the plant on display at his residence and hold a charity benefit before the big Chiang Rai Spring Orchid Show. Chiang Rai is a city north of Chiang Mai. That show is a charity event and will be open by invitation only and only the crème de la crème of Thai society is ever invited to that event."

"And who is Mr. Guildenhuis and what is the Swansdown Group?" I asked.

"Charles Guildenhuis is the current president of SCORE. The Swansdown Group is one of the richest pharmaceutical companies in the world. They own the patents on half a dozen of the newest rejuvenating cosmetics. Don't you know the slogan ...*for a skin as soft and clear as Swansdown...?*"

"No, never heard of it."

"You are impossible. How does Matilda put up with you?"

"What do I put up with?" Matilda butted in.

"Your husband, he has never heard of *Swansdown*."

"You mean the cosmetic company?"

"Charles Guildenhuis will need to be persuaded of your worthiness for membership, George, so I suggest you get to know a bit about *Swansdown* and his other products, if you want to come to Chiang Rai," she advised and then continued, "Oh dear, I must admit, that I am not sure that you will be acceptable to SCORE for membership, but at least we can try. I will propose that you give an address at the banquet. You will have to wear a suit. You do have a suit don't you?"

"Oh, I was thinking of wearing a loin cloth and swinging from the chandelier," I replied sarcastically.

54

"Now you sound like William. Which of you gives the other your weird ideas?"

"Great-aunt, I'd like your opinion on something..." And Matilda cleverly drew Bertha aside, saving me from escalating our exchange.

Back at home, as we were getting ready for bed, I said to Matilda, "I don't know how I am going to spend a whole weekend brown-nosing these SCORE members. I have no patience for excessive snootiness."

"I know my dear, but I am sure they will all love you."

"More likely, there will be some horny males, clamoring for your womanly wiles." I pointed at her breasts.

"If so, I will charm them and maybe if you wear an unbuttoned, open neck shirt to show off your manly chest, the women will be swooning, too. Maybe if you talk very enthusiastically about your orchid work, they will overlook the fact we don't actually grow any orchids for a hobby."

"And you can distract the men by smiling at them? Get their minds off their orchids." I was not sure I liked the direction the conversation was taking even if I was promoting it. It was almost as if we were prostituting ourselves to get our accreditation.

"How sexy do you want me to be?"

"Just batting your eyelashes should be sufficient." Matilda would look at this as if it were a game but it certainly made me feel a little uncomfortable. Of course, William never missed an opportunity to tell me that I was an old fuddy duddy. It was a good thing he would not be present. I could see him flirting with both the men and the women and Jake getting very upset, again. I was not sure that the incident with Jennifer had blown over yet.

The next day at work I asked William to phone various orchid nurseries in Southern California to see if he could locate any flowering plants of *Paph. rothschildianum* or one of its hybrids that might be similar in size and shape. While he was doing that I phoned Jake and asked him to organize adding Matilda and Great-aunt to our microbot team. I was anxious to start with our training. William found that there was one nursery in San Diego County that might have suitable plants ready in a few week's time. I hoped that by then we would have enough expertise so we could direct the microbots sufficiently to get them to climb up the plants to the flowers and retrieve the pollen.

Meanwhile, Jake had been able to access the confidential files that Tylo and Associates had built up about Vicknes bin Osman. Apparently, Tylo had kept him under surveillance from before he had run off with Ester. He had phoned me at school and asked if he could come over for a chat. He wanted to run some information by me, but not on the phone, and without William being present. This did not bode well.

We were sitting in my somewhat cramped office on the third floor of the research building. He was in the plush padded armchair that I kept for visitors and I was in my swivel desk chair. My computer was on a credenza behind us and for once, the surface of the desk was almost clear. I had a small pile of lecture notes for the afternoon's lecture neatly stacked to one side. Jake looked across the desk at me. He seemed almost hesitant.

"I went out to Denver for the day, yesterday. Paul," referring to his boss, "gave me total access to all the documentation on bin Osman and I spent several hours going through it. That man is a nasty piece of work. He has the equivalent of his own small private army, perhaps as many as two thousand men trained as a militia. He has free access to several South-east Asian countries like Indonesia, Malaysia, Thailand, the Philippines and perhaps even southern China and moves through them with impunity. He has lavish residences and military detachments in each of them. Paul confided in me that perhaps he has set an impossible task for you. Surprisingly, he is concerned about Great-aunt Bertha travelling with you. He does not want her exposed to any danger."

"That is indeed a surprise, considering that in the past he threatened her with bodily harm if we did not do his will in Africa," I said, referring to one of our previous adventures.

"He claims now that it was just a ruse to get us to look for that damn disa orchid," Jake said.

"I assume he is not concerned that Matilda, William, you and I would also be in considerable danger, too." I could not help sneering.

"Actually, I think he has a lot of respect for you and Matilda. Perhaps he sees William and me as being more expendable."

"Why do you work for that man?"

"It's a living. I needed to do something once I got out of Afghanistan and I seem to have a talent for this."

"Unfortunately, Great-aunt is our only ticket to get near that albino roth. Without her, the entire project is a no go." I returned to that subject.

"Tylo understands that, but he is concerned about her. He wants me to talk to her to see if she can get SCORE to substitute you and Matilda for her."

"Knowing Bertha, that is most unlikely. She would be more concerned about exposing Matilda to danger than herself."

I told Jake that Great-aunt had wangled an invitation for us to go to a SCORE meeting outside of Julian, where they were going to consider us for membership to fill the vacancy in the organization. But I asked him to discuss Tylo's concerns with Great-aunt. I had noted that Tylo had not suggested that he buy the reserve for us if we made no attempt to get the pollen.

"So, why did you not want William present?" I broached the other subject and Jake shifted in his chair as if uncomfortable.

"If he understands the real danger of the situation he will be adamant that he comes along. He will always be certain that his job in life is to cover your and Matilda's back. As you know he is unpredictable enough so he will not follow orders. Can you see him dealing with an armed militia? He has never even held a gun."

"You know I don't like guns either, But we both survived that shoot-out in the Richtersberg." I referred to our recent African trip.

"That was pure luck and you know it." Jake was adamant. "I am not going to grieve for another lover. William is not going to come with us."

"Then why is he learning to control a microbot?"

"That is just to keep him quiet for the time being."

"I think you are asking for trouble."

"I will deal with it when I have to."

As I expected, Great-aunt pooh-poohed Tylo's concerns. She was certainly not going to let Matilda go where she feared to tread.

When I related everything to Matilda that evening she merely nodded but did not comment, not even about Jake and William.

The next morning at nine we were all gathered together at Microbotics for our first lesson in controlling the bots. Again Jennifer Pandit met us. She smiled broadly at William who grinned back at her. I was aware of a soft warning growl rumbling in Jake's throat. Jennifer was introduced to Matilda and Great-aunt Bertha. Then she turned and beckoned us to follow, leading us down into the building and to yet another room. It was another small conference room and we sat around a table waiting for Max Fiercely. When he came through a door at the far side of the room Jennifer asked us to place our smart phones on the table in front of us.

"Good morning." Fiercely said and then all business. "Our first exercise is to install the bot control apps in each phone. They are only to be used while in this building and will be deleted when you have finished here today. Remember, they utilize top secret programming and will have to be uninstalled before you can leave Microbotics today."

He turned to Jennifer, "Will you collect the phones and bring them to me, one at a time, and I will install the guidance apps?"

She picked up William's first and carried it over to Fiercely, who turned his back to us while he programmed in the link to the app. The phone was returned to William. He seemed to linger a moment while taking the phone from her. At first, I thought it was my imagination, but a grumble on the part of Jake confirmed my suspicions. I decided that I needed to talk to William at the first opportunity. Eventually, all of the phones were programmed and we were herded into another laboratory. Here there was again, a large table in the center of the room and laid out on it at intervals were five fairly simple Tee mazes chalked out on its surface. Matilda and Great-aunt Bertha looked curiously at the row of little bots arrayed at the entrance to each maze. Each had a number painted on its back.

Fiercely addressed us all, "If you touch the 'GO' icon on your screen you will see a joystick represented there. Your dossiers say that you are either left or right handed and the app has been installed specifically for each person. Let us start with you, Matilda. You are right handed, correct? Good, now slide your right index finger slowly over the joystick in the direction away from you and look at the spyder bot with the number three."

"Why is the joystick only on the bottom half of the screen?" Matilda asked.

I looked at my phone and sure enough there was a black square taking up the upper half of my phone. Surely it would be easier if the joystick covered the entire screen?

"The top half will show you what the bot sees," Fiercely said. "For now you are to use your eyes to guide the bot, but eventually you will have to drive the bot using the bot's camera for navigation."

Matilda's microbot was positioned about eighteen inches from the entrance to the 'T' maze in front of her on the table. She put her forefinger on the joystick and slowly slid her finger towards the top of the screen. The number 3 bot rose up on its legs and started to walk away from her.

"If you slide the joystick to the left the bot will turn to the left and if you slide it to the right it will turn right. Try doing that," Fiercely instructed.

Sure enough the little machine crawled away from her and she had it turning left and right.

"This is easy," she said at first.

"Okay, then drive your bot to the opening of the 'T' and set it going down the stem to the cross passage. And make it turn left. You may not touch any of the chalk markings, the bot will stop if the tip of any leg touches chalk. If it stops you will need to pick it up carefully, by holding onto the rounded carapace or hump, and set it back down in the center of the runway. Under no conditions can you let the tip of any leg touch your skin. In that case the bot will attack you. William learned that the hard way a few days ago." And William scowled. Jennifer shot him a look of concern and I saw Jakes eyebrows inch together into a frown.

The guidance task sounded so simple at first but the stem of the tee was only two inches in diameter and the bot itself about one inch wide. Matilda's bot also seemed to have a bias to move to the right and Matilda had a devil of a time avoiding the chalk and steering it back to the center of the maze's passageway. It took five attempts merely to deliver the spyder bot to the choice point of the tee and then several more attempts were needed to turn it properly and reach the goal at the end of the left arm of the maze. Matilda finally accomplished the task but it took great concentration. She looked around at us as if to say, "There you are. Now it's your turn. Not as simple as I thought it would be."

I knew that if she had difficulty then the rest of us were in serious trouble. An hour later, no one other than Matilda had accomplished the task. The room was filled with moans of frustration as the bots appeared to have minds of their own and resisted our attempts to guide them.

"Oh, shit," William groaned as his bot flipped onto its back as he attempted to guide it into the right hand arm of his tee. "How can I upright it without touching the legs?"

"Here, let me show you," Jennifer reached for his phone and ran her finger along the left side of the screen and the bot rocked itself over.

"Remember there are more than two dimensions. You are working on a flat surface now but eventually you will need to learn how to move and climb in three dimensions," Fiercely said.

Jennifer handed the phone back to William and I noticed her finger trailing across William's palm as he took possession of the device again.

"Thanks." He grinned back at her and she winked at him. I saw Jake grimace. If this continued I could foresee an explosive argument. Time for me to assume Big Brother and scold William, but not in front of everyone. It would have to wait until we were alone.

We each had to learn our bots individual idiosyncrasies, but by the end of the first training session we had all mastered our individual bots to the point where we could navigate the simple maze. Fiercely said that because of the AI induced differences in each bot, the bot we were using for now for training and practice would be the bot that we took on our mission.

Halfway through the morning we took a very short coffee break in a nearby common room. Other people were in the room but they only looked at us curiously and avoided interacting with us.

On our return to the laboratory we were shown how to signal the bots to turn on their cameras and the screen above the joystick showed us the world through each bot's camera. Because the camera aperture was the equivalent of a pin hole, they had amazing depth of focus.

"Now turn away from the table and using only the phone's field of view, try and negotiate your way through the maze. For the first attempts you all turn left when you get to the junction."

It was not as easy as one might have thought but after several attempts everyone succeeded in the task of working their bots through the maze. We were feeling quite self-satisfied.

"What else can the spyders do? I mean, types of motions," Matilda asked.

"Well, they can jump."

"Oh. How does one make them jump?"

"I have to install a small icon on your screen. Give me your phone." And Matilda handed her phone to Fiercely. He fiddled with it and handed the device back to Matilda.

"That is cute."

She now had a small icon in one corner that was of a little green frog.

"Tap the icon."

Matilda did this and her robot leapt about six inches straight up into the air.

"Tap in a forward direction."

And the spyder leapt forward but not quite so high in the air. It managed to land upright and Matilda made it scramble away. It was possible to change the direction. They could even jump backwards.

"Would this be useful to you?" Fiercely wanted to know.

"Possibly. It might make an easy way to get off the plant," I suggested.

So all of the phones then had the jumping command installed and we practiced the motions. William and Jake figured out how to play leapfrog with the little machines. Actually it was great fun and not at all like work.

"Anything else these little guys can do?" Great-aunt Bertha wanted to know.

61

"Yes, they can pick up other small objects."

"What's great is if one spyder gets in trouble and becomes inactive, it can be picked up and carried by another."

"Yes, let me show you how. Matilda will you turn off your spyder please. And William let me borrow both your bot and your iphone."

She did this and Fiercely demonstrated how to pick up and carry small objects. He was able to make the front limbs elongate and bend to the front of the bot. Now for the first time I noticed that the leg ended in a tiny claw. It was rather like a scorpion or crab's front limbs. Fiercely guided William's bot over to Matilda's inert one. He lowered William's spyder's front legs and pushed against Matilda's robot slipping the front limbs under the bot's body. Then he lifted up the front legs and carried her bot for two feet.

"Now you all try it. Practice in pairs."

This was more difficult, but we mastered the task.

"Tomorrow we will do more practice on jumping and lifting and then try to find your way through a more complicated maze," Fiercely said. "If you succeed in that then we will try some competitive races. It should be fun. Now give me your phones so I can uninstall the driver apps for today."

Jennifer returned with us to our car but as we reached our vehicle Great-aunt Bertha pulled her aside and whispered to her. Jennifer turned red in the face and stalked away, without saying good-bye.

"What was all that about?" William asked.

"I told her that you were newly engaged to Jake and to stop flirting with you."

"Thank you, but we can look after ourselves," Jake muttered tersely.

"Maybe, but you don't really understand William, he gets excited by anything he can rub against. He is like a puppy." Great-aunt was never afraid of calling a spade a spade.

"I was just playing. It meant nothing," William said.

"Maybe to you, but maybe not to Jennifer. It is not fair to her," Great-aunt countered.

"Jeez, I'm not a little child," William was argumentative and I could see the bantam cockerel coming to the fore. This was going to get interesting but not in front of the security gate at Microbotics.

As if reading my mind, Matilda said, "Can it everyone! This is not the time or place for an argument with the potential of erupting into an all-out fight. William, you and Jake can sort this out when you get home. Somehow, I don't think Jennifer is going to be a problem again."

Chapter 6 – On the Way to Julian

The next few days went by in a whirl. We had training sessions with the bots in the mornings and I attended to university work in the afternoons. I was preparing for a new set of lectures in Tropical Ecology and had an enormous amount of library research to cover to get the information I needed for my course. At Micobotics, we advanced from simple table top mazes to more complicated designs and then on to three dimensional mazes where we had to get the bots climbing around on tree-like structures. It was all going very smoothly, in fact much better than anyone had anticipated. Even William was behaving himself and Jennifer, paying attention to Bertha's admonitions, stayed out of his way. Fiercely had decided that we were now so competent that he and Jennifer no longer needed to be present to guide us. If we got into trouble he could be summoned by pressing an alarm switch on the wall.

We had worked out this day's exercise ourselves. Fiercely still did not understand the true nature of our mission, but we needed to be able to climb to our target without being seen by the militia guarding the orchid. The bots were going to be camouflaged to blend in with the plant's green color, but now they were still unpainted. We needed to be able to move the bots around the plant, but at the same time, out of any guard's field of vision. So in today's exercise, I was pretending to be the guard and stood to one side of the tree-like artificial plant we had built for the bots to climb in. The bot drivers had to maneuver their little robots up the tree, among its branches, so that the little buggers stayed hidden from me. Each was given a goal on the tree that they had to reach while staying out of my line of vision until they reached their target position. In the exercise today, four of the bots were all in the tree structure at the same time. Everything went smoothly and for the most part I was unable to detect where the bots were in the structure. This was good because the branches in the tree had been made quite narrow and about the same diameter as a strong *Paph. rothschildianum* flower stem.

I think we were all pleased with our efforts when the unexpected happened.

"You know, Great-aunt," William said, "it seems my spyder is very attracted to your spyder. It keeps sidling over towards yours. It is hard to keep it away from yours. I think it's in love with your spyder."

"Don't be absurd, William, it's a machine. What does it know about love?"

"Well it's damn difficult to keep it away from yours and also keep hidden from George at the same time."

"Don't make excuses for your incompetence."

"Look, I'm not touching the controls and its heading for your bot again."

Then before we realized what was happening, William's bot rushed at Great-aunt's, lifted it up and threw it off the tree with such force that when it hit the floor it broke into pieces. I had no idea that a bot could throw with so much force.

"My spyder!" Great-aunt wailed and turned to William. "You killed my spyder!"

"I did not. I didn't touch the screen," William said. "It's got a mind of its own."

We stood around looking at the splintered robot on the floor with goggle eyes.

"I better get Fiercely in here." I strode across the room and pressed the alarm, but that was not the end of it.

"William," Matilda squealed, "It's going for my bot now. Turn yours off. Now! Quick, turn it off!"

"It won't turn off." William was jabbing his finger, helplessly at his screen.

"Stop it."

"I can't."

William's bot was advancing relentlessly towards Matilda's spyder and had almost reached it when Jake leaned forward and tried to flick William's bot off the branch. In a flash the little robot twisted around to grab hold of Jake's finger and dug its claws in around the bed of his nail.

"Ouch. It's slicing my finger." And in horror we watched as the bot rapidly shirred its legs, each one making a slice through the skin of the finger. Jake tried to shake the bot off, but it clung on and

65

started working its way onto the back of his hand gauging grooves of open flesh as it cut through the skin. Jake was yelling and scattering drops of blood around the room.

"I think it is trying to bury beneath my skin," he yelled.

Just then the door burst open and half a dozen armed guards, their weapons at the ready, burst into the room. They were followed by Max Fiercely. He quickly assessed the situation, put the men at ease, and had his tablet out. After a few deft strokes the bot ceased to move but its legs were curled tightly beneath its body and half-buried in the back of Jake's hand.

"First aid!" Fiercely commanded and one of the guards left the room and returned promptly with a kit. Matilda took it from him and went to Jake to try and staunch the flow of blood. The bot was still partially embedded in the flesh of Jake's hand. She tried to pull it loose and Jake grimaced.

"Sorry. I know it hurts."

Great-aunt was also searching in the kit and found a small spray bottle of Novocain. She quickly sprayed the anesthetic over the wounds.

"Better," Jake said after a short while. "Less pain now."

"I am going to try and pull the bot free, tell me if it hurts," Matilda said. She had held pads of absorbent gauze against most of the wounds which were still seeping blood but now reached over to try and grip the bot again.

"Ouch."

"No use, it is firmly embedded in his hand. I will rip through more flesh if I try and pull it loose."

"We need to get Jake to a doctor to stop the bleeding," William said, his face ashen. "Is there an urgent care facility near here?"

"How do they get the bot off his hand?" Great-aunt wanted to know. "Will it have to be cut out?"

"You cannot go to urgent care," Fiercely said. "The bot is top secret. No ordinary doctor is allowed to see it. I have contacted the special Microbotics emergency doctor. He has clearance for the bots program and should be here very soon. Jake you need to sit down. We will have someone take care of this promptly. I know it's difficult but try and relax."

"Easy for you to say," William grumbled as he led Jake solicitously to one of the few chairs in the room.

"Hold those pads firmly against Jake's hand," Matilda instructed William. She looked at the blood seeping onto William's hands and looked down at her own hands also stained red with blood.

"So tell me Jake. What is your HIV status?"

"Negative."

"Thank God."

"How can you worry about that at a time like this? He's seriously injured," William cried.

"Exactly, now we don't have to worry about that for ourselves at least."

While we waited for the arrival of the medic, Fiercely looked around the room trying to piece together what had happened and then he realized that the remains of Great-aunt's spyder bot lay on the floor in front of him. He looked up at me.

"Now George, please tell me exactly how this all happened. Don't leave out any details. And how did this bot get damaged? We may not be able to replace it."

I recounted the whole morning, trying not to leave anything out. From time to time Fiercely muttered, "I see" and "I was scared this might happen" and "Too much AI, I kept warning them."

After the medic arrived, Fiercely was able to get the little bot to relax its legs and the doctor pulled it free and handed it over to Fiercely, who examined it with a "Thank God, its undamaged," and placed it back on the table with the other bots that we had forgotten. He switched them all off.

Meanwhile the doctor tended to Jake's wounds, washed them and applied some antiseptic before bandaging the hand. After writing an anti-pain prescription that he handed to Fiercely, he hurriedly left. It was peculiar for he had neither introduced himself nor wanted to know Jake's name. It was all business and conducted as quickly as possible.

"How is he going to get the prescription filled without a name?" Great-aunt asked.

"We will take care of it," Fiercely assured her.

As we left, Fiercely came over to me and said, "Perhaps we need to rethink your project? At a minimum I will need to discuss this with Mr. Tylo. After that I will get back to you. I am not sure we have either the resources or time to replace the bot that was destroyed and William's bot will need to be reassessed, too. Its brain may have to be washed and that will take time and special expertise. I am going to call a halt to your training sessions until everything has been reassessed. This is a great pity because your human team was performing up to standard. No one on your team is at fault. I will make that perfectly clear to Tylo. This has to be due to equipment malfunction. Though of course, Jake should never have tried to flick that berserk bot away, but then at least he did save Matilda's bot from being destroyed. Perhaps we have to look into the possibility of sabotage, too. I don't see how that is likely. Again, Tylo will have to make the final decisions."

"What a pity," Matilda said that evening during dinner. "And everything was going so well. We could all maneuver those little bots so nicely. Now what are we going to do? And poor Jake's hand is a real mess."

"How much damage was done to Jake's hand?" I asked. "It looked dreadful. It is his right hand too."

"Oh, it should heal eventually, though it may leave some scars."

"That's his gun hand. I hope none of the muscles were compromised."

"Time will tell. Wish the doctor had given a prognosis. I suppose that will go to Tylo."

"And the orchid reserve? If the project is called off, will that no longer be in the cards?"

"I don't know about the fate of the reserve. Hope it is not in jeopardy. Perhaps Tylo will let us continue but with fewer bots."

"What will happen to William's spyder? Is he out of the picture now, too? I hope not. I bet that William feels that this is his fault. He probably blames himself for Jake's injury as well. You know how sensitive he can be."

"Depends if they can reprogram the brain in William's bot."

"And Jake, will Tylo replace him with someone else? Perhaps we will have to leave both William and Jake behind."

"That may be for the best, if we can get a competent replacement for Jake?"

"I wonder about Grace Mposa. What is she doing these days?"

"Last I heard she was working for Tylo and Associates in Penang."

"That's Malaysia isn't it?"

Grace had been a very competent security agent who had helped us on a previous mission. It would be nice to see her again but not at the cost of replacing Jake and William with her. She was not regarded as family the way William and now Jake were considered. Of course they were not blood relatives, but no one in our group really was, not Great-aunt and Matilda nor William. Cousin Ernie was probably the closest to a blood relative of Matilda's but even she was not really sure of that. But we were all, instead, related by history and close association and sometimes those ties bind a family together stronger than blood.

A few days passed without hearing back from either Tylo or Fiercely, but Great-aunt continued to push Charles Geldenhuis of SCORE to invite us to their mini conference in Julian. In the end she was successful and I received a very formal invitation to address the conference on my research at the opening banquet of the meeting. I had chosen a topic, "Orchids and Deceptive Marketing," that I thought would be appealing to the moneyed members of SCORE, though the topic was really on how orchids deceived and enticed their pollinators. Everyone seems to like the accounts of how certain orchid species persuade their pollinators to visit them by posing as receptive female bugs. And there are many even stranger adaptations that helped to make for a riveting story.

The gilt rimmed envelope that bore the invitation had an embossed XX in gold foil on the reverse. Inside, the invitation was handwritten in beautiful calligraphy. Matilda looked it over and echoed my thoughts, "This is most pretentious. I don't think these are really our sort of people."

"Agreed, but they are our ticket to Mr. bin Osman's albino *rothschildianum*, so we had better be nice to the gentry and get along with them."

69

"You mean brown nose them. God, I hate this."

"Unfortunately, we have little choice in the matter now. But how can we get to the pollen if we have no microbots at our disposal? This may be all for naught. I suppose you have not heard from Max Fiercely about the fate of the bots yet?"

"Nope, I called him this morning and he said to contact him on our return from Julian. He is still having talks with Tylo, but the Feds appear to be involved too, so it may take a while."

Matilda was driving Great-aunt Bertha's S600 Mercedes Sedan, a sleek silver body sitting on top of a 6.0L biturbo V12 engine. So what if it only got 12 mpg in the city, it got all of 22 mph on the open road. It was a good thing that William was not with us as he would have ragged Great-aunt mercilessly about her carbon footprint. As it was, Great-aunt sat in the front with Matilda, chatting away at this and that the way two people do, when they are very comfortable in each other's presence. I sat in the back reviewing my PowerPoint presentation on my iPad. The lecture was also on a flash drive that I had been instructed to bring along. That was safely snuggled in my chest pocket. I felt it from time to time to assure myself that it was safe. We were travelling to Julian to meet with SCORE and let them vet me on my suitability for being offered a membership. At the moment, the car was gliding along Interstate 5 and heading for Interstate 8. We were driving through the Camp Pendleton Naval Reserve, a 17 mile stretch of military protectorate that creates a buffer between the coastal cities of San Diego and Orange counties and protects the area from urban development.

To our right was the Pacific Ocean. A few warships and destroyers were off the coast. It must be a military exercise of some sort. The air buzzed with a variety of helicopters. I could recognize a couple of Boeing CH-47 Chinook choppers. It is a heavy duty craft used for ferrying troops in combat zones. It is an oldie but still in production and a trusted craft. Then I saw an MV-22 Osprey taking off from a destroyer, and got quite excited. Jake had talked about them recently. It is an odd looking craft with two rotors, one on each side of the cabin. I pointed it out to the women still chatting away and paying no attention to all the activity in the air.

"Look at that. One doesn't see an Osprey every day."

"Is that an experimental craft?" Great-aunt asked. "Looks weird."

"It's made by Boeing and is a cross between a chopper and a fixed-wing plane. It has been in production for several years now. It can swivel the propellers so it can take off and land vertically but with the rotors shifted to the front, it flies at high speed like any turboprop plane. Best of both worlds. Can carry over 20 passengers."

The cabin suspended under the wing looked ungainly with a small cube in front holding the pilots and a larger boxlike cabin behind it. A rotor was placed near the tip of each wing. I watched intently as the rotors first swiveled on the wings before the craft went zipping through the sky.

"I didn't know you were interested in military craft, George. Aren't you supposed to be a pacifist?"

"Well you know Jake has a military past and he has a pilot's license and is enthused about this particular craft. He says that Tylo has just bought one for his private use. He wants to fly it."

"Does that mean William is egging Jake on to persuade Tylo to let him ride in it? You know William. He loves roller coasters. Anything for a fun ride. He'd want to fly in it," Bertha said.

"Boeing military will sell one to private citizens?" Matilda asked.

"I don't know. But you know Tylo better than we do. Anything Tylo wants, Tylo eventually gets," I said to Bertha.

The Osprey flew towards us, the thud of its rotors increasing as it approached. For some reason it reminded me not of the bird of prey for which it was named, but rather a gigantic dragonfly.

Spring comes early in Southern California, usually several months earlier than in the rest of the country. We had enjoyed good rains this winter and the hills were green, for a change. Along the verges of the road, small yellow and orange daisies flowered. They were not natives but rather alien invaders from Africa, yet they made for a cheerful drive. No doubt some nature lovers would soon be preaching eradication and the flowers' years are probably numbered. I glanced at them from time to time as the car silently slipped along the road. Their common name is Namaqualand Daisy and in Southern

Africa the acre upon acre of carpeted with flowers would remain very welcome each spring. Here, modern sensibilities made them out of place.

Oceanside was the first of the small coastal cities to appear after Pendleton, and from here on it was continuous urbanization. The area is built up. In the old days there had been acres of plastic covered structures housing carnations and roses; it is an ideal climate for cut flower production, but those crops have moved to South America and now, the old growing areas have been replaced by condominiums and high-density housing. Ever more concrete and tile. But there were gaps between some of the built-up areas where the land was not suited for building. The terrain was unusual. When the Spanish invaders settled in Southern California, one of their goals was to "save" the heathen, and to that end they built a string of missions from San Diego up to San Francisco. The road connecting the missions was named El Camino Real, the Royal Road. Today, the remnants of the road are identified by cast iron bells hanging from posts. The problem with the road was that in the southern regions, in particular near San Diego, there was a series of lagoons running perpendicular to the coast. Roads in the early days had to detour around these stretches of marsh and water. Many of the lagoons still exist, but the interstate traverses them with bridges, of which most of the commuters are unaware as they drive along the freeway. As we approached San Diego, the traffic grew ever denser and I was glad Matilda was driving and not me. One of my pet peeves is stop-and go traffic.

Some thirty-five miles past Oceanside is Mission Bay and here the interstate gives rise to a branch that runs due east. This is Interstate 8. This freeway runs along a low lying area called Mission Valley that is now an area of malls and hotels. Perhaps it once housed a lagoon that was an extension of Mission Bay and perhaps with rising sea levels, it will become a lagoon again in the future. We turned onto Interstate 8.

"How far away is Julian?" I asked Matilda.

"About sixty-four miles. Somewhat more than an hour."

"It's quite a drive. I wouldn't want to do this too frequently."

"Ah, but Julian has its own special atmosphere. I think you will like it," Great-aunt chimed in.

That remains to be seen, I thought to myself.

The drive out of San Diego along Interstate 8 had little to recommend it; the few towns, while not drear, were nothing special. It was only after turning onto route 78 and heading north that the scenery started to change and we were climbing into the mountains and along a winding road. At one time this must have been densely forested but now I saw many dead tree trunks. I guessed that the woods were originally a mixture of pine and oak species. California is known for its many species of oak trees. There had been repeated forest fires in recent years but one earlier in 2003, called the Cedar Fire, had devastated much of the original mountain forest. Some fifteen years later it was being replaced by bush but it would be many years before the forests could return to their earlier glory. Eventually, the road ran out from the woody area to a high grassy plain. Here was Lake Cuyamaca. It seemed quite extensive. I wondered if it had been stocked with fish.

"That's Lake Cuyamaca," Great-aunt Bertha said. "We are getting close to Julian. It is situated in forest, again. We have to go right through the village to the road that leads up to the branch for the Whispering Oaks Inn and Spa."

The forest surrounding the town seemed to have escaped the fire and the trees were intact. The town was essentially a single street and a couple of side streets with shops. Care had been taken to make sure that a rustic and historic Old West atmosphere was preserved. Nevertheless, it was also clear that the economy of the area depended on the influx of tourists from the surrounding cities. I suspected that it survived because it was the exact opposite of the cosmopolitan major cities of Southern California. Later, I learned that Julian had been declared a California Historical Landmark.

Chapter 7 – Whispering Oaks

Whispering Oaks Inn and Spa was a rambling set of buildings. The architecture looked like something that Frank Lloyd Wright might have designed, with walls of plate glass interspersed with tan sandstone slabs. The main structure was elevated on a grassy knoll with a cantilevered second story that jutted out over a large Koi pond. The road, paved with tan and beige flagstones, curved around the hill, making a circular driveway to and from reception. Clumps of late spring daffodils were scattered along one edge of the road and they nestled at the base of mauve lilacs. Every plant looked as if it had been manicured to draw attention to the lines of the buildings. Behind the Inn one could see parts of the bright greens of the private, nine-hole golf course, reserved solely for the guests. To the right, but closer to the main building complex, was a tennis court. Matilda took this all in as she guided the Mercedes towards reception, where a liveried bell boy waited patiently for our arrival.

"This place should be called the Pampered Palace. It reeks of luxury and we have not even stepped out of the car yet," Matilda remarked.

"And what is wrong with a little luxury? Especially if one has earned it," Bertha challenged her.

"N...nothing, I'm not complaining," Matilda said.

"Funny name," I remarked, "I cannot see any oaks, let alone whispering ones."

"If you look at that hillside over there with the trees," and Great-aunt pointed to a slope on the left, "there are some oaks in there. On windy nights one is supposed to hear them rustling and complaining."

"Can one?"

"I've never been here in a windstorm, so I don't know."

Matilda braked the sedan in front of reception and a young man rushed over to Great-aunt's side and opened the door. He was beaming. "The great lady returns. Oh, it is so nice to see you again." And he held out a hand to assist her out of the car. "Are you keeping well? I must say you are looking well. I believe you get younger every time I see you. What is the secret of your ageless beauty? Your usual rooms are waiting for you."

Matilda and I exchanged curious looks at the blatant fawning and pawing from the bell hop.

"And it is nice to see you too Jeffrey. Is Miriam doing well? And the little ones, also? That is so good," and she turned to us. "This is Matilda, my Great-niece and Professor George, her husband. They are also here for the SCORE meeting. And this is Jeffrey." She gesticulated at him. "He is the concierge, *cum* bell hop, *cum* barista, etc. If there is anything you need to know or if you want help, this is the young fellow to ask."

Jeffrey beamed and then addressed Great-aunt, "Most of the other members have already arrived. It is requested that everyone meet in the lobby at 7 p.m. for wine and hors d'oeuvres."

"Good, we will have time to change into evening wear. Jeffrey, do you know which suite Matilda and George have been assigned?"

"I believe that it is the Escondido Suite."

"That is nice. They will enjoy it. Doesn't it have its own private hot tub?"

"Yes ma'am."

Jeffrey loaded our cases onto a trolley and beckoned for us to follow. Meanwhile Great-aunt started off towards the lobby and then turned to us, "Follow Jeffrey and get changed. I will meet you back in the lobby about seven. I need to see someone first."

Our suite turned out to be sumptuous. It was in a separate building from the main hotel. Also of modern architecture, there was a broad veranda that encircled the building. It was made of made of the same flagstone as the driveway. The edge was marked by a boxwood hedge neatly clipped and geometrically perfect. It was no more than three feet tall. At intervals along the veranda were the front doors that each led to a set of rooms. I reckoned that there were no more than five of these suites. They were separated widely to give a sense of privacy. From the veranda one could look across the expanse of lawn towards the forest.

Inside our suite, Jeffrey demonstrated how one could turn on a romantic fireplace in the wall by the mere flick of a switch. There were fresh flowers on a desk and a bowl of fruit on a coffee table centered between a love seat and the large television screen suspended on another wall. A king size bed took up the center of the room. Off to one side was a small kitchenette with the equipment to make coffee and a supply of freshly baked pastries and cookies. A set of French doors opened onto a small balcony, screened for privacy that held an inviting Jacuzzi. I gave Jeffrey a tip and he slid out of the door, closing it gently.

Matilda plopped herself down on the bed. "This looks like the honeymoon suite. Pity this is supposed to be a business weekend."

"Well it does not have to be only business…"

"I can tell that from the lust already glazing your eyes. You better just have a shower and get dressed and concentrate on delivering a good talk tonight. After that we can play, if you are still up for it."

"I won't have any trouble getting it up for it."

"You never do," she smiled.

Matilda was glorious in an off the shoulder, bold floral print outfit. There was enough scarlet-red in the design to contrast with her blonde hair and make it stand out. The skirt, ending some inches above her knees, emphasized her long, shapely legs. The dress clung to her hour-glass figure and I noticed several men kept glancing at her. "Keep off!" I wanted to shout. "She's mine, she's mine." Her long, bright blonde hair was piled high and off her slender neck. I was used to it cascading around her shoulders, but this style showed off her earrings. Besides her wedding ring, the only other jewelry she wore was a pair of large, pendant, tear-drop diamond earrings that Great-aunt Bertha had given her one birthday. I could never have afforded them on my salary and Matilda hardly ever wore them. I looked her over. She was ravishing. I could have forgotten about the meeting and taken her then and there.

"Don't look at me like that." She teased as she tossed her head at me, making her hair shimmer. I suspect she got a kick out of my reaction to her when she was all dressed up. She focused on my groin.

I gulped and she said, "No time for that now. Let's go lover-boy. You have a job to do first."

76

For a small hotel, the lobby was cavernous, with high walls and floor to ceiling plate glass windows on two sides. The lobby led into a very large alcove with *trompe d'oeil* painted walls of a forested landscape. Here, a bar had been set up, as well as tables mounded with hors d'oeuvres. This was not cheese on crackers. There was caviar on minced egg; seared mahi mahi with a wasabi reduction; steak tartare dressed with a slice of bright green, Sicilian Castelvetrano olive; small crimini mushroom caps stuffed with shallots and blue cheese, and a variety of paté, some with a truffle glaze. The hotel knew how to spoil its special guests. As we walked towards the small cluster of people talking to each other, Great-aunt Bertha separated from the crowd and came over to us.

"These are the people you need to impress," she said as she took me by the elbow and steered me towards them. The first was Charles Guildenhuis, President of SCORE. I recognized his tall, thin and gaunt figure from newspaper reports. His long blond hair was turning grey. I figured him to be in his mid-fifties. He reminded me of a Viking, quietly going to seed. I had researched him on Google. Charles Guildenhuis was a major financial contributor to the political party that I abhorred. Here, he extended a limp hand unenthusiastically as he looked me over.

"Pleased to meet you," I murmured unenthusiastically myself.

"Likewise," and he turned away to make a comment to an elderly old dame dripping in pearls. She nodded at whatever Guildenhuis had said. It was too soft for me to catch.

I looked at the older woman. Her hair was snow white and piled high on her head. Despite her age, her face was unlined. Her neck, without a vestige of sagging skin, showed off the myriad pearls. I suspected some Beverly Hills cosmetic surgeon was driving a new Bentley as reward for fine tuning her face. The woman smiled something to Guildenhuis and then turned to Bertha and asked, "And who is this fine looking young man?"

Guildenhuis made a quiet "Hurrumph," and walked away.

"This is my great-niece Matilda's husband, Professor George, from the Irvine branch of the University of California. He will give the banquet address tonight. George, Matilda, may I introduce you to Happy Forrester. She is the famous romance novelist. Every book makes the New York Times bestseller list."

"I know," Matilda said shaking Happy Forrester's hand. "I just read *The Spurned Lover*. Enjoyed it immensely. You do write well."

"Thank you. I'm glad you enjoyed it." She looked over at me, speculatively. "You, professor, would make a marvelous model for the cover of one of my books, especially with your shirt ripped open. Look, he is going bright red! How charming," and she smiled.

"I'm afraid my husband is not into romance stories," Matilda came to the rescue. "He only seems to read textbooks and scientific papers."

"And who is this exquisite young blonde with the good taste in dress?" It was a thin woman with horn-rimmed glasses, wearing a beautifully tailored tweed suit. She stared at Matilda as if undressing her. Her eyes scanned Matilda's dress but narrowed as they took in the pendant diamonds. Was she trying to figure out if they were real or simply well made cubic zirconium.

"This is Phillipa Madison, editor-in-chief of *Fashion Digest Magazine*," Happy said. "If you have her approval, you are well dressed indeed. Phillipa, this is Matilda, the pretty wife of tonight's speaker, Professor George. So she is taken, Phillipa. Stop salivating."

"Pity." Madison turned away and strode around to Guildenhuis. "Charles, can I have a word with you?"

"Don't pay too much attention to Phillipa. She can be very abrupt. Bertha, Hillary Herschel has just entered the lobby," She looked over to the entrance and we followed her glance. Hillary Herschel carried herself proudly as she stepped over to the registration desk to make some remark to the clerk before turning towards where we were standing. Happy Forrester herded us away to the bar. "Probably a good time for us to get a cocktail or some wine. What would you like to drink, Professor and you too, Matilda? Oh, Jeffrey is tending bar tonight. Good. That means double shots."

Jeffrey had changed his bell-hop uniform to that of a barista and must have overheard her. "Ah, Ms. Forrester, a Vieux Carré as usual tonight." And he reached for bottles stored under the counter. I knew about the drink. The base for the drink was equal parts of rye whiskey, brandy and sweet vermouth, to which one adds a little Benedictine and dashes of both Angostura and Peychaud's bitters. I noted that the brandy he selected was *Armagnac Hors d'age*, a very fine brandy indeed. "Ms. Forrester, I assume you want your usual three Luxardos?"

"I don't know this drink," Matilda said, looking at me.

"I had one once in New Orleans," I explained. "It was invented there at the city's famous Carousel Bar sometime in the 1930s. Try one. People describe it as delightfully complex."

"What is a Luxardo?" Matilda asked Happy.

"They are the original Maraschino cherries. There are no better. I am a sucker for sweet things and I do love cherries. In the early1800s, or thereabouts, a woman, Maria Canevari, developed a wonderful cherry liqueur. This led to a business named after her husband Girolamo Luxardo. It's a long story that starts off in, what is now, Croatia and goes to the Austro-Hungarian Empire, where a massive distillery was built. It was destroyed by the allies in the Second World War. The sole survivor of the family fled to Italy with one small cherry tree, where he met up with a contact who had a copy of the secret recipe book. The firm is now in Veneto, Italy and still makes liqueurs and maraschino cherries. The story might make a good foundation for a romance novel. The company takes sour marasca cherries and candies them, the end product being Luxardo maraschino cherries. They are not the bright scarlet of the cherries to which you are accustomed. Luxardo cherries are like opulent rubies, almost black in color and so yummy. I love them." Happy finished the story.

"As do I," Great-aunt Bertha chipped in.

"I thought that maraschinos trace their way back to some convent in medieval times in Dalmatia," Matilda butted in. I am not sure how she knew that.

"Ah yes, that was rosolio maraschino, the liqueur."

After the story, both Matilda and Great-aunt Bertha had no option but to order a Vieux Carré.

I decided to be more conservative and ordered a simple gin and tonic with a twist of lime.

"Bombay Sapphire is good enough," I said to Jeffrey.

While he was mixing the drinks, a voice from behind me said in a strident voice. "Tippling again, Happy?"

It was Hillary Herschel and there was obviously no love lost between Happy and Hillary.

79

Happy merely replied, "Don't be a bitch, Hillary."

"And who are these people?" Hillary stared intensely at Matilda and me as we turned around to confront the voice.

"Professor George and his charming wife, Matilda." Happy informed her.

"What are they doing here? I understood this was a closed society. Perhaps they should leave?"

I could see Bertha starting to bristle. "Professor George is a world famous orchid biologist," she said sharply. "He has been invited to address the gathering tonight. You should be honored that he even deigned to come and meet with our group."

"I can just imagine what Boris will have to say about this. You know he wants to be restrictive about SCORE. He was just saying that we should not bother replacing deceased members. The smaller the group the more kudos for being a member. He will be irate to learn new people were invited to the meeting."

"Well, Boris is not here. He had to stay in Russia, thank God, and is missing our gathering this weekend."

"Who is Boris?" I asked.

"Boris Prokov, is a Russian entrepreneur, fabulously wealthy, who believes the world must kowtow to all his wishes. Of course he is wrong," Bertha informed us.

It was becoming clear from both Herschel and the president, Charles Guildenhuis's attitudes that I might have an uphill battle to get accepted into the group.

"This is not the way to make our guests feel welcome," Happy said. "I, for one, am looking forward to hearing what the professor has to say tonight. We must apologize for Ms. Herschel's rude behavior. Please ignore her, she cannot help being uncivil." At that, Hillary Herschel stalked off, leaving us feeling uncomfortable in her wake.

Happy looked after her, saying, "What can one expect? After all, she was brought up in the slums of Detroit and is only here by the grace of marrying the CEO of one of the world's leading automobile manufacturers. She is one of the most stuck up people I have ever met, and I bet she believes that she farts 4711 eau du cologne."

Bertha laughed.

Happy turned to us, "Bertha, you and your guests must be careful. That woman means to cause trouble tonight. Melinde Berser confided in me that bin Osman would like to have you banned from the grand orchid exposé in Chiang Rai. Apparently, he knows of your friendship with Paul Tylo. SCORE may attempt to have you and yours blackballed. They are afraid that they will lose the invitation to come to the unveiling of bin Osman's fabulous new paph."

Melinde continued and Happy concurred, "Yes, and Hillary has Guildenhuis in her back pocket. He will do whatever she asks."

This was a new wrinkle that we had to deal with.

However, as other members of SCORE and their spouses and partners appeared, there was no indication that anything might be amiss. The SCORE secretary Mercedes Grilling appeared in a frumpy, long, blue skirt spoiled by a slit seam along one leg, showing a bit more thigh and her dumpy legs than was necessary. I could imagine Phillipa, eyes narrowed and sneering at her.

We were introduced to her. "If you need to know anything about SCORE, this is the person who you must ask. She knows absolutely everything." Great-aunt introduced us. Next was Morris Quicker, a Hedge Fund Manager, and his date for the weekend, an aspiring starlet named Felicity Fay. I wondered if that was her real name. Among the group was also Willis Formby, the well-known clothing designer, who had a handsome young man on his arm. I think William would have called him a vanilla twink. Melinde Berser, another member, was apparently a movie producer. One person who went out of his way to charm us was Horace Terkhamian, the famous plastic surgeon. Most of these people seemed pleasant enough and we put 'the bitch,' as Happy described her, out of our minds. After introductions and nibbles on a few of the hors d'oeuvres, we were summoned in for our meal. The audio-visual tech asked for my flash drive for the talk I was to deliver. I asked him about the projector quality. Great-aunt had told me I would be expected to talk when the others started on their desserts. The tech assured me that my dessert, an English Trifle, would be kept fresh for me until after my talk had been delivered.

I always get a fit of the jitters before a public performance and this was no exception, especially as we had so much riding on it. We were seated at a table with Happy, Great-aunt, Morris Quicker and his companion, who looked like a starlet and gave the impression of a bimbo blonde. I thought it was merely an act to impress the wealthy Hedge Manager, but she made some inane comment about chocolate being non-fattening and how she just hated the idea of having to learn her lines for a small walk-on-part in an off-off-Broadway production. I was not sure why she combined the two thoughts and I saw Matilda raise an eyebrow. The meal came and went. I thought it was probably delicious but was too nervous to do more than push my food around my plate.

Great-aunt Bertha noticed this, kicked me under the table and said, "Just relax. You will be okay. Remember you know more than all of them combined."

The tables had been cleared for the dessert and Charles Guildenhuis arose and cleared his throat. They all looked at him expectantly and then they looked at me.

"Tonight," he started, "we have been promised a lecture by Professor George from the University of California. Actually, I have no idea what he is going to talk about, but I have been promised by our esteemed member," and he pointed at Great-aunt Bertha, "that it will be educational, provocative and also entertaining. We will take a ten minute break while the tables are being cleared of our dinner dishes and desserts are brought in."

There was a general rustle as several members got up and headed for the toilets or to have a quick cigarette break. After the desserts were set out on the tables, the lights were dimmed slightly. I had been reassured that the projector could throw enough lumens to give a bright picture. I walked over to a podium that had been set up. It was a small enough audience and so I did not need a microphone. "Good evening, ladies and gentlemen." I pressed the button on the slide clicker to bring the title slide to the screen.

As the screen lit up, the title slide slowly came into focus.

"Orchids and Deceptive Marketing"

Pollination

Enticement and Deceit

Rape and Fulfillment

Sex Among the Orchids

There was a gasp from someone in the audience. It turned out to be Hillary Herschel who stood up and glared around the room, "What is this filth?"

I jumped in, "Miss Herschel…"

"It is Mrs. Herschel!" She corrected me.

"Er…Mrs. Herschel, I assure you I am not going to talk about anything salacious, merely how orchids are able to persuade insects to carry their pollen from one flower to the next. It will be very respectable."

She made a loud hurrumph sound … and settled back down, leaning over to an elderly gentleman and saying loudly enough in a stage whisper for everyone to hear, "We will see how respectable he is."

As my talk progressed I pointed out that many orchids do not offer rewards to the insects that they enticed to carry their pollen. They often deceived their pollinators by pretending to be flowers that gave rewards. So some of the cymbidium orchids in the wild have the same color as rhododendrons that flower at the same time and offer nectar. Many of the slipper orchid species have markings or bumps that look like aphid infestations and can even have crystalline shiny areas around a central 'aphid' (it is actually a raised bump in the center of the staminode) that mimic the honey dew that aphids produce. The reason for this is that they are pollinated by female syrphid flies that lay their eggs among 'aphids' because their larvae normally feed on aphids. The flies get trapped by the flowers and in their efforts to escape, are forced to pollinate them. I showed close up pictures of various flowers and their parts to illustrate my lecture.

Looking around the audience, I found that many of the members seemed enraptured by the topic, but Mrs. Herschel was sitting rigidly and scowling from time to time. Even Guildenhuis appeared to be interested.

But then I showed them pictures of various species of *Ophrys*, European orchids where one petal takes on the appearance of a hairy female bee. They even have shiny blue wing patches, and I told them how the male bees emerge from hibernation ten days before the female bees, when the orchids are in flower. It was then that I noticed Herschel becoming more and more agitated.

"The orchid flowers even smell like female bees and they produce the exact same pheromones," I said. "The male bees swoop down onto the orchid and actually mate with the flower, to the point that they often deposit sperm on the flower. While they do this, if they have pollen stuck on them from a previous visit to another blossom, they can transfer that to the flower with which they are currently copulating and effect pollination."

By now Mrs. Herschel was positively squirming.

"So you see," I continued, "while the bees are raping or masturbating on the flowers they are doing nature's work." I saw her jaw drop and her eyes open wide. I thought I could even see flecks of saliva spurting out her mouth.

"The interesting question," I asked, "is this. It's easy to see what the orchids gain from the encounter. They get pollinated. But what do the insects get, other than a good time?" And I grinned. "Why and how does something like this evolve?"

Mrs. Herschel was slowly rising out of her chair. She was in slow motion and I decided I had better finish quickly.

"Female bees will only allow a male bee to mate one time, so he had better be good at it when he gets his chance. The orchids allow the males to get practice so that when the females emerge, they are ready to go at it. Both parties win and evolution can account for it." Several members of the audience chuckled.

Hillary Herschel drew herself up to her full height. She was red in the face. "What utter rubbish," she screamed. "There is no evolution. And there is no way God would have designed such a thing. Take your heresies and your masturbating bees and get out of here. Go

84

back to your university where Satan reigns and take your impure thoughts with you. You disgust me!"

All hell broke loose. It became clear in the resulting fracas that SCORE was divided into two camps, those for us and those against us. Several members had raised their voices.

"Perhaps we should leave," Matilda suggested to Great-aunt Bertha.

"Yes, that would be best. I will stay and try to take care of everything. Leave it to me." She kissed Matilda on the cheek and blew a kiss at me.

Matilda took my hand as we left the dining room. No English trifle for me that night.

"Sorry no trifle tonight," she said. "We can do better. Skinny dipping in the Jacuzzi."

I smiled despite the rising tension in the dining room. I had done my best.

As we walked back to the room we discussed my talk.

"I thought I gave a good talk tonight."

"Yes. Most of the audience was riveted. As good as any you have given recently. Pity that bitch had made up her mind, before she even came into the room, that she would try and sabotage it."

"I suppose so. Hard to predict the outcome now."

"Most of the audience was on your side."

"Can Great-aunt Bertha do anything, do you think?"

"She can be a formidable lady. We will just have to wait and see."

"I suppose so."

"It might be a blessing if we cannot go with SCORE to see the orchid. I think the microbots are very iffy. Are we going to be able to get them working reliably? I'm not sure we can pull it off."

"Yes, but I hate to give up on getting the preserve."

"I know my dear. No point on brooding about it. Let us wait and see what develops next. Maybe it will all work out."

Back in our suite, there was a surprise. On the desk was my dessert, a large helping of trifle with a note from Jeffrey.

85

Great talk. I was listening from the back of the room. So fascinating. Enjoy.

Jeffrey

At least the help thought I had done a good job, even if the bitch from hell did not think so. I needed this comfort food and blessed Jeffrey as I set about devouring it. Meanwhile, Matilda had already gone onto the deck and I heard splashes from the hot-tub. Remembering her promise I quickly spooned up the dessert, relishing the rich custard, layered with crisp slices of kiwi and juicy raspberries, all with thick slabs of sponge cake soaked in both cream sherry and cognac. The whole thing was covered with lashings of whipped cream. It was heavenly.

Dessert did not last long. I hurriedly discarded my clothing, and strolled out towards the hot tub. Matilda had turned on the pumps of the vat. She sat leaning against the wall of the tub, submerged almost up to her shoulders. Her breasts bobbed up and down in the swirling water. Matilda looked up at me, scanning my body.
"My, you are eager. Good thing no one can look onto the deck."

Chapter 8 – Downtown Julian

The following morning Great-aunt Bertha was uncharacteristically subdued when we met for breakfast at the spa's coffee shop. There was also a formal restaurant, but breakfast was not served there. Some of the SCORE members greeted us politely, but a few ignored our presence altogether and pretended we did not exist.

"So what happened after we left?" Matilda asked Bertha, her tone a little apprehensive.

"We had a very frank discussion."

"And where does that put us?"

"It is too early to tell. Guildenhuis wants another meeting behind closed doors. I suggest that you and George go and visit the village today. Take in lunch at one of the local cafés. I think that Herschel will be in full dragon mode. Not sure who rubbed chili peppers up her ass but she will be doing her best to black ball you. I know that Guildenhuis is on her side too. And Herschel also has a proxy vote from Boris Prokov. Something about a letter that she will produce at the business meeting early this afternoon."

It was all enough to make me lose my appetite and I only asked for coffee and whole wheat toast.

"Are you still thinking of staying for the entire weekend?" Matilda asked.

"We cannot give up now," Bertha answered. "That is what the other side is hoping for, and they don't know the reasons for which we we need their endorsement and I cannot give them the real details."

I glanced around the room. Fortunately, no one was within hearing range. "I will not let Herschel have her way," Bertha insisted.

It must have been some time after ten in the morning when we drove the Mercedes South along Banner Drive back into the village. Main Street itself is only four blocks long and runs in an East-West direction. Weekend tourists were already present, making parking difficult. Finding a side street away from the main road to park, I turned left onto B street and drove the two blocks to 5th avenue, turned left again and parked in front of a house. The entire tourist part of

Julian probably encompasses less than fifteen not very big city blocks. The town still looks very much the way it must have been in the 19th Century, very frontier in style.

We walked back down to Main Street. A few weeks earlier there had been a daffodil festival with a flower show in the small, almost dilapidated Town Hall. The banners flying across the street were still present. The street appeared to be lined with cafés and restaurants proudly touting their apple pies.

"Let's stop and get a cup of coffee," Matilda suggested. "I read about a quaint café on the last block of Main Street that is known for its baked goods and it has a small outdoor patio where we can sit and have our coffee."

"Sounds good to me."

"It's on the other side of the road."

So we crossed the street, dodging a string of cars looking for places to park. One modern feature was the presence of parking meters. I felt smug knowing the Mercedes was safely locked away from all the traffic and in an unmetered area. City folk, up from San Diego for the day, filled the street, strolling the sidewalks, peering into all the shops selling souvenirs or antiques. Many of the people appeared to be young couples, some with children, and others without. I found we had to dodge around them as they often stopped in the middle of the sidewalk to gawk at something, completely oblivious to other people attempting to walk on by.

I suppose I have a naturally suspicious view of the world but it seemed to me that every time Matilda and I stopped to look in a shop, a pair of women half a block behind us stopped at the same time but they were not looking at any of the store windows. They sometimes talked together but usually were silent, just watching other people strolling along the sidewalk. I figured they were both in their mid-thirties and were quite attractive. Perhaps that is why they caught my attention. They both wore boots, tight denim jeans and cowboy shirts, casual clothes that one might wear on an outing at a dude ranch but not really the clothes for a day in Julian. Each woman had a roomy bag draped over one shoulder. I wondered for a moment if they might be a lesbian couple, but they seemed to pay equal attention to both the men and women who walked by them. Their purses were large enough to hold a Derringer or something larger and more deadly.

"Let's go into that shop," I pointed to a news store.

"Why, what do you need?"

"Nothing, I think we are under surveillance. Need to check it out." And we slipped into the store. "We need to stay in here for at least five minutes. Find something that interests you."

"Can I help you?" The proprietress asked with a smile.

"Just browsing," and I smiled apologetically.

"No problem, just make yourself at home."

Matilda whispered, "How do you know someone is watching us?"

"There are two women, half a block behind us, but always keeping a constant distance between us. When we stop they stop. Something funny is going on. We must be careful."

Matilda looked at the magazines while I found a small printed guide to the town and its tourist spots. I am not sure that I ever mentioned that I have a sweet tooth. By the time I had selected a Milky Way candy bar, about five minutes had passed. This should have been enough time for the women to have walked past the news store to a position ahead of us, but I had been watching the store window and had not seen them go by. We paid for our purchases and I warned Matilda not to look back down the street. However, as I held the door open for her, I took a quick backwards glance, trying to act casual. The women were not to be seen.

"It's okay. They seem to have moved on," I said to Matilda. "I must have been mistaken. It was a false alarm."

"You are quite jumpy today. Try and relax this morning. Why would anyone want to keep us under surveillance anyway?"

As we walked along, Matilda held my hand and I felt like a teenager again, lucky to be in love, and contented to be away from the worries of the world. But it was really just an act. I did not want Matilda to think I was a worry wart. However, I could not get the two women out of my mind. I was so sure that they were stalking us. But I could not come up with any reason why they should do this. Who would set them after us?

We walked along, peering into shop windows, and stopping every now and then to smell bunches of lilacs that many stores offered. I relaxed and started to enjoy myself. Unfortunately, it was not to last.

We had covered much of the distance to the café when I saw the women again. It was a car honking its horn that made me glance back down the street. There were the two again, playing at being tourists. Both had put on dark glasses. They were crossing to the other side of the road, chatting together animatedly like recently reunited, intimate friends. They ignored the cars coming towards them. In California, pedestrians always have the right of way and those two looked intent on testing the law to its limits. Had I been too paranoid about them? The driver of the car that honked at them raised a fist and was probably swearing at them, but the women appeared oblivious to his threats. Surely, if they were stalking us, they would be more careful and not draw attention to themselves. Once on the sidewalk again, the women continued chatting like long lost friends who had finally found each other again. They were walking in the same direction that we had covered, albeit nonchalantly.

We turned to enter the café, but before I followed Matilda inside, I glanced surreptitiously over to the women and saw that they had stopped at the crosswalk at the corner of the block across from the café. But they did not bother to cross to our side, merely glancing across the road to the café. I supposed they would be able to see through the large front window at customers sipping coffee while seated at tables scattered about the shop. Did I imagine them pretending indifference while keeping an eye on the people, including us, within the store? Then both shifted their bags as if for easier access and reached inside them. My alarm levels went into overload.

"I think those women mean us harm," I said to Matilda.

"Sure you are not being paranoid?" she said echoing my own thoughts from a few moments earlier. "They look pretty harmless to me."

"Find a table that lets us look across the street at where they are standing," I suggested. "I'll order the coffees."

At the counter I said to the pretty barista who looked like a college sophomore, "One café Americano and one café au lait. No sugar. Thank you."

She asked for my name. "We will call you when your drinks are ready."

I paid and went over to Matilda.

"Any action?" I asked.

"No, they are just standing on the sidewalk over there, talking up a storm."

We watched for a while until the barista called out my name and I went to pick up the coffees. Suddenly both women froze as they noticed me getting up to fetch the drinks. At the side of the shop was a small garden patio screened off from the street by a tall hedge. I carried the cups out there calling to Matilda to follow. I selected a small table behind a large, leafy lilac bush. I could watch the street from there through a few gaps in the foliage but we should have been hidden from view of people outside the cafe. We could see them but I hoped they could not see us. If I was indeed mistaken about the women, they should just ignore the fact that we had disappeared. If not, our disappearance should spur them into action.

For a while it appeared that the women were unconcerned about our disappearance, but then they started to walk hurriedly across the street towards the café. Each had a hand in her purse and it was pointed in front of their bodies. They must have had guns that they were holding hidden from the surrounding pedestrians. I glanced around the enclosure. The only exit appeared to be back through the café. Some of the shrubs at the rear might be thin enough for us to squeeze through.

"Forget your drink. We need to get out of here fast. Through the bushes at the back."

We raced towards the back. The customers at other tables looked at us in surprise.

"Here." Matilda had found a place in the hedge at the back we could squeeze through and she slipped between the bushes. I had scarcely managed to squeeze through into the narrow alleyway behind the store, when I heard the women burst onto the patio.

91

I could hear one of the women announce loudly, "FBI. Where did that man and woman go?"

No time to ponder if they were really FBI. I doubted it, but expected one or more of the other customers would point to where we had left the patio. Matilda was racing down the alley, beckoning at me to follow and I needed no encouragement. She slipped between two buildings and I followed just as I heard the discharge of a gun.

"Stop!" One of the women commanded.

Hell no! I was not going to stop for them. The space between the buildings was too narrow for two people. Matilda had reached the end of the structures and turned to the right. There was a large garbage dumpster alongside one wall reeking of rotten food. If we ran along the wall our pursuers would see us. There was no choice but to hide in the dumpster. Matilda climbed in. I followed and we crouched down. We motioned to each other to be quiet and I pulled the lid closed. It was not the best of hiding places but we had no choice. One of the garbage bags had split open, releasing the most awful stench. I thought I was going to vomit. Matilda laid a hand on my shoulder and I gripped it. There was a small hole in the wall of the container and I could see a speck of light. I bent down and peered out. There, standing a few feet from the dumpster, were the two women. Each had a gun that she was waving around. We could hear them.

"Where did they go?"

"They must be in the dumpster."

"That stinks so much we would have heard them retching."

"Well, there is nowhere else they could be."

"Cover me while I open the lid."

The lid was too heavy to be lifted with one hand. She would have to put her gun down while she did it. It was our chance. As the woman struggled to throw the lid back, I quickly pushed the lid open, surprising her. She gasped, stumbling backwards. I grabbed the open bag of garbage and springing up, hurled the contents at the woman's head, drenching her with the rotten stuff. It looked like chunks of rotting fish. She shrieked. Matilda pitched a second but unopened bag at the other woman, as she squeezed the trigger of her gun. The bag connected with her head, messing her aim and the round ricocheted harmlessly off the wall. We both vaulted out of the dumpster. The first woman was vomiting and I was able to kick her gun away from her and it also discharged, harmlessly. Meanwhile, Matilda had slammed into the second of our pursuers and thrown her to the ground. They wrestled for the second gun. Matilda could always handle her own fights so I went over to the first woman, leaning and heaving against the dumpster. I retrieved her gun.

"Who are you and what do you want with us?" I asked, pointing her own gun at her. I hated guns (it's a long story for another time) and would never pull the trigger but she would not know that.

She looked at me sullenly, her chest still heaving; some vomit had stained her shirt.

"Go to hell!" She spat out at me. And suddenly, she swung around and grabbing the straps of her purse slammed it against my head, the clasp slicing open my cheek. I felt the blood well up and start dripping down my face. Involuntarily, I put my hand to my face and it came away red with blood. I could feel a giddy shock coursing through my body.

While I was still reeling, she ran over to where Matilda, on the ground, had just taken possession of the other gun. She kicked Matilda, the heavy boot raking alongside her head. Matilda gave a cry and collapsed, knocked out cold.

The woman helped her companion stagger up.

"Come on Olive, we better get out of here."

She stared back at me, challenging me to use the gun and then without further ado, both women ran away clutching their purses but leaving their guns behind.

I could not give chase, Matilda needed my attention. I sat down and cradled her against my chest. She groaned and slowly opened her eyes.

"G…George. What happened? Your face. You're bleeding. Where are those women?"

"They ran away. How do you feel?"

"Like I was kicked in the head."

"Actually, you were. Do you think you can walk?"

"I can try."

"We need to get back to Whispering Oaks."

"You need a doctor to see to your face. Otherwise, you will have a scar across your cheek."

"We can call a medic from the hotel."

We made our way back to the car. The few people we encountered looked away. I suppose they did not want to get involved. I drove back to the spa, hoping I was not smearing too much blood on the upholstery.

Jeffrey was aghast when he saw us, helped us back to our suite, and phoned for the house doctor, who it turned out, was away from town that weekend. Unfortunately, his locum was busy with an accident, so Jeffrey pulled Horace Terkhamian out from the SCORE meeting to have a look at us.

It was a polite knock on the door that signaled his arrival.

"Come in. The door is unlocked," I called out.

Terkhamian poked his head around the door and his eyes widened when he saw us, "What have you two been up to? My, you do smell ripe. Is that rotting fish I smell? Been dumpster diving?"

Little did he know that was exactly what had happened.

"We were attacked in Julian." I kept it as short as possible. "Look at Matilda first. She was kicked in the head."

"I am okay," Matilda said firmly.

"Let me check, anyway." Terkhamian pulled a small flashlight from his medical case and shone the light in her eyes. He muttered to himself, "Reflexes seem okay but she has a nasty bruise just above her left ear." He felt her skull gingerly. "Sorry if I hurt you. Skull does not seem to be fractured. Do you remember what happened to you Matilda? Both just before and just after the attack?"

"Yes, everything."

"Good. No amnesia. Do you have a headache or migraine anywhere besides the bruised area?"

"No."

"Excellent. I don't think you have a concussion. But the side of your head will be tender for a day or two. Take it easy for the rest of the day. But don't go to sleep until later tonight. If Matilda falls asleep this afternoon, Professor, wake her up and if you have trouble rousing her, send for me at once. Now, Professor, let me have a look at you."

He held my head at a slant and peered at the cut on my cheek. "Lucky it is a clean cut with no jagged edges and fortunately not deep enough to require stitches. I'll disinfect it first and then align the edges of the wound. I have some butterfly bandages and will use two to hold the edges of the wound tightly together. With luck you should not have a scar."

He cleaned the wound and applied the bandages, placing some more gauze over the whole thing and held that in place with some tape. Then he packed his unused supplies back into his carryall.

"Thank you doctor. What do I owe you?"

"Goodness, nothing. I have known Bertha for a long time and she has rescued me on numerous occasions. This gives me a chance to repay her and luckily you guys are not too damaged. Have you reported the thugs who attacked you to the police? Did they steal anything?"

"No."

"Well, you were lucky. But still, you should report this, we don't want hooligans on the streets of Julian. This is normally such a safe community. Now stay out of any more trouble. You have given Bertha enough to worry about as it is."

"What do you mean by that?"

"I should not tell you this but you seem to have made some powerful enemies among the SCORE members. I cannot imagine why, but then... you have lots of strong supporters, too. I am one of them. I will pop in later and see how you are doing. By the way, that was a really great lecture you delivered last night. Even if it did end in a general ruckus. I think you will be a great addition to our group, provided they vote to admit you, that is. Seems you have a reputation for getting into trouble. Don't worry I will say nothing about your current situation when I return to the meeting. That would jeopardize your chances. Mrs. Herschel, who leads the opposition, really does not like you. I don't understand why and she has not brought up any cogent reasons for excluding you, but she has rallied a good number of the group to her side. She would love to bring up this incident even if it is not your fault. I don't want to give her any ammunition. Don't let anyone see you until after the vote."

"When will that be?"

"Probably close to five or six this evening."

"Thank you for your support and advice," Matilda said.

"I don't know what it is worth. The final vote is yet to come."

After Terkhamian left, I helped Matilda undress and then did likewise and followed her into the shower. We needed to clean up but I kept my head out of the water. I helped Matilda shampoo her hair, being careful about cleaning around her bruise. We were still too shook up for any hanky-panky. We needed to dispose of our clothes. Perhaps have them burned.

We had scarcely dried off and climbed into fresh clothes when there was another discrete rap on the door.

"Who is it?" I called out.

"Me, Jeffrey. I brought you some lunch," and he came in after I unlocked the door. He delivered a plate piled high with an assortment of finger sandwiches. I saw whole wheat bread with English cucumber slices, others with tomato and cheese, and even some with shrimp salad and crackers heaped with liver paté. It was garnished with fresh raspberries, juicy strawberries and crisp grapes.

"Thank you," Matilda said. "George, do you think you can chew with your cheek all cut up."

"Lucky for me I can chew on the other side of my mouth. I had no idea how famished I am. Are you hungry, too?"

"I think I can eat a little. That paté looks quite nice."

"Good."

We relaxed in the suite for the rest of the afternoon. I watched a documentary on TV about a lost tribe in the Amazon. It amazed me how they kept finding new tribes, still living under Stone Age conditions. It must have been close to five that afternoon when the phone rang. I lifted the receiver.

"Sir, this is Jeffrey."

"Yes, Jeffrey?"

"There is a delivery for you at the front desk. Shall I bring it to your room?"

"What is it?"

"A bouquet of flowers. I think they are roses."

"From whom?"

"Don't know, sir. There is a sealed envelope."

"Who is it addressed to?

"Mrs. Matilda, sir."

"Very well. Bring it to the room. Thank you."

I turned to Matilda, "Seems some admirer has sent you roses."
"Curious, I wonder why."
"And I wonder who."

Jeffrey delivered half a dozen yellow roses in a simple crystal vase. At least they were not red roses. A small envelope was attached to the stem of one of the flowers with a simple yellow sateen bow. It had Matilda's name scrawled on it. She detached it and slit the cover open, pulled out an ivory card and read it. Without saying a word she handed the card over to me.

TROUBLE IS SPAWNING

THIS IS FAIR WARNING

BEGONE BEFORE MORNING

OR ELSE!!!

AND TAKE THAT DAMN PROFESSOR WITH YOU!

Chapter 9 – Whispering Death

I don't take kindly to threats and neither does Matilda. It puts my back up and is sure to make me do exactly the opposite, but was this something we could ignore? Was this warning from Mrs. Herschel? Who did those two female operatives we had encountered in Julian work for? I could not believe they were from the FBI. That made no sense whatsoever. And it was not a casual hold-up. They had staked us out and spent quite some time following us. This was one of those times that I wished Jake was with us. His insight was invaluable in these situations.

In the end, however, the matter was taken out of our hands. A half-hour later, Great-aunt Bertha came storming over to our room. She was irate.

"What is this? Horace says you were held up in town. Matilda might have a concussion and you, George, were sliced open. Are you both alright? Why didn't you call me as soon as you got back to the Spa?"

"You were busy and our injuries were not life threatening."

"But bad enough that you required a physician. I don't need this sort of worry."

"And that is exactly why we did not inform you of our problems."

"Matilda, let me see your head," and Great-aunt made a close examination of Matilda's bruise before finally kissing it and adding, "I suppose you will live. And you…" She turned to me…"You look like Frankenstein with your face all bandaged like that."

"Gee thanks," I said.

"So, tell me everything, and don't leave anything out," she commanded as she settled into the chair by the desk. We gave her a minute by minute account of our day, ending with the vase of flowers and handing her the card. She held it, staring at the script as if she could divine who the writer might be.

"I wonder how this is all connected," she mused. "Only the members of SCORE and the hotel staff know you are in town. I suppose those two women could be independent operators looking for some innocents to mug, but the way they followed you, I must admit it seems unlikely."

"We were wondering why Hillary Herschel was so upset last night. That was an extravagant display of bitchiness. It's unusual for even a fundamentalist bible thumper to allow themselves to freak out like that, and merely because George alluded to the evolution of some flowers. I was surprised how emotional that woman became," Matilda said.

"I can answer that now," Bertha offered. "Melinde Berser told me after our meeting today that Herschel has sued her husband for divorce. Apparently she walked in on him humping one of the maids in the master bedroom. I gather she even burned the sheets afterwards. It is going to cost him a pretty penny. She was looking for a fight last night even before she met you. And you were talking about sex. Even if it was sex between bugs and flowers. But it does not make sense that she would have hired someone, let alone two people, to try and take both of you down. That seems to have been preplanned. And why the warning for you to leave town? This has to be more complicated than we suppose."

"What do we do now?" Matilda asked.

"Well, we were supposed to go home tomorrow anyway. So we may as well stay here and try to enjoy ourselves. I am going to make reservations in the spa's restaurant for tonight. I'll make them for 8 p.m.," Bertha said.

"Are we secure at Whispering Oaks?"

"Probably. But before I came to speak to you I contacted Jake, so he and William are driving to Julian as we speak. They will join us for dinner tonight, and will be staying in the suite next to yours. All complements of Paul Tylo."

"So, you know about our day. Now tell us about yours. How did your meeting go?" Matilda asked.

"Well, it was not quite a disaster."

"What does that mean?"

"I was hoping that offering George membership in SCORE would simply be *pro forma*. It is true that neither of you have great wealth but George does have great prestige. After all, he has an international professional reputation as an important orchid biologist

99

and that should mean a great deal. But we have a clique in the membership, who for no good reason, or so it seems to me, are scared that George's considerable orchid knowledge will make them appear very amateurish and inconsequential. They have brought up a number of arguments, none of which I find very convincing. They say that once it becomes known that George became a member, that others will point to the fact that they have relaxed their standards. In the past we have refused to admit academics to the group. They simply cannot afford most of our activities which are usually very costly, five star resorts, etc. You must remember that SCORE makes no pretenses that it is an egalitarian group. They argue we need fewer members, not more; the fewer we are, the more exclusive we become."

"I have heard of snobbery," Matilda said, "but this is ridiculous."

"Sounds as if they have rejected my application," I added.

"No," Bertha said, "They have tabled consideration of your application until the entire membership gets a chance to vote. A number of members were not present and they will have to be polled. We had more than a quorum to take a vote and I think it would have passed today, but Herschel presented a petition from the Russian, Prokov, for a delay and a full membership vote. Unfortunately, it only takes three members to ask for a full vote. Prokov, Herschel and Charles Guildenhuis together demand the full vote and so for the moment we are at an impasse."

"Is there time for a vote before the Chiang Rai Orchid Show, which is only a few months away?"

"Oh yes, it can be done via email."

"So all hope is not lost, yet."

"Anything else transpire at the meeting?"

"Yes. Bin Osman has been corresponding with Guildenhuis about his fabulous orchid. Apparently it has a strong spike showing and it will be ready for the Chiang Rai Show."

"I thought he was going to have a private showing for SCORE?" Matilda mused.

"Apparently, he has changed his mind. Now all the attendees at the charity opening evening benefit will get to enjoy the flower."

"That could make it easier for us to get the pollen."

"Perhaps, but it could work against us as well."

"How do you reckon it will make it easier?"

"I was wondering how we would get Jake and William in to help us. Now we just have to buy admission tickets."

"Admission is by invitation only. How do we get the extra invitations?"

"I know a guy who is a big player in the Thai orchid world, Channarong Bunyasagaboon. He has one of the largest orchid nurseries in the country. I'll bet he can get me several invitations if I ask."

"Thai names always seem so unusual to me. They are so long, I never know how to pronounce them," Matilda commented.

"Thai names are not too bad once you understand them," Great-aunt added. "This is not the time for a lecture, but before we go to Thailand we will have to talk about them. You remember, as a young woman, I spent some of my time in Thailand when I did South East Asia – spent quite a few years there before I met my first husband. Most Thai peoples are only addressed by their first names and these can have specific meanings. For example, Channarong, means 'experienced warrior' but everyone addresses him as Kani. They like to use short nicknames of one or two syllables. Family names were only introduced during the early Twentieth Century and the government wanted each family name to be different, so in order to do that people resorted to very long names. Kani's family name is an exception. When written in Roman script, it is not unusual to have family names with fifteen or more syllables. Most family names are unique. I'd say nearly eighty-five percent of Thai family names are one of a kind. The same name means that people are related. No equivalent of Smith or Jones, with thousands of unrelated families. However, few people use family names."

"All very interesting, Great-aunt. However, if this Kani, or whatever you call him can get invitations to see the roth when it goes on display, why are we worrying about SCORE?" I asked.

"Because SCORE members will be allowed to get a closer look, and I am hoping that bin Osman will allow a SCORE member to measure the flower so we can write it up for a good orchid magazine. And it makes sense to ask a Professor to do the measuring."

101

Apparently Great-aunt had been working on how we would get access to the plant. She continued, "I am sure that after measuring the flowers bin Osman will get someone to examine the flowers to make sure that the pollen has not been disturbed but it will give us an opportunity to secrete one or two of the bots into the potting mix."

It was late afternoon when both William and Jake arrived at the spa. They had made good time despite the dreadful Southern California traffic. They stormed into the center of our room and ignoring Great-aunt Bertha, who was reading quietly in the corner by the desk, rushed in to confront us.

"Oh my God, George, you look a mess. You sure you are okay? See, you need us to look after you. The guys that jumped you must have been brutes. Are you going to have a scar? Jake, we need to go into town and see if we can locate those ruffians and teach them a lesson! And what about Matilda? Great-aunt said she had been knocked unconscious. How did you get away? Did you have to carry Matilda?"

"Calm down William. You are cackling like a demented hen. No need to freak out. We are both fine."

"You don't look fine."

"I have a little scratch and Matilda did not get concussed."

"Then why did Bertha call us to get here right away?"

"That was before she saw us. She was told we had had medical attention and she over reacted, sort of like what you are doing now."

William went over to Matilda and took her hand, "Honey, are you sure you are alright?"

"I am fine, William dear."

"What did those guys look like?"

"Actually, it was two ladies."

"Two women?"

"It is sort of embarrassing."

"Sort of embarrassing? How did two women beat up a big hunk like you?" Jake exploded.

So I decided that I might as well recount the entire saga all over again.

"Does not seem like a regular hold up – sounds more like a contract, but odd using women to do the dirty work," Jake thought aloud to himself.

'Oh, I don't know. In this day of sexual equality? If women can do the job, why not, and it looks as if they almost pulled it off." William was all for equality for everyone.

It was Jake who then suggested, "If you guys are okay, then we may as well drive back to our apartment in Orange County tonight."

"No Jake, there is more to it. Matilda received a threatening note this afternoon." And Great-aunt handed the card with the rhyme over to Jake, who shared it with William.

"This changes the complexion. Who do you think wrote this note?"

"We don't know."

"Well, to be safe, you guys should go home tonight too."

"I don't want anyone to think they can push us around. We will go home tomorrow as scheduled." I was adamant. No one was going to push us around, especially as we now had reinforcements.

"Well then, I suppose we had better stay here tonight, too," Jake said. "But if we do stay, then I want to make a suggestion. This is what we will do..."

Great-aunt Bertha made reservations for dinner that night at Les Chênes, the restaurant run at the Spa. We were told that suits and ties were *de rigeur* and I had been warned to bring a dark suit with me. Matilda wore a conservative but rich maroon outfit with a high neckline which nevertheless still revealed her hourglass figure and contrasted with her blonde tresses. Her hair now cascaded around her shoulders. She wore no jewelry. She did not need anything. She simply looked stunning in her own right. Both William and Jake also wore dark suits, Jake with a narrow reddish paisley-patterned tie and William, also, with a similarly colored and patterned bowtie. They made a stunning couple. Bertha must have told them to bring suits. Normally, William would have fought against having to wear a 'monkey suit' as he called semi-formal wear. Bertha must have been very persuasive.

"Are you packing?" I whispered to Jake, referring to his favorite Berreta, usually with a silencer.

He nodded, "Of course."

I wondered where on his body he had secreted it. Must have taken the silencer off to make it smaller.

Like everything else at Whispering Oaks, the restaurant was top cabin. Great-aunt Bertha had invited Happy Forrester and Melinde Mercer to join us. We waited for them in a small foyer. Many of the SCORE opposition, as I thought of them, were also eating at the restaurant that night. I watched their reactions as they passed us, hoping to get a clue about who might have sent the threatening card. Guildenhuis nodded briefly to us and then looked away. Melinde Berser and Morris Quicker came in together and while they scrutinized my face with its bandages, they did not say anything or even acknowledge us verbally. Dr. Terkhamian came in next. He inquired about how we felt and noted we seemed to be improving. He then went into the dining area and I saw him sit down at Guildenhuis' table. We were still waiting for our guests when Phillipa Madison, Willis Formby and Hillary Herschel arrived as a small group. They tried to ignore us but I saw a look of both surprise and shock pass across Herschel's gaunt face when she took in my bandages. The other two studiously ignored me. From her reaction, I was almost prepared to remove Herschel from my list of suspects.

We introduced William and Jake to Happy and Melinde as our very close friends and we went in to dinner. Our large table was draped in a beautifully embroidered linen cloth and had dark carved chairs around it and was positioned under a magnificent chandelier of cut crystal. I noticed that each table had its own chandelier and of a size that matched that of the table. The lights glinting off the crystal pieces dangling from the ceiling were, in turn, reflected off beautiful Waterford water and wine glasses at each setting. The place settings were of Royal Doulton bone china with a ribbon of gold around the rim of each thin plate. The main serving plate was surrounded by sterling silver cutlery polished to mirror sharpness. The array of knives, forks and spoons would have made the most fastidious English butler proud. I looked around the room again. Each table had one or two Ikebana arrangements, depending on its size. They were exquisite and must have been made by a master arranger. A number of large floral arrangements were set around the walls of the room. Everything was elegant, almost too elegant.

I noted that Jake had selected a seat opposite William, from where he could keep the room under surveillance. He was on alert although others in the room probably only saw him as slouching casually in his chair. William and Matilda were chatting happily together as was their wont. Great-aunt and her friends were talking quietly among themselves at the far end of the table. Bertha sat at the head, the matriarch, in her proper place.

After a while, William looked around, "There is no menu," he complained.

"William, tonight is a fixed menu," Great-aunt explained. "Armand, the chef, will decide what we are to eat."

"What if I don't like what he prepares?"

"At $350 per head, you will like it," Matilda warned under her breath.

William looked at her, "Yes ma'am and I will not complain that there is also no salt or pepper on the table, either. Wow, three hundred and fifty. I guess we are not getting hamburgers tonight."

The empty dinner plates were taken away and replaced with smaller plates, each covered by a lace doily upon which the first course, a small bowl filled with a milky-green, creamy liquid was set.

William looked at it suspiciously.

The waiter approached him, "A dusting of nutmeg, Sir?"

"What is this?" He pointed at the bowl.

"It is a cold avocado bisque, Sir."

"Don't call me Sir, You are old enough to be my father."

"Yes Sir, err... Nutmeg... young man?"

"I'll try a little. Thanks"

William tentatively selected the correct spoon after watching Great-aunt pick up her spoon. He dipped it into the bisque and sipped at the creamy soup. "Ah, this is yummy."

After the bisque was cleared away, the setting was prepared for the next course. This time the base plate was covered with a small napkin and the next course on a small saucer was placed in front of the diners. It was *pâté de foi gras*, from France and served on dry Melba toast so as not to interfere with the taste of the pâté.

"I thought you could not import fresh meats into the country," Matilda said.

"It is tinned," Great-aunt explained. "Nevertheless it really tastes freshly prepared."

"Poor geese, tortured for the pleasure of a few gourmands," William interjected.

"You mean gourmets?"

"No. I know what the word means and I used it correctly."

However, I noticed William seemed happy enough to eat his serving of goose liver.

"What is the next course?" William was waxing enthusiastic.

"Usually a small sorbet to cleanse the palate." Great-aunt knew what to expect.

The meal progressed from sorbet to Chilean Sea Bass glazed with caviar in *crème fraiche* then onto the mains, a serving of Chateaubriand, the pink meat tender enough to melt in one's mouth. Alongside the meat and on the plate were two shallow dishes, Japanese style, one with Béarnaise sauce and the other with the more traditional crapaudine sauce normally served with Chateaubriand. Each course had its appropriate wine. The meal ended with a brilliant dessert, an apricot mousse accented with just a hint of cognac.

"A most memorable meal. Thank you so much Great-aunt. That was wonderful and truly worth wearing a suit for." William was smiling blissfully. "However, the meals you and Matilda serve at home are every bit as good. Thank you, thank you and my tummy thanks you too."

"William, you are too much," but Great-aunt Bertha was smiling.

We all made our thanks and retired to the lounge for a liqueur, before retiring for the night.

It must have been shortly after midnight when I was woken up by the soft but persistent rapping at the door. I slipped out of bed.

"Who is it?"

"Me. Jake. Open up quickly, please."

I unlocked the door and he stepped in closing the door behind him.

"What's up?"

106

"As I suspected would happen, there was an attack on your room."

At Jake's insistence we had switched rooms with them. William and he had taken turns staying awake and being on guard while the other slept.

"Is William okay?"

"Yes. He was asleep but on the floor in the bathroom. I heard the front door being opened. The perpetrator must have had an electronic master key card."

"Didn't you have the deadbolt on?"

"No. I was setting it up for an invasion. I thought an attempt would be made and wanted to catch the person."

"Anyway, before I knew it there was a rapid succession of five shots at the bed. We had piled extra pillows under the covers to look like two people asleep."

"I did not hear any shots."

"The person had a suppressor on the gun, just made *Ph...tttt*! sounds."

"Did you see who it was?"

"No. It was dark and the person stood silhouetted in the doorway. I'd say about five-nine and medium build but the head was in shadow. I could not see the face. I yelled, 'Stop or I'll fire,' but the person ducked down and fled. He or she was very fast. By the time I got my six strides to the door, there was nobody I could see. It all happened so fast."

"Male or female, and only one person?"

"Could not tell the gender, may have been wearing a ski mask."

By this time Matilda was awake and listening, "Where is William?" she demanded. "Why did you leave him alone?"

"He is also armed."

"That is ridiculous. He does not even know which end of the gun to point."

"Not any more. Since Africa, he has been spending time with me at a shooting range."

Just then, there was a loud report, a gunshot apparently coming from the room next door."Oh God, William."

107

We all rushed out of the room, Jake in the lead brandishing his Beretta. He turned to us quickly and commanded, "Stay back! Go and lock yourselves in the bedroom."

We were in no mood to obey him. If William was in danger, we were not going to run and hide.

It was no more than a hundred feet along the veranda to our original bedroom. A small nightlight near the door of the suite barely lit the way. We were half way there when a round smacked into the wall in front of Jake, blasting a sizable hole. He dove to the pavement and we followed suit. The sound of this shot reached us after the bullet had hit the wall. It was coming from the forest across from the lawn. We were sitting ducks. Jake pointed the Beretta, aimed along the silencer at the night light ahead of us and pulled the trigger. At least we were now in the dark. A second round smashed into the wall behind Matilda, again followed by a report. The sniper must have been using a Browning Mac-10 rifle, also known as the *Whispering Death* because its rounds found their target before the sounds reached their victim. I prayed whoever this was did not have an infra-red scope that would let him target on our body heat.

"Flat on your belly and wriggle towards the door." Jake set the pace and it was hard work. Snakes do not have it easy. After this, I would see them with new respect. That is if I survived this.

The third round struck the wall lower than the first two, but still behind us. The sharp shooter was lowering his sights closer to the floor of the veranda.

"George, Matilda, crawl next to the hedge. Make it difficult for the sniper to see where you are." Jake whispered urgently and we wriggled over to the boxwood. I was not sure that the hedge would be any protection against an infra-red scope. The next round found a window and glass flew over the pavement.

"Continue to stay down," Jake said in a hushed voice. "He may be waiting for you to make a move." And we lay prone alongside the hedge. I wriggled backwards until I was parallel to Matilda. Jake continued his progress towards the bedroom where William should be hiding. I put an arm around Matilda's shoulders and drew her close to me. We were both fighting the temptation to jump up and try to run away. Instead, I pressed Matilda closer to the pavement and then insinuated my body between her and the sniper. I was trying to shelter her but I knew it would be futile. One round from the Whispering Death could slam right through both of our bodies. I whispered in her ear, "Always remember this, I love you very much." The next moment the veranda in front of us, where I had been only a moment before, exploded, tearing out chunks of the hedge as well. The sniper had lowered his sights trying to guess where we were hiding.

By now the noise had roused many of the residents at the spa and lights started popping on all over the place. Jake had reached the bedroom door but he could not stand up to unlock it. Someone must have called 911 because I could hear sirens approaching in the distance. I wondered how many first responders a small village like Julian could produce. Would the sniper try to flee? We all continued to hunker down where we were. There was no more gunfire.

Chapter 10 – Another Attempt on our Lives?

It was a local sheriff's deputy who was first on the scene and he found us still hiding behind the hedge. As soon as Jake heard the deputy approaching, he called out to the man to take cover because the sniper must still be in the forest area. The deputy went around the corner of the building and we heard him phoning for reinforcements. The forest was now silent, and after a short period I thought I heard a car start. The sniper must have had a car on the other side of the forest. I could hear it moving off into the distance. By the time additional officers arrived the sniper had fled.

We found William hiding in the bathroom as Jake had ordered him. It turned out that William had not discharged his weapon. We had mistaken the report from the sniper's first shot as being from William. The sniper had tried to blow out the window of what he thought was our room. There was a small crater under that window. Perhaps we were lucky the person was such a poor shot.

It was five a.m. by the time we had given our statements and had answered what questions we could. Other members of the sheriff's department were called in from neighboring towns. We also reported the attack in town by the two women and were reprimanded for not having called it in earlier. I made the excuse that we needed medical attention. The principle investigating officer to whom we had given statements asked for a possible motive. We could suggest none. It was ridiculous to assume that it had anything to do with my lecture. No one was going to take a contract out on a university professor no matter how much they disliked his lectures. It had to be something else. But what? To make things even more complicated, surely the person who fired the shots into the bedding would have assumed that a kill had been made. So then why the sniper as well? Were two independent parties out to get us? If the women were separate, that might even mean three different parties were after us, and what had we done to deserve such singular attention?

We were advised to return to our homes in Orange County as soon as feasible, but to keep in contact with the investigators. In turn, they would also make contact with the Orange County Sheriff's Department. We could expect more questions. They promised to keep us informed of their investigations.

As soon as he was able, Jake phoned headquarters in Denver. He had a direct line to Paul Tylo's home and was not shy to use it. He gave a running account to his boss. He figured that there were three attempts but we had no information on whether or not they were separate or combined into part of a single operation. There had to be more to this than pollen stealing.

Great-aunt suggested that Jake and William drive us home right away. She would bring our luggage when she returned later that day. But first she had some more SCORE business to attend to and it could not wait.

It was Matilda who turned to Great-aunt Bertha as she came out to the car. "What makes you think we will be any safer at home than we are here?"

'True," Bertha said. "You are not going home. Jake is taking you somewhere safer. You will see when you get there. I will say goodbye to Jeffrey for you and give him a generous tip on your behalf. Leave it all to me."

"Where are you taking us?" Matilda asked, once we had settled into Jake's sleek BMW.

"We thought it safer for you to stay with us in our new condo for a few days. It is a gated community that is very concerned about its resident's privacy. Also it is close to the university, but I do not want you to go there. Call in sick for a few days. We want you safe and sound until we have a better feel for what is going on and why you have been targeted."

"And if you find out, then we don't have to worry about being safe?"

"You know what we mean. It may give us a chance to have the threat neutralized."

Neither Matilda nor I had visited their new living quarters before. There had been no reason to do so. They always came to visit us. Neither one had any cooking skills, and Matilda loved feeding the two men at either our home or at Great-aunt Bertha's estate. She spent hours designing new meals to try out on them and, of course, the two men appreciated her cuisine. Jake drove up to a security gate for the underground garage of one of the new condo towers on Jamboree Boulevard in Irvine. A guard was on duty who demanded to see Jake's identity card and driver's license before admitting us. Once the car was parked we followed the two men to an elevator and Jake held his card in front of a scanner before pressing the button for the fifteenth floor.

The condo was sparsely furnished and as they said, half apologetically they had only moved in a few months earlier and had only purchased the bare necessities. They led us to the spare bedroom, dominated by a king-sized bed and a chest of drawers.

"This is to be your room for the next few days," William said. "It will be nice to have you with us until it is safe for you to go home. Come let me show you the rest of the condo."

The condo was situated facing the back of the building away from the busy street and with no adjacent buildings opposite. It meant that no-one could look in through the windows from across the way. The living room led onto a small balcony. The view was wonderful. We looked down on a small lake that doubled as a bird sanctuary. I could just make out ducks and geese swimming near the rushes at the water's edge. It really was quite close to the university that I could make out on the other side of the lake. For the first time I realized that Tylo and Associates must pay Jake Seemore an exceptional salary. Certainly, William on a research assistant's meager income could only contribute a small fraction towards their rent, if anything. Even a full Professor, like myself would have had trouble making the monthly payments. Of course Jake often had to put his life on the line for Paul Tylo, so I suppose he earned a commensurate salary.

"This is very nice," Matilda said to William after we had been shown around. "I suspect that your colleagues must be green with envy."

"Actually, no one at the school is aware that we live up here. Remember that Jake is a very private person. His job, you know."

"Of course."

"Can I make you a cup of coffee?" William asked both of us. "Jake bought me a fancy espresso machine for my birthday. I have just

112

figured out how to use it. I want to show it off." He pointed to a stainless steel device on the kitchen counter.

"It is a Breville BES870XL Barista Express Espresso Machine," Jake said proudly. "Nothing but the best for my baby."

"I did not know you were a coffee connoisseur William," I said. "Thought you were always happy with instant."

"I am learning," William countered. He went to a cupboard near the machine and turned to Matilda. "You choose the beans you want." He pointed to half a dozen different packages and while Matilda selected one, he collected some special espresso glasses from another cupboard.

While we waited for the coffee to brew, I turned to say something to Jake, but he was wearing his phone's ear buds and waved me away. His face was very serious and his brows beetled. After a few minutes he got up and went onto the balcony. He appeared to be arguing with someone. I hoped it did not concern us. For the life of me, I could not understand why anyone would want to try and kill either or both Matilda and me.

"How long do you think we are going to have to be holed up here?" Matilda asked me.

"I don't know. But we can't stay here too long. I have work at school to attend to and we still need extra training with the microbots. And neither of these can wait."

"I have things that need to be done at home, also."

William produced two small glasses of espresso. They were double walled to keep the liquid warm. He handed one to each of us and then filled another two, one for himself and the other for Jake, still talking on the balcony.

I sipped at mine. "Whoa, not too bad. You'll make a barista yet," and William glowed.

When Jake rejoined us he looked glum. I raised an eyebrow at him questioning and he took a deep breath and answered, "That was Tylo on the phone. Max Fiercely is dead. It seems that Fiercely was in a freeway accident on the 405. Except it may not have been an accident. Tylo suspects that it was some sort of revenge killing, but he is not sure."

"When was this?"

"Just this morning while we were driving back home."

"What happened?"

"He was driving in to work. It was an open stretch when suddenly his car accelerated and slammed into the central divider. They think he was doing well over a hundred when he hit the wall. He must have been killed instantly."

"Accelerator got stuck?"

"Unlikely. The car had front avoidance collision radar and should have braked automatically. It did not."

"How do they get to a revenge killing from the accident?"

"They think a nearby car was remotely able to jam the radar system and turn it off."

"One can do this?"

"Apparently. I cannot give you all the details. Some of it is classified and even I don't know the whole story."

Matilda was listening with a look of concern on her face as she sipped her coffee. She spoke up. "Does Tylo think that our problems at Julian are connected to Fiercely's death? If so, how and why?"

"Tylo thinks it's possible but he appears reluctant to say how or why. He says the two could also not be connected. He is not sure."

"What about our bot training?" William wanted to know. "Is that over?"

"No. He wants us to continue. Jennifer Pandit knows almost as much about the little bots as Fiercely did, but there are other people involved with the development of the bots. Tylo has confidence Jennifer can finish training us, but he will assign someone else, as well, if there are problems. Apparently, the malfunctioning bots are being rebuilt. It will be about a week before we can resume training. I was not happy that Pandit had been assigned as Fiercely's replacement and tried to get us a different trainer but Tylo was adamant. Pandit will also work with us." Jake scowled at William. "And you are going to have to stop flirting, and you must tell her that you are not available. Maybe I should just tell her you are my fiancé?"

I could tell that William was about to let fly with some snide remark, but then he thought better of it and merely nodded in acquiescence before mumbling, "Bertha already told her I had a jealous boyfriend and that it is you. She thinks it is sweet that you have a jealous streak where I am concerned."

114

"You certainly don't act as if you care." Jake was not going to let go.

Sometimes William is like a little bantam rooster. I could almost see the feathers of his neck starting to inflate. In another minute we would have a full fledged cock fight on our hands. Jake was also bristling. Our presence was not going to censor their behavior. Luckily, Matilda stepped in to cool the situation.

"Boys," Matilda warned, "Get serious. We have some really nasty problems to deal with. People are trying to kill George and me. And now Fiercely is dead. Tylo thinks that Fiercely may have been murdered. We have no idea why or what any of this is about, and ... you two... are arguing because William smiled at some woman. It is time to get your priorities straight."

"Sorry."

"Matilda, why don't you phone Bertha and see what time she expects to arrive here?"

"Good idea, and then we can make some plans about this evening."

She tapped the contact number on her cell phone and then glared at it. "Her phone went straight to voice mail. She must still be busy in conference or she is driving back and has turned off her iPhone."

There was not much to do but sit and wait. I felt like a prisoner marking time. Jake went off to buy us lunch, a fast food meal of crisp tacos and green bean burritos with extra salsa. Simple, cheap and filling. While we waited for him to return, William put on a radio station that specialized in 80s music. He knew that both Matilda and I liked that but it did nothing to soothe our anxiety. What sort of mess had we gotten into this time? This seemed so much more serious than a simple caper to steal some pollen. Now it was a matter of life and death. I mused over a variety of scenarios that might explain what had happened, but I kept drawing blanks. Maybe it had nothing to do with pollen. Could it, instead, have something to do with the microbots? That might explain Fiercely's death, but then why should we be involved? We had been very careful not to tell Fiercely the real reason we were going to use his bots. Whatever the true situation, we could not remain in hiding. We needed to get on with our lives.

It was William who came up with an idea. "Do you think that Microbotics was also training anyone else to use the bots and we have been confused with that other party?"

"I don't know," Jake said. "That is a possibility. I will see what I can find out. It may take a couple of days. If there is another party involved I hope it is not classified. Sometimes when there are military operations it is kept top secret. Even Paul Tylo, himself, does not always get clear access to everything, especially where the Feds are concerned."

In mid-afternoon, Great-aunt texted Matilda to let her know she was on her way. We were to meet her for supper at seven o'clock and she gave us the name and address of a little Italian restaurant on Seventeenth Street in Costa Mesa. Orange County is a jigsaw of interconnecting cities; one running into the other, and often it is difficult to tell which city one is in. Distances are not that great and everything is usually within an easy drive, provided it is not rush hour. One measures how long it will take to get anywhere, not by the distance, but by the hour of the day.

"Texting us instead of phoning suggests that she does not want to talk. I suppose whatever business she still had with SCORE did not go very well," Matilda said.

"Let's not prejudge anything," William added.

I did not say anything. The last few days had left me totally bummed out with everything. Perhaps I should just give up on getting the orchid reserve? Life was certainly much simpler before I took on that burden. And with global climate change, who knew if any reserve would be viable anyway. I was driving myself down into a spiral of depression. Matilda, who is normally ultrasensitive to my moods, was totally unaware this time. All I wanted to do was curl up in a corner and ignore the world.

"Hey, hey!" It was William coming to the rescue this time. "Stop that."

"What."

"Don't you dare slip into a blue funk. I can tell."

I looked up at him and shrugged. "People have been trying to kill me. Fiercely is dead. SCORE hates me. And you want me dancing a jig in the corner with a smile on my face?"

116

"No. I know it is serious, but we have faced far worse before. Where is the good old George that I know? The one who does not give up without a fight."

"It just seems so pointless. We have to risk our lives so Paul Tylo can get his revenge jollies. Why can't he just get his rocks off some other way? What have I come to, that I place the people I love in jeopardy and ... for someone I don't even like?"

William laid into me, "I knew a George once; the old George who could not resist a challenge. He would get up and come out of his corner swinging, even if he had been knocked down many times before. The old George never, ever gave up."

"Well, maybe it is time for the old George to act his age. He is no immortal teenager any longer and he has responsibilities to those nearest and dearest to him."

I was suddenly aware that both Jake and Matilda were staring at William and me, trying to figure out what was going on.

"What are you looking at?" I would have snarled but I felt a great ennui sapping my strength.

"George. Are you feeling sorry for yourself?" Matilda asked.

I looked back at her. Did she expect me to be her Superman all the time? "No, but I need some down time. I don't want to have to look over my shoulder every second of the day. Suddenly I don't like where I am at. It is like my world is spinning out of control."

"You have the three of us to support you," Jake reasoned. "William and I are here to cover your back."

"That's right," William agreed. "No one expects you to do everything on your own. This is ultimately all for a very good cause. The old George would fight with his last breath to save an orchid species from extinction. So what if Tylo thinks he is using you. In reality we are using him too. And it is costing him a pretty penny. Where is the man who once said he would sleep with the devil if it allowed him to save one species from extinction?"

"I don't think you are helping me, William."

"But it is very difficult for someone who is used to being in control all the time to find everything suddenly going out of control." Matilda continued. "It's understandable that you feel bad about things. Maybe you just need a bit of a rest. You did not sleep much last night. We were awake for most of the night. I think I am going to take a power nap. I'll set the alarm for two hours from now. It will give us time to freshen up for supper. I do hope that Bertha has our luggage with her. George, come and rest with me."

I stomped off to our bedroom and threw myself onto the bed.

The Ristorante della Toscana was a tiny bistro hidden away in a corner of a strip mall and had Bertha not furnished the actual street address we would never have found it. I looked around for Great-aunt's Mercedes but it was not to be seen. It would not be unusual for her to have switched cars after arriving home. She had several autos and always seemed to be buying a newer model.

Jake asked us to stay in our car with the motor running while he slipped into the restuarant. After a moment he came back out and climbed into the driver's seat. "Yep. This is the right place. Bertha has reservations, a table for five. No one else is in there."

He turned off the engine and once we got out, locked the doors. He looked around cautiously and hearded us over to the restuarant. A small bell attached to the front door signaled our entrance. Inside I was surpised how small it was. There were only eight tables in the dimly lit room. A small oil lamp flame on each table scarcely spread enough light for the clientele to see what they were eating. A middle-aged woman greeted us and showed us to a table in one corner of the room. There was no one else in the dining room. Jake selected a chair were he could survey all of the tables and from where he could also keep watch on the sidewalk outside the front door. I looked around the room for an exit other than the front door. A swing door across from the front entrance led to the kitchen. It did not look very big. The woman who had seated us had disappeared into the kitchen. The entire restuarant was quiet. No sounds came from the kitchen.

"This is odd. Normally Great-aunt is very punctual. I wonder what happened to her? I hope that she is okay. Let me call her." But Bertha was not answering; the call went directly to voice mail.

"Perhaps we are at the wrong restaurant. I must have misread the address." Matilda reread Bertha's text on her smart phone. Suddenly, she gasped and whispered to Jake, but loud enough, so that both William and I could also hear, "Why did Bertha select this place?

She has never mentioned it before. It looks like a trap. Let's get out of here." She stood up, "Come on, everyone. Out NOW! Fast!"

We got up hurriedly and followed Matilda out the front door. Once outside, she hurried across the parking lot to where Jake had parked the car. "Hurry!" She called out frantically, and ran towards the car. Jake unlocked it and we all tumbled in.

"Drive, Jake, drive." He threw the car into reverse and then jack rabbited out of the lot just as the restaurant burst into flames and exploded, scattering glass fragments over the sidewalk.

"God," William cried, "That was close. Let's get out of here before the cops arrive.

"What about the staff? Shouldn't we go back and see if we can help?"

"No point. I glanced into the kitchen as we left. There was no one else in the place. This was all a set up," Jake confirmed.

While driving he used the blue tooth in the car to report back to Tylo and we listened in to the brief conversation. Other than to tell Jake to take us to a safe place he did not say anything that might enlighten us as to what was going on.

"Matilda, what was the clue that made you realize it was a set up?"

"When I kept getting voice mail from Bertha's cell phone, I thought maybe she could have misplaced her phone and I called the landline at her house. She answered her phone right away. She was at her house. She said, 'Thank goodness you called. Someone seems to have stolen my cell. Where are you?' At that point I figured we had better get out. Could have been wrong but glad I did not take the chance."

"You had better let her know what has happened," I said and she busied herself on the phone.

As we drove back down Seventeenth Street we could hear sirens converging on the strip mall from which we had just fled. I hoped that there had been no surveillance cameras to catch us running away from the restaurant.

"Jake," Matilda tapped him on the shoulder. "Great-aunt wants you to drive us to her place. She wants to report back on SCORE and we need to pick up our luggage."

119

"I'm hungry," William complained. "Can we just stop for burgers somewhere?"

"We just escaped from a fiery death and all he can think about is his stomach."

"Be grateful. It means he is still alive."

"Of course."

Matilda consulted her smart phone and selected a nearby eatery with a drive through. Jake stopped at the drive through window and William ordered a cheese burger and a soft drink. No one else felt like eating. We then drove back to the Interstate and headed south to Lake Forest and Great-aunt Bertha's estate. She met us at the door.

"Come in, come in," she beckonned, and escorted us into one of the smaller and more intimate lounges.

"Where is your cell phone?" Matilda demanded.

"I don't know. I was rushing, late for my meeting and thought I must have left it in my hotel room but when I returned at the break to retrieve it, it was gone. Maybe I dropped it somewhere."

"It was not misplaced. It was stolen." And Matilda ran through the account of how we thought we were texted from Great-aunt's phone to meet her at the restaurant and what had happened there and of our narrow escape. "A table for five had been reserved under your name," Matilda told Bertha. "We became suspicious when the staff all seemed to disappear. That's when I phoned your house and when you answered, I realised we were being set up for something. So we got out of the restaurant as fast as we could and we were just in time before it blew up. It was a close call."

"Well, thank God you are all safe now."

"Yes, but whoever these people are, they are not willing to give up," I said. "Just wish I understood why they think they need to kill us. I cannot think of anything we might have done to deserve this attention. This cannot have anything to do with bin Osman, or can it?"

No one could come up with any rationale about why we were being singled out or what any of us might have done to warrant these attacks on our lives. We stared at each other glumly.

"What's next?" Matilda asked. "Great-aunt, you may as well tell us what happened with SCORE today."

"Well, I have some good news. SCORE voted to admit George as a member, but in a temporary capacity, until he proves himself."

"Yay," said William.

"What made them change their minds? I would have made a bet that they would turn me down," I said.

"It was touch and go, but I pointed out that because of the attempts on your lives yesterday, that if they also barred your membership it might throw suspicion on some of the SCORE members. It was helped by the fact that everyone had to account for all their time yesterday and last night. We all had to give statements of our activities to the authorities. Fortunately, most of the membership bought my arguments. It would not have mattered anyway, because Channarong emailed me that he will provide an additional four invitations for the opening festivities of the orchid show."

Chapter 11 – More Spyder Training

The local news services had blamed the explosion at the Ristorante della Toscana on a faulty gas leak in the kitchen, and no one seemed to have noticed our lucky escape from the strip mall. They noted that no casualties or injuries were reported. The explosion was considered an accident and not a case of arson.

The following week was relatively quiet with no more attempts on our lives. We had an electronic surveillance system installed in our home. We moved back into our house, made sure that the security alarm system was working, but kept everything locked up all the time. I managed to spend some time in my office at school, but everyone continued to stay on high alert. I must admit that it was stressful, but what else could we do? William, in the meantime, had located several plants of *Paphiopedilum* St. Swithin in flower at a Santa Barbara Orchid Ranch and he made arrangements to drive up and collect them. The plants cost over two hundred and fifty dollars each but I figured Tylo would not even notice those paltry amounts. These slipper orchids were hybrids that had one parent being *Paph. rothschildianum*. In the absence of that species they would make a good facsimile for our target flowers. We were anxious to see if we could get the microbots climbing the plants to extract the pollen. Each plant was made up of several fans of about six leaves, each nearly a yard wide. Out of the center of one fan emerged a pencil thick stalk, itself nearly three feet tall and bearing four flowers. The plants were growing in clay flower pots about twelve inches deep and ten inches wide.

So it was that all five of us, together with three plants in tow, turned up at the T & A Robotics plant on a Tuesday morning, wondering what the day would bring. This time we were met by a young Asian man who, with his shoulder length hair dyed blond, looked as if he would be more comfortable on a surf board than in the paramilitary uniform he wore.

He introduced himself saying, "Hello, I am Brian Kim, one of the engineers at this plant. I have been assigned to help train you."

We introduced ourselves as well and then he led us into the building and down to the laboratory where we had trained during our last visit. We passed Fiercely's office, but the door was closed and his name plate had already been removed. No one mentioned his demise.

Jennifer was already in the lab and she greeted us somberly, merely nodding to William and Jake. She smiled at Matilda and Great-aunt, saying she was happy to work with them again. Then she reached into a leather case and extracted five microbots and showed them to us. The bots were now painted a dull green with some camouflage brown markings. Each had a different pattern and, in addition, there was a single black dot placed in a different position on each one so that we could identify them individually. There were also slight differences in shape, so even without their new paint jobs, I recognized Matilda's, Jake's and my own as they were placed on the table in front of us.

Jennifer pointed at one of the new ones, "This will be yours from now on, to replace the one that William's bot destroyed," she said to Great-aunt Bertha. "And this is your new one William. Hopefully its AI is in good working order this time. Max Fiercely reprogrammed it before his unfortunate accident."

"Please be seated." Brian gestured to a semi-circle of chairs in one corner of the room. "I want to make sure that I understand what this project is all about. I was told that you want to be able to collect pollen from a rare orchid species growing in dangerous terrain in a forest somewhere in Borneo. Is that correct?"

"Yes," I dissembled.

"On a cliff, I have been told."

"That is right."

"I don't understand why one would want to do this. But I suppose that is none of my business."

William and Jake had carried in the three plants. The man at the gate had merely grunted when he saw them. He was no longer as suspicious or officious as on our first few visits although he still insisted on inspecting our passes as if he had never seen them before. He had gesticulated to the three orchids, "How much more herbage are you going to bring in?"

"Oh, a whole forest, eventually." William could not resist the jibe.

"I hope those approximate the wild orchids you want to get to," Brian Kim said.

William answered, "Yes, they are about the same size."

"If you pass your cell phones over to me, one at a time, I will reinstall the app you need to control your individual bots. While I am doing that Jennifer will help you set up your plants. Jennifer, please space the pots as far apart as possible."

He fiddled with the phones and handed them back to us.

"Take turns, select a plant and see if you can guide your bot over to the plant that you have choosen. And see if you can climb the flower pot, find the flower stem and climb up it to a flower."

It took a while to get used to the guidance systems again, but eventually we were able to get the bots not only to the correct plant but also to clamber up the sides of the pot. I had some concerns that the bots might damage the leaves as they climbed around them getting to the flower stalk. I remembered how William's previous bot had attacked Jake's finger and almost shredded it to the bone. We could not afford to have the bots make obvious damage on the leaves of bin Osman's albino *Paph. rothschildianum*. I examined a leaf that my bot had just crossed and, sure enough, I could see two rows of puncture marks.

"Brian, we need to minimize the damage that the bots cause to the plants," I said, pointing to the tracks across the leaf. "Is that possible?"

"Why do you need to do that?" he asked.

I came up with a reason. "We borrowed these plants and I promised to return them unscathed. Their owner will be upset if we return shredded plants. Also the plants we want to collect pollen from in the wild are an endangered species and the conservation rangers will be really upset if we damage them. It was hard enough getting the permits to collect the pollen."

"I see. Perhaps I can adjust the force produced by the legs to try and minimize how far they penetrate into the plants' leaves and stems. Everyone, take a break while I fiddle with the settings. Jennifer, why don't you take everyone to the common room for some coffee? It may take a while. I will come and call you once I have made the necessary adjustments."

The common room was scarcely fifteen feet by fifteen feet, and was one level up, but as with all the rooms in the building, there were no windows. A counter along one side held a microwave, a small coffee machine and a small sink. A cupboard above the counter contained coffee mugs, sweeteners, creamers and even a few packages of cookies.

"What. No teas?" Great-aunt asked.

"Sorry, no one here seems to like tea," Jennifer answered.

"But they can be forgiven. There is a large selection of cookies, so I am content," William said.

The chairs scattered around the room hardly seemed designed for relaxation. They all had hard backs and a minimum of padding. It was a room designed for quick breaks.

Jennifer measured out coffee grounds and set the coffee maker to brew and turned to us saying, "You may as well all take a chair. I don't know how long it will take Dr. Kim to adjust the tension in the legs of the microbots."

I selected a chair but as I suspected it was not comfortable. Jennifer pulled up a chair herself, and waited for the coffee.

I turned to her, "It was a shock to hear about Max Fiercely. So unexpected."

"Yes, and it is a great loss to the company. He was the brains behind many of our products."

"He seemed a nice person, too." Matilda added.

"He was." Jennifer gulped, fighting to hold back her tears.

"Sorry, I did not mean to upset you," Matilda said.

"Do we know any more about what caused him to lose control of the car?" I asked. "It seems so bizarre for that to have happened. Could it have been foul play?"

Jennifer thought for a moment. "That's what the FBI suggested…" And then she realized she had said too much.

"The FBI? Why were they called in?" Jake jumped at the lead she had dropped.

"I should not have said anything. Please forget what I said." She jumped up and hurried over to inspect the coffee urn.

"Jennifer, you know that I am a security agent for Tylo and Associates. But you are probably unaware that there were several attempts on George and Matilda's life last week. And the four of us barely escaped an explosion in a restaurant the other night." Jake stared directly at her as if it might be her fault.

She looked at us in shock. "No one said anything about that."

"We don't want to advertise it."

Jake jumped in again. "I was wondering if there might be a connection between the attempts on George and Matilda with what happened to Fiercely?"

"I would not know. Can't think of any reason. I am sure that it is company policy that we do not discuss this anymore."

"Well, we need to know who is behind these attacks and if we can expect more attempts. You must tell us what you know." Jake persisted.

"I really don't know any more. Gossip at the lab suggested that the FBI had been called in but no one knows why; Fiercely always kept his cards close to his chest. We normally only know about those projects we are working on. And then we only know what the clients are prepared to tell us. We often have requests for bots for many different uses. We don't usually know exactly how or why they will be used. I suppose that in some cases we are not given the real reasons for their use."

That was true. After all, we had not told them the true purpose for which we wanted the bots. I was starting to feel a little guilty about that.

Matilda noticed that the coffee was ready and that Jennifer was not prepared to pour. She got up and filled a cup for each of us. Jennifer looked very unhappy and gazed off into the distance. No one felt like talking, but I was willing to bet that all sorts of scenarios were running through Jake's mind. I don't remember if the coffee was good or bad.

126

Back in the lab we each ran through the exercise that Brian Kim set up for us. The bots were able to climb around on the plants without producing any obvious damage. Soon we were all able to reach the flowers.

Tomorrow, we would try to do it stealthily without the bots being obvious. I was not sure how we were going to explain that to Brian. After all, if we were in the wild we would not care if the bots were noticed or not. Maybe we could just set it up as a bot agility competition between all of us. We left the plants in the practice room until the next morning.

The next day, Jennifer called in sick and Kim, who was busy with other things, was happy to leave us to our own devices once we had all the bots operational. Jake and William were working well together without Jennifer, and I hoped that she was not very ill but sick enough to stay away for a few days. We were all learning to handle the little devices very well and none of the earlier problems surfaced. Before his death, Fiercely had been able to adjust all of the AI programs so that they no longer caused any problems. At the same time, we were getting very adept in avoiding physical contact between any two bots and that probably helped. For the most part Kim tended to leave us alone and we could practice getting the bots to climb up to the flowers while keeping them on the underside of leaves where necessary, and out of sight on the sides of the flower stems facing away from us. We were all getting the hang of operating these little robots or, as William insisted on calling them, spyders. And I must admit they seemed to become more like mechanical spiders every day. Even Great-aunt Bertha became very skillful at driving her little bot. On one occasion she and William had a race to see who could get to the very top of the same flower stem first and she beat him hands down.

Our skills at manipulating the robots would have to be concealed when we were trying to get pollen from Bin Osman's plant, so we now had to practice driving the robots without obvious swipes on the phone touch pads that might draw attention to our actions. This was going to be a covert operation in the midst of a crowd of people. We would be pretending to read Facebook or study our emails while actually operating the bots. That turned out to be relatively easy to master, too.

By the end of the week our control of the bots was excellent. Jennifer had still not returned to work. Brian Kim confided to Jake that he was getting worried about Jennifer's illness. I had not thought overly much about her absence and when I did I considered it a good thing that she was not present. This meant we did not have to be so secretive about our training and I did not have to worry about William messing with her. But William had missed her and Matilda always asked of Kim about her when we came in the morning. William had her phone number (as one might have expected), and on Matilda's urging had tried to call her. All calls went directly to her voicemail. There were no replies. She was either very ill or else the phone had been lost, stolen, or its batteries allowed to run down. Brian mentioned that he was going to drive over to her home to make sure she was okay. Jennifer had been Fiercely's right hand person and we wondered if she was still brooding about the accident. Jake said she had been trained as a Tylo operative and one should expect total reliability. The fact that she had not checked in, even to say that she was so sick that she was taking sick leave, was troubling.

After our training session, Jake offered to accompany Brian Kim to Jennifer's apartment in nearby Costa Mesa to check up on her. William had wanted to go with them, but Jake insisted that he go home with us and Great-aunt Bertha. William insisted on going with them. There was a troubled look on Jake's face that implored me to take William back with us. Matilda whispered something to William and he complied. He would drive us home in Jake's car. Later, Jake would ask William to pick him up and then join us for supper.

Costa Mesa attracts a more diverse citizenry with more affordable middle class neighborhoods than some of the other coastal communities in Orange County, which can be very expensive and pretentious, and cater to upper class executives and well-off retirees.

We were quiet on the drive home. No one wanted to talk about the possible reasons for Jennifer's absence. But I think we were all worried that something untoward may have happened.

At home, Matilda busied herself in the kitchen and Great-aunt went straight to the liquor cabinet and looked through our array of bottles.

"What would you like?" I got up and went over to help her.

"Do you have any dry sherry?"

I found the bottle and poured a small glass for her. Meanwhile William, who had followed Matilda into the kitchen, returned carrying a couple of bottles of Dos Equis. He handed one to me. I thanked him and excused myself. It was only mid-afternoon and I retreated to my den to try to work on the final chapters for the textbook, but I could not concentrate. William and Great-aunt always had things to say to each other and I wanted some solitude.

It must have been close to five when I got a call from Jake on my cell phone.

"George?"

"Yes, Jake. Are you ready for William to pick you up?"

"Jennifer is dead."

"What…how?"

"It looks like an execution."

"What makes you say that?"

"Her wrists were duct taped behind her back, as were her ankles. She looked as if she had been kneeling on the floor, and there was a single wound to the left side of her temple."

"A clean kill."

"I did not say that. Her brains were splattered against the wall. Thank God William was not with us."

"He would have had trouble dealing with that. It will be bad enough as it is. He was very fond of her. When do you think it happened?"

"It must have been several days ago. It was the smell outside her apartment that led us to get the manager to open her door."

"I assume you called the police."

"Yes, they are here in force, and only now gave us permission to leave. I expect that they will want to talk to us again tomorrow."

"Do you want me to tell William and the others what has happened?"

"Please. I know it is difficult. If you'd rather, I suppose I can. Can you come and pick me up in half an hour? Dr. Kim will drop me off back at T & A Robotics. Ask Security to phone for me when you get there. I'll be inside."

I popped into the kitchen to tell Matilda I was going to fetch Jake. She looked at me inquiringly. I grimaced. She said a quiet, "Oh," and I gave a quick synopsis of Jake's phone call and left through the kitchen door to the garage and the car. Her last words were, "I'll tell William and Great-aunt."

We had had a quiet meal and now sat in the living room trying to understand what had happened. Jake had recounted his grim afternoon.

"What I don't understand," Great-aunt Bertha said, "is why no one else at the apartment complex noticed the stench."

"It was a small penthouse isolated on the upper floor. You know along the coast there is always an onshore breeze starting in the early afternoon. It was simply an accident of situation. No one else had reason to go up to her apartment."

"And what about noise? No one heard the gun firing?"

"They must have used a silencer, a suppressor. Remember, Jake always has one on his Beretta," William offered. "Whoever did the deed must have used a sound suppressor too."

"I think that the most important question to ask is if either Fiercely's or Jennifer's death is related to the attacks on George and me?" Matilda asked.

"It is hard to find a connection. Of course both of them were Tylo employees and they were helping to train us. Who would have known that? We have no idea why Matilda and I were targeted. The possibilities all seem so unreasonable. It is hard to believe that some member of SCORE was so scared we would get membership that they put out a contract on us..." I paused.

"Is there any way that bin Osman could have learned of Paul Tylo's plan to steal the pollen? And if so, then why target T & A Robotics personnel?" Jake wanted to know.

"It must all go beyond that," Great-aunt said. "Remember Jennifer, poor girl, said that she thought the FBI were investigating Fiercely's accident. There must be something else going on, of which we are totally unaware."

"After Jennifer let slip about the FBI, I contacted Cousin Ernie. He was unaware of any FBI investigation about the accident. He said he would ask around but has not gotten back to me. I suggested that he

130

also look into any other government concerns to see if T & A Robotics was under investigation," Jake added. "I phoned him last night but he has not had any leads yet."

"What should we do now?" William asked.

"The only good thing is that our training is completed. We need to get Tylo to release the bots to us and store them in a safe place until we need them."

"Do you have a date yet for the Orchid Show in Chiang Rai?" I asked Great-aunt.

"Yes, Channarong sent me an email yesterday with all the details. I forwarded them to Paul Tylo and he said he would arrange plane tickets and will send an itinerary in the next few days."

"Jake, have you reported in to Tylo yet?"

"No. Brian Kim was going to do that once we returned to Robotics."

"Perhaps you should call him yourself now and see if he has any insight into any of this?"

Jake agreed and said he would do that on a secure line once he got home.

There seemed little else to discuss. We said goodnight to the two men and bade them be careful. Matilda insisted that Great-aunt spend the night with us.

Chapter 12 – Running from the Cartel

A couple of days later Jake came to my office at the university. I had given a lecture earlier in the morning and had then gone out for a cup of coffee with some of the students. I always like to socialize with the undergraduates. I sometimes think they learn more during those discussions than in the formal lectures. Too many of the professors are stuffy and resent the students taking up their "precious" time. I never do. I look back fondly at some of my earlier mentors and how they took time to interact with me. Now I was taking a moment to relax before returning to my writing. The various chapters I had been assigned for the textbook were finished, and my next task was to review them for grammatical correctness before offering them to my co-authors for their input.

Jake arrived unannounced, and looking particularly grim and stressed out.

"What's wrong?" I asked, thinking that perhaps William had gotten up to some mischief again. But then, on reflection, Jake would simply have handled that himself without dumping on me.

"Cousin Ernie phoned me about an hour ago. He said he had tried to contact you but without success. It was very important."

"I was probably in lecture. I always turn my cell off. Once Matilda rang me just as I had told the class to put their phones on vibrate or I would kick anyone out of class if their phones rang while I was lecturing. They thought my phone ringing at that time was hilarious and wanted me to expel myself and cancel my lecture for the day. Since then I always switch it off."

I pulled the phone out of my pocket. It was still in the 'Off' mode.

"Did he tell you what this was about?"

"Sort of…He tried to contact you a second time without success and then he phoned me. He is in L.A. and wanted me to see if everyone was okay. I called Matilda and William first. They are fine. But when I tried to call you there was no response. Fortunately, I was in the area and so thought I should check up on you and make sure you were also okay."

"Well, I am fine. Sorry to put you to all this trouble. Just forgot to turn the phone back on."

"Well now that I am here, there are a few other things that we need to talk about. Let's go outside". He wrote with a finger on the palm of his hand…BUGS!

Maybe my office was bugged. I doubted it but then remembered in Africa that one of our houses had been bugged. Better safe than sorry.

The campus has a central park and we walked down the stairs and out into the park. There are green lawns and huge eucalyptus trees as well as other smaller trees and shrubs. It covers a ten acre area with lots of meandering paths. We chose one that had no students loitering along it.

"It looks as if Cousin Ernie has been nosing around. Apparently there was a big drug bust in San Diego about six weeks ago. The Federal Drug Enforcement Agency was involved. One of the DEA agents shot one of the dealers, who turned out to be the baby brother of the head of the Guatemalan Cartel. The Guatemalan Cartel heads an international drug smuggling ring. You name the drug and they either manufacture it or can sell it to you. They specialize in designer drugs. Anyway, the big boss man in the organization has sworn revenge for his baby brother and wants to 'off' everyone who was involved. Cousin Ernie thinks that T & A Robotics cooperated with DEA and supplied microbots that were used to get a lead on the Cartel. That might explain both Jennifer's execution and Fiercely's fatal accident."

"But why would they be after us too? We have nothing to do with DEA."

"Maybe the cartel does not know that. They may have spied on T & A Robotics and seen us going into and out of the Robotics plant. Perhaps they think we work there or are part of that system?"

"Has Tylo confirmed any of this?"

"I have not had time to speak to him yet."

"I think that has top priority. If we are threatened by some international group of gangsters then our little home warning systems are useless. I assume they do not know where we live yet, or they would have attacked our homes already. It is only a matter of time before they discover our addresses. Maybe we all need to go into hiding?"

I continued, "The orchid show is only a few weeks away. What about us going to Thailand now and hiding out there?"

"Problem with that is we don't want to be brought to bin Osman's attention early. Great-aunt says that the orchid community in Thailand is a very close knit community. They will all know we are in the country within days of our arrival. We must have as little to do with bin Osman as possible."

"Okay, let's stop off in Singapore first, for a week or two? We should be safe there. Drug possession is a capital crime in Singapore."

"I don't know anything about the reach of the cartel. Does it extend into Southeast Asia? We will need to be sure that Singapore is safe. That will take a day or two to find out."

"Back in Julian, do you think the cartel was involved there?" I asked. "Those two women did not look like druggies to me."

"George, you are being naïve if you think you can recognize members of one of these organizations simply by their appearance. They are like the proverbial octopus, with tentacles that can ensnare and manipulate anyone."

That gave me something unsettling to think about. All I wanted to do was save some orchids and now my family seemed to be targets of an international band of drug runners who demanded revenge and were mistaking us for G-men of the Federal Drug Enforcement Agency.

"What about my responsibilities here at school? I still have another three lectures to give and I must put together the final exam."

"Can't you just modify an old exam, and what about asking one of your colleagues to fill in for you with the remaining lectures?"

"I will have to get permission from the department chair, Dr. Petersen. He might expect Tylo to give the department money again like he did when I was released to go to Africa."

"It can probably be arranged. I will let you know. And in the meantime keep your eyes and ears open for any suspicious people or activities. I will get back with you after I consult with Tylo." He walked me back to the department and then took his leave. I was starting to regret the entire affair. What can of worms had I opened up? It was getting worse and worse.

Matilda and Great-aunt listened carefully when I reported my conversation with Jake.

"Looks as if there is no point in backing out of the agreement with Tylo at this point," Great-aunt said. "It does not matter anymore. There is no way we can explain to the Cartel that this is a case of mistaken identity. Will you get early leave from the department?"

"I talked to Petersen already. He has agreed. He'll do anything for money. There is someone who can give the last three lectures and the TA will administer the final exam. The exam will be machine graded and the TA will assign the letter grades. I can give instructions about what to do about the borderline grade cases."

"When do we leave and is it to Singapore? Is that the right place to go to?" Matilda asked.

"Jake wants us to stay put for a few more days until all arrangements are secure. And as for Singapore, it is densely populated and has a very diverse population with lots of tourists, so we should blend in. I have been told that Tylo and Associates can easily organize a safe-house for us there."

"Do we go back to T & A Robotics again? How are we going to get our spyders?" Matilda wanted to know.

"Not sure. We need to wait for instructions."

We did not have to wait very long. The next day Jake delivered the microbots. We each received our little machines wrapped cozily in a small velvet bag. I would wear a hip bag for my passport and some of my money. There was more than enough space in there for my bot. It could hide in one corner. Matilda had a similar, although more fashionable, leather travel purse that she carried over one shoulder. She had packed some jewelry in that bag and the bot would be mistaken for another piece in the TSA scanners. In a separate package, was a little charging cord. We were advised to keep the charge cords separately in our checked luggage. I assumed the other three would carry their bots in a similar way. The bots were small enough that TSA would not know what they were looking at in the x-rays.

Three days later, Matilda and I were seated at the departure lounge of the Tom Bradley terminal at LAX. We were waiting for Eva Air to take us to Singapore via Taipei. There appeared to be no direct flights between Los Angeles and Singapore. I found this surprising. One would have thought that these two important commercial cities would have direct links. Jake and William had escorted Great-aunt Bertha the previous day. Hopefully, at least one of them would meet us at Changi Airport that served the city state of Singapore.

Jake wanted to get to the city earlier to make sure that our safe house was really safe and that included debugging, if necessary. It turned out, and not unexpectedly, that Great-aunt had an old paramour who lived in Singapore that she wanted to visit without explaining about her entourage. She would pretend to travel separately and would contact us the day after our arrival. Great-aunt seemed to have connections all over the world and usually those were the people known as 'rich and powerful'. In Singapore it was a Mr. Wie Wee, an investment banker. I chortled when told the name, but one glare from Bertha made me hold any further comments. William, however, was not as responsive to her threats as I was and anyway, he loved to bait her.

"Is he a little man, Great-aunt?"

She glared at him and William explained, "That's a pun."

She merely harrumphed then and retorted sharply, "Gǔnkāi!"

William looked at her with raised eyebrows. "What does that mean? Is it Chinese? I did not know you could speak Chinese. Is it Mandarin or Cantonese?"

"Enough with the questions! William, sometimes you annoy me. I am telling you to piss off! And it is Mandarin."

"Yes ma'am."

Jake had texted us that they had all arrived safely. Great-aunt had been whisked off by Wie Wee. The safe house was clean and ready for us. Great-aunt was not told where the safe house was situated. But we could speak to her if necessary using encrypted phone lines. This was all getting to be too high tech for me. Jake and William would meet with us at Changi after we had cleared customs.

I looked around the waiting room. Was someone here a member of the cartel? Were they still looking for us? It might be anyone, perhaps the middle-aged couple in the corner with the toddler? Did the husband keep looking at us, albeit surreptitiously?

136

And what about the young Latina a few seats away, who could not have been more than twenty. She kept looking at Matilda. I was so paranoid. But paranoia had kept us alive in the past. Of course if we were being tracked, care would be taken to make sure we were not aware of our trackers. We were safe in the airport but what about when we left Changi at our destination.

In our backpacks were some simple disguises, but we could not use them yet. Matilda had a dark black wig. Her passport photo was of a blonde and she needed to be blonde to get through immigration checks at Changi, but after that she would go to a toilet and put on the wig. Similarly, I had a blond mustache I could attach to my upper lip. These were simple disguises but they should help put any surveillance team off the track for a while once we got to Singapore.

Tylo had supplied business class seats and we settled down before the general herd of passengers boarded the plane. Matilda and I were in separate little seating nests. This made it difficult to talk and I wondered if it might not have been better to travel in 'main cabin extra,' as some of the economy seats with extra leg room were called these days. At least there we could hold hands and lean against each other when we tried to sleep. Of course, the food and service was better in business class, even if travel was less romantic.

I relaxed in my seat and put on dark wraparound sunglasses. They allowed me to track boarding passengers without them realizing I was observing them. The passengers travelling economy had to pass through the business cabin. Several of the passengers filing past seemed to be interested in us. Were they merely curious or were they actually keeping us under close watch?

Once everyone had squeezed down the aisle past us, Matilda leaned over to me and whispered, "There seemed to be at least three people who scrutinized us as they went past."

"I thought I saw two, a Latina woman and a youngish man. He was a hippie type with torn jeans and a beard. The Latina was a younger girl intent in keeping up with the hippie but she paid no attention to us. Are those the ones you saw?"

"I also noted them back in the lounge. But there was also a rather swarthy, middle-aged man."

He had not registered with me. Matilda was so gorgeous that any red-blooded male would automatically focus on her. It could just have been a sexual thing and not surveillance. However, one could never be sure.

The flight would be broken for a few hours at Taoyuan International Airport in Taipei. We would watch for our suspects when we got off at that terminal to transfer to the flight to Singapore. If they were not on that flight perhaps there was nothing to worry about.

Traveling business class, we were entitled to use the lounge at Taoyuan and we hid out there for most of the airport stay. However, when we went to the gate to board for Singapore I noticed that all three of the people we were wary of were already seated there. What did this mean? We deliberately went to sit close to the Latina. The hippy was on the floor nearby organizing his small backpack. I noticed it because he had a small toy monkey clinging to one of the pack's straps. From time to time he passed a package to the woman. So they were a couple. I looked around the gate area for Matilda's swarthy man and found him engrossed in a newspaper. All three appeared to pay no attention to our presence.

Flying time from Taoyuan to Changi is slightly more than four and a half hours and we arrived on time, just past seven-thirty in the early morning. I hoped one of the men would be there to meet us. William was by nature a late riser so I thought Jake would probably be the one to greet us. At the airport, as we were herded through the various lines of people, I kept a look out for our suspects. Matilda surreptitiously pointed out the swarthy man. He looked once at Matilda but ignored me and ended up some distance in front of us for passport control. He did not look back at Matilda again. Of the other two there was no sign. Near the luggage carousels was a set of toilets and we both visited them before picking up our small suitcases. I looked for a possible camera in the stall but could not find one, so I applied the mustache. It was quite bushy and only a little darker than my auburn blond hair. When I came out I went and washed my hands, looking in the mirror. The mustache looked quite good. Maybe I should grow a real one. It was amazing how Matilda's wig changed her countenance. We went to the carousel and found our luggage and

138

wheeled it past the custom officials and out into the foyer where many greeters stood, each with their tablets spelling out names. William was there, but with no sign of Jake. His tablet read **Corbett** in bold. We walked over to him. I wondered where he had pulled up that name.

"Mr. and Mrs. Corbett?" He asked.

I nodded, playing along, and he extended his hand to shake mine as if we were strangers.

"Nice to meet you. How do you do? Did you have a pleasant journey? International travel can be so tiring these days. Such long flights and such little rest. Will you please follow me?" William was hamming it up and enjoying himself. He reached for Matilda's luggage and led us out of the airport and towards a row of cars waiting at a passenger loading zone. He steered us towards a limousine. As we approached, the chauffer open his door and climbed out. He was in uniform and raised his peaked cap at us in greeting. I saw that it was Jake. He pretended we were strangers to him and he went around to open the passenger door alongside the sidewalk. Then he touched a button on his car key and the door to the trunk raised open for our cases. William placed them in the trunk and climbed into the front seat beside Jake.

As we slid onto the back seat, I turned and saw the swarthy man rushing towards a small blue Audi parked about 500 feet behind us. Someone already inside, opened the door for him and I caught a glimpse of the hippie guy pulling the man's suitcase onto the backseat. The swarthy man opened the driver's side door and climbed in and revved up the engine.

"Home, James," I said to Jake. "Do you see that blue Audi pulling out behind us? I think he will try to follow us. We may have to shake him off."

"Only one tail?"

"Who knows? I'll keep my eyes open."

"Where are we going?"

"AMK."

"What's that?"

"Ang Mo Kio Town. It's a suburb with a lot of high rise condos. Our safe house is in one of the towers and hopefully we will be lost in there," William answered.

139

Jake pulled the car out onto Airport Boulevard and headed towards the town. The traffic in Singapore follows the British system of driving on the left side of the road. At the exit from Changi, Jake had the choice of going straight, parallel to the shoreline, on the East Coast Parkway, or veering inland to the right on PIE , the Pan Island Expressway. Singapore does not number its main roads and highways. Instead they use a three letter designation like PIE. Jake chose the PIE turnoff and some distance behind us, the Audi continued on our trail. It was keeping a constant distance behind us. The expressway had a healthy compliment of autos filling every lane. Jake tried changing lanes and found that the Audi did likewise. We were convinced we had a tail. So much for the efficacy of disguises.

"May as well take your wig off," I said to Matilda as I reached to remove my mustache.

"No, leave it on," Jake said. "We are not sure they are certain who we are."

"It may just be coincidence that they are going the same route that we are."

"Are you carrying heat?" I asked Jake.

"Yep. T and A supplied me once I got here. It took a special permit. I could not bring my own into Singapore."

"Hurry. They are catching up with us. Speed up!" William shrilled at Jake.

"Speed limits in Singapore are strictly maintained. If I go very fast over the speed limit we will have a traffic cop on our heels in no time. They give demerits for speeding. Enough demerits and you lose your license." Jake replied. "Anyway, there is too much traffic and it's all going at a moderate speed.

"Well how else can you shake them?" William cried anxiously.

"Wait and see."

Jake moved into the fast lane closest to the center of the road but again there was so much traffic that he could not accelerate significantly. Nevertheless, the Audi moved into that lane, too, and was only about three cars behind. It was slowly catching up to our limo. Jake scanned the road ahead. A major exchange was coming up fast. It was for KPE, one branch of which went towards downtown. At the last minute Jake slammed his foot down on the accelerator and veered across all the other lanes, squeezing between cars and trucks to take the exit ramp for KPE south.

"Oh my God," shrieked Matilda, "You almost hit that truck."

"But I did not," Jake said cool and steady. He glanced in his rear view mirror to see the Audi come swerving onto the KPE ramp as well. "Damn, it did not work."

We were now on Sims Way which was a separated double boulevard with traffic flowing in both directions

The first major intersection was confusingly called Sims Ave. It turned out to be a wide one-way street with four lanes of traffic travelling westwards back towards Changi. Narrower side streets, called Lorongs, also one-way, led off to the right. Elsewhere they might have been called lanes or alleys. I looked at the street signs. They were confusing as well – Lor 11 Geylang, with the next Lor 13 Geylang, and it was followed by Lor 15 Geylang. The Lorongs all had odd numbers. To some civic architect it probably made sense but to a newly arrived visitor I did not know what to think. The architecture lining Sims Avenue was a mix of modern multistoried buildings, but also older, two-storied shops probably constructed at least half a century earlier. The ground floors were a mix of small stores, often with the iron shutters so common in many tropical and third world countries. Many of the shops carried a range of tropical fruits piled on tables lining the sidewalks. Second floor windows sometimes had laundry hanging in them but there was still a sense of genteel prosperity. Presumably the shop owners often lived above their businesses. The streets were very clean.

We must have been six blocks along Sims Avenue when I looked behind and saw the blue Audi turning onto Sims Avenue from Sims Way. They would see us. I cautioned Jake, who merely grunted in reply and turned down the first alley to present itself. It was a one way street and we were travelling in the wrong direction. Fortunately, there were not too many cars and no trucks. A few angry drivers honked their horns at us as Jake, never slowing down, squeezed around them. This narrow street led to Geylang Road which was another one-way street but running in the opposite direction to Sims Avenue. Side streets here were even-numbered lorongs. There was little traffic here and Jake floored the accelerator.

"If we can get back to KPE before the Audi sees us we can make a beeline for the PIE. He won't find us then."

The Sims Way intersection came into view and Matilda turned around and looked out of the rear mirror as Jake merged with the northbound traffic.

"Damn, there is the Audi," she said.

Jake swerved around a slow truck in front of us and then turned right, back onto Sim's Avenue again. Three blocks down Sims, Jack came up behind another slow truck signaling that it was going to turn right into the next narrow alley. Jake overtook that truck and swung in front of it into what was probably Lor 15 or Lor 17 Geylang. The truck slammed on his brakes, swearing volubly at Jake, and sounded his horn angrily. Jake ignored it. Half way down that block he had already spied a small hotel. He sped up to it, noticed an underground parking garage, slung the steering wheel around and managed to turn onto the sloping entrance without flipping the car and slammed on the brakes. The truck driver honked again as he passed the hotel.

"Can you see the Audi? Is it in the alley?"

"Cannot see anything."

"Okay, then lets chance it," and Jake drove down into the garage. It was dark and he parked the car, turning off its headlights.

"Everyone out of the car," he said urgently and we complied. He locked the car and beckoned us towards a door in one wall. It led to a staircase back up to the hotel lobby. There was no receptionist and only a bell to summon one. Cautiously, I went to the front door and looked out just in time to see the blue Audi driving by. Warily, so as not to be seen, I peered around the door and watched as the car drove slowly down the street and turned right onto Geylang Road again.

"We will stay here for about half an hour. That should be enough time and it should be safe then to get back to PIE," Jake announced.

There was a small lounge area near the reception desk with a sofa and two side chairs. I sat next to Matilda on the sofa and the two men took the single seats. Jake kept looking at his watch to see that sufficient time had gone by. The hotel appeared to be deserted. We had been there a half hour when Matilda frowned and asked. "I wonder if the blue Audi represents the Guatemalans or bin Osman's agents?"

"No idea, but how could the Guatemalans know where you were going and what flight you would be travelling on?" William pondered.

"Who bought the tickets?" Jake wanted to know.

"That was Tylo's admin assistant. I spoke to her over the phone when she wanted to know what times we wanted to fly," Matilda said.

"Was it on your landline or cell phone?" Jake asked.

"No, we did it all by email."

"Some person has been phishing in your computer."

Our conversation was interrupted by a tiny Chinese woman who came through the front door, looked at us, and slipped behind the counter. She addressed us, "I am sorry," she said. "We do not have any vacancies."

"Actually we came by because we thought one of our friends was staying here and we would like to see him." William was good at dissembling.

"What is his name?" I will look him up in the computer.

"His name is Mr. Soh Fat. Actually he is not very large, in fact he is quite thin," William grinned at her.

Dutifully the receptionist, not seeing any humor in this, typed in the name, peered at the screen for a moment and said, "I am so sorry none of our guests have that name. Perhaps you are at the wrong hotel?"

"Is there another hotel in the Lor Greylang area?" William asked.

"Oh yes. It is the Pearl Hotel."

"Do you know the Lorong number?"

"I think it is Lorong 18 Greylang. Ooh no, that is the ladies of the night's street. It must be Lorong 19."

"Good. We will look there. Thank you."

We got up and trooped back down the stairs to our limo. Once belted in, Jake started the car and we nosed our way cautiously up the ramp and back into the alley. There was no sign of the blue Audi. We must have given them the slip.

143

"William, you sure are having fun making up Chinese names. It's not nice to denigrate other cultures," Matilda challenged him.

"Let's go and look at Lorong 18. I have never visited a real red light district. That might be very interesting," William said, changing the subject.

"No way – we are not looking for trouble of any kind," Jake vetoed William's suggestion with a steely voice.

"It seems to find us anyway," Matilda muttered to herself but loud enough for the rest of us to hear.

Back on the PIE we headed off toward the northeast.

"Where are we going?" I wanted to know.

"The safe house is in an area called AMK, short for Ang Mo Kio. It is near the lower Pierce Reservoir in northeastern Singapore."

The reservoir was on the left hand side as we drove along. There were few buildings and the trees and remaining small patches of forest, reminded me that originally this area had been tropical rainforest. Then, small farms had been cut in the forest which in turn gave rise to villages and then towns. AMK was now an ultramodern part of the city.

Chapter 13 – Singapore Safe House and a Visit to the Botanic Gardens

Ang Mo Kio Town was once a rural district in northeast Singapore. The original small holdings, farms and country homes had steadily been replaced with blocks of apartments, civic buildings and parks. Now the older blocks of apartments were being replaced with more modern and taller towers of apartments, albeit, often with less floor space per unit. Today, Ang Mo Kio is a bustling community of nearly two hundred thousand souls and the four of us would need to hide among them. The apartment building had an underground garage with a steel gateway. Jake clicked a remote and the gate slid to the side and he drove down two levels before he parked the car. Meanwhile William opened the glove compartment and fished around in it, withdrawing four pairs of wraparound sunglasses and several baseball caps. He handed a pair of shades to each of us and caps for the men.

"It's too dark in here for sunglasses," Matilda complained.

"This is mostly an Asian community, people with round eyes and non-black hair tend to stand out. Eye and hair coverings are *de rigueur* whenever we are out of the apartment," Jake explained, slightly misusing the term. I figured he meant obligatory.

"It's bad enough that you and I are so much taller than the average Singaporean," he said to me. "It is a good thing Matilda never wears high heels. Of course, William is not that tall."

"Are you calling me a runt?"

"No William, it's just that you are not a giant he-man like George. And my dear, you are just the perfect size for me."

I noticed Matilda rolling her eyes.

We rolled our suitcases to an elevator in one corner of the garage. There was an electronic key for the elevator and Jake pulled a card out of his wallet, swiped it over the call button and we waited for the elevator. He also pulled out his cell and selected a number, whispered something into it that I could not hear and put it away as the elevator door opened. A couple stepped out, nodding to us as they strolled past and we entered the lift. This time a security code had to

145

be punched in before the door would shut and then he selected the fourteenth floor.

When the door opened again it was onto a wide, carpeted hall that might have been in any high quality hotel anywhere in the world. On a credenza an arrangement of exotic tropical flowers stood across from the elevator door. Of course, I took note of the stems of *Arachnovanda* and *Opsisanda* orchids that are used as long lasting cuts in this part of the world.

"Come on," Jake said impatiently and he walked several hundred yards down a corridor towards our apartment. A number on the wall to one side indicated discreetly that it was number twenty-five. On the door itself was a buzzer which Jake pressed.

"Who's there?" Came a rather tinny voice.

"Genesis."

And the door opened and we went in.

"Genesis?" I asked.

"It's my code name."

"There was a camera mounted discreetly above the door, why also a code?"

"If I was being forced against my will or if something was wrong, I would have used another word. Cannot be too careful."

"I assume there is someone else in the apartment that makes the decision whether or not to let one in."

"Yes, you will meet him in a moment. He is our host for the duration of our stay."

The door opened into a short, but narrow passageway that led into the living room. It was sparsely furnished with just the basic necessities of sofa with a table, several additional recliners and a flat screen television in one corner. There were no pictures or hangings on the wall and no carpeting on the floor.

"I apologize for the sparse furnishings."

And we turned to the source of the voice. It was a slender Chinese man. I guessed he was probably thirty-five or forty, no more than five-foot four tall and I doubt that he weighed more than a hundred and thirty pounds. He looked like he might be in his mid-thirties but like so many Asians who appear ageless, he could have been in his mid-fifties, too. He had a round baby face that seemed

146

even more circular because of his drastically receding hairline. In another five years he would have a smooth, shiny, bald pate.

"Meet our host, Mr. Soh Fat," William said grinning. It was not a name that he had made up after all. William continued, "Soh Fat has two brothers, Loh Fat and Noh Fat." And he giggled.

"William, I have already explained to you that my family name is Soh, not Fat." He smiled, not taking offense at William's attempt at a joke.

"Let me guess, you are the delightful Matilda," Soh turned to Matilda, "and therefore you," he turned towards me, "are the famous orchid Professor." And he stretched out a delicate hand. It could have been that of a young woman. I took it hesitantly, but his grip was surprisingly strong and I winced as he pumped my hand up and down. "If there is anything you require or need, do not hesitate to ask. I must apologize for the poor furnishings in the apartment but getting this apartment ready in time was a rush job."

I looked around and wondered if there was an IKEA in Singapore.

"Oh yes it is IKEA," Fat said, as if reading my thoughts. "There are several branches in Singapore. That's where most of this furniture comes from. I was not given much time to get the apartment ready for you. My budget was not very big either. Here, let me show you your rooms and the apartment."

There were three small bedrooms. Each led to its own even smaller bathroom. There was a small kitchen with a table that looked as if it could not seat five persons. Were we to be hidden in this sterile apartment for the duration of our stay in Singapore? I hoped not.

As if to echo my thoughts Matilda said. "We cannot stay locked up in here for the next week. We are going to have to get out of here from time to time. Being cooped up is going to drive me crazy."

Jake heard what she said and looked troubled. "We will all be safer if we stay here."

"There is only so much television I can watch," Matilda replied. "And Singapore has so much to offer. We can wear disguises. Surely we can just melt into the crowds?"

I could see Jake starting to put up his back and stepped in to calm things down.

"We can discuss that later. After all, we have just arrived. I could do with a shower to refresh myself and then a small nap would not go amiss. I did not sleep enough on the plane last night."

That seemed to settle it for the moment and we retired to our respective bedrooms. I threw myself on the bed and fell asleep almost instantly. When I gradually awoke several hours later I found myself clasping Matilda and one of my arms had gone to sleep. Slowly, I tried to get my arm free without waking her. She just snuggled more deeply against my chest, grabbed my arm and refused to let go of it. When I tried to pull my arm free she groaned a little. She must have been deep in a dream because she muttered, "Don't leave me, I need you."

So I tried to settle back without disturbing her, but my arm was now dead and I wondered how long I had until gangrene set in. That did nothing to help my disposition. I knew that gangrene was not going to set in but merely the thought of it was stressful. About fifteen minutes later she suddenly turned over and I quickly extracted my arm. As blood circulation was restored, intense pins and needles sensations flushed through my limb.

"Ouch! Ouch!"

She opened her eyes lazily, "What's your problem?"

"Pins and Needles," I answered.

"Then don't sleep with your weight on your arm."

I knew from previous experience simply to shut up at that point.

"That was a great power nap," she said. "I feel refreshed. We should have had a shower before the nap but you seemed so tired. I think a shower now would be good. Would you like to join me?"

Of course I could not refuse.

Jake, William and Fat were poring over a map when we eventually joined them in the living room.

"What are you studying that map for?" I asked.

"Mr. William wants to visit the two major gardens in Singapore. I was showing him where they are situated," Fat said.

"Oh, both the Singapore Botanic Gardens and the Gardens by the Bay?"

148

"Yes, there is the famous orchid garden in SBG and everyone acknowledges that Gardens by the Bay is the number one tourist attraction in Singapore."

"Well, I want to see the Merlion," Matilda added about the famous fountain that spurted into the bay and was Singapore's icon.

"What's a Merlion?" William wanted to know.

"You know what a mermaid is, half maid and half fish? So a merlion is similar, although this mythical creature is a fish with the head of a lion, and it is the symbol of the Singapore tourist industry," Fat volunteered. "Which Merlion do you want to see, Matilda?"

"There is more than one?"

"Yes, in fact there are five Merlions."

"I suppose the original one. I read it was at the mouth of the Singapore River."

"True it was, but they moved it some years ago. Singapore has been reclaiming part of the sea and the mouth of the river was shifted."

"Where is the Merlion now?"

"It is sited on a promontory that now fronts Marina Bay."

"That is the one I want to see. If it is on Marina Bay then it should be pretty close to the Gardens by the Bay. We can do both in one trip."

"I wonder why Singapore chose a Merlion for its symbol?"

"Well, the city was originally a fishing village so the fish part recalls its history and the lioness head alludes to *Singapura*, the original name that means lion city. So you see we get Singapore from *Singapura*. In Malay it is called *kota pura*. *Pura* being lion."

"Thank you," William said, "I think this is more information than I need."

"Whatever, I still don't like the idea of leaving the safe house," Jake asserted.

"Don't be a worry wart," William said. "Singapore is an enormous city. How could those people ever find us again. We lost them, didn't we?"

"Do you think they trailed us to the safe house?" Matilda threw in her two bits.

"No, but… I want to be sure everyone stays safe," Jake said.

Soh Fat jumped into the conversation. "I would like you to spend most of tomorrow in this condo. Let us assume your pursuers

149

will still be looking for you. Don't risk them finding you. After all, Singapore is a relatively small city."

"But Singapore has over five million people in it," William said.

"Yes, but it is a relatively small area," Fat countered. "I'll tell you what. Here is a deal. Stay in the apartment at least for tomorrow and in the evening I'll take you out. There is an excellent dim sum restaurant in AMK. We will go there for supper. It needs reservations and I can sneak you in without anyone seeing us."

"Dim sum, yum," William enthused. "Okay but we do need to visit those gardens on the next day."

"All right," Fat agreed reluctantly.

"It's settled then. We can go to the Botanic Gardens day after tomorrow. I want to see their orchid collection," William got up and went towards the kitchen. "What do we have to eat Soh Fat? I am getting hungry."

"He is always hungry, Soh Fat, don't go to any trouble over him," I said.

"There is a packet of cookies in the cupboard next to the oven. William, why don't you bring them out here?"

William returned with a package of Oreos.

Fat noticed Matilda looking at the cookies in surprise, "What, you wanted Fig Newtons? This is Singapore, a modern city in the modern world. We all share in the global culture."

As if to stress that fact, Fat said, "And tonight we are going to have a salad and pizza!"

"I thought Singapore was famous for some of its traditional foods," Matilda said,

"Oh yes, there is Hainanese chicken rice and *Nonya laksa*. The latter is flat rice noodles with a broth of prawns in coconut milk. But Singapore uses recipes from all its major ethnicities."

"I approve of the idea of *Nonya laksa*," William said. "Can you cook us some?"

"Alas no, I have no cooking skills," Soh Fat admitted.

"That is a bummer," William remarked. "Can't we go out for our supper tonight?"

And Jake frowned. Keeping us in the apartment was not going to be easy.

150

The meal that night was simple pepperoni pizza. Soh Fat had phoned the order in and it was delivered. The delivery man seemed to know Fat and they exchanged a few minutes of conversation. The pizza was not bad but I thought the crust might have been a little thinner.

The next morning dawned with clear skies. From our windows we could look down on an array of tropical trees, which were dotted with either pink flowers or yellow flowers. I recognized the pink as those of a *Bauhinia* species, sometimes called the Poor Man's Orchid but it was not an orchid at all. Its flowers merely resemble one. Singapore boasts that it is an urban forest with over two million trees planted alongside its roads and in its parks. I assumed this was supposed to compensate for all the natural forest trees that had been destroyed to make the city state. But I had to admit that the current greenery was very pleasant.

We passed the day watching television and I must admit that there are only so many movies one can watch before it becomes tedious. Matilda was reading a small booklet on Thai etiquette and from time to time she would interrupt to discuss various behaviors. Apparently it was considered an insult to show anyone the soles of one's feet. Then there was the *wai*, a greeting gesture, in which the palms of one's hands are placed flat, together and with fingers pointing up. They are then brought to one's face with finger tips raised no higher than the levels of one's eyes. For royalty or images of the Buddha finger tips are raised higher to the level of one's forehead as a sign of extra respect. We were informed how to say "hello" in Thai. Women say "*sawasdee kah*" and men, "*sawasdee krap*". William had a field day with that one. He strode around the apartment *waiing* and greeting each of us with a slurred and mumbled *sawasdee* followed by a clearly and loudly enunciated *krap*. He continued this until both Matilda and Jake could not take it any longer and they yelled simultaneously, "William, cut that crap!" It was clear that we would go crazy if we were to be cooped up in the condo for more than the one day.

That evening, Soh Fat was true to his word, and hired a taxi to take us to the Seaside Palace, a restaurant that must have been miles from the ocean but specialized in dim sum and also seafood. Its clientele was mainly local Chinese.

"I thought dim sum was only for breakfast or brunch," Matilda remarked as we were seated.

"These days dim sum is also taken as an evening meal, especially in some of the more modern restaurants," Soh Fat explained.

I noticed that the waiters pushed small wheeled trolleys around from table to table. Each trolley was piled high with little bamboo baskets each of which held various steamed delicacies for which dim sum was renowned. Customers were selecting food from the trolleys. No waiter with a trolley approached our table.

"We are being ignored," William almost wailed.

"Dim sum is supposed to be an accompaniment for tea. We will be offered the dim sum once we have selected and poured our tea," Fat explained patiently to William.

He looked questioningly at Fat and turned to Matilda who is always everyone's authority on food. "Is that so?"

"Yes, we need to select our tea first," she said.

"What sort of tea would you like?" Fat passed a menu to Matilda who scanned it quickly and she decided. "I like *guk pou*."

"I beg your pardon?" Jake enquired. "What is that?"

"It's a tea made by infusing chrysanthemum flowers."

"And that tastes good?"

"It's one of the most popular teas in Southeast Asia."

Fat ordered a pot of *guk pou* as well as one of jasmine tea, just in case, we Westerners might not appreciate the flowery taste of *guk pou*.

The tea arrived and was poured. I lifted up my little cup smelled and sipped the tea. I thought it a little strange. There was a mildly pungent aftertaste but it was not too bad.

"What do you think of the tea?" Soh Fat enquired.

"Not bad. Is it made from the leaves or the flowers?" I asked.

"Actually it is the flower buds. Here let me show you. I'll get one out for you," and Fat opened the lid on the tea pot and fished out a round, plump bud. Once it had cooled he passed it on to me to examine. I pried the bud open to reveal a simple daisy that probably would have been white.

"It is much smaller than I would have thought," Matilda opined.

"You were expecting a large football-sized mum in the tea pot?" That was William.

"No, but the chrysanthemums I see in gardens and as potted plants have much bigger flowers."

"Sometimes the petals of those larger flowers are used to flavor autumn snake soup," Fat said.

"Snake soup!" William was horrified, "What species of snake?"

"All I know is that it is a poisonous snake."

"Hope you have not ordered any snake soup for us," Jake finally added his two bits, "I am against eating reptiles"

"No worries. It is not autumn."

Despite its slight pungency I thought the tea had a palate cleansing effect and with further sips I decided that the jasmine tea was unnecessary. The others agreed with me.

"Are there any other times chrysanthemum tea is drunk?" Matilda turned to Soh Fat. She is always fascinated by recipes and special foods.

"When I was a child and had a sore throat, my *nainai* would make me drink *guk pou* with honey and gold and white needle flowers. It was very soothing."

"What are needle flowers?"

But Soh Fat did not know.

Once the tea was served, a waiter appeared with a trolley laden with little baskets and we were shown dainty dumplings of various kinds.

"We will eat family style so everyone gets to taste," Fat said as he looked into several of the baskets on our server's trolley.

"Do you have any *har gow*?" He asked and turned and explained to William, "Shrimp dumplings – the one's they make here are exquisite."

"Yes sir," and a basket was placed in the center of the table. The server placed a card on our table and stamped it in one corner. William looked at Matilda with a raised eyebrow.

"Haven't you eaten at a dim sum restaurant before? That is how they keep track of all the baskets we order."

The server offered several other baskets.

"Those look good," Jake pointed to what appeared to be small round buns with a rich shiny brown glaze.

"*Char siu bao*, filled with barbecued pork. You will enjoy. Everyone likes *char siu bao* – very popular," Fat said and selected two baskets of that.

New waiters appeared, each with a different trolley laden with baskets and we were tempted with ever more culinary delights.

And so the meal went. We must have tried eight or nine different types of dumplings and little buns. Each new basket arrived with another stamp on the card.

"Why are there different stamps on the card?" I asked Fat.

"They reflect the price of the basket. Some are little and others bigger."

"But all the baskets were the same size."

"Little baskets are the least expensive, medium baskets are those that cost a little more and bigger baskets are the most costly."

"The size reflects the price and not the volume of the basket," Matilda explained.

It was an excellent meal.

"I am full – that was so good," William had a smile on his face.

"Pity you have no room left," Fat said with a sly grin. "I was going to order red *fung zau* for you to try."

"What's that?"

"Ah, phoenix claws. Actually they are chicken feet that are first fried, then boiled in black bean sauce, and finally steamed until they are moist and tender."

"Just as well, I am so full I cannot eat another morsel," William said with some relief in his voice. "I will have to wait for another day to try the claws."

"William you are so full of it. I cannot see you putting a chicken's foot anywhere near your mouth."

We set out for the Singapore Botanic Gardens the next morning. Jake was driving again. We were all wearing sunglasses and

Matilda had on her wig. As we were leaving the apartment Soh Fat came running up. He held out a brightly patterned scarf to Matilda.

"I brought you a nice hijab. If you have that and your glasses on, no one will know you. Here, let me show you how to wear it." He wrapped the square of material around Matilda's head so only her face showed. The remainder was draped casually around her neck and over her shoulder. Then he deftly partially exposed a lock from the black wig. Now she looked like some wealthy Middle Eastern lady.

I noticed that as we drove south on upper Thompson Road and past the MacRichie reservoir that Jake kept scanning both the road ahead as well as the road behind.

"Looking for the blue Audi?" I asked.

"Not just that, any car that seems to be paying attention to us. Perhaps we should have changed cars for today? Our pursuers probably have."

"We will just have to keep alert."

As the road rounded the flank of the reservoir it changed names. It was now called Lornie Road. Ahead of us was the PIE motorway that we had driven two days before. The road changed names again. Now it was Adam Road that took us via the Farrier Flyover, an overpass, across the PIE.

William was looking out the window and said, "There is a blue Audi coming off the PIE and in our direction, too."

But it was a false alarm. The blue car took a side street away from us.

We were now driving along the western flank of the botanic garden.

"Soh Fat suggested that it would be easier to find parking if we go in at the Nassim Gate. That is on the other side of the park. We will need to go around to it," Jake said.

"Jake, isn't the Burkill gate closer to the orchid garden?" I asked.

"Yes, but there is no public parking for cars near the Burkill, only for motor coaches. I Googled it last night. This means we will have a long walk through the garden to get to the orchid display. But we have the whole morning."

"Only the morning? We can spend the whole day here. There are no other plans."

"Yes, there are. I plan to keep you all safe and sound. This morning's outing is against my better judgment and I want to keep it as short as possible."

"You are no fun," William spouted.

"It's more important to stay alive than have fun. Remember, our mission is in Thailand. That is going to be tough enough and we will need everyone in one piece if we are to accomplish that."

The Singapore Botanic Garden is over a hundred and fifty years old and is now recognized as one of only three World Heritage Botanic Gardens. It is famous for two things. It was here that Ridley was able to figure out how to grow rubber trees. During the 18th Century the rubber market was dominated by Brazil, and natural rubber latex was harvested from wild growing trees that were often very widely spaced in the forests. In one of the most famous cases of biopiracy, seeds of rubber trees were smuggled out of the Amazon and ended up at Kew Gardens in London. These eventually provided the rubber tree seedlings that were planted out in the Singapore Botanic Gardens and from there, throughout Malaya, as it was known in those days. In the end, Brazil was unable to compete with Southeast Asia for rubber production.

The second important historical fact about the gardens and the reason we were there now had to do with the orchids. The director of the gardens from 1925 until 1949 was Professor Eric Holttum. He was fascinated by the orchid wealth of the area and realized that the island had the ideal climate for growing orchids as a cut flower crop. He encouraged the development of the industry through hybridizing and introduced modern techniques. For a time, Singapore became one of the world's leading orchid cut flower producers. Exceptional hybrids were named for both Singaporean and world famous people. More than a hundred celebrities have been honored in this fashion, ranging from Emperor Akihito of Japan to Margaret Thatcher of Great Britain. Today, there is a section of the garden devoted to those named hybrids. Singapore became the model for Hawai'i and especially Thailand which also developed enormous orchid cut flower industries.

We had heard about the orchid garden but had never had the opportunity to visit before.

Singapore appears to have its interests intertwined with orchids. The floral emblem of the city state is an orchid, *Vanda* Miss Joaquim, sometimes called *Vanda* Miss Agnes Joaquim. This is a pink and mauve confection of a flower that to some resembles a butterfly in flight. It used to be used for making floral leis, especially in Hawai'i.

We were standing in front of a bank of *Vanda* Miss Joaquim admiring the display of flowers and Matilda was reading a label that said that Miss Joaquim was, indeed, the national flower of Singapore when Jake turned to me and asked, "Do you know anything about this Miss Joaquim?"

"Oh God, don't ask George questions like that," William implored.

"Why not?"

"It will put him into professor mode. He will talk for half an hour now."

I cleared my throat, "William you exaggerate. Actually I know very little about this flower. First of all it is not really a *Vanda*. It belongs to the genus *Papilionanthe* which means butterfly flower."

"See, what did I tell you," William said. "Enough now, George."

"Respect your elders," I bantered back. "Probably sometime in the mid to late 1880s, the flower appeared in the garden of a Miss Ashkhen Hovakimian (whose name is now anglicized to Agnes Joaquim) an Armenian lady."

"What was an Armenian lady doing living in Singapore?" Matilda asked.

"Actually, there was a very small Armenian colony in Singapore in the early 19th Century." And I continued, "In those days there were two closely related orchid species, *Vanda teres* and *Vanda hookeriana* that were widely grown in Singapore gardens. The hybrid flowers were more spectacular than both parents and it became very popular. The plant was vigorous and ideally suited to the climate here. It is assumed that Miss Joaquim actually made the cross but one cannot be certain. She certainly would not have had the current tissue culture techniques we use today to grow the babies. Those techniques

157

were not known at that time. It is more probable that the orchid appeared spontaneously in her garden. At any rate, she gets credit for making the hybrid."

"He is a veritable font of trivia," William announced to all.

"George actually kept it quite short and succinct this time and his knowledge really adds to our appreciation," Matilda said coming to my rescue, but she continued with a grumble. "This wig is very uncomfortable. The wig and the hijab are making me sweat. Its damn hot and the humidity doesn't help either."

"We appreciate your suffering for our cause," William grinned.

"Well I hope you appreciate it."

"What were you saying?" Jake turned to me.

I continued pontificating, about how people had used modern DNA techniques to figure out which had been the original pod parent and which the pollen parent when I noticed Jake's eyes starting to glaze over, so I brought the discussion to a stop. Then I heard an excited voice behind me. "Why, it is Professor George. What are you doing in Singapore?"

We all turned around to see an old man walking towards us. He had a round beaming face as if he was delighted to see me, but for the life of me I could not recall either his name or his face. At a guess I would have thought him a Malaysian gentleman. He must have been at least seventy years old, with a mop of silver hair.

He reached out his hand to me and I took it and asked, "Do I know you?"

"You don't remember me, do you?"

"No."

"Raymond Wong, we met in the Rio Conference in 2004."

"Goodness." I dredged up what I could. "You reported on work you were doing on floral pigments in *Paph. liemianum*. I remember you now. Rio... wow, that was more than ten years ago."

"And I suppose that this must be William, your associate." He turned to William with an outstretched hand. "George talked about you but you were not at the conference." Raymond looked around our small group. "I don't know who these other two are." He looked up at Jake and I introduced him without designating any sort of relationship.

He scrutinized Matilda. "I thought you were married to a blonde lady. Have you changed partners?"

"No, no. I am still married to Matilda. This is Miriam, a research associate. She has severe laryngitis and cannot talk at the moment." It saved trying to explain why my wife was in a disguise.

"Which is good because otherwise she never shuts up," William grinned at Matilda, who glared back at him. He knew he was safe at the moment but would probably get a sharp cuff to the head when she had the chance.

Raymond gave a stiff little bow to Matilda and she inclined her head.

I turned to Raymond, "What are you doing in Singapore? Aren't you at the University of Kuala Lumpur?"

"Singapore is a nice place to visit and get away for a weekend. It is so safe. Cannot say that for most cities these days. Thought I would visit the Orchid Garden. And surprise, I find you here. What are you all doing in Singapore, if I might ask?"

Rather you did not ask I thought, but said instead, "We are on vacation, too, but combining it with business. Scouting for a new research project. I am thinking of looking at the effectiveness of nature reserves for orchid conservation in either Malaysia or Thailand."

"That makes for a nice excuse to come and play in Thailand," Raymond said and winked at me.

"Of course." And I smiled slyly back at him. Thailand does have a reputation and I might as well utilize that to my advantage with Raymond.

William, who had been watching us very intently, raised an eyebrow. I hoped I had not planted some seed of expectation in him. Thai dens of vice were well known around the world and some might appeal to him, but they did not feature in any of my future plans.

As we walked around the various sections of the orchid garden, Raymond babbled like a long lost relative. Then he started gossiping about the orchid growing community in Malaysia and I only paid attention with half an ear. Finally, he worked his way to the orchidists in Thailand. We had barely entered the section of the garden devoted to wild species when I heard Raymond mention a man that he apparently did not like. It was Vicknes bin Osman and I pricked up my ears.

159

"Who is this bin… what did you call him, bin Osman?" I said pretending innocence.

"Oh. A dreadful man. Very wealthy, but totally narcissistic person. He has no empathy for anyone. However, I must say, he has probably the best orchid collection in all of Thailand. And that is saying a lot, considering how crazy that entire country is for flowers and especially orchids."

"Do you know him personally?"

"It is all hearsay about his personality but he did visit with me at the university several years ago. It was quite unnerving. He wanted to know all about *Paph. rothschildianum* in the wild on Mount Kinabalu. He said he had come to me because I was an authority on color in slipper orchids and he wanted to understand albinism in slippers and their value. He kept coming back to roths, asking who might have an albino roth. I kept assuring him that no one had ever found an albino roth. I felt he did not believe me. He kept asking me in different ways where he could buy an albino roth. He thought I was lying by saying there was no such thing. It felt like I was being cross examined by a King Cobra just looking for an excuse to strike. Also, he has what I would call snake eyes. Iris so dark it looks as if the eye has a giant opening into it. I was so uncomfortable in his presence, I felt a wave of relief when he walked out. He never even thanked me for all the information I had happily given him. I should have charged him for consultation." Raymond was indignant.

I did not have anything to add to the conversation.

"The funny thing," Raymond continued, "there are rumors now, that perhaps bin Osman has an albino roth."

"Any idea if that is true and if so how he got it?" I asked.

"I'm not sure. I suppose that it could have been a mutation in a line bred roth. Much like the way that the albino *Paph. fowliei* was found. It appeared spontaneously in a flask of seedlings in someone's greenhouse. However…"

"However, what?"

"There are some other rumors too."

"And these are…" I encouraged him.

"This seems unlikely but I have heard that a new locality for the species was discovered, but then destroyed in a forest fire shortly after it had been found."

160

This all seemed to confirm what we had been told earlier. Raymond continued, "I am surprised that you have not heard anything of this. After all an albino *rothschildianum* would be the orchid find of the century."

How was I to answer that without giving the game away?

"There are rumors but I thought it might just be the discovery of a new undescribed species. I heard the plant would be shown at the big orchid show in Chiang Rai. If we can spare the time, maybe, we will visit that show. But that has relatively low priority," I lied.

I thought of inviting Raymond to take lunch with us. There are a number of eateries at the garden. But that would mean that Matilda would have to keep quiet, pretending to have her sore throat.

I was saved the decision when Raymond looked at his watch and said, "Oops, look at the time. I promised my wife I would meet her for lunch. George, it was great meeting you and talking again. Please give my regards to Matilda."

And he hurried away.

Matilda, William and Jake had wandered off away from us but I noticed that Jake kept looking back at us, perhaps to make sure that I was safe. When he saw Raymond moving away he hurried over to me.

"Where has he gone?"

"Lunch with his wife."

"While you were talking to him I ran a search on the man on my phone through the local T & A security branch."

"What did you find?"

"They are not a hundred percent sure, but there is a Raymond Wong that may have ties with bin Osmin."

That left me feeling very unsettled. What was going on? If what Jake found out was true then what was Raymond Wong up to and was our meeting purely accidental?

Chapter 14 – William Goes for a Swim

Back in the safe house apartment after lunch, Jake received more disturbing news. Tylo and Associates had a new message for us. There were rumors that the Guatemalan Cartel now had several agents in Singapore. This was troubling on a number of levels. Singapore was known to have a zero tolerance policy against drugs. What was a powerful drug cartel doing in this territory?

"I knew it," William exclaimed. "That blue Audi, I knew it was the cartel. They are following us."

"The big question is why?" Matilda wanted to know. "We have had nothing to do with the cartel."

"Why would they risk coming here? Why do they think we are so important?"

"Who knows? But this is a big city," I said, "and I don't see how they can find us now. I am sure we threw them off our tracks on our way to Ang Mo Kio Town on our first day here."

"I hope you are correct," Fat said, "but T & A are concerned, and what worries them worries me. It is my job."

"I think we need to tell Great-aunt Bertha," Matilda said. "Jake, how do we get in touch with Bertha?"

"She has her cell with her doesn't she?"

"Of course." And Matilda went into our bedroom to phone Bertha.

I turned to the others and said, "None of this makes sense to me."

"Is it possible that bin Osman and the cartel or perhaps some members of SCORE are all in bed together?"

"Why do you say that?"

I told them about my conversation with Raymond Wong in the park. How could he know that I was going to be at the gardens that morning? Was it really happenstance? Why would he bring up the topic of the albino roth? Surely only the cartel would know we had made it to Singapore. SCORE members should think we were either still in Southern California or maybe in Thailand. But they were the ones who might guess about the albino roth. Or was it a mole at T &

A? Once before we had been jeopardized by an informer working at Tylo and Associates.

"Soh Fat," I turned to him, "you are the only one who knew we were going to the Botanic Gardens today. Who have you spoken to? "

He thought for a while. "I am most careful and I am always discrete. Except for reporting in to T & A early this morning, I have not been in communication with anyone else."

"Did you tell them of our plans? With whom did you speak?"

"Head of security."

"There are no bugs in the apartment. Both Jake and I carried out a very thorough sweep of the rooms before he went to pick you and Matilda up at the airport." Soh Fat was adamant.

"Did you mention to security that we might be going to the Gardens by the Bay tomorrow?" I asked.

"No. I was not sure of your plans for tomorrow. I know you were talking of going but I hoped to talk you out of it. It is too risky."

"Matilda's disguise worked very well. No one recognized her at the Botanic Gardens, today." Dr. Wong did not recognize her, and he had met her several times before during the Rio Conference and he has excellent recall.

"With wrap around sunglasses and if we dye our hair dark black we should be okay too."

"No need to worry about your hair color. Haven't you noticed that many Asians now color their hair? Fair hair does not stand out the way it did ten years ago. Glasses will help for William but both George and Jake are so tall and large they will draw attention to themselves in any crowd of Asians."

"There are so many tourists in downtown and by the Gardens at the Bay, I don't think they will stand out," William argued.

"We will leave the decision up to Jake and the Professor." Fat left the room and that cut the discussion short.

"Matilda is taking a long time with her call," Jake remarked.

"Not really, when she and Bertha get going they will spend hours talking to each other."

"Where is she staying?"

"With Mr. Wie Wee. They have rooms at the Marina Bay Sands Hotel," Jake answered referring to the world famous hotel that is a landmark of the city state. It is built of three separate curved towers, containing the guest rooms that support a giant sun deck called the Sky Park on the top. It is reminiscent of an ocean liner supported in the sky on the three pillars, but the entire structure looks like some futuristic dream scape, perhaps a giant Stonehenge. The deck has palm trees among the sun lounges and it spans all three of the hotel's wings. The deck has a large infinity pool that runs along the length of the deck with the edge of the pool some hundreds of feet above the street level below. It is the largest infinity pool in the world.

"Isn't that the hotel next to the Gardens by the Bay?"

"Yes, across the street from it."

"You said ...rooms. I thought they were old lovers," William asked.

"Separate rooms – for appearances' sake. They still have old fashioned ideas and, probably you know, it is more fun to sneak into each other's suites."

"It boggles my mind, to think of old people having sex. I mean it's not a great visual," William said.

"You visualize Great-aunt Bertha doing it with Mr. Wee?" Coming out from the bedroom Matilda had overheard William's comments. She was astounded. "Do you visualize George and me going at it too?"

"Er...um..."

"Come on William, that is gross. We certainly don't imagine you and Jake getting your jollies. Do we George?"

"It's a visual I can certainly do without," I added.

"Everybody does. Otherwise you must be dead and without any imagination." William was adamant. "You just don't want to admit it."

"Can we talk about something else?" Jake wanted to change the subject. He seemed a little embarrassed by the turn the conversation had taken.

"If Bertha and Wee are staying at the Marina Bay, perhaps they can invite us for lunch on the Sky Park before we go to the gardens?" William, taking the hint from Jake, decided to pursue one of his goals. He had mentioned earlier he wanted, very badly, to go up there. "I hear it's only open to residents and their guests, although there is the Observation Deck that one can pay to visit but then you cannot swim.

That is reserved for residents." William had obviously done his research. I was careful not to mention that the hotel also housed one of the world's largest gambling casinos. If William knew that we would never get away to the famous Gardens by the Bay. Or maybe I was denigrating my young friend.

Matilda answered, "As it happens, Great-aunt has invited us all to lunch poolside on the sky deck of the Marina Hotel. We can go there after visiting the Merlion. It is not too far from the hotel."

"Yippee. High five!" William prompted Jake. "We should have brought bathing trunks. I really want to be able to say I have swum in that pool. Isn't there a mall close to us, perhaps I can buy a Speedo? I must ask Fat."

Soh Fat was not happy about us wanting to have lunch with Bertha and Wee and he did not want to take William shopping for swimming gear. In the end, he wrote down William's waist measurements and said that he would pick up something for William to wear, saying it would definitely not be a Speedo. Fortunately for Fat, no one else had any intentions of swimming. He was going out anyway to pick up Chinese take-a-ways for our evening meal and would visit a nearby sportswear shop and select what he felt was appropriate swim gear for a young man.

Fat was as good as his word and returned, not only laden with food, but also a very conservative pair of red Bermuda trunks. Of course it was not what William would have selected but it was adequate and would not offend the Singaporean sense of modesty.

After the meal we all sat in the modest living room and tried to plan our next day. We finally settled on first visiting the Merlion in the morning and then a visit to Great-aunt Bertha and Mr. Wie Wee for a light lunch, after which we could stroll through the Gardens by the Bay.

The Marina Bay waterfront is the jewel in the crown of the city-state of Singapore. The hotel itself is across the street from a giant convention center that lines part of the bay. And close to the end of the convention hall is the curious science art gallery building, itself looking somewhat like a partially disemboweled clean white globe artichoke. I had been told that the design was an abstraction based on a

165

lotus flower but for some reason it has always looked like a partially eaten artichoke to me. While it has its own permanent collections, its main function appears to be that of displaying important travelling art collections.

In the distance, across the water, stands the Merlion, gushing a stream of water into the bay and farther off, a giant Ferris wheel based on the famous London Eye but of course being Singapore, that bastion of wealth, this wheel is the largest in the world. I was once told that one could reserve a single cabin on the wheel, which holds up to twenty-eight people for one revolution for a cool grand. Within an easy walk from the convention center and past the hotel, one comes to the famous Gardens by the Bay.

The Gardens by the Bay must surely be on the bucket list of every serious horticulturist and botanic garden aficionado in the world. There is simply nothing else on the planet remotely like it. Among its attractions are two of the largest glass greenhouses in the world, themselves looking like engorged silver insect larvae. There are no supporting pillars inside the structures and they are large enough to accommodate multistory buildings inside them. In one part of the park is a modest forest of five giant steel trees with a suspended walkway between them. Each tree is many stories high and one contains a restaurant in its crown. As I described the Gardens, I could see Jake trying to figure out if the park posed any security problems, but he kept his thoughts to himself.

Soh Fat seemed to acquiesce to our program for the next day, though somewhat reluctantly.

"Isn't there rail service that can take us downtown or to the Bay?" William asked. "It would give us a better feel for what Singapore is really like. No one would suspect us of taking city transport."

"Yes," Soh Fat replied, "but the terminal at the Bay is still under construction. But with a car, you can park at the hotel and take a taxi to the Merlion. All the other attractions are within walking distance of the hotel."

"Can we get a different car? The cartel will be on the lookout for our limo."

"Will do. Later on this evening. Will see what I can arrange," Fat obliged.

William changed the subject. He turned to Soh Fat and asked. "I am curious…"

"Aren't you always?" Matilda muttered.

He ignored her. "Soh Fat, what does the name Ang Mo Kio really mean? I tried to Google it and found that *ang mo kio* means 'red tomato.' Is this development really named after a veggie?"

"Maybe. It does mean red tomato but there are other possible derivations as well."

"What's this about veggies?"

"Remember the area was rural and known for its market produce and, in fact, grew a lot of tomatoes. But the name also could refer to rambutan. It is '*ang mo dan*' in Mandarin."

"What is a rambutan?" Jake asked.

"It's a tropical fruit, somewhat like a lychee but larger, and instead of short bumps on the shell, it has longer, incurved bristles. It reminds me of a gorilla's balls, like a hairy scrotum…" William said and added, "I like rambutans. The flavor is better than lychees, more refreshing and not so sweet. Another relative is the longan or longaan. Those are smaller and somewhat fragrant… Of course there are also longkong and longsam. Very similar in having a shell and an inner succulent flesh."

"Enough, William and you complain about me?" I added.

"There is another story about the name of Ang Mo Kio. The word 'kio' means bridge. The Kallang river flows into the Pierce reservoir. You passed it driving into Ang Mo Kio. Back in 1923 there was a Lady Jennifer Windsor who lived in what was then called the Upper Thompson area. Thompson had built a bridge over the river. Anyway, Lady Windsor had three children. One day while the children were playing near the river there was a storm and the river came down in a flash flood. The children were swept away by the swirling waters. Only two bodies were ever recovered. The locals thought the area was haunted and on certain days one could hear the little girl, whose body was never found, calling out for her mother. Lady Windsor became aware of the rumors and took to frequenting the bridge hoping to hear her lost daughter's voice. The name is sometimes thought to refer to the bridge and is called Ang Mo's bridge."

"How tragic. But somehow it does not make sense. It should be called Windsor Bridge then." Matilda was being local.

"But that makes for a really sad story," William said. "Thank you Fat. It is like a ghost story. I can hear the little girl's plaintive voice crying in the distance … Mommy, help me… help me."

"Really! William you have too much imagination," Fat declared as he got up, "I need to arrange your transportation for tomorrow." And he left the room.

I turned to the group. "We should make sure that our individual bots are charged. Probably won't hurt to do that this evening. Also, I wonder if we need to practice driving them sometime."

Later that evening, as we were undressing in the bedroom, Matilda turned to me. "Remember the walls in this apartment are very thin. We had better be careful not to alert William to any activity. His imagination drives too many fantasies."

I merely chuckled. "He still has the hormones of a raunchy, teenage, horny dog."

When Matilda climbed into bed, I snuggled next to her, inhaling the clear springtime fragrance of her skin and buried my face in her hair, luxuriating in its silkiness against my face. Matilda slipped her hand over my chest playfully tweaking one of my nipples. It was unexpected and I gave a gasp.

"Quiet," She giggled and slipped her hand lower.

I bit her neck in an effort to stifle a groan and she arched her back.

We had just started to get going when I became aware of the bed squeaking and with an effort stopped my motion. The rhythmical bed noises continued.

"It's next door," Matilda whispered. "Must be William and Jake, going at it. I wonder which is the top and which the bottom?"

Just then there were some loud groans in two different voices and I could not help giggling. Matilda joined in and we both ended up roaring with laughter. The bed next door became silent. It quite put me off my stride, for a while. Then I thought, "What the hell," and we continued with our own game to its delightful conclusion.

At breakfast the next morning, Jake blushed when William announced, "Boy you two sure made a racket last night. I had trouble getting to sleep."

"We made a noise? It sounded like a freight train barreling down the tracks in your room, until it got derailed," I threw back at him and Jake's face became a stunning shade of carmine. William merely shrugged it off.

"It's just human nature. Did you have a good visualization?" And he grinned.

The Merlion looked like all the pictures I had seen on the web. We walked around it looking up at its head. One's first impression is of the head with its gaping mouth and the stream of water spitting out into the bay. Only later does the lower covering of scales and a fish's tail sink in.

"The head reminds me of a Pekinese dog with its squat face and bulging eyes," William said.

"The head is typical of an ancient Chinese guard lion. You see them all the time outside Chinese restaurants at home," I lectured.

"Well, I don't think the ancient sculptors ever saw a real lion. They just wanted to portray something they thought had a fierce expression. The majesty of the lion just is not there. All I see are the bulging eyes, similar to some caricature of a fierce ancient warrior."

I could not help agreeing with William, until he said. "When I was a kid, a friend's mother had a Pekinese, and he told me that we were not allowed to hold the dog upside down by its tail because its eyes would drop out."

I have never been able to go past a Chinese restaurant since without thinking of a blind Pekinese and a pair of eyeballs lying on the sidewalk. So much for how friends influence our lives!

While we were playing tourist, Jake kept scanning the crowds. He never seemed to let his guard down and I was grateful for his presence. We kept our visit to the Merlion short and caught a taxi for the quick ride back to the Marina Bay Sands Hotel, where we had used valet parking for the modest silver Toyota Camry that Fat had hired for us.

The ground floor of the Marina Bay Sands is immense and stretches under the three residential towers. Great-aunt Bertha came down to meet us and took us back up to her rooms.

"You look very fashionable, today, Great-aunt," Matilda smiled at her. She was wearing a simple but svelte afternoon dress that showed off her still youthful figure. Her hair had been styled recently.

She held up her hands up for inspection by Matilda. "What do you think of my nails?"

"Longer than usual, but beautifully manicured," Matilda replied.

"There is a beauty spa at the hotel. Wee suggested that I indulge. If we had more time I would treat you."

"Thanks, but security at T & A seem to think we should not interact too much with you. They say too big a group draws attention."

"Well there is unlikely to be any one that we know at the hotel."

Her suite was both luxurious and spacious with a lounge and balcony giving a wonderful view of the gardens below and part of the harbor in the distance. Behind a set of closed doors must have been the bedroom and bath. As we entered, a tall thin man stood up and tossed long black hair off his face. He smiled broadly at us. He had been seated on a sofa looking at his cell phone. It was hard to pinpoint his age. I assumed he was probably close to Bertha's age but on reflection he might have been ten to fifteen years younger. Now he strode forward with the vigor of a much younger man. "Hello, I am Wee."

I waited for William to say, "No you are not wee, you are quite tall." But for once he was silent and looked at the gentleman warily.

"How do you do, I am George," and I stretched my hand forward to shake his, but he surprised me by pulling me into a quick hug, and then turned to Matilda who was removing her hijab. She felt no need to wear it in the hotel. Hopefully her darkened hair would offer some disguise as well.

"You, of course, are Matilda. Bertha is correct, you are quite lovely. I thought you were blonde but, whatever, you are still gorgeous." Wee kissed her on both cheeks and she glowed. "Now you two boys, I assume, are William and Jake. I have heard quite a lot about the two of you. Most of it good, I must say."

170

"Pleased to meet you, sir," Jake was his usual polite, gentlemanly self.

William, however, seemed at a loss for words as he was also drawn in for a hug. Obviously this was not the man he had been visualizing the evening before. I felt we were perhaps meeting and greeting an important person. But the importance was not defined.

"Shall we go up to the Sky Park?" Great-aunt asked.

"I brought a bathing suit. I have to swim in the infinity pool," William said.

"Of course you do," Bertha agreed. "Do you need to change? You can use my bedroom."

"No need. It is under my jeans"

"Well you need to take off your underpants first, or your jeans will be wet for the ride back to Ang Moh Kio."

"No need, I am going commando."

"Huh?"

"He means he isn't wearing any underwear, free balling, you know," Matilda volunteered.

"William, William, you certainly are full of surprises. Whatever happened to tidy whities or is it tighty whities?"

"It depends how firmly they hold the family jewels. Anyway whities became unfashionable. You should see the silky colored underwear men wear today."

"I don't think I need to. But William, I worry about you."

"Don't worry about me Great-aunt. Jake keeps an eye on me."

"I bet he does. He has to, poor man."

The Sky Park on the top of the Marina Bay Sands Hotel is one of a kind. We sat round a table in the shade, sipping drinks. Spread along one side of the deck ran the infinity pool. I could believe the publicity, that this was the highest and largest infinity pool in the world. It was flanked along one side with two rows of deck chairs for the sun lizards and others reclining in the tropical sun and risking skin cancer in order to get a *healthy* tan. The recliners were interspersed at intervals with living palm trees that had been transplanted to the roof. The other side had a roof, with tables for those who wanted to enjoy the pool, sip drinks or have a light meal, without being in the sun.

You probably know about infinity pools. They have one or two sides where the retaining wall is just a fraction of an inch lower than the surface of the water. The water looks as if there is nothing holding it back and actually there is not. It overflows and drains into a catchment container before being recycled back into the pool. If the pool is higher than surrounding buildings, like on the top of a skyscraper, the water surface can create an illusion of meeting with the sky in the distance; hence the name infinity pool. In the pool, one thinks one can swim to the horizon, or right out of the pool and in this case fall over fifty stories to the earth below. Not for people who are scared of heights.

There must have been nearly a hundred people in the pool that day, all enjoying the tropical sunshine and the heady knowledge they were among the very few who could enjoy swimming in the sky. William was somewhere out there in the mass but the pool was so large that it was difficult to identify individuals unless they swam close to our table. I could tell that Jake was fretting. He kept scanning the pool.

"Relax Jake. William is a good swimmer," Matilda advised. "In his late teens, William was a lifeguard at the Newport Wedge. George taught him to swim and George is a brilliant swimmer."

"I don't like it when any of you are out of sight. Then I cannot do my job."

"And what is your job?" Wee asked.

"He works for Tylo and Associates. He is our security detail," Great-aunt answered and then quickly changed the subject.

I saw Jake blink. He was not happy having Wee know anything about his job. I wondered how much Bertha had confided in her paramour. Bertha, herself, was sharp enough to notice Jake's concern.

"It is okay, Jake. Wee is like family. I can vouch for him."

This surprised me because we had not met Wee before. Bertha must have seen some look cross my face, because she turned to me and said sharply. "George, you of all people should know that family is not defined by blood."

Yes, but then I realized that perhaps each member of a family defines the constituents of their family differently. Some family's children do get disinherited and others adopted and brought into an all embracing circle. Lovers come and go but for a while they too become part of a family before they move on and sometimes disappear, forever lost in the mists of old memories.

"Can you see where William is in the pool?" Jake asked Matilda.

She stood up and looked over the pool. There was a knot of people in the far corner but they were too far away to discern properly. As she turned back to sit down she noticed a woman walking out onto the deck and being seated at a distant table.

"Don't look now," she said to me. "I think that is Hillary Herschel who has just been seated at that table over there on the left."

"The bitch from hell! What the fuck is she doing here?" I reacted in surprise and turned around and there the woman demon sat looking down at a menu. She was unaware of us. It was a table set for two and I wondered who would be joining her.

"Do you think she knows we are here?" and I turned away, "Be careful not to draw attention to ourselves." But everyone had to take a surreptitious peep at the table. Fortunately, she was still engrossed in the menu.

"Wow," Matilda said, "Charles Guildenhuis is joining her."

Sure enough there was the president of SCORE. Herschel rose to greet him as he reached the table and he lowered his head to kiss her. This was no mere peck on the cheek but a full blown smooch that looked as if it probably also involved tongues. Guildenhuis held onto her hand as she sat down and lingered there before taking his own seat.

"Oh my!" Great-aunt whispered.

"I thought he was happily married. Where is Guildehuis' wife?" Matilda murmured.

"From that kiss, I don't think she is with him. This is going to be interesting," I smiled to myself and was about to stroll over to their table to greet the couple, when Jake became agitated.

"Something is happening in the pool. Looks like a fight is breaking out. Where is William?" Jake was out of his chair. Frantically, he raced down the paving towards the end of the pool, where people were shouting at each other, and the water was being churned into a froth. I heard him calling William's name.

"William, I'm coming, I'm coming." I heard Jake gasp as he ran.

173

Herschel and Guildenhuis followed Jake's stampede along the length of the pool. They, of course, would not know who he was.

"Is that someone actually now on the edge of the pool?" Matilda pointed.

I could just make out the figure of a man wearing red shorts climbing onto the wall. He had tousled hair like William. If it was William, he was in trouble, trying to maintain his balance but teetering back and forth. Then suddenly someone jumped out of the water at him and pushed the man on his chest. As if in slow motion, we followed the person's arms being flung in the air as he screamed and plunged down the other side.

"Oh my God! William has been thrown off the building! " Matilda was standing up yelling, "William!" at the top of her voice. We all looked at each other, eyes wide and mouths open.

Chapter 15 – Fun in the Gardens by the Bay

No one said anything – we just stared at each other in shock. How on earth could this have happened? I saw tears starting to gather in Matilda's eyes, brim over and trickle down her cheeks. I got up and pulled her into my arms as she started sobbing.

"He…was… my….best friend. How… could this… happen?"

"Don't know." I was fighting back the tears myself and we clung to each other.

Wee was holding both Bertha's hands in his. She would not cry. I had never seen her lose control, ever, but the way her mouth was turned down spoke volumes.

All the noises and sounds in the background simply faded away, out of focus, and time stood still. Half of the laughter and joy in my life had been taken. I could feel it draining away. "Oh William my little brother, what will we do without you."

I don't know how long we stood holding onto each other. I needed Matilda and she needed me, but we were not giving each other comfort. Simply it was some ill-defined form of support against this new emptiness that was gnawing inside our hearts.

I suppose barely fifteen minutes had passed when I felt a hand tap my shoulder and heard a familiar voice I thought I would never hear again.

"Hello. What's going on here? Why is Matilda crying?" William was standing next to us.

Matilda pulled herself free from my arms and rushed over to William and grabbed him into a bear hug. "Oh, William, I thought we had lost you. I thought you were dead. "

"Dead? I just went to pee. No big thing. You always insist that I never pee in the pool. I have never understood all the fuss about that. It gets so diluted anyway. What's all this commotion about? And where is Jake?" He noticed his lover's absence and looked around the deck. His eyes narrowed as tried to focus on the melee at the far end of the pool. "What's going on there?"

"Thought you were in the middle of all that... A man who looked like you... He was on the edge," Matilda explained.

"Then someone pushed him off the pool wall. We thought it was you. He screamed and must have fallen all the way to the ground. Must be dead now," Great-aunt added.

"Nonsense. The wall is only about five feet above the next level. No one can fall out of the pool and all the way down to the ground. Think of the liability. Don't be silly. No one can fall off the deck." William pronounced.

"Hurrumph." It was Great-aunt. "I was sure your days were over. Wasn't surprised. You are always asking for trouble. Your fiancé is way over there." She waved towards the end of the deck and continued. "He went running to rescue you. You had better go look for him. We all thought you were a goner. Be a nice boy. Go and reassure Jake that you are okay."

William trotted off to find Jake. There was still some sort of melee happening at the far end of the pool and lifeguard whistles were finally being sounded. There was no sign of Jake.

I turned my attention back to the table where my nemesis had been seated. There was no one there. They probably noticed us when Matilda screamed William's name, but they probably thought we had not seen them and made their escape. Damn, I was looking forward to confronting them.

"Why would someone want to kill William?" Mr. Wee finally asked the question that no one else wanted to pose.

I answered. "We don't really know why William should be singled out but there were several attempts on our lives in California. After all, that is the reason for our coming to Singapore. We thought we would be safe here. But we were tailed on our way to Ang Mo Kio after we arrived at Changi, and it took quite an effort to shake them off our tracks. We are all on high alert. And that person did look like William. I suppose it could have been a coincidence. After all, how would anyone know that he would go swimming in the infinity pool?"

"If you are all in danger, who is behind these attempts on your lives?"

"The problem is that we are not sure."

176

"It could be the Guatemalan Cartel, but why would they be after us? We have nothing to do with designer drugs. Maybe some members of SCORE are responsible. Herschel and Guildenhuis certainly cannot stand us. They really hate us; however, it does not make sense that they would take a contract out on William. It might be Vicknes bin Osman. I suppose Great-aunt has told you about him, and our involvement there?"

Wee nodded. "Ah, the emerald orchid! But why would one want to kill anyone over an orchid – it's only a plant."

"Perhaps, but we are not dealing with just a plant here. It is a passion and the values of passions are usually hyperinflated. What this plant signifies has different values for each person. For Paul Tylo using this plant to get revenge over bin Osman is worth the several millions of dollars it will cost him. For bin Osman protecting and cherishing this living jewel that is one of a kind, might for him easily be equated to the value of several human lives. It is thought that he does not even value human life."

"Nevertheless," Wee said, "I have trouble visualizing any passion that drives one to these lengths over a plant or anything other than one's lover."

"That is because you are more noble than the egomaniacs we have to deal with. And I love you for that old man," Bertha said looking into his eyes.

"But, how would bin Osman have learned about us?" I continued. "Or it could be some other, as yet, unknown party. We just don't know. So little of this makes sense."

"I must tell you," Wee asserted, "if Bertha is in danger there is simply no way that I am going to let her go to Thailand on her own, even if the rest of you are there with her. I must go as well."

"My dear," Bertha said, "that is very sweet and I know that you mean well, but you will just get in the way. We can handle ourselves. We have been in much worse situations than the current one."

"We will talk about this again." Wee was adamant. "Later."

I could see the sparks in Bertha's eyes. She rarely lost her temper but she was also used to getting her own way and she was subservient to no one. I was not quite sure how she would handle Wee who was obviously smitten with her but I was not so sure that Bertha was equally enamored with Wee. She was one independent lady. In her earlier years she had progressed through several husbands. Some left through natural causes but at least one had been deliberately discarded.

We had not ordered our meal yet and a waiter was hovering in the background.

"We may as well order and when the boys return they can order for themselves," Bertha decided.

"I am not hungry," Matilda said and I felt the same. We were still recovering from the shock of thinking we had lost William.

"Nevertheless, you need something. Order a light salad." Great-aunt pointed to an item on the menu. A Caesar salad, either with cold prawns or chunks of salmon. Either would do for me but Matilda simply shook her head.

"I could not keep it down."

When our food arrived she leaned over and helped herself to a forkful of my salad and merely commented, "Not too bad," and then got up and excused herself.

"Where is she going?" Wee asked.

"Probably after William and Jake." Both Great-aunt and I said simultaneously and smiled at each other. We knew Matilda's mind.

When Jake and William returned with Matilda in tow, I noticed that William was dressed in his jeans again.

"Where are your bathing trunks?"

"I left them in the changing room. Don't see myself wearing them again."

Bertha was lifting a small slice of Melba toast, covered in pate to her mouth but she paused, her eyes narrowed and she peered at William. "Are you free-falling?"

"Huh, oh you mean free balling." He grinned. "Yep. And don't look at me like that, you won't see my junk."

"Heaven forbid."

"Speaking of junk, have you ever wondered why you never see underwear model's junk through the cloth?"

"Oh, do tell. I have gone all my life wondering about that," Bertha said sarcastically.

"Well it's quite simple." And we were going to learn about it whether we wanted to or not.

He continued, "The model cuts the crust off a slice of soft bread and inserts the bread between his junk and the cloth of the underpants."

"I will think of that every time I take a bite of a sandwich from now on," And she took a sharp bite out of her pate. After swallowing she added. "Perhaps it is a shame you did not fall off the building."

"So tell me," I turned to Jake, "what happened over there?"

The story as far as he could figure out and as told to him by the man who had been pushed off the wall, was that a couple of older youths were rough housing when this man swam over to them and told them to stop it. They did not take interference gladly and told him to piss off. He then said he would get the lifeguard to expel them from the Sky Park. Whereupon the two became even more upset and threatened to beat him up. One of them clenched his fist and took a swing at the man who tried to escape by climbing onto the wall. The top of the wall was slippery and while he was trying to maintain his balance the youth sprang out of the water and slammed him against his chest and knocked him off the retaining wall.

"Was he badly hurt?" Matilda asked.

"Mainly some bruises, scrapes and a few cuts. He was lucky. He could have damaged his back when he fell or even broken a limb."

"At least he is alive and did not fall very far, then."

"Yes, it was not too far a fall."

"And the youths, were they arrested?"

"No, they managed to run off before they could be apprehended."

"It sounds as if this had nothing to do with William, then," Wee said and Jake nodded.

"Well that is a relief."

After lunch, we decided to set off for the Gardens by the Bay. It was a very short walk from the hotel and both Bertha and Wee decided to accompany us. Neither had seen the gardens yet, although they had been living in the hotel for nearly a week. I wondered if they had spent the entire week making up for lost time, stuck in the hotel. They had not mentioned that they had visited anywhere away from the hotel. We strolled leisurely across the elevated pedestrian walkway that led from the hotel across to the park. Except for William, who seemed as exuberant as ever, the rest of us were subdued, still recovering from the shock when we thought he had been killed. It is called Lion's Bridge and it takes one across Shearer Ave, the motorway that flanks the park. Directly ahead of us we could see across to the unique 'Supergrove' of giant artificial trees and off to the left the giant greenhouses looking for all the world like two enormous silvery clams. The larger greenhouse is the Flower Dome and the somewhat smaller but much taller one is the Conservatory Cloud Forest. It is big enough to house a small mountain supporting a rainforest. These structures all stood out stark against the expected greenery of the park. We had heard much about all three of the attractions. When last I had visited Singapore it was to attend a World Orchid Conference and we had been treated to a preview of the Flower Dome. I wondered how it had matured in the intervening years. At that time the Supergrove and Cloud Forest were still under construction.

The Lion Bridge brought us down at a small central area by an entrance to the park. I had the feeling that we were entering a theme park rather than a botanic garden and in truth it was a bit of both. Nevertheless, I knew that it also had the serious focus of educating the public about the wonders of the plant world.

From the entrance, a short path led to another bridge that spanned a narrow waterway. At first I thought it might be a river or some inlet from the bay. It could not be the latter because it was flanked by marginal plants that would only grow in fresh water.

"This is apparently Dragonfly Lake and it runs along all three sides of the park." William was reading from a map on his cell phone. "Somewhere here there are supposed to be giant, life-like sculptures of dragonflies as well."

But I would be more delighted with live ones and sure enough I could see some dragonflies dancing in the air close to reeds protruding through the water. "They have also introduced fish and I think I heard somewhere even a family of otters," he continued.

This bridge led us to a path that indicated it went to a garden of Malaysian plants. "Can we get to the Supergrove this way?" Bertha asked.

William consulted his map. "Yes, I think so."

As we approached the Supergrove the density of people increased. The park was really the City's major tourist attraction. While Matilda, William and Bertha insisted on reading nearly every interpretive sign on the traditional uses of various plants by the local peoples, Jake was doing his thing, scanning the crowds for trouble makers. Wee seemed uninterested in the plants and rather bemused by Bertha's enthusiasm for them.

There were twelve 'trees' making up the Supergrove with another two clumps, each of three, positioned elsewhere in the garden. Each tree was constructed from a central concrete cylinder and an outer framework of metal rods. The trunks of the trees were fashioned into living walls of plants, bromeliads, orchids, ferns, creepers and other vegetation, with bare metallic branches making up the crowns. They were immense. The largest reached up sixteen stories, some fifty meters high, and supported a large restaurant in its crown, said to provide spectacular views of the park, bay and city skyline. The crowns of the smaller trees held banks of photovoltaic cells so like living trees, could harvest the energy of sunlight, but instead of sugars they converted the light into electricity, part of the park's efforts to be sustainable. The trees were connected underground to the Cloud Forest Conservatory and helped vent heat buildup from that conservatory. Two of the larger Supertrees are connected by an aerial walkway, called, with the Singaporean penchant for initials, the OCBC Skyway. Except for where it is attached to the trees there are no other obvious supports. Actually, from the walk one can see that it is suspended by wires to nearby tree branches. Great engineering. At a height of 22 meters (some seventy-two feet) above the park and some 128 meters long (slightly more than 400 feet), the skyway affords a great view of the park. It is a favorite attraction but at this time the crowds lining up to pay admission and be whisked up to the skyway were not excessive. We lined up for our turn. Bertha and Wee were ahead of us in the line when William turned to Matilda and asked, "Did you see how long Bertha's nails are? I thought she always wore them short."

"A lady is allowed to change her mind."

"Maybe Wee likes to have his back scratched when they are going at it."

"Stop William."

"What, you don't care for the visual?" And he grinned at her wickedly.

The view from the Skywalk is all it is touted to be.

"Good thing no one is acrophobic," Matilda said as we wandered slowly along taking in the view.

"I wonder how often they get a jumper?" William asked. Of course it was a typical William question. "This railing is quite low, nearly anyone can climb over it."

"Sometimes I think you are sick," Matilda told him.

"Just stating the obvious."

I expected the banter to continue when I felt Jake stiffen next to me.

"What is it?"

He turned towards me and said casually, "Don't look now, but we are being watched."

"Where?"

"Down below, near the third tree to our right. It is the hippy guy who was in the blue Audi."

"You sure he is watching us?"

"Yes, he has a small pair of opera glasses and he pretended he was bird watching but he kept coming back to check us out. I also saw him take a picture of us with his phone."

"Do you think he is aware that you noticed him?"

"No, I just looked casually past him."

"Do you think he can hear us?"

"Nope. We are too high up."

I glanced casually about. Sure enough it was the same slender young man we had noticed at LAX by our gate. If not for the fact that he had also followed us in the blue Audi, I would have assumed it was a coincidence meeting him here. But now I was not so sure. Trying not to stare, I took in his slender figure and scruffy beard. He had the same small backpack that he had carried onto the plane with him. He swung his binoculars around looking at the trees and scanning us on the Skywalk. I gazed off into the distance as if looking at the scenery.

"Is there anyone else with him?" I asked Jake.

"I don't think so. I would like to ask him a few questions."

"Do you think we can catch him?"

182

"Maybe, later, if he keeps following us."

"Best chance will be if he enters one of the greenhouses after us."

"Yep."

"Should we tell the others?"

I looked at Matilda who was talking animatedly with William, Great-Aunt, and Wee. They seemed unaware that Jake and I had pulled away from the group.

"I will tell Matilda and ask her to keep the others busy and out of our way."

"We will get flack afterwards from William when he finds out."

"So be it. When we get off the Skywalk, let's see if he follows us and look out for possible companions of his."

We rejoined the group and I pulled Matilda aside, alerted her and said what we were going to try to do. She nodded in agreement with only a brief caution to be careful. Once back on the ground, we set off towards the Flower Dome, stopping every now and then to admire various bushes and trees. This also gave Jake the opportunity to make sure that our suspect was still tailing us. He was.

You have to pay to visit the Skywalk and the conservatories, but Great-Aunt Bertha had arranged for our tickets through the concierge at the hotel. We showed them again at the entrance to the Flower Dome and entered. In front of us was a display of flowers worthy of a bulb farm in Holland. Despite the fact that it was late spring, there was an enormous array of tulips packed closely together in a more-or-less semicircular bed. It was surrounded by a path and then an arching narrow bed containing a row of mature, tall cypress trees. In front of and between the trees were taller, modern intersectional lilies, each carrying several gigantic flowers in clean white, interspersed with plants bearing equally large flowers of baby-ribbon pink. Floating above the flowers were several large sculpted dragonflies with bright blue eyes and transparent wings. It made for a fantastic floral display.

In the distance we could see a few visitors wandering along the paths, but for some reason there were very few visitors in the conservatory. It could work to our advantage if we wanted to tackle our spy.

I knew that in some adjacent areas there were also sculpted mushrooms on which other colorful giant insects were perched. We walked along the path, tulips on our left and on our right the entrance way to an events hall. The roof of the events hall is planted with a collection of adult baobabs and other Madagascan tree species with swollen trunks. They had been imported from Madagascar and established in this garden of the Flower Dome. It had been an exceptional undertaking and gave the plant collection in this giant conservatory a unique flavor. Behind the tulip field and its border of lilies, the rest of the garden was divided into areas representing the major Mediterranean ecosystems of the world and regions were planted with the flora of Chile, Southern Africa, California, etc.

Jake seemed to be keeping an eye open, but so far our tail had not entered the dome.

"We will need to set a trap," Jake murmured to me. "The guy is not going to come in while we are standing here in the center of the flower field ogling the pretties. He would know that we could see him. You have been here before, right? Are there any darker areas where we could take this guy once we have him? I am worried about surveillance cameras, although I have been looking but cannot see any. But they must be here somewhere."

"Well, there is a hallway under the Baobab garden, where the walls are made up of screens upon which are projected large flower images," I remembered and pointed to the entrance door to that presentation.

"Good. I will persuade him to accompany me there and as soon as we go through the door you will join me. Tell the others that you need to pee or something so that they don't follow you."

"Okay. I suppose our group needs to be visible when he comes into the dome. We can go over to the palm collection. It is close by and not so far that I cannot get back to you quickly."

"I will go with you towards the palms, but hide behind one of the cypress trees, where I can watch for our friend and from where I can quickly get back to the front of the flower field when he passes by it. I can pretend to be fascinated by those big flowers. So the rest of

184

our group won't suspect what we are up to. What are those flowers anyway?"

"Intersectional lilies."

"What does that mean?"

"It will take too long to explain right now. Ask again later if you really want to know."

"Okay."

"How will you signal me when I need to join you?"

"I'll send a simple text on your cell. Just the word 'NOW'. Then you make your excuse and join me in the exhibit room."

"Got it."

Matilda and the others were only a few steps away when we joined them, and I suggested we go and look at the palm collection. Again, these were mature trees that had been dug up in countries half a world away and moved here at great expense. No one seemed to notice that Jake was lagging behind. We had nearly reached the palms when I saw the hippie stalker walking cautiously through the entrance and seemingly scanning the conservatory. It was the same young man I had noticed on the flight over. He still had that little toy monkey attached to the strap of his backpack. He reached into the outermost pocket of the pack and extracted a smart phone and proceeded to take pictures of the flowers. I watched carefully from the corner of my eye and saw that he had registered where Matilda and I stood and tilted the phone in our direction, snapped a few pictures and turned back to the flowers again.

"It's time," I told Matilda, "Take everyone down that path towards the South African garden. When you get there tell them what we are doing. We'll join you before too long."

The odds were still in our favor. There were no other visitors coming in through the entranceway.

I saw Jake slip back to the main path where our tail still stood, pretending to be entranced by the floral display. I felt the phone in my pocket vibrate, signaling Jake's text message. The man was now staring at Jake bearing down on him and he did not notice me hurrying round the other side to block any escape back through the entrance. Jake reached him, put a hand on one of the young man's shoulders and gripped him firmly. With the other hand, Jake flashed an open ID

185

wallet in front of his face, but too quickly for him to be able to read it and then returned the wallet to the front inside pocket of the thin windbreaker he was wearing. In one smooth movement he put the wallet away, retrieved his Beretta from its holster and jammed it into the man's side. I saw the hippie's face blanch. He looked little more than a kid. Perhaps he was only in his late teens.

"Come with us young man. I won't hurt you as long as you cooperate."

"I ain't done nothin'," the hippie protested. "Lemme go."

"Not until you tell us what we want to know. Then I will think about it. Maybe… maybe not."

We were walking towards the entrance to the flower corridor. It was like the dim mouth of a cave beckoning. I helped to hurry him along by gripping his elbow and pulling him forward. The guy did not seem to realize that Jake could not shoot him without possibly hitting me as well. Knowing Jake I suspected that the gun was not even loaded. It was all for show.

"Who do you think you are?" The young man was starting to resist being pushed towards the dark entranceway ahead of us.

"I ask the questions," Jake said firmly. We pulled the guy in through the open entranceway and into a darkened corner of the room next to the doorway. The other walls of the hallway had screens, upon which were projected an array of flowers and dancing butterflies. Jake released his grip on the man's shoulder but kept the gun centered on his chest.

"What's your name?"

"Jimmy."

"Well Jimmy, if that is your real name?"

"It's my name," he said adamantly, "not ashamed of my name."

"Okay, Jimmy. Why have you been following us?"

"Not following you. … just a tourist. On holiday. Seein' the sights, makin' pics."

"If that's the case, show us your pics."

"I don't have to…"

"Oh, but you do. I have this pointed at your heart." And Jake waved the gun over Jimmy's chest.

"Can't, phone is dead. Needs to be recharged."

The man hunkered back into the corner and against the walls with both Jake and myself looming over him. I was hoping our larger bodies would be intimidating.

"I'm running out of patience. George pat him down and see if the phone is in his pocket."

I ran my hands down his legs but there was nothing in his pockets. Not even a wallet."

"Must be in his pack. Take off his backpack and find his phone," Jake instructed me and I turned Jimmy around and removed the backpack. He was limp and unresisting. I twisted him around to face us again. I found the phone quickly and turned it on. It was fully charged. He was pale now and he seemed scared shitless.

"No juice? You lied. What are you hiding?"

"Run through the photos and see how many pictures there are of us," Jake said.

Sure enough there were some telephoto shots of Matilda and me on the Skywalk and then in the Dome looking at the palms. I scrolled back and there were a few shots, again of Matilda and me sitting at the table near the infinity pool. The pictures seemed to focus on only the two of us. There were no photographs of Jake or William, Bertha or Wee.

"He even took pics of us next to the pool," I said. "I did not see him on the Sky Park deck in the hotel."

I scrolled further back and found pictures of me talking to Raymond Wong at the Singapore Botanic Gardens, and then further back waiting for the plane at the airport lounge in Taiwan. This man had been following us everywhere we went. How did he know where we were going? Who was the informer? And to whom did this man report?

"Bring up his recent phone calls," Jake suggested.

Suddenly Jimmy lunged forward and grabbed for his phone.

"No, no." I held the phone high up, beyond his reach and he tried to pull my arm down.

Jake pushed him back into the corner.

I stepped back away from both of them and pulled up the list of his contacts and took a snap shot of the list with my own phone. Then I looked at his recent calls and took several snaps of that as well.

"Give me my phone back." The young man insisted.

"Ooh, I don't think so," Jake said. "We can and will learn a lot from your phone."

Technology is a two edged sword as the man was now discovering to his horror. I had a record of nearly everywhere he had visited in Singapore.

I slipped his device into the pocket of my jeans together with my phone and leaned towards him, my body towering over him from the side but not between him and Jake's gun.

"Who do you work for?" I wanted to know.

"Let's start with something more simple, like, – what is your real name, Jimmy?" Jake asked.

"I don't have to tell you nuttin'," the young man answered finding a scrap of courage.

"In that case, I may as well just call security and tell them that you were trying to sell me and my friend here some '*spice*' and you know what? Here in Singapore – drug dealing carries the death sentence."

"Go ahead. I ain't got no drugs on me. You got nuttin' on me."

Despite his bravado, he looked terrified.

"Your grammar is dreadful," I could not resist commenting, but he was too tense to pay any attention to my criticism.

"Oh no? No dope?" Jake pointed out, "What is this then? Looks like *spice* to me." And he extracted a small plastic self-sealing bag with a little white powder from his jacket, held it in front of the man's face and dropped it into a pocket of the backpack.

"I'll tell them you planted it."

"Come on, look at you. Look at me. Who do you think they are going to believe? I showed you my ID. I am security. You, you are just some little hippie punk? You think they will believe you? No way. So I have a deal for you. You just have to answer a few little questions and we will let you go. You can get yourself home and hide away from the bad guys. What do you say? Is it a deal?"

"I done nothing illegal." He was still defiant.

Jake put on his bully mask. "If you don't, I am going to cut off your little balls and stuff one down each ear. You are never going to fuck a girl again."

Now he extracted a switch blade from a pocket and flicked it open, waving the blade in front of the kid's face. The kid tried to shrink against the wall.

"I am not kidding." And Jake grabbed the man's crotch through his grubby jeans.

The kid gasped.

"You are going to tell us everything," Jake insisted.

"I...I...,"

"Good then. Here is the first question. Who are you reporting to?"

"I don't know... I just have a phone number and I speak to voice mail."

"What do you report about?"

"I have to tell them what you are doin' and who you are talkin' to." He pointed to me and added "You and the lady. And I have to take photos of you guys and message them to the phone number."

"Why?"

"I don't know why. I does what they tells me to and I doesn't ask too many questions."

"Okay, and who tells you where we are going to be?"

"The place comes in a text from a number. I dunno whose sends it."

"Who works with you?"

"Uh..., Carlos, he drives the car." That must be the swarthy man.

"His full name?"

"It's a funny one, di Sorrento or do Soilento... something like that... not sure."

"And the woman who was on the plane with you."

"Oh that's Rosie, she's my squeeze. She doesn't know we are supposed to follow and report on you guys. She's just along for the ride."

He now seemed willing to talk but we did not seem to be getting anywhere or any closer to what we needed to know. This kid was obviously only one of the bit players.

"Man, I don't means you no harm. I am just trying to make some bread. Mans got to eat."

"So, how did you get up to the Sky Park deck?"

189

"Carlos gave me the pass."

"And of course, you have no idea how Carlos got the pass?"

"No, dunna know."

It was clear that we were not going to get much more out of the kid. What was apparent was that there was someone prepared to go to a lot of trouble and spend a great deal of money, having us tracked. But why? It did seem unlikely that Jimmy and Carlos were working for the Cartel. They would not want to know who we were meeting. They were more likely to shoot and get rid of us and not worry about our contacts.

"You can go. But we are keeping your phone."

"Man, I gotta have the phone. Rosie cannot find me if I have no phone. Please sir... She don't know the city. I gotta find her and we gotta get away before Carlos beats me up. He is goin' t'be real mad at me, bein' caught an' all."

Did I catch a snivel as well? I was too damn soft hearted. Matilda always said, I tried to play macho but am really just a teddy bear. I made sure that the snaps I had of his screens were legible and handed the phone back.

"You can go," Jake said. "Clean up your act and if I ever catch you tailing us again..." He left the threat hanging in the air as Jimmy gratefully scampered off.

"Is it wise, letting him go free? Won't he just inform his bosses that we questioned him."

"Yes, that is a problem, but I don't see what else we could have done. I was not going to shoot him."

"Of course not."

As we walked back towards the palm garden, I turned to Jake. "Sometimes you really scare me, pulling that switchblade and the way you threatened the kid."

"What did you expect of me? He was endangering our family."

"He really thought you were going to cut off his balls. Especially when you grabbed them."

"It's a tough game and you have to play rough, or you don't have any effect. He needed to know that my threats were for real."

190

"And are you really carrying a sachet of *spice* in your pocket, in Singapore?" I asked Jake incredulously, referring to the synthetic cannabinol he had used to threaten Jimmy.

"Naw, it was just some artificial sweetener, I made up this morning. Thought it might come in handy."

"You knew we would meet up with whoever was tailing us? And you had already decided how to use it?"

"Pure luck. But you know me, I like to be prepared."

We found Matilda, William, Bertha and Wie emerging from the South African garden.

William ran up to us excitedly. "What happened? Did you find out anything? What did you do with the guy? Where is he now?"

"Slow down. Let's find a place to sit and I will tell you everything."

We ended up perching on a low wall that bordered a flower bed.

Jake and I recounted our encounter with Jimmy and what he had said.

When we finished Bertha summed it up with, "Well it seems unlikely that the cartel is involved, but who stands to gain from any of the information that Jimmy relayed, and why bother to collect it? Something does not make sense."

"And where does that leave us now?" Matilda echoed.

"Well we know of Jimmy and Rosie, and they seem to be lightweights. And then there is Carlos, the swarthy older man. Jimmy seemed scared of him. What is his true role? There was no mention of the Latina woman; maybe she is not in the picture? How were they able to track us?"

It was Wie who finally put it into words, "If it is not the cartel then who else stands to benefit? Perhaps you have to confront Carlos or whoever is orchestrating their entire operation."

"Maybe it is SCORE," Great-aunt Bertha said and then added thoughtfully. "After all I certainly was surprised to see both Guildenhuis, and what's her face, on the Sky Park deck today."

"It just means we have not eliminated anyone yet from our long list of potential perps," Matilda analyzed and the others all nodded in agreement.

Meanwhile I was scanning the list of recent phone numbers. One of them had a Singapore area code and a call had been placed at about eight-thirty each morning. Later each day Jimmy had phoned another number and sometimes had attached a document of some sort. I assumed it was pictures he had taken of us. I showed the pattern to Jake. He pulled out his phone and compared the number with his list of contacts. I saw his brows beetle when he recognized a match and his face grew grim. He showed me the contact's name and raised a finger to his lips to signal I should not say anything.

William, sharp eyed as usual, was about to say something but Jake managed to signal him to be quiet too.

The others had not noticed, and as we walked towards the mountain forest conservatory, I pulled Matilda aside and quietly said to her, "We have a real problem."

She raised an eyebrow, "What do you mean?"

I explained about the phone numbers and she gasped.

"Don't say anything yet to Bertha or Wie. We need to decide how to handle the situation. No need to upset them unnecessarily."

She nodded, "Does William know?"

"Jake will tell him soon enough."

Somehow the enjoyment of the gardens and their spectacular conservatories was spoiled for the rest of the day. Nevertheless, the rain forest conservatory was mind boggling. A small mountain had been built in the center of the tall domed glass house. Air temperatures were cool unlike the torrid heat one could sometimes expect outside in the park. Waterfalls cascaded down the sides of the mountains, which were covered with the kinds of vegetation normally found at high altitudes in the tropics. Some orchids had been skillfully placed among the begonias and ferns and other vegetable delights. But the sights did not distract me for long. My mind kept returning to the telephone number we had recognized on Jimmy's phone. What the hell was going on and who wanted us under surveillance and why?

We had an early meal with Bertha and Wie and learned that Bertha had been in contact with Channarong Bunyasagaboon, her Thai nursery friend, who invited us to come and visit him outside of Chiang Mai for a few days before the show. Apparently all the preparations for the show were proceeding very well and he expected it to be a spectacular display of orchids. This was a good suggestion because I felt anxious to leave Singapore. This city was no longer a safe haven for us. However, I thought it, was it too soon to head for Thailand? What to do?

Chapter 16 – Poisoned by Pizza?

As Jake drove us back towards Ang Mo Kio, we told William and Matilda about the telephone number we had recognized on Jimmie's phone.

"It came as quite a shock," Jake said, "when I realized that it was Soh Fat's phone number."

"At the same time that he was pretending to be worried about us going out on the town, he was informing them about our daily activities and proposed trips. Really two faced. And I believed that his prime job was to insure our safety." I echoed Jake's anxiety.

"I cannot believe that Soh Fat is the informer. He is so nice to us. He even went out and bought William his swimming trunks. Are you sure it is his phone number?" Matilda wanted to know.

"Yes it is his number. I double checked. And come to think of it, the guy who was pushed out of the pool was wearing almost identical trunks. Maybe those hooligans thought that other guy was William, who they deliberately wanted to injure. He could have been badly hurt. They disappeared quickly after the incident, too."

"Well," William said, "When we get back to the safe house we can force Soh Fat to tell us what this is all about. Maybe we can learn who is behind all of this and do something about it?"

"But you guys let Jimmy go," Matilda added. "I expect that he has already told all his associates what has happened."

"I don't know about that. He will probably get into bad trouble if they think he was careless to the point that he allowed us to catch him. These people are ruthless. I would not be surprised if they kill him outright. My guess is, he will fetch his girlfriend and then try to get the hell out of Singapore as fast as he can."

"If Jimmy has owned up to what happened today – then I will be surprised if Soh Fat is still in the house when we get back there."

"Jake," William said, "have you informed Tylo about your suspicions involving Soh Fat?"

"Not yet. I want to confront Soh Fat first."

"Well I hope he is still there then."

194

After the car had been parked, we went up to the condominium and let ourselves in. There was a note on the table near the front door. It was addressed to me and I opened it, read it and turned to the others.

"A note from Soh Fat. He says he hopes we had a fun day. He has been called back to headquarters. He suggests we call out for a pizza for supper. There is a phone number here for a pizza delivery service. He says he has already ordered it we just need to call when we are ready for it."

I had scarcely finished when Jake had his cell out and sent a call through to Tylo and Associates, Singapore branch.

"I'm really hungry," William said. "I am going to call them right now and ask for delivery now." He fished out his phone and asked. "What's the pizza number?"

I gave it to him and turned back to Jake. He had a serious look on his face. Kept nodding as he replied with several yeps and an occasional yes. He saw me looking at him and raised an eyebrow and grimaced. Something was dreadfully wrong.

He continued speaking for a while longer before returning the phone to his pocket. He turned to us with a serious expression on his face. We all looked at him expectantly.

"The shit has hit the fan. Looks like the bird has flown the coop. Soh Fat was not asked to report to headquarters. He no longer answers any calls."

"What are we going to do?"

"We had better pack up and get out of here, pronto."

"No. T & A want us to stay here tonight. Two new agents are being dispatched to protect us. Under no circumstances are we to let anyone into the apartment. Keep the door locked and make sure the latches are on too. I have been given the safe word to recognize these new agents. Tomorrow we are to be moved to another location. I said we wanted to go on to Chiang Mai tomorrow, but Tylo seems unhappy about us leaving Singapore. At any rate we will need to pack everything tonight."

"What about Bertha? Is she safe where she is?" Matilda asked.

"Phone her and tell her everything that has happened," I suggested.

Matilda pulled out her phone and retired to our bedroom.

195

Then a thought struck me. "Does everyone know where their microbots are?"

I had been carrying mine with me everywhere but William had left his in the safe house because he had wanted to go swimming. I did not know where Jake had stowed his. I assumed Matilda's was in her hip purse.

Both William and Jake scurried to their room to look for them.

"God dammit! It's gone." That was William's voice and I hurried into the room to find him next to his open suitcase. In his hand was the small box that should have contained the bot. It was open and empty.

"That fucking Fat bastard," he stormed. "He went through all my things and he has taken the bot. Left the charger though. Wonder why he did not take that?"

"And yours?" I turned to Jake.

"He did not find mine. I hid it inside the pillow, on my side of the bed. Here it is."

I hurried to our bedroom. Matilda was still on the phone. She looked at me querying.

"Where is your microbot? Did you have it with you today?"

"I'll get it after I finish talking to Great-aunt," and she dismissed me, so I returned to the other bedroom where both men were carefully unpacking their luggage and inspecting all their items.

"The fucker left a tracking device in the lining of my suitcase, and one in William's too."

"Now we are checking for other bugs," William added.

"Who do you think Soh Fat is working for?" I asked.

"Probably either SCORE members, bin Osman or the Cartel."

"What would SCORE or the cartel want with a microbot?"

"As far as the Cartel is concerned, it confirms our ties to Robotics. I don't think anyone at SCORE would figure out what we hoped to use the bots for. If bin Osman is aware of our mission, that means he not only has a mole high up in Tylo and Associates that knows what we are going to do, but he now has proof of how we want to achieve our mission and that makes it so much more difficult." Jake dissected our options and their relevance.

196

At this point Matilda hurried into the bedroom. "What is going on?"

"William's microbot is gone. We think Soh Fat took it."

"Mine is safe." Jake said when Matilda turned her head toward him.

"I have mine," Matilda said with relief in her voice. "I had left it in the small jewelry case I travel with. Nothing was taken. The case is still there with the bot. I still have the charger. He did not take that either. George, where is your bot?"

I patted the case on the belt around my waist.

"So we are down to four bots, if Great-aunt Bertha still has hers," Matilda said. "I will phone her again and make sure she knows to take extra care of hers."

"He also put GPS tracers in the boys' luggage. We need to check ours for them too," I said.

"Before we do that, tell us what Bertha and Wie have decided upon," I asked.

"She and Wie will change hotels tomorrow, and are thinking of driving out of Singapore into Malaysia, perhaps going to Kuala Lumpur for a few days before travelling to Chiang Rai. I had better phone her again with this latest disaster."

While Matilda was back on the phone to Bertha, Jake helped me inspect our cases and sure enough, each had a tracer cunningly hidden inside the cloth lining. The devices were flat and we could easily have missed them if it were not for Jake's expertise. Once all the inspections were completed and no more devices found we settled down in the living room to await the arrival of our new guardians. William turned on the TV and selected a news channel that broadcast in English. It was mostly mundane local news and I hardly paid any attention to it until a newsflash came on. Two tourists crossing Victoria Street in downtown Singapore had been struck and killed by a hit and run driver late in the afternoon. A tourist had been filming the street at the time and had captured the scene. The police were looking for the driver of a blue Audi who had abandoned the car. The dead tourists were Americans, a Mr. James Blakely and his fiancée Miss Rosalie Hernandez. A hollow sick feeling expanded in my belly. Were we now somehow responsible for Jimmy and Rosie's deaths? This

197

also demonstrated how truly ruthless our adversaries must be, but it did not really absolve us from a role in those deaths either.

"I wonder when that pizza is going to arrive. I am starving," William complained. I had forgotten that William had phoned in the pizza order.

"Was that the pizza company that Soh Fat recommended?"

"Yes."

"Why would he do that if he was running out on us?"

"Maybe it's just a ploy to let us open the door to an assassin? He would not have expected us to phone T & A as soon as we got back from the gardens and discover that he had skipped out."

"Perhaps it's a poisoned pizza?" William pointed out and continued. "That would be an easy way to wipe all of us out at once."

We looked at each other. And as if on cue the buzzer rang to announce a visitor who wanted access to the complex. I walked over to the intercom which had a small screen above it and I peered at the screen. There was a person in silhouette holding a pizza box. Why was the light which should have been illuminating his face pointing away from him?

"Who are you?"

"Southeast Pizza. Special delivery. Can you let me in please?"

There was something familiar about the delivery person.

"Wait a moment."

I turned to the others. "It's the pizza, but being delivered by someone who looks a lot like Carlos di Sorrento, Jimmy's friend. I have him waiting downstairs. Jake, what do you think we should do?"

"Do you think he is armed?"

"Picture is too fuzzy to be sure."

"If we could take him down, we might learn what is going on."

"How would we do that?"

"Easy. I have a suggestion. Tell him to come up. It will take him at least five to ten minutes to get here."

I gave him directions and we set up the trap.

"Matilda, William we want you both in the kitchen and lock the kitchen door behind you. On no condition come out unless either Jake or I ask you to. Hurry in there now. If you open the window you

198

will see a small balcony one floor below. You can drop onto it if you need a way out – an escape."

"I am not going to abandon you," Matilda was adamant.

"Same for me," William said.

"Don't argue. Now go."

And they went into the small kitchen and I heard the deadbolt snap into place. Thankfully the safe house had deadbolts on every door.

I quickly retrieved my hoodie and stuffed a pillow into it and filled the head with a dark shirt and propped it up on the sofa with the head facing away from the door. We dimmed the lights to a very low level. We had left the TV on as this would draw the man's eye first. We both took up positions on either side of the front door. Jake pushed himself up against the wall, next to the latch. I was on the other side of the door next to the hinges. We waited. The door was heavy and soundproof so we would not hear the footsteps approaching. Jake switched on the intercom and camera for the front door.

Eventually we saw a figure approaching, cautiously looking around; he was carrying the pizza box with one hand under the box and the other on the lid to steady it. But it also looked as if he held something else as well, under the box. He was moving too cautiously to be a normal pizza delivery guy. When he stopped in front of the door and pressed the buzzer with his elbow, Jake could see what was in the other hand. The man was armed. Jake signaled me to unlock the latches and then as I had been instructed I rapidly opened the door, slipping behind it and out of sight as it opened.

There were two *pffiitt* sounds as bullets slammed into the head of the hoodie knocking it off the couch and onto the floor. The gun must have had a suppressor attached and that is what Jake had recognized. Damn, there went a perfectly good hoodie and shirt! With hands clenched together, Jake slammed his arms down hard onto the assassin's hand on the top of pizza box. The gun discharged again harmlessly, as both it and the pizza box dropped to the floor. Pushing the box downwards had forced the man off balance and he was leaning forwards.

"Now!" Jake yelled as he jumped backwards, and I slammed the door as hard as I could into the man, connecting with his head. I heard him crash to the floor outside the door. In a flash, Jake reopened the door. The man was staggering backwards. Jake slammed a fist into the man's stomach and as he doubled over Jake delivered an uppercut to his chin. With a loud crash the man fell to the floor. He was groggy as he went down. Quickly, Jake turned him onto his stomach and bound, first his wrists, and then his ankles together with double zip ties, before dragging him back into the apartment. Thankfully, nobody else had come to investigate what the noise was all about.

"You can come out now," I called to William and Matilda who slowly opened the kitchen door and peered out before stepping into the lounge to join us.

Jake was busy frisking the man, patting him down and carefully turning out all of his pockets but the man had little on him to give a name or identity.

William reached for the gun. "Stop! William, don't touch it!" And William stopped in mid reach.

"We don't need any other fingerprints on that weapon. Matilda, can you get a clean plastic zip-lock bag from the kitchen and using another bag pick up the gun and place it in the bag without touching it directly."

"Sure." She went to the kitchen, and returned with the bags, and carefully retrieved the gun, engaging the safety lock at the same time.

"What are we going to do with him?" William wanted to know.

"Well a little intense interrogation is in order," Jake answered.

"I don't think he is in any shape to be questioned. He is too groggy," Matilda assessed the situation.

"Maybe not now, but certainly in a little while."

When the pizza box hit the floor it had burst open and scattered slices on the floor.

"We had better clean the floor," William said.

I bent down and sniffed at one piece without touching it. Was that a faint smell of almonds I could detect?

"Again, don't touch any of it unless your hands are protected. Are there any more plastic bags in the kitchen?"

"Yes, a boxful."

"Good, get several and use them as gloves to handle the slices of pizza."

200

"Jake, do you think they might be poisoned? If so why would he bother to have a gun as well?"

"I don't know. But let's not take any chances."

"After all this excitement, I am still hungry," William groused.

Jake pulled out his cell and tapped a number.

"Jake here. We have had a problem, an armed intruder pretending to deliver a pizza. Yes, we are all okay. Managed to subdue him. He will be your problem after you arrive. But we are hungry. Can you find some fast food? Hamburgers and fries will do. Thanks. Yes… yes…"

He turned to William. "Food is coming. T & A agents will be here in about fifteen minutes."

A loud groan came from the man on the floor. He struggled against his bonds for a while before giving up and then glared around the room.

"Ah, Mr. di Sorrento, or should I call you Carlos? I see you are awake." Jake had plastered a grim sneer on his face. It made him look cruel. I had never quite seen this side of him before.

"Wrong name." But his eyes widened at the sound of his name, giving him away.

"I have some questions for you. If you cooperate, maybe I will go easy on you. First, where is Soh Fat?"

"Who's that?"

"Don't play stupid. We know he set you up to come and deliver the pizza. Of course you know who he is."

"I know nothing."

"Okay, who is your boss? Who are you working for?"

He stared stubbornly into the distance.

"Is it the Guatemalan Cartel?"

His mouth remained firmly closed.

"Look, you are in a bad situation. We know about the blue Audi. You ran down Jimmy and Rosie. It was caught on someone's phone. We saw the video on TV. If you don't talk we will just hand you over to the police."

Of course even if he did talk we would hand him over anyway, but Jake did not mention that. I could see Carlos' jaw clenching.

"That was not me."

"I think you are lying."

I took over. "So if you are not working for the cartel, then who are you working for?"

He stared at me, stubbornly.

"Is it Mr. bin Osman?"

"Who is that?" He said.

"In a few minutes security will be arriving. If you cooperate we might help you."

He simply sneered back.

"You know, I think he looks hungry," William said. "Why don't we feed him a piece of pizza? I'm sure he would like that." And William placed the bag with the pizza slices on the ground near the man's face. He blanched.

Jake turned to us and said slowly and distinctly, "George you hold his head steady and Matilda if you pinch his nose tight he will have to open his mouth and then I can force feed him a couple of slices of pizza."

The man started shaking his head and body, vigorously from side to side as if he wanted to get up. I grabbed him by the shoulders and forced him firmly flat against the floor. He still squirmed a little but I was able to hold him steady.

"Looks like it will take all four of us to feed him. Never mind, we can do it. I don't know why he does not want to eat. Almost everybody loves pepperoni pizza."

Jake held his head firmly while William pulled out a slice and Matilda reached forward to close his nostrils.

"W…wait. I'll talk."

"Say something we want to hear. Then I will release your head. But if you lie it will be no big deal to force you again to eat."

"It is not the cartel. I know nothing about any cartel."

"Then who is your boss?"

"I don't know. I get my instructions from Soh Fat."

"Why did you follow us all the way from LA then?"

"There are a couple of dames in our gang. One of them offered me big money if I was to follow you to Singapore and report back on what you guys were doing here."

"And Jimmy and Rosie?"

"Same women hired them. Pity about Jimmie, he was a nice kid."

"And Rosie?"

"She was just along for the ride. Claimed Jimmie was good in bed. Who would have thought it? Such a scrawny kid."

"So you just got rid of both of them?"

"They were warned not to compromise our operation. Sad, but that's the way things are."

There was no real remorse in the man's voice, simply matter of fact. I believe there are some people totally devoid of empathy. They are so self-centered that they cannot imagine what it must be like to be in another person's shoes. There are two warring sets of genes in the human population, there is an altruistic set and the other set has selfish genes. The altruists have great empathy and work on the assumption that their survival is enhanced when people work together, they take care of each other and protect one another. Selfish people, on the other hand, see only limited resources and damned be the needs of anyone else. They know that they must get their share of the pie in preference to anyone else. Carlos di Sorrento seemed to be one with the selfish set.

"So let me go back to the beginning. Where is Soh Fat?"

"I don't know. I take direction from him. He doesn't report to me. I don't know anything more." And then he added hopefully, "You going to let me go now?"

It was Matilda who answered that question. "Mr. di Sorrento, you killed two young people; you shot bullets into someone you thought was a person and you delivered poisoned pizza which could have killed all of us. Do you really think we are just going to let you go?"

"But you promised."

"No, sorry, we simply lied. You understand don't you?" She smiled gently at him.

"May as well finish me off then."

"Oh, no. That would be too easy. We will let the authorities take proper care of you."

Our two new Tylo and Associates security agents arrived fifteen minutes later carrying burgers and fries. They introduced themselves as Peter Wang and Kevin Ahmed and we left them to look after Carlos di Sorrento while we repaired to the kitchen to eat. We suggested that they call their contacts at the nearby Ang Mo Kio police precinct to come and take delivery of Mr. di Sorrento. We assumed that the police would want statements from us as well.

Here we were in Southeast Asia, now eating hamburgers, having narrowly missed being poisoned by pizza. Whatever happened to the exotic foods and recipes of the Asian countries?

It was Matilda who started the conversation during our meal. "You know I thought that Soh Fat was on our side. He seemed so caring and helpful. Are we sure that he is the real serpent in the woodpile?"

"I'm afraid so. How else would the pizza delivery person be di Sorrento? And he admitted that Soh Fat was the person giving him and Jimmy direction," Jake said.

"But who would have put the cyanide in the pizza?"

"Probably di Sorrento. He knew it was in the pizza. Pretending to force him to eat the pizza got us some information out of him."

"The real question is, from whom does Soh Fat take orders?" I asked.

"While we are busy with questions, I have one or two of my own," William added. "Who do those women in California, who hired di Sorrento and Jimmy, report to? And what were those two SCORE people doing in Singapore besides obviously making out with each other? Maybe that was just a ploy on their part."

"I suppose the only thing we can be sure of at the moment is that events in Singapore have nothing to do with the Cartel," I contributed.

"I hope so," Jake said.

Jake placed his burger back on his plate and reached into a pocket and pulled out his phone, which was vibrating. "It's Tylo. I'll take it in our bedroom." And he left us in the kitchen.

We finished our meal, tidied the table and cleared away the food packages.

"I'll put Jake's meal in the microwave and keep it warm for him," Matilda put what was left of the burger and the few fries into a plastic dish and put it into the appliance.

We had scarcely finished when I heard the front door bell ring. We walked back into the living room to find four uniformed police officers crowding into the living room. Peter Wong addressed them speaking what I assumed was Malay. When he saw us emerge from the kitchen he switched smoothly to English. English is one of the four official languages of the city state and nearly everyone is fluent in it. Peter turned to us, "I am telling the officers why I called them. They are impressed that you were able to overpower Mr. di Sorrento."

"Mr. Seemore, who is in that bedroom over there..." And he pointed to the doorway that Jake had closed. "...is also a security agent for Tylo and Associates. He is a very experienced operative. He played the major role in subduing this perp."

The police cut the bonds on di Sorrento's ankles, leaving his arms bound behind his back, and raised him to his feet. With an officer holding each elbow they propelled him towards the open front door of the condo.

As they reached the door di Sorrento twisted his head back towards us and said, "We will meet again, amigos. And next time I will win."

I thought that was just bravado. A policeman pushed him out and they hurried down the hallway, leaving one policeman to take our statements.

We recounted the sequence of events, from arriving back in the evening to find our 'housekeeper' Soh Fat had left a message and what had happened since then. We avoided mentioning what had brought us originally to Singapore, suggesting we were tourists on our way eventually to Thailand. Matilda pointed out we had seen the video of the blue Audi running down the two tourists on Victoria street and that when the pizza delivery man arrived she recognized him as the same man who had fled from the scene after mowing down the two people. Of course the fact that the first thing he had done was fire into the dummy on the sofa would play heavily against him. It might take the authorities some time to realize the holes in our story. Once the policeman had our statement he cautioned us against leaving the city without getting permission first and then left.

Matilda pulled out her cell phone, "I had better update Great-aunt and Wee about our current situation and excitement. Need to warn them to be on their guard too." She went into the kitchen for some quiet.

I turned to Jake and asked, "What did Tylo have to say?"

"He now thinks there could be a tie in between bin Osman and the Guatemalan cartel."

"I thought we were discounting the cartel."

"He pointed out that the cartel used to deal in heroin before they switched to designer drugs, and that bin Osman's father controlled heroin production in Northwest Thailand."

"Damn. Just when I thought we were starting to make some progress…"

"Tylo isn't sure. Perhaps Soh Fat is working for someone else."

"What does he want us to do?"

"He suggests that we head for Chiang Mai as soon as we can get permission to leave Singapore."

"Did you tell him that Soh Fat took one of the microbots?"

"Yeah, but Tylo thinks that Soh Fat probably does not know what we planned to do with them. After all he won't have the app to control it."

"How long do we have Peter Wang and Kevin Ahmed with us?"

"Probably until we feel confident that we don't need them. They will be on sentry duty tonight so we can get a decent night's sleep. Oh, Tylo wanted to know if we want Grace Mposa to join us."

Grace had been a member of our security team on a previous mission in South Africa. She was a very smart intelligent lady, and also a natural beauty with the most beautiful skin of glowing toffee gold.

"Do you remember Grace is currently in Penang and could easily fly in and join us."

"Didn't someone say that she was also a helicopter pilot?"

"Yes, she trained originally in the South African military. Well, should we get her to join us?"

"I don't think that will be necessary. I do like Grace, and Matilda would certainly be happy to see her, however, the more people in our group the harder it is to keep everyone focused on a single goal."

"Okay, but I will keep her contact info, just in case…"

Chapter 17 – Chiang Mai Interlude

We had a peaceful night. It was nice being able to delegate sentry duty to Wang and Ahmed.

The next day Tylo and Associates had worked a miracle and the authorities agreed to let us proceed to Thailand the following morning, as long as Jake was prepared to return as a material witness when di Sorrento's case came up for trial. As a T & A employee they had the company's assurances that Jake would appear when commanded to do so. Jake contacted Channarong Bunyasagaboon as soon as our tickets were confirmed and he agreed to meet our flight at the airport in Chiang Mai. The four of us would stay as guests at his nursery outside of the city for the few days, until the weekend of the orchid show. Then we would move to the Golden Lotus Hotel at the city of Chiang Rai, where the orchid show was to be held. Chiang Rai is the northernmost city in Thailand and is more provincial, whereas Chiang Mai is much more cosmopolitan. Both cities are on the tourist routes, but Chiang Mai seems to be the better known.

We flew from Singapore directly to Chiang Mai. The skies over Thailand are frequently covered with smog, mist or the smoke from burning harvested rice fields, and the smoky grey air makes the land below look uninviting, but on this day the sky all over the country was crystal clear. Perhaps there had been an unseasonal rainstorm that had cleaned the air. March, while the start of the hot season, is still normally quite dry. I was sitting by the window and looked out over the city trying to locate the unusual square canal that I had read surrounded the original old city, but now the old city is in the heart of modern Chiang Mai. The old city had been confined to a square area, and part of the Ping River had been diverted to form a defensive moat outside the city walls. As the plane dropped lower towards the airport, I scanned the city trying to identify the canal. I could not see it but at the same time could not help noticing the new neat housing developments springing up on the periphery of the city. Chiang Mai is spreading out into the surrounding countryside and is now a bustling urban metropolis with a population of over a million. From the air, one had a sense of prosperity and orderliness that is lacking in so many other nearby countries.

The Chiang Mai International Airport is a sprawling white building. One portion is for international flights and the other for domestic flights. We hurried through immigration and customs, coming out at a narrow area where people waited to meet arrivals. Our host was waiting for us. He held a tablet with my name on it and we hurried over to greet him. He was a middle-aged man, slightly under six foot tall, with silver hair that framed a square face with a small straight nose. His lips were generous and there was a twinkle in his dark eyes.

"Mr. Bunyasagaboon?" I struggled to pronounce his name smoothly.

His face lit up and he extended his hand. "Just call me Kani. Formal Thai names can be excruciatingly long, so we all use simple nicknames."

We shook hands and I introduced the rest of the party. "This is my wife Matilda." And she executed a nice *wai* and then gave him a charming smile, followed by a shy *"Sawasdee kah."* Kani smiled back at her.

"These are my associates William and Jake.

"Sawasdee krap," William said, but spoiled it with a goofy grin and a very sloppy *wai*.

"Pleased to meet you," Jake followed and shook Kani's hand, western style.

"I am so pleased that you will be staying in Chiang Mai for a few days. I am sure that we will have fun."

I later learned that 'having fun' was an important Thai concept.

"Have you known Great-aunt Bertha for a long time?" Matilda asked as we followed Kani to a large passenger van that awaited us. It was chauffeured and the driver helped to load our luggage.

"Oh yes. Many, many years. We have been close friends for a very long time. I am so pleased that I can help you, who are so important to her."

I was no longer surprised at the number of men that all seemed to have great admiration and affection for Bertha. I have no idea how many of these men, it seemed of all nations, were ever intimate with her, but would not have been surprised if most were. How she juggled all these people and still retained their affections was a mystery. The men never seemed to show any jealousy and simply accepted that it was not their turn if she appeared with someone else in tow. So, I did not expect Kani would feel put out when Bertha finally appeared, and probably in the company of Wie. I did not know at that time that Kani was also married.

"I am so glad you are here to attend the orchid show. It is going to be a simply smashing event. Best one we have ever organized." He must have learned his English from British television. For where else would he have picked up the phrase, 'simply smashing'?

We had been told by Great-aunt Bertha that our host had a guest apartment on the grounds of his orchid nursery and so that is where we expected to be taken. His business had a reputation for holding an outstanding collection of Southeast Asian orchid species and I was looking forward to strolling through his nursery and hoped to see many orchid species new to me.

"Is it a long drive to the nursery?" I asked.

"Not really, but I was able to find a nice condo in town which will be much more convenient for you. You will be within walking distance of several restaurants and shopping. If you need to travel farther, well there are taxis and they are not very expensive. If you are adventuresome you can always ride in a tuk-tuk."

"What are those?" William wanted to know.

"Tuk-tuks are small motorized tricycles that seat two passengers, or at a squeeze three, in the back and the driver sits in front. Very common and also cheap. Locals use them all the time. It is a motorized rickshaw." Kani explained.

"Sounds like fun," William said.

"Yes, fun is important. People in Thailand always want to have fun."

"We would like to visit your nursery," I said. "I have been told that you have a very good collection of *Bulbophyllum* species."

There are more species of *Bulbophyllum* than any other kind of orchid. The numbers exceed two thousand, making it not only the largest orchid genus but actually larger than any other known plant genus. Southeast Asia is particularly rich in these plants.

"Yes, perhaps tomorrow, I will come and pick you up. What is a good time in the morning? Do you have a mobile phone? We must exchange phone numbers."

Our residence was on a side street, a narrow lane, and a few blocks from Nimmanhaemin Road. Kani told us that Nimmanhaemin had many restaurants and shops and was the 'in' place for the younger crowd. It was a busy thoroughfare both day and night.

Our home for the next several days was a small two bedroom townhouse. It was very modern, spick and span with a modest kitchen area. We unloaded our cases and exchanged telephone numbers. He suggested we be ready at ten o'clock the next morning for the visit to his nursery. Before leaving, Kani also gave Matilda a visitor's guide and map.

"There are lots of fun things to do in this city. I suggest this afternoon you go and visit the old city. It is not too far from here. Also there is a good breakfast place a few blocks away. Let me show you," and he took Matilda out into the lane and explained how to get there.

We said goodbye and he left us to our own devices.

"First, I need a shower," William said.

"You always need a shower," Matilda responded.

"And just what do you mean by that?"

"Nothing! Just an observation. You always seem to want to have a shower."

"Haven't you ever heard, cleanliness is next to Godliness?"

"Well you will never make Godliness, so I suppose you had better go and have your shower if it's your next best thing."

Fortunately, Jake's phone ringing interrupted any further exchange, and William scuttled off to the bathroom that was *en suite* to their bedroom. Jake muttered into his phone but I could not tell anything about his call. I looked at him expectantly after he hung up.

"That was T & A, Singapore. They have traced Soh Fat. He is here in Thailand, maybe even in Chiang Mai."

"How did they find where he is?"

"He used a company credit card to buy a plane ticket, Singapore to Chiang Mai. Interesting coincidence, isn't it? Apparently he flew out two days ago. Police helped get that information for us."

"Well, we had better keep an eye out for him."

"Yes, there is a conversation that I need to have with that little man."

We played tourist that afternoon and took Kani's advice to visit the Old City, where we found a museum that explained the history of the area. Originally, much of what is now known as Northern Thailand, together with adjacent parts of Myanmar on its Western flanks, Laos to the East and a portion of China on the North, was called the Lanna Kingdom. It was bordered by high mountains, but much of the land was a fertile agricultural plain that was fed by numerous rivers. The name Lanna itself referred to the multitudinous rice fields that gave the country its wealth. The city designated the capital of Lanna varied from time to time, until 1296, when King Mengrai founded Chiang Mai, as his capital and it has stayed the most important city of the region to this day. Lanna was eventually incorporated into the kingdom of Siam in 1892. In the 20th Century the area included the infamous Golden Triangle, known for its crops of opium poppies and heroin production.

The defensive moat that had once surrounded the old city was still there. Now there were several bridges that gave access and remnants of the old wall which still existed in places between the canal and the modern paved streets. Today, the moat is more of an elongated pond, replete with waterlilies and fountains. The wall must have been quite impressive when first erected. It was made from uniform terra cotta bricks, different in size from the bricks we use today. Those were much thinner but otherwise of similar dimensions. They must have been fired at high temperatures to have withstood the centuries since they had been laid down. What little of the walls that still remain are illuminated at night, giving only a hint of their ancient splendor.

It is fascinating how much is known and how detailed the history of the region is and how far back in time it goes. King Mengrai was been born on October 2nd in the year 1238 as the 25th king of a region called Ngoenyang. He expanded his holdings and founded several cities which served in turn as his administrative capitals. In 1262 he founded Chiang Rai in the Kok River basin in the north. But Chiang Mai itself which was only established decades later, retained preeminence.

While King Mengrai was successful in expanding his own territory by subduing surrounding countries, he was also something of a peacemaker. He was able to broker a peace between the nearby countries of Phayao and Sukhothaj and this he did in the face of a royal scandal. Apparently King Ramkhamhaeng of Sukhothaj had seduced the Phayao queen. It is not recounted if the queen was a willing participant or not. Understandably the Phayao king. named Ngammuang, was upset. War was imminent. Exactly how Mengrai was able to mend fences between the two royal families is not clear, but not only did he do that, but at the same time he also managed to forge a lasting detente between his and the other two kingdoms. All three kings are today honored with their statues standing tall, together in friendship, in a square in the Old City. I looked at them and marveled at the canny abilities of King Mengrai.

There are many Buddhist temples in Chiang Mai. They are very colorful and some are incredibly elaborate. A few are very ancient, being erected in the 13th and 14th Centuries. Matilda, always a history buff, was anxious to visit the oldest in the Old City. This temple, Wat Chiang Man, was erected in 1297. It is still in use today and houses two famous statues of the Buddha, one carved from crystal and the other from marble. It is amazing that this wooden building with peaked roofs and a double arched entrance still looks in good condition some seven hundred years after its construction.

One temple that I found particularly interesting was that of Wat Suang Dok. It is close to the Old City and was built about one hundred years after the Wat Chiang Man. This temple is renowned for housing one of the largest bronze Buddha statues in all of Thailand. It is an enormous 500 year old rendition of the Buddha. One always slips off one's shoes when entering a temple and we left our footwear among that of the many other tourists. Like most of the other tourists we ogled at the giant statues. Of course Matilda and William executed

213

perfect wais of respect to the statues. William must have been practicing. The inside of the temple was adorned with colorful frescos.

Most tourists come to the temple, I suppose, to inspect the statues or the many white bell shaped *stupas* in the grounds that house ashes of long dead members of the Lanna Royal Family. What fascinated me, however, was the fact that the temple was built on grounds that used to be a royal garden for growing flowers. Thailand has a modern reputation for horticulture and flower breeding and it seems they have been doing it for centuries, long before the west, perhaps creating and selecting flowers while our own ancestors were still barely clothed, painted savages. I wish I could have found out more about what plants were being grown for the royal family, but did not have a clue how to start researching that information.

Chiang Mai is an interesting mix of traditional and modern as are its restaurants. That evening we were enjoying our evening meal on the veranda of a sidewalk cafe that specialized in Thai style curries. It had the pretentious name of the Royal Thai Curry Palace. Across the narrow street, a fast food hole in the wall proclaimed that it sold 'world famous' burgers. We were seated on benches on either side, at one end, of a long trestle-type table, looking at photographs of the food offered. None of us could read the Thai descriptions. Another family with several children occupied the other end of the table. There always seemed to be children around.

"I never realized how many different kinds of curries are available," Jake said perusing the menu. "They seem to come in different colors like red, green and yellow."

"Yes," Matilda said, who we have always regarded as the font of all things culinary. "But there are other kinds of curries as well that have nothing to do with color, like Kaeng Khua curry and Mussamum curry as well as many others."

"I need to know what to avoid, so that I don't burn the roof of my mouth."

"You can usually ask for mild, medium or hot and the cook will adjust the amount of curry paste added to the dish to suit your taste. But Jake, a big strong man like you is expected to enjoy macho style curries."

He looked uncertain at that comment and I could see a mischievous glint in William's eye when he turned to Jake and said, "Ask the waiter to only use the littlest chili peppers when they prepare your meal."

"William, stop that," Matilda said sternly, and turned towards Jake. "Jake, usually the smaller the pepper, the hotter its fire. The Thais have a special little chili that they call the *prik kee noo*. They eat it with nearly everything. Often they cut it into little circles and float them in a dish of fish sauce."

"What does *prik kee noo* mean?"

"I'll tell you after the meal."

"Oh, oh. That sounds ominous. Do I want to know?"

"There is always value in education," she said.

"Here is some trivia for you," I said. "At one time the *prik kee noo* was considered the hottest chili in the world, some fifty to a hundred thousand Scoville units."

"And you want me to eat a sauce made from those?" Jake raised his eyebrows in mock horror.

"At least these Thai chilis are not as hot as the Trinidad Scorpion or Carolina Reaper chilis, both hotter than two million Scoville units."

"Why would anyone want to eat one of those?"

"Beats me."

"I will order something nice and tasty for you that is not going to incinerate your mucous membranes," Matilda offered Jake.

"Thanks"

She ordered *kaeng ka vi kuang* for Jake. It turned out to be prawns in a mild yellow curry. I chose roasted duck in a red curry. It was delicious, the curry being sweet and salty in perfect balance, with hint of lychee and the tang of tomatoes. I noted a few little circles of *prik kee noo* hiding among slices of cherry tomato and fragments of basil leaves. Jake carefully avoided them.

"This is so good," Matilda pointed with her spoon at her dish of green curried chicken.

"What are those things that look like giant green peas, floating around the chicken chunks?" William asked.

215

"It's an eggplant relative. You will not like them."

"Can I try?" And he reached over with his spoon and scooped up one of the little green spheres. Popped it into his mouth and bit down.

"Yuk. That is sooo… bitter. You sure it isn't poisonous?" He took a big swig of water and rinsed out his mouth, swallowing the liquid and wiping his lips repeatedly with the back of his hands. "Ugh!" And William returned to his own meal of beef in a mussamun curry sauce.

"I told you that you would not like it. Why don't you listen to me sometimes? I know what you like and what you don't like."

We were back at our residence discussing what to do that night.

"What is the night life like here in Chiang Mai?" Matilda wanted to know.

"You want to go to a night club or a bar?" I asked.

"I was looking at our options on line and Chiang Mai is renowned for its lady boys," William informed us. "One of the bars, called Heroes, is said to have the most famous lady boys in all of Thailand, even better than Bangkok."

"Lady Boys?"

"Female impersonators."

"I am not sure I am up for watching some old drag queens," I said.

"Don't be such a stick in the mud George. And these are not just any old transvestites. They are beautiful creatures. It will be fun. Come on, lets go."

I looked around at the others. They all seemed eager for a night out on the town, even Matilda was nodding.

"I suppose you already have the address written down?"

"Of course."

"Okay. Is the bar far away?"

"Don't know, but I'll phone for a taxi," Jake volunteered.

Jake sat in the front seat of the taxi. I am almost the same size as Jake but somehow the three of us, Matilda, William and I were squeezed into the back seat.

216

Jake said to the taxi driver, "Heroes, please. Do you know where it is?"

"Heroes, everyone knows where Heroes is. That is great fun place."

And we were off. He drove down the lane to Nimmanhaemin Road. The street was filled with vehicles. Motor scooters were weaving between cars and tuk-tuks and even pedestrians were walking in the streets rather than on the narrow sidewalks. Another feature of Thai traffic is the small pick-up trucks that act as buses. There is a shell over the rear compartment and two rows of seats along the walls on the sides. Passengers face each other. The Thai term for them is *song teaw*. They seemed to be everywhere and were often overflowing with passengers. For some reason in Chiang Mai, all the *song teaw* were painted red. I was glad that I did not have to drive in that traffic.

"So tell me Matilda, how did you rate that meal we just had? I mean the curry restaurant," William said. Those curries are different from the Indian curries we get back at home."

"Yes, the Thai ones are much sweeter and some of the spices seem to be different."

"They use a lot of coconut milk, don't they?"

"Yes and it is quite nutritious too."

"Before I forget. Matilda, how does *prik kee noo* translate into English."

"Roughly it is… mouse shit chili."

"Huh. Thanks for waiting until after the meal to tell us."

"Does it really have mouse poo in it?"

"No, no. It's just the name given to the little narrow chili peppers that they prefer."

"I wonder how they got that name."

"It is a long story. They consider mice playful and the little pieces of chili hide in the meal waiting to surprise one."

"But why shit?"

"It does not have the same connotations here as we have at home. Anything that is secreted or excreted is considered *kee*, like ear wax or even tears. I think it refers to the chili seeds being pushed out of the chili when it is sliced open."

"Oh, that makes sense of a certain kind," I added.

217

We arrived at our destination where a neon sign proclaimed 'Heroes'. The bar was situated on the corner of a block, with its open windows facing both streets. Music blared out into the street. It was crowded to overflowing. Patrons clustered outside clutching glasses and bottles while they peered through the windows towards a small curtained stage raised at the far end of the room. Alongside one wall was the bar with maybe fifteen stools and three bartenders doing very good business. There were as many as twenty-five small round tables scattered on the floor in front of the stage, with four to six seats squeezed tightly around each table. If there was a fire code limiting the occupancy of the room I don't think it was being observed. Maybe a hundred and fifty to two hundred people, shoulder to shoulder, filled nearly all available space. I did not see how they could fit any more people in, but I was wrong. We were led to a tiny table with four stools jammed around it. Somehow we pushed our way towards the table; apologizing as we bumped into strangers as we wound our way to our perches. Disco music pounded in our ears – it was too loud to carry on any meaningful conversations. Several mirrored balls suspended from the ceiling revolved, scattering shards of different colored, bright light around the room. The clientele was a mix of locals and tourists, both men and women. Some people were drinking tall glasses of strange tropical cocktails. I nursed a bottle of Chiang beer.

Suddenly the music stopped and the lights were stilled. In response, people in the room started to talk and the level of noise increased. I could make out some rustling behind the closed curtains on the stage and they waivered as someone on the stage brushed against them.

"Ah, time for the Lady Boys," William grinned at Jake.

More people were leaning expectantly through the windows.

A drum roll climaxed, with a clash of cymbals, and the curtains drew apart. On the stage were what looked like eight gorgeous young women, each wearing a different but tight sequined gown. The audience applauded lustily as a petite performer in a scarlet dress started to belt out Madonna's classic tune "*Like a Virgin*" while the other seven strutted around the stage posing with various arm stances that were reminiscent of Balinese dancers. If the actor was lip-synching she was excellent but perhaps she was actually mimicking the great singer's voice. It was difficult to tell. When she finished, the audience broke into enthusiastic applause. It must have been a Madonna night because in turn each of the Lady Boys slunk sexily into the center of the stage and performed one of her songs. "*Open Your Heart*" was followed by "*Papa Don't Preach*" and then my favorite "*Material Girl*." At the end of each performance, the audience gave the 'singer' a standing ovation. At first, I had assumed that they were lip-synching, but as different actors took central stage, one could make out slight differences in the tonal quality of their voices. Perhaps they were actually singing.

"Stop ogling their breasts," Matilda warned me.

"They look so real," I whispered back and indeed we could see the exposed portions of flesh not covered by cloth.

"It's called hormone therapy," William added. He must have overheard me.

"But there is nothing in their crotches." Jake remarked. He had exceptional hearing. Three of the performers' costumes included tight lycra panties that were exposed and seemed to show nothing stowed inside. I wondered for a moment if they were using slices of crustless bread.

"Maybe they have had their frankfurters and beans removed," William surmised.

"Ouch. I did not want to think about that."

"Maybe they really are women," Jake offered.

"If you look at the conformation of their legs it gives away their sex. Their legs are very straight. Women are usually somewhat knock-kneed," I pointed out, "Also some of them have shoulders that are a little too wide for real women. And that one there has an adam's apple."

"Shush. Can't you just relax and enjoy the show? No need to analyze everything so critically." The woman at the table adjacent to me glared and turned back to her companion, a rather stout gentleman.

I focused my attention on the stage, where a raven haired beauty thrust her breasts towards the audience and began to sing the racy "*Justify My Love*."

And then it happened. All hell broke loose….

Chapter 18 – A Tuk-tuk Chase

An elderly white man suddenly stood up and snarled at the top of this voice, "You fucking perverts are all going to burn in hell and I am going to help you get there."

And he pulled what looked like a small rifle with a wide barrel from a backpack and used it to shoot a smoking cylinder against the back wall of the stage. It missed the lady boys, who screamed and jumped off the stage into the crowd of spectators. Later I learned that the 'gun' was a 37mm 9 inch ST-9 Havoc Launcher and it certainly created havoc.

"It's a bomb!" Somebody shrieked as a cloud of smoke gushed from the canister. I grabbed Matilda and thrust her under the little table that collapsed on top of us. I covered her body as I waited for the explosion. It never came, but the entire room erupted into chaos. I could feel people pushing against the table as they desperately tried to exit the bar. One woman made an earsplitting scream at the top of her voice. The tumult increased. Someone to the right of us yelled. Others were screeching. Somebody else stepped on my arm and toppled over on top of us. I pushed him off of me. People were desperately scrambling to escape. And then – my eyes were burning. Matilda coughed and I realized it was not a bomb. It was a canister of teargas that the deranged individual had thrown onto the stage.

"Keep your eyes closed, its tear gas."

There was a pathway opening up towards the back of the room.

"Matilda," I gasped, "Let's try and crawl towards the exit."

"No, stand up, the gas is heavier than the air. Where is William?" She asked.

I tried to look around but my eyes were burning, with tears streaming down my cheeks. William had been sitting on my left. I groped around in his direction but could not find him. I grabbed Matilda's wrist and pulled her out from under the table. I was vaguely aware of police sirens converging on the bar. Matilda had pulled her blouse over her head. She always seemed to know the correct thing to do and I loosened my shirt and covered my face with it too. We felt our way between tables, not sure what direction we were moving. We kept bumping into people. It hurt to breath and I was trying to take little gasps. We were not making much progress getting out of the building. There were too many other people and I could not see where to go. I made sure that I held Matilda's hand. In some recess of my mind I knew that no one died from tear gas and if we could get away from the horrid stuff we would recover. At least we had not been badly trampled on. People do get killed in the surge of a mob hysterically trying to escape from a crowded theater.

It was a policeman, wearing a gas mask, who finally lead us out into the street where the bar's former clientele were still milling around. People were crying, some panting for breath, it was still chaos.

"There you are," I heard Jake's distinctive voice but I could not see him, my eyes still burned.

"Matilda, George." Then I felt William's arm gripping my shoulder. "We will take care of your eyes now."

"Tilt your head back and keep your eyes open," Jake commanded. I felt water splashing onto my face. "Eyes open!" He commanded again and the pain eased to the point I could see again. William was washing Matilda's eyes. They had taken bottled drinking water from a store nearby and using it to wash our eyes.

Tear gas is not a gas. It is a dry acidic powder ground into micro-fine dust and that dust can be transferred back to one's eyes from dust on one's clothing. We needed to get out of our clothes and under a shower. But first the police wanted statements from as many people as possible.

"How did you get out so fast?" Matilda asked William.

"Jake grabbed me and pulled me out with him before the gas spread from the stage to the audience. He recognized it for what it was. Everyone else thought it was a bomb and freaked out. First thing we did was run to a nearby store and buy several bottles of water. He knew that washing one's eyes with water was the best treatment. Luckily we got out before the tear gas hit. Then we looked for you. Could not see you anywhere."

"We were probably under the table."

"Bad choice. Teargas is heavy."

"I know that now."

"When the police arrived they had masks and helped evacuate everyone."

"Did they get the perp?" I asked Jake.

"Don't think so. I looked for him outside but could not find him."

"That sounded like a Southern accent, maybe Georgia?"

"It was certainly American."

"What do we do now?" My breathing had eased and I could see again, although my eyes still felt irritated.

"We need to get you and Matilda out of those clothes when the police let us go."

I am always amazed that if one knows that one should not touch one's face that it becomes almost impossible not to touch one's face.

It turned out the police were expecting trouble. There had been an American Evangelist group in the city preaching their gospel of hate for all things that do not conform to their narrow views of what makes for approved and appropriate behavior. These killjoys certainly did not approve of the Thai concept that having fun was a good thing.

We had just been cleared to leave when a tuk-tuk turned into the crowd. The people parted to let the vehicle through. Out of the corner of my still watering eye I saw a small, balding Chinese gentleman was the passenger. I grabbed Jake and pointed towards the tuk-tuk.

"The passenger, that looks like Soh Fat."

"After him." We ran for an empty tuk-tuk who was looking for passengers. Jake and I clambered aboard.

I yelled back at Matilda. "Go home, we'll see you there."

"Follow that tuk-tuk," Jake pointed to the vehicle now turning the corner at the end of the block.

"Four thousand baht if you catch up to that tuk-tuk. The one with the blue flag flying on its back." Four thousand baht was slightly more than one hundred dollars.

Our driver nodded with enthusiasm and accelerated, swerving around a couple still rubbing their eyes in the middle of the street.

"Hang on," I yelled to Jake and clung to a railing to avoid being thrown out of the rickshaw.

"You sure that's Soh Fat?" Jake asked when he had a chance.

"Think so. Sure looked like him."

Tuk-tuks have a roof and a rear wall, so it is difficult to observe the passengers from behind. Several other tuk-tuks also had pennants flying but none were blue. Unfortunately, the pennant colors were hard to make out at night, except for when the vehicle passed under bright streetlights or close to bright illumination from store windows. It would take concentration not to get the rickshaws confused.

Jake's offer of a reward must have been the best offer our driver had had in a long time. He was taking risks, weaving between pedestrians, other tuk-tuks and larger trucks and vans. Usually the traffic in Chiang Mai is laid back and no one seems to be in a very great hurry. The drivers are courteous and make allowances for others using the road. One taxi honked at us when we cut in front of him while trying to keep Soh Fat's ride in sight.

I was sure that we were going to collide with a large trash container being wheeled into the street, but at the last moment the tuk-tuk careened out of the way. The street ahead of us was congested and I thought we had lost sight of the little blue flag, but luckily we got to a corner just in time to see the other tuk-tuk turn to the left, a block ahead. There was little traffic and we were able to make up part of the distance between the two vehicles. Although tuk-tuks are motor-tricycles, they are not really built for speed. Most tuk-tuks' top speed is only thirty-five miles an hour but they can get to forty or even fifty miles per hour, especially when going downhill. Unfortunately our part of the city was perfectly flat. Trying to do thirty-five miles an hour in congested traffic where everyone else is happy at twenty, can at times be hair-raising.

The vehicle ahead of us seemed unaware that we were in pursuit but it was like a race through thick molasses. We were overtaking it so slowly that I thought we would never catch up. As we were approaching the left hand turn, a car suddenly swerved down that street ahead of us. We were in a narrow lane and could barely make out the pennant on the tuk-tuk ahead of us. There was no room on the sides to overtake the car in front. My frustration grew in reciprocal proportion to our slow progress. Would we ever catch up with Mr. Soh Fat?

Fortunately the car turned off the lane. Our quarry was still ahead of us but had gained distance and was approaching a well lit street and turned onto it.

Jake swore at our driver. "Shit. Can't this bucket move any faster?"

"Going as fast as I can, boss. Driver ahead cannot go faster. We will catch him." He said confidently.

"If you want your money, you had better do that," Jake growled.

The tuk-tuk ahead turned onto a busy street. I thought I knew where we were headed. It was towards Wang Mui Market that lined one side of Wang Sing Kham Road, a busy street noted for its many fresh fruit and vegetable stalls that spilled out onto the sidewalk. It had been on our 'to visit' list. However, I had not expected to visit it during a slow speed tuk-tuk chase.

Wang Sing Kham Road is a one way street but the driver ahead on Soh Fat's tuk-tuk turned against the flow of traffic. Our driver looked at Jake for direction. The street was filled with both vehicles and pedestrians. Traffic was inching its way along the road.

"Follow him," Jake urged.

Our driver shrugged and turned into, but against, the flow of the traffic. A taxi slammed on his brakes to avoid colliding with us. The driver glared at us as we slowly moved out of his way and turned alongside the taxi to drive past it. We inched our way past the taxi. On both sides of us were people on motor scooters, but moving slowly, so that they could talk to pedestrians walking alongside. In typical Thai fashion everyone was taking their time. There was no rush except for us, scared we might lose our quarry. Ahead I could just make out the flag on the back of the other tuk-tuk. Between us was a group of maybe as many as twenty teenage girls crossing the road. What they were doing at that time of the night in a tight group was beyond me, but there they were. And here we were, stymied in our chase.

"Get out," Jake said to me, "we continue the chase on foot." He reached over and thrust the promised money into our driver's hand

and leapt out of the tuk-tuk. I ran ahead and pushed my way into the crowd. Jake was behind me. I kept losing sight of Soh Fat's tuk-tuk when cars came between us and our quarry. If it was not for the flag standing up from the tail of the tuk-tuk we would have lost him altogether. Only when I managed to catch up to the rickshaw, now stalled by a mob in front of him, did I realize that something was wrong.

"There is no passenger in that tuk-tuk," I yelled back at Jake.

He immediately spun around and tried to survey the crowd. There was no sign of any one remotely resembling a little half-bald Chinaman in that crowded road. Soh Fat had given us the slip. Nevertheless, Jake hurried up to the now passengerless tuk-tuk and had a few words with the driver. I kept looking at the crowd hoping to catch a glimpse of Soh Fat but without success. I turned back to the tut-tuk but, by the time I reached it Jake had already retreated and was making his way towards me.

"Any information?" I asked.

"George," Jake said, "The driver was unaware that we were following and trying to catch up with him. So Soh Fat probably does not know that we are on to him."

"Where is Soh Fat now?"

"He got off when the tuk-tuk was stalled, about half way down Wang Sing Kham Road, I figure that must have been five minutes ago. He must still be in this area."

"I don't suppose the driver knew his passenger's name?"

"No. I asked but he said that he had never met him before."

"Where did he pick him up?"

"Damn. I didn't ask."

I turned away from Jake and looked for the tuk-tuk, but blue pennant and all had disappeared in the mob. The rickshaw was nowhere to be seen.

We retraced our steps, looking at the faces in the crowds and peering into the fruit stalls. I wondered if any of the sales people manning the stalls would remember seeing Soh Fat. It seemed unlikely, there were so many people. I approached a few and asked if they remembered anyone fitting Soh Fat's description. No one had seen him. I approached another stall near to the corner where we had turned onto Wang Sing Kham Road.

225

An obese woman sat in a chair behind the counter, looking out at the crowd from within her stall. She looked directly at me and noticed me glancing at her fruit. She smiled at me. I noted piles of mangoes in many varieties, small red bananas and fat green plantains, dragon fruit in both red and yellow varieties. But it was not all tropical fruits, there were also plastic boxes of blueberries, grapes and apples, probably all from California.

"Do you speak English," I asked her.

"Yes."

"I am looking for a small man…"

"Many small men out there," and she gestured towards the street, "What kind do you want? How much can you pay?"

"I don't want to buy a man. I'm straight and married."

"So? Have you any idea how many straight and married men still want to play with another ma…"

"You don't understand. The man I am looking for. He's a… a friend, an acquaintance."

"Oh, why did you not say? What he look like?"

"Short, only so high," And I held my hand in the air to approximately Soh Fat's height. "He is half-bald, no hair on front of his head, Chinese man, maybe forty years old."

"I saw such a man, fifteen minutes ago. Right in front of my store."

"What happened to him?"

"He look at my yellow dragon fruit, but he no buy."

"And…?"

"He walk to taxi and drive away."

We had reached a dead end. However, I bought a punnet of blueberries for Matilda, they were her favorite fruit.

When Jake caught up with me I shared my new information. It was a dead end, a wild goose chase, because we really did not know if it was actually Soh Fat that we had been chasing. It might have been some innocent stranger.

We took a taxi back to our apartment, where Matilda and William were waiting anxiously. They had changed out of their clothes and Matilda's hair still looked damp.

"How are your eyes?" I asked her.

"Better. The shower helped."

I hurried to the bathroom and she followed me. I recounted our exasperatingly slow tuk-tuk chase and our lack of success.

"Put your clothes into this bag. We have to wash all the tear gas off the clothes," and she produced a large plastic bag. "Into the shower, now and don't touch anything else. Don't touch anything. Now!" Matilda commanded.

She watched me undress, made no comment about my natural glory, picked up the laundry bag and left me to have a thorough scrubbing. Normally I would have invited her to help me but did not want to expose her to any more of the contaminating acid dust.

"What do we do now?" William enquired when we had all gathered once more in the living area.

"Kani is sending a car tomorrow to pick us up to visit his nursery. He wanted to know if we wanted to visit an elephant park and go riding on an elephant."

"Huh?"

"There are a number of elephant parks outside of Chiang Mai. One is near Kani's nursery."

"That would be exciting. An elephant ride might be great fun," William said.

"It sounds like fun but we are certainly not going to encourage any elephant parks," Matilda insisted.

"Why not?"

"Have you ever heard of how they train the elephants? They use pain to make them obedient. Common thing is to stick roofing nails through their tender ears. Elephants are very intelligent and also have exceptionally long memories. The mahouts separate baby elephants from their mothers at an early age and they are confined to narrow pens where they are brutally starved and tortured into submission. The process actually has a name – *Phajaan* or crushing. And of course bullhooks are used to hurt them as well. Because of their long memories elephants that have been trained this way remember the pain, when threatened, even long after they have reached adulthood and old age. Also elephant backs are surprisingly weak and have trouble supporting a two hundred pound adult." This time Matilda had taken over my role of pontification.

"You have convinced me. No elephant rides," William agreed. "I had no idea that something like *phajaan* actually existed."

"It is almost never discussed. They are aware of the sensibilities of modern eco-tourists and know it will bring bad publicity, but elephant rides are very popular and there will be a market for them as long as the tourists remain unaware of *phajaan*," Matilda said.

"The practice probably goes back hundreds if not thousands of years," I added. "Some elephant camps today claim to treat their animals 'responsibly' but remember, even if they are looking after them kindly now, they still had to be trained using *phajaan* methods."

"Animal acts in modern circus are banned in many countries now because of the cruel methods needed to train elephants," Matilda drove the point home.

We decided to give the elephant parks and camps a miss. I knew however that some elephant parks are actually sanctuaries for rescued pachyderms where they can be rehabilitated but I hate animals in captivity and prefer to see my animals in the wild. Unfortunately there are very few wild elephants left in Thailand. But some nature preserves do boast small numbers of them.

It was Jake who helped us make up our minds. "Let us go to Kani's nursery. While you are looking around and enjoying the plants, I need to have a conversation with Mr. Channarong Bunyasagaboon." The long name rolled off his tongue as if he had been practicing, and knowing Jake, he probably had. Jake looked directly at me as he continued, "We need more information about this flower show that is coming up next week and also we need more recent background information about Mr. bin Osman. That is what is important, and I think that Kani will have most of the information we need."

Chapter 19 – Flying Snakes

The following morning we had breakfast around the corner at a little cafe a block away from our apartment. On our return, there was a large mini-van waiting outside our residence. The driver got out and approached us. "Are you Professor George? I have come to drive you and your friends to visit Kani's Orchid Nursery. I will bring you back here after your visit."

"How far out of town is the nursery?" Matilda asked.

"About an hour's drive. We will take the road to Doi Inthanon. It is on the way there."

"Where or what is Doi Inthanon?" William asked.

"Doi means mountain in Thai," Matilda had been reading her tourist guide. "Doi Inthanon is the tallest mountain in the country. Actually it is the farthest endpoint of the Himalayas. I read in the guide book that it is covered in forest and is a large nature reserve and tourist spot. One can drive close to the very peak and take a leisurely walk to the top along a nature trail."

"Probably has cool growing orchids in the forests then?" William supposed.

"Yes, one of my colleagues said he saw *Coelogyne nitida*, some dendrobiums and oberonias, even *Pleione praecox* growing in the forests high up." I replied.

"Maybe we should think about going up there, if we have a free day."

"That might be fun, but remember this is not a fun trip."

"Perhaps afterwards?"

"Are there elephants up there?"

"Don't know, but I heard that there might be Himalayan sun bears."

"Aren't those creatures the basis for the Yeti, the abominable snowman?"

"Not enough snow on Doi Inthanon for a Yeti, although it can drop to freezing."

"Jake, when did you last report in to Tylo?" I changed the conversation.

"Soon as we got into Chiang Mai."

"Did he have any advice?"

"Only to stay low and keep out of trouble until we get to the show."

We drove south of the city on the road to Doi Inthanon passed the suburbs where houses gave way to fields and the fields then gave way to sloping lands and then trees and the trees became denser and clustered into forests. Doi Inthanon is somewhat to the southwest. These woodlands are not like the lush lowland forests with big leaved trees. Here the leaves are small and branches not as heavily clothed in foliage. We left the main road and wound our way into the foothills. Trees got taller and taller. This was mixed forest, some dipterocarps and even some conifers.

Jake and William sat in the very back of the van. They were both quiet. I turned around and looked at them from time to time. Jake kept looking back out of the rear of the car but also at the surrounding forests. I assumed he was being careful looking for cars that might be following us. There was a lot of traffic but our driver was very careful and most cars seemed to pass us. Others stopped at the a few small villages we drove through and yet others turned off to the entrance ways of large resorts and tourist parks. It did not look as if anyone else was interested in us and I hoped that we had left all that behind in Singapore.

"What are you doing William? You are awfully quite," Matilda remarked.

"Found this field guide back in our apartment and I borrowed it." He held up a book and I squinted at the title. It was a guide to the snakes of Southeast Asia.

"I assume there are hundreds of different species."

"Yes, and some are very unusual."

"Did you know that there are two species of flying snakes?"

"Flying snakes?" Matilda interjected. "I don't want to meet those."

230

"Well they don't actually fly. More like gliders. I saw a video once. They climb trees and launch themselves into the air. Contract their belly muscles in and the body acts like an elongated parachute. They look like they are swimming through the air. Can direct where they hope to land," I went into professor mode.

"George, I don't need to know that. I don't need to have anything to do with flying snakes."

"You remember the spitting cobra in Africa?" William reminded her of one of our previous encounters with one of those nasty reptiles.

"Yes."

"Well they have spitting cobras here too."

"Ugh. I need a gun." Matilda was a sharpshooter and I thought she could probably even dispatch a flying snake in mid-air. Being a biologist, I secretly hoped we would see flying snakes. That would be so rad.

"Have you ever seen a flying snake?" William asked our driver. "They are supposed to occur in the forests over here."

"No sir. I am a city man. I don't want to have anything to do with snakes."

"George, are flying snakes poisonous?" Matilda wanted to know.

"Yes, but they have back fangs and would have to chew for a while to inject sufficient toxin to harm you." I knew a bit about these snakes. They are so interesting.

Our driver pulled in to a narrow side road and followed it into a community of maybe twenty small holdings. The road was so narrow that two cars would not be able to pass each other. We passed one household, surrounded by nearly an acre of dragon fruit cacti. It must have been too early in the season for ripe fruit, but one could see that some of the oval fruits were already blushing red. Dragon fruit is very popular in Thailand, but I find it bland and overrated. Nevertheless, it was interesting to see how it was farmed.

"Must have lots of bats in the area," William muttered referring to the fact that these cacti are typically pollinated by bats.

A small poster on a fence revealed that 'Kani's Orchids' were to be found around the corner and there the van turned into an open driveway. The nursery backed on to what looked like wild forest at the edge of the town. Here were set a number of high roofed poly tunnels with open sides. Running along their length were metal benches jammed full of plastic pots holding an enormous assortment of orchid plants. Kani came out to greet the car and, as we alighted, strode forward to shake our hands.

"Welcome to my nursery," he said. "So glad to have you here."

We expressed our delight in the opportunity to visit.

"May I get you some refreshments? Perhaps some juice or bottled water?"

"That would be nice," Matilda said politely and he led us to a covered veranda near a potting shed.

"Would you like ice?"

"No thanks. We are staying away from unbottled water."

"Okay. I have refrigerated bottled water. Will that do?"

"Lovely," Matilda answered for us.

We settled down in some comfortable chairs around a small table.

"This is my wife, Charlotte," he announced, as a short woman came forward bearing a tray with bottles of water and a plate of cookies. She placed them on the table and smiled shyly at us. I was no longer surprised at the names that some Thais selected for themselves.

I stood up to greet Charlotte but she waved her hands at me to sit down again.

"Don't bother getting up. We are very informal here."

"Thank you," I said.

"You are from America?" She asked.

"Yes, California."

"I like California, except for Los Angeles. I do not enjoy your freeway traffic."

"Neither do we," William grinned at her.

"Do you all like orchids?"

"Most of us, except for him," William pointed at Jake. "Jake here is just along for the ride."

"Yes, I am long suffering," Jake said.

"It cannot be so bad?" Charlotte asked. "Why is Jake with you?"

"Oh. He is my boyfriend," William answered.

"That is understandable. Everyone has to make sacrifices for love."

"Words of wisdom," William grinned again and Charlotte smiled back at him.

We finished our drinks.

"I suppose you will like to go through the nursery now?" Kani suggested. "I have a very fine collection of bulbophyllums and many are in bloom now."

"We would like to see them,"

"I must return to the house," and Charlotte got up and left us.

"This way," Kani stood up and led us towards one of the growing houses.

Jake walked alongside him and glancing up at the nearby forest asked, "Do you have flying snakes in this region?"

"You mean *ngu kieo ron*? Oh yes, they are very common. Sometimes they land on the ground near the orchid houses."

"That must be unsettling."

"Only at first. After a while one gets used to them."

"I would love to see one flying," William ventured.

"Perhaps it could be arranged."

"Really?"

"Yes."

"If we disturb the trees, maybe they can be scared into flight."

"How does one disturb the trees. They look so fixed."

"Simple, we chop one down. As it falls it will bump and shake other nearby trees. The shaking and noise might frighten them into flying."

"Have you ever done this?"

"No, but I have always wanted to. It would be a great experiment. I think that must be how the wildlife photographers coax them into the air."

"I am not sure I want the sky full of flying snakes," Matilda objected.

"Think of the stories you can tell when you get home," William reasoned.

233

"That's the point. I want to get home without encountering any snakes, let alone ones flying through the air towards me," she said, determinedly.

"I agree with Matilda, I don't need any snake encounters," Jake agreed.

"You are acting like a wuss. They don't bother you if you don't bother them."

"But is cutting down a tree going to be enough to frighten the snakes into flying?"

"I also have some powerful firecrackers. Both shaking and explosions might work."

"Maybe we can arrange to chop a tree later? It would be fun." Kani said, despite both Matilda and Jake's reluctance at the idea.

"I hate the idea of killing a tree simply to look at a snake," Matilda said.

"We have some trees in the patch of forest that are so old they are partially dead already. The next storm will probably bring them down. It is no sacrifice to cut one down. Any orchids on the branches, will be rescued and grown in the nursery. In fact, there is one we were going to cut down because it has a big clump of a coelogyne orchid on it. By luck, my workers have already cut through most of the trunk. It will not take long to bring the entire tree down."

"Isn't there also a flying lizard in this region?" William asked.

"Yes, they are small, only a few inches long, maybe as much as eight if you include the tail. They have long ribs that they can extend along their sides with a flap of skin between the ribs. They can glide through the air. Sometimes they are mistaken for birds."

"The genus is *Draco*," I added, "It means dragon."

"I had no idea there were so many flying reptiles," Jakes said. "But I can live without them."

"People who are afraid can stay back in the office," and he pointed back to the veranda where we had had drinks. "Only problem with snakes is when you don't see them, and accidently step on them or brush against them. Snakes don't like that."

I saw Jake staring around at the ground as we walked towards the growing houses.

"Better watch your step," I told him, half amused. He was such a big strong man and here he was almost admitting he was scared of

234

something. It evoked a teasing streak in me that I had not realized I possessed. Actually, from travelling so much in the wild, I always did watch where I walked, but Jake was a city boy.

Kani led us over to a fence running down the center of the nearest growing house that was covered with orchids, making a hedge of plants. Plants were mounted on rectangles of rigid plastic netting and then hung on the fence. It was a mix of both hybrids and species. Benches running down alongside, but separate from the fence, were laden with potted orchids. In other areas, vandaceous orchids were suspended in wooden baskets from wires strung at head height with their roots hanging down in the air, straining towards the gravel floor. With the high humidity of the region there was no need for potting media for the vandas. They would not dry out. I envied the ease with which one could grow orchids in this benign climate.

"This is an amazing collection of bulbophyllums," Matilda cooed.

"Yes, I have nearly all the known species in Southeast Asia," Kani said proudly.

"This must be the best collection in Thailand."

"No, I believe that bin Osman has many more plants than I do."

"Have you seen his collection?"

"No one sees his collection. He is a very private man."

"How do you know about it then?"

"We all have our spies."

"And what do your spies say about this fabulous new plant he is going to put on display at the show in Chiang Rai?"

"It is supposed to be an albino form of a large multifloral *Paphiopedilum* species. But no one knows for sure exactly what it is."

"I heard that it might be an albino *rothschildianum*. Do you think that is so?"

"An albino *roth* would be fabulous. We will have to wait and see. There are lots of rumors. What have you heard?"

"Do you know Dr. Raymond Wong?"

"Yes I met him at one of the big Pan Asian Orchid shows. They have them every three years."

"We bumped into him recently, at the Singapore Botanic Gardens. He seems to think bin Osman might have a special *roth* coming into bloom."

"What do you know about Mr. bin Osman?" Jake asked.

"Only that he is fabulously wealthy and lives on a big estate outside of Chiang Rai. They say his father made all the money during the days when the Golden Triangle was the world's largest opium producer. He is not a nice person. He never forgives anyone for making a mistake and so we all avoid getting on his wrong side. So no one ever challenges him on anything. We are all surprised that if he has an extra special orchid that he would put it on show for anyone else to see. It would have to be something very special and I think only an albino *Paph. rothschildianum* can fit that bill."

"Maybe he needs to boast about it? An albino *roth* would make news around the world. Could you imagine how much such a plant would be worth?"

"Surely, an astronomical amount."

"If he is showing this plant – and everyone thinks that he is – I wonder how he plans to deal with security," I asked.

"Security would be easy for him. He commands his own private army and they are all licensed to carry guns."

"So, there will be armed guards protecting the plant?"

"Most assuredly."

"What will the orchid show be like? I was once at a show in Kuala Lampur and it was merely a row of tables with individual plants on it."

"The show is to be held in the Five Star Golden Lotus Hotel in downtown Chiang Rai. Different societies, nurseries and some individuals will make landscaped displays and arrangements of flowering plants just like western flower shows."

"So bin Osman's special plant will be part of a floral display?"

"I don't think so. Often special plants are displayed on their own on an isolated table. I have heard that this plant will only be on display during the first night of the show. The opening night is a special charity event, tickets are very expensive and the people come more to be seen than to see the orchids. If it is an albino roth then it will probably be removed back to the safety of his own nursery after the guests have left the first evening. At least that is what I would do if I had an albino roth." Kani said. It made sense.

If that was the case we would have to get our hands on the pollen during the opening event while the display hall was filled with visitors and in front of crowds of people. This would make our task even harder. But I did not want to appear too interested in the *roth* and so I changed the subject back to Kani's collection and exclaimed several times in delight at some of the rare species in flower. Many were new to me.

We wandered down the aisles between the plant benches. Every plant was in pristine condition. Kani was indeed an expert grower.

"I don't see many slipper orchids in your collection," William observed.

"No, we are too warm – they do better at higher altitudes."

"Does that mean that bin Osman lives in a cooler climate?"

"Yes, he lives on the road to Doi Chaang, about forty-five minutes drive from Chiang Rai. Doi Chaang is known for its coffee production. The temperature and rainfall there is also ideal for slippers and bin Osman owns many hectares in that region. He built his estate there. If you like coffee you should visit Doi Chaang. They grow and sell many different kinds of coffee there."

"Can one buy *kopi luwak* in that region?" Matilda asked.

"No, normally *kopi luwak* is from Indonesia. But I have heard rumors that one farm in Northern Thailand does market *kopi luwak*," Kani answered.

"What is *kopi luwak*?" William demanded to know.

"It's coffee made from beans that are partially digested by the palm civet cat."

"What!"

Matilda explained that the fresh coffee fruits are force fed to the civets and their feces collected and the partially digested beans washed from the fecal material and then roasted. It is the most expensive coffee in the world.

"I don't believe it," William exclaimed. "That has to be a load of crap."

"Actually it is a load of civet crap. And I shit you not." I backed her up.

"Have you ever had any?"

"No, I have never ever even seen it offered."

"So how do you know that this coffee is for real?"

"Look it up on Wikipedia," Matilda added.

"And if you ever try it and like it," I said, "you might want to try panda poo tea, too. It's the most expensive tea in the world."

"Now… you are teasing me."

"Me lie? I only speak the truth." But I was not going to tell him that the tea bushes were only fertilized with panda dung. There was no need to be any more explicit than that.

"Does bin Osman farm coffee?"

"No, he is so wealthy, that if he grew any it would be for his own use."

"Is he still living off his father's money? I heard rumors that he was following in his father's footsteps but now is more modern and manufactures designer drugs, like *spice*," Matilda ventured.

"How does a nice lady like you know about *spice*?" Kani wanted to know.

"Oh, I know about the modern world. After all, we are from Southern California."

"Well there are rumors," Kani admitted. "I had heard he has connections with some Central American drug lord."

That could be the Guatemalan Cartel, I thought to myself.

"What about bin Osman's personality? What sort of man is Mr. bin Osman?" Jake wanted to know.

"He is a man who is used to getting his own way," Kani said. "And if he does not then he gets very upset. I have heard stories, but we do not need to go into them here."

"Ruthless?"

"Exceptionally so. One does not want to get on the wrong side of that man. Some of his rivals have disappeared. He lives in a dog-eat-dog world."

"I heard that he is a great womanizer. Do you think that is true?"

"All I know is that at nearly every formal function I go to, he has a different lady with him, always very beautiful. Models. That sort

238

of thing. With his wealth, of course, he can afford only the very best. If I were you Professor, I would not let him near your wife. Matilda here is the sort of gorgeous woman he is attracted to. I think he scouts the world for his women, but the odd thing is you almost never see them a second time."

"Didn't he have an American wife once?"

"Yes, but that lasted for a very short time."

"They got divorced?"

"No, it was a tragic end. The poor woman committed suicide."

I had not realized that Charlotte had come into the growing area and was listening in on our conversation. She joined in.

"There are rumors." Charlotte added. "Some say that she might have been killed in a weird sort of sacrifice. There is supposed to be a sect that worships demons. People think that bin Osman gave his wife to that sect after he got bored with her."

"That is just nonsense. Old wives tales. Such sects do not exist."

"Well what about the Black Temple?" She insisted.

"That is simply due to the artistic license of the monk who built it. Demons are common in temple art."

We wandered up and down the aisles. At one point there was a loud rustling among some small bushes under a bench and it startled Jake, who jumped and automatically reached for his gun, pulling it out from the holster hidden under his loose shirt. This raised Kani's eyebrows. A small cat jumped out from the bushes and ran between Jake's legs. He sheepishly returned the gun to its hidden holster.

"You carry a gun?" Kani observed with astonishment.

"Our lives were threatened in Singapore. I am not taking any chances," Jake explained.

Kani continued to look at him dubiously. "But this is Thailand..."

"Yes, but the other night in Chiang Mai, we think we saw Soh Fat. He gave us the slip," William announced, unwisely.

Kani's eyebrows were still raised and Jake explained. "Soh Fat was the man who organized that attack on us in Singapore. Great-aunt Bertha must have explained to you?"

"Yes, yes, but she did not mention any people by name. Soh Fat – that name sounds familiar. Where have I heard that name before?"

"He is a small Chinese fellow, so tall – going bald." Jake raised one hand to about Soh Fat's height.

"Ah yes, now I remember. I thought he was a secretary for bin Osman. About five or six years ago."

Jake and I exchanged glances. Matilda was about to say something but I gave both her and William warning shakes of my head. Kani was looking at Jake and not at me so he did not notice me. He already had too much information. We had to keep him out of it. If Soh Fat was a double agent, then bin Osman might already know everything. We could be in serious trouble.

Quick on the uptake, Matilda intuitively knew that we needed to change the subject. Kani did not need to know what was actually going on. "Kani do you have the white form of the Burmese *Dendrobium fytchianum*? I have only seen the pink form but I know there is a white one and I would love to see it. The white form must be particularly beautiful."

"Yes, but it is not their season, although there might still be a few unseasonal flowers. Let me take you to them and see if there are any late flowers."

"You have species from Myanmar?" William asked.

"The Thai people do not discriminate. We love flowers from everywhere."

We walked to the section where he kept them, while Matilda kept the conversation focused on dendrobiums and away from our problems in Singapore. There was only one lone straggler still in flower, but Matilda dutifully went into raptures.

We had gone through most of Kani's collection and were running out of safe topics to discuss. Luckily Kani decided it was time for more refreshments and indeed I was thirsty.

"Let us go back to the veranda. Charlotte is preparing some refreshments and while you are enjoying a snack or two, I will organize one of the workers to chop down a tree in the forest and another to light some crackers when that tree starts to fall. With luck we will see a flying snake or two," Kani guided us back to the covered

240

veranda. Charlotte must have seen us approaching because she came out with a tray bearing several plates. There were some small cupcakes on one plate and tropical fruits on the others. The bananas were about half the size of those we normally see in the west but much more flavorful, fruity with a hint of acidity that cut through their normal blandness.

"Can I come with you to select the tree?" I asked. "It will give me a chance to look at the forest."

"Certainly," Kani turned to the others. "While we are in the forest, the rest of you will be looked after by Charlotte. She needs the opportunity to practice her English."

Kani and I left the others to make light conversation with Charlotte and enjoy the snacks.

We returned about fifteen minutes later. Charlotte, who turned out to be perfectly fluent in English, made it clear that while she had some misgivings about our experiment, she thought it might be fun. Nevertheless, she admitted to having closed all the windows in the house to preclude any flying reptiles. I could tell that neither Jake nor Matilda were looking forward to our experiment and I half expected them to insist on staying safely on the veranda. When we had all finished our snacks, Kani told us what he wanted us to do. We were all to assemble in the clearing about fifty feet from the forests edge where we would have a clear view and could capture any flying creatures on video.

Since Charlotte was coming out with us, both Jake and Matilda had no option but to join us without admitting to be scared. We walked over to the spot he recommended and spread ourselves out so as not to obscure each other's view. William had his cell phone out and set it to camera. He held the phone out at the end of extended arms, holding it with both hands, to steady the device. He scanned the tree tops.

"This is good," he said. "If they glide into the clearing away from the forest, I should have an excellent view."

"I will give the signal," Kani said and dialed his phone.

Shortly after that we heard a few loud thuds. Someone was chopping down the tree. Then there came a sharp, crackling sound and we could hear branches breaking as the tree came down, bashing into the surrounding forest. A flap of wings followed and dozens of birds took to the air. Then two almighty explosions almost deafened us, as the fireworks were exploded, and a cloud of snakes and lizards jumped into the air. They came flying fast and furious and directly down towards us.

Chapter 20 – What Does Soh Fat Know?

I had no idea there might be as many as a dozen snakes in the trees at the edge of the clearing. They ranged in length from only a foot to as much as three feet. And it is true they looked as if they were swimming as they dropped down through the air, their bodies bending side to side in sinusoidal curves. But they were also moving fast because they had gravity to assist them. While their body shape helped them to plane through the air they were not getting very much lift. It just slowed them down a little so that they could select and aim for a landing site.

"Woo hoo!" William yelled in excitement, as he tried to keep his camera on one of the plummeting serpents. He was moving about, arms extended and waving like a windmill as he tried to select which snake to follow on his screen. Once he had done that, he then had to keep his arms rigid and steady while keeping the gliding reptile centered on his screen. Not an easy task because the snakes were dropping so fast.

I was trying to work out trajectories, in case some of the snakes might land directly on or near us. The little draco lizards were also sailing in spirals down to the ground. They were aptly named because they resembled miniature dragons sailing through the air. The lizards scarcely made it twenty-five feet from the forest edge, but because of their lighter weight and lateral sails, would actually stay airborne longer than the snakes. However, the snakes were better at maneuvering and directional gliding. It looked as if some might land among us. Everything was happening quickly. I think most of the snakes could see us. Flying snakes have large and very well developed eyes and I expected them, like other snakes, to make an effort to avoid us.

One snake, however, did not live up to my expectations. It was one of the larger creatures and William was simply unaware of it. All his attention was focused on another snake that he was photographing.

Suddenly coming down from the side, the snake banged against William's outstretched arms and wrapped around them. William gave a shriek and dropped his phone. Time stood still. The snake seemed undecided. Was this warm and somewhat hairy appendage it had coiled around an unusual tree branch, or was it part of an animal, albeit a very noisy animal, jumping up and down? Fortunately for William, this snake was either stupid or very slow. Perhaps the impact with William's arm had jolted its brain. It did not seem to know what to do other than hang onto the hairy branch. William was frantically waving up and down, trying to shake the reptile free. The snake coiled around William's arm more tightly. I was surprised it had not bitten him.

The snake had pebbly grey and white scales with a row of bright red markings running down its back. The large head supported on a relatively narrow neck, had a pair of big eyes.

"Get it off me!" William begged.

For once Jake did not know what to do. His face had blanched and he stood there in shock.

We had to do something for William, but he was beside himself and could not take direction.

I saw Charlotte jumping to one side, trying to get out of the way of another snake that appeared to be heading directly towards her. The reptile smashed into her midriff before crashing to the ground, landing on a pile of leaves. It righted itself and immediately headed away from the human now shrieking at the top of her voice.

"That snake must have been flying with its eyes closed," Jake remarked.

"Don't be silly. Snakes can't close their eyes." Matilda muttered.

Charlotte was pale, almost in shock, and shaking. I thought she might throw up, but Kani gathered her in his arms and talked soothingly until she calmed down.

William, however, was not calm. He was still jumping up and down flailing his arms around but both were pinioned together by the snake. Meanwhile other snakes were still circling around, looking for a place to land, but fortunately, they sensibly avoided us. At this point,

William's snake finally decided it had had enough and needed to do something drastic. So it pulled its head away from the shaking arms and looked around. I thought it might try to jump free but instead, it stretched its slender neck up away from William's arms. Sighted on his hands and opened its mouth wide and looked for a suitable place to bite.

Matilda screamed at the top of her voice, "William stand still." He heard her and made an effort not to flail his arms holding them as far from his chest as possible. I could see him gritting his teeth as he tried to steady his arms. Matilda sprang into action and grabbed the snake just behind its head, her fingers clenched under the snake's jaw and her thumb on the top of its head between the eyes. She forced the snake's mouth shut. With her other hand she gripped the snake's narrow neck. Now we had somehow to unwind the creature from William's arms.

"For God's sake William, keep still, don't you dare move!" And she turned to me and commanded, "George, help me unwrap this beast." I stepped forward and reached for the coils around William's arms, looking for the snake's tail. It would be easier to start at that end of the animal.

No matter how many times I have to handle a snake, and there have been several, I am always surprised by a number of things. Snake's bodies always feel cool. Intense muscle activity generates heat but snakes don't seem to warm up very much, unless they have been basking in the sun. Their scaly skin is very dry. They are surprisingly strong and even if they are not constrictors, they can apply considerable pressure, squeezing and holding on. I pulled the tail loose from William's arm and started to unwrap it. The snake did not like this and struggled to tighten its grip. Meanwhile, Matilda was pulling the head end away from William's arms, also trying to unwrap it from the front end. Jake had come up behind William, who was now standing still with his eyes shut and his arms outstretched. Jake was crooning in William's ear and he leaned against his partner trying to comfort him. Somehow, we managed to disentangle the creature from William's arms and together, Matilda and I gingerly carried it towards the forest, looking for a place to release the creature.

"When I say 'now,' drop it on the ground and step back quickly," Matilda advised.

"Now!" And we released the snake, which looked around, thought about it for a moment, and then darted away towards the forest's undergrowth.

When we returned to the others, Jake was still hugging William and whispering in his ear, trying to calm him down. Charlotte had recovered from her scare. Both she and Kani were looking on, bemused at the two grown men still clutching each other. The Thais are very accepting of the gay lifestyle but somehow this very large, almost giant, man comforting the much smaller and lithe William, struck a humorous note for them that I did not quite understand.

"William, where is your phone? Was it damaged?" I asked.

"Nope. Luckily the screen was not cracked."

"Hope you got some good footage."

"Better have something to show for it. Not everyone gets attacked by flying snakes."

"Actually, I don't think it was an attack. More of an accidental impact."

"Whatever."

"Experiment was a great success, I think," Kani said with a smile as we approached him.

"No more experiments," Charlotte scolded him. "Snake hit me. Not good."

"I agree and I will be very happy if we never repeat that experiment again," Matilda said, "That was excitement I did not really need. And I hate snakes too!"

Later that afternoon as we were driven back into town William asked, "What I want to know is, to what species did my snake belong?"

"There are two species of flying snake in Thailand. This one was *Chrysopelea paradisi*, the paradise golden skin," I translated the scientific name. "Also those we saw today were rather small. That species can achieve a length of five feet."

"Thank goodness it was not five feet long," Matilda remarked. "It was difficult enough handling it as it was."

"It was not really gold," Jake observed.

246

"Yes, but that is the generic name and it probably refers to the first snake of the genus to be described. I thought the snake was beautiful, with that row of small scarlet diamonds running down its back."

"The professor knows everything," William said. "I did not see any red diamonds."

"Of course not, you had your eyes closed," Matilda observed.

"Matilda, I owe you one. I think that snake was going to bite me. Thank you for your quick presence of mind."

"It was nothing. You would do the same for me. Right?"

"You mean grab the head of a snake as it is preparing to strike? I don't know," he answered truthfully. "My reflexes are not as fast as yours. And me not knowing how to grip the head? Probably not."

"Matilda, you are one remarkable lady and I am so glad you saved my baby," Jake said.

"You would have done the same for me, Jake, wouldn't you, if you were closer?" William asked.

"I don't think I could," Jake admitted.

"Not even for me?"

"Well maybe I could shoot at it?"

"And then William would probably have lost an arm," I interjected.

"Well the thing to do is stay away from all snakes from now on. They are evil," Jake insisted.

"They serve a useful purpose. Eating rodents, other snakes and even help to keep lizard numbers down."

"Enough about snakes. Let us talk about other things."

"Okay, what?"

"Something neutral, how about food?"

"What type of cuisine do you want to try tonight?"

Back at our house, after a pleasant meal and after we had all more or less recovered from the day's excitement, we were sitting in the small lounge when I turned to Jake and asked him, "Have you communicated with Tylo about the possibility that Soh Fat was also working as an agent for bin Osman?"

247

"I sent him a text almost immediately and asked for instructions and asked if perhaps we should consider aborting the operation."

"What was his reply?"

"Nothing yet."

I thought about it for a moment and then said, "I hate to pull out at this stage. All the effort and time spent will have been for nothing. What a waste. No reserve in South America, either."

"I think that the major question now is; what does Soh Fat actually know?" Matilda said.

"Actually, probably very little."

"Then why was he having us followed?"

"That is probably because he wanted to know what we were up to. He was trying to learn why we were in Singapore."

"Did anyone at Tylo and Associates know anything about our operation and its goals?" I asked Jake.

"I don't think so. No one except for the operatives ever knows the actual mission."

"So Soh Fat knew we were worried that we had been followed to Singapore and knew he had to keep us safe, but he did not know why," I continued.

"We did let slip that we liked orchids and wanted to visit botanic gardens," William pointed out.

" – but he should not have connected that to bin Osman's plant. In fact, I would be surprised if he knew anything about bin Osman's orchids at all," Jake argued. "Soh Fat was probably just a general mole who reported everything that happened at T & A back to bin Osman no matter what."

"How did he know that the Americans, presumably from the cartel, would be trying to keep track of us?"

"I wonder if di Sorrento and Blakely were taking orders from Soh Fat or giving him orders?" Jake asked.

"Whatever, we must now assume that bin Osman knows George's name. He could easily research George on the web and find out all about him. After all he is a famous name in orchids. I guess that bin Osman also has a list of the attendees at the upcoming gala benefit for the first night of the orchid show."

"So what? He wants recognition for his special orchid. What better than to have a famous authority like George, acting as a witness for his plant."

"Problems only arise if he connects George to Paul Tylo, and that may be the major damage that Soh Fat has done. Besides that, Soh Fat and di Sorrento tried to poison us with that pizza. Who initiated that? It could have been bin Osman. Having George killed in Singapore would not have reflected back on him at that stage."

"So George was the target and the rest of us were – what? Just expendable? Gee, that makes me feel good."

"Remember, Soh Fat also knew that our Great-aunt stayed at the Marina Bay, because he went and bought the swimming trunks for William."

"We can also assume that he may have identified her and Wie Wee, and passed that on to bin Osman."

"Don't forget, we must also assume that Soh Fat took William's minibot."

"But he would think it was just a small ornament or toy and not a remote controlled robot. And even if he knew it was a robot, he would not connect it to the use we wanted to make of it."

I wondered if we were we simply trying to rationalize away our fears.

"That may be what Soh Fat knows or does not know. What does bin Osman know or suspect about us? That is the critical point now."

"Let us consider the worst case scenario. Soh Fat has relayed all of our names to bin Osman including that of Great-aunt Bertha, and has told him that the four of us work for Paul Tylo. He cannot be sure of Great-aunt and we never gave him her full name. She was not with us at the Botanic Gardens, only at the hotel and Gardens by the Bay. Before we had wiped Jimmy Blakely's phone clean of all photos of us I had looked through them. There were none of Bertha or Wie. In fact, they were only of Matilda and me; none of Jake or William, either."

"I wonder if Soh Fat thinks that Jake and I are simply your security detail?" William added.

"Perhaps, but more likely he knows of our association through the university."

"What about the members of SCORE? Are they tied in with bin Osman?"

"Yes, to the extent he invited them especially to come and report on the show. But we have not ruled any of them out with regards to the attacks on us."

"Don't forget about Chris Guildenhuis and Hillary Herschel. We know they hate us. Was their appearance at the Marina Bay merely accidental? Even if that is the case, they may have or will still inform bin Osman of our relationship with Great-aunt Bertha." Matilda added. "Great-aunt Bertha was very surprised to see Guildenhuis at the Marina Bay. Guildenhuis's wife had told her that she would have been flying directly to Bangkok. Maybe Great-aunt assumed, incorrectly, that husband and wife would be travelling together."

"Do we know how many of SCORE's members and their spouses will be at the show?" Jake continued with another question.

"Probably not more than half. If I remember correctly, that is what Great-aunt thought," Matilda added.

"I think that I need to talk to Guildenhuis and to Herschel. Perhaps I can persuade them to level with me. Tell them I have video of them kissing in the Sky Park," Jake said.

"You have video?" I was surprised.

"Did you think I was just looking at Facebook while we were having lunch?" He grinned at me. "That may get us some cooperation."

"Better not lose your phone."

"No worries, everything is stored in the cloud."

"We have to find out what Soh Fat knows. I still cannot get over how nice he was to us in Singapore when we first arrived," Matilda said.

"We have to find him first," William pointed out. "We don't even know if he is still in Chiang Mai or even if the man George and Jake chased was actually Soh Fat."

"Jake, does Paul Tylo have a mole working for bin Osmin? After all, turn around, is fair play," I asked.

"I am not sure."

"Well then how did he get his information about the albino roth in the first place and how did Tylo know how bin Osman got his hands on it?"

"Seems likely to me," William said. "Tylo must have his own spies."

"Phone Tylo when you can, and see if the mole can locate someone called Soh Fat. Maybe we can still find him?"

"Okay, I would like to get my hands around Soh Fat's scrawny throat and throttle the truth out of him." Jake was quite angry about the situation. "There are minus fourteen hours difference between Chiang Mai time and Denver. I will call him when it is about eight, this morning."

Matilda turned the discussion back to bin Osman. "If bin Osman is unaware that we are after the pollen, then he may simply think our job will be to destroy his plant."

"You think he is scared that we will try and spray it with an herbicide like Round-up?"

"Unlikely. That would create an enormous scandal that would reflect badly on George. It would destroy his reputation. No, bin Osman will not expect us to destroy his plant. He probably has no idea what to expect, unless there is another mole at Tylo and Associates in Denver who has told him about Tylo's scheme. But that is highly unlikely, Paul has been ultra-careful not to discuss our plans with anyone else. The guys at Microbotics knew we were after pollen but they thought we were going off into some jungle. They were never told exactly where. The cartel might have ties to bin Osman but it is more than probable that they are simply after revenge. It is unlikely that bin Osman has any detailed knowledge of what we hope to accomplish. My guess is that he merely suspects that we will be up to something but he cannot know exactly what we want to do." Jake summed it up.

"In the best case scenario, he will probably try to keep us physically apart from his plant."

"So many probables," Matilda mused.

"In the meantime, we should try to keep a low profile until we leave for Chiang Rai," I suggested. "And we need to continue with a low profile after we get there too."

251

"When should we head for Chiang Rai? The charity night is next Friday. How many days before that should we plan to get there?"

"Our reservations at the Golden Lotus Hotel start on Thursday night, don't they? I expect the show set up is Thursday afternoon and until sometime on Friday morning. Then they will be judging the show on Friday afternoon. The preview charity party starts at seven, Friday evening."

"Maybe we can help with the judging?"

"Not according to Kani. Local members normally do all the judging. However to honor SCORE, three of the senior SCORE members will be asked to do the paphiopedilums and phragmipediums. As we are all aware I am not senior enough to be a judge."

"I wonder who they will choose?" Matilda wanted to know.

"I am sure the president, Guildenhuis, will be one of the judges, but we won't know who the other two will be. Kani has been told that they will be drawn by lot."

"When did Kani tell you all this?"

"Today, during our visit when we left you eating snacks, and we went to check on which tree to chop down for the snakes. We need all the information we can get and we need to know how the show will be set up. So I asked lots of questions about the show. We discussed this while we were in the forest."

"So what is the set up of the show?" Jake wanted to know.

"It is a large banquet room in the hotel on the ground floor. Tables are set around the perimeter of the room and they are to be draped with a heavy black fabric. Each table is about eight feet long and three and a half wide. He wasn't sure how high they might be. He said normal table height. Each table will have a landscaped display of flowering orchid plants."

"Seems just like the shows we have stateside," William said.

"Yes."

"Do we know where in the room the albino roth will be presented?"

"No, but because it is only to be shown for the first night, he expects it will be placed on a table of its own, that can be easily removed, together with the plant when it is no longer on display."

"I have been thinking," I said.

"Oh oh, that sounds ominous," William offered.

"That we should only have one or two bots attempt to remove the pollen," I continued. "William has already lost his little robot…"

"Not my fault. Soh Fat stole it," William interjected.

I continued, "The more robots clambering over the plant, the more likely one of them will be noticed. Also, we will need to toss the bots onto the base of the plant itself before they are activated."

"You just cannot walk up to the table where the plant is displayed and throw something at it," Matilda objected. "You will have the armed guards down on you in no time."

"I have thought about this and here is what I think we can do. This is where William comes into play." And I told them of my idea. They thought it might have a fifty-fifty chance of working. We would also have to cluster in front of the plant and try to block our activity from other people in the room. That might work if Great-aunt Bertha and Wie were to join us.

"Another problem." Matilda brought up. "We simply cannot stand in front of the plant and pilot the robots on our iPhones. People will wonder what we are doing. We have to be discreet. They probably need to be piloted from another room."

"William, can you research the hotel's floor plan on your iPad and see if there is a restroom near the display hall?" I asked. "Maybe they can be piloted from within a toilet stall? If the toilet is next door to the show venue, the range should be good enough."

"Sure." And he set to work.

"While William is doing that, we need to come up with a plan on how to retrieve the robots, assuming of course that we are successful and they have the pollen."

"That is indeed a problem. Someone other than the pilots will have to retrieve the bots and do it unobtrusively at that."

"If the table is set against a wall, then the bots can climb down the table cloth at the back out of people's sight. They could even hide under an adjacent table and we could retrieve them the next morning."

"But we don't know where it will be placed."

"So we will just have to play it by ear and deal with it at the show."

This was a serious complication that we had not foreseen. One could not just bend down and pick up what might look like a large insect crawling across the floor in the middle of a cocktail party.

At this point, William looked up from his tablet. "Got it! Complete floor plans for the Golden Lotus Hotel, convention floor. We are in luck. The men's room is right next door to the ballroom where the show is to be held."

"And the women's?" Matilda wanted to know.

"Hmm. It's at the far end of the hallway about as far from the ballroom as can be located on that floor. Sorry Matilda. I think you will be too far away to pilot your bot. You may as well let me use it," William said.

"No way. It would take you too long to get used to its idiosyncrasies anyway. Don't you remember during training how they kept emphasizing that each bot was an individual and one could not transfer training from one bot to another? That's why we always had the same robot with which to work."

"Let me play psychologist for a moment," I said. "Mr. bin Osman is so enamored with his plant that he has organized this special orchid event, even to the point of specially inviting not only the rich and famous of the local community, but also members of SCORE from around the world. Won't he be anxious to see their reactions to his plant? He will probably be keeping an eagle eye on his botanical treasure most of the time. He considers it so precious that he is only putting it on display for a very limited time. We need to find some way of distracting him when it comes time to retrieve our little robots."

"George. I can read your devious mind," Matilda interjected. "You want me to distract him. Go over and waft pheromones in his direction until he is so sex crazed that he forgets about his orchid?"

"Well, err…perhaps you can flirt with him? As you are unable to pilot your bot, at least it would help us, while we are in the toilets playing with ours."

"Why does that sound obscene?"

"You know what I mean."

"Okay, I suppose I had better turn blonde again, too."

"That always helps."

254

"We are forgetting one thing," Jake said.

"What is that?"

"Great-aunt Bertha also has a little robot."

"We cannot have too many people involved at this point. Someone will need to dissuade her from attempting to get the pollen. Maybe she will consider herself our back-up in case we fail?"

"There is still the problem of where she can safely pilot her bot from. The lady's room is too far away."

"Who is going to worry about a little old lady looking at Facebook on her iPhone in the hallway outside the display venue?"

"Better not let her catch you calling her a 'little old lady,' she will hate that."

"But it is true."

"So let me sum it all up," I said. "Jake and I will use our bots, because the women have no place from which to pilot theirs and William has lost his. We need both William and Matilda to act as distracters. We will have to lob our robots surreptitiously to the base of the plant. We still don't know how to retrieve the bots after they have done their job. Problem is, not knowing the exact placement of the plant in the room."

The odds of pulling off this scheme did not look very promising. In the meantime, we needed to practice tossing our little robots at a target some six to ten feet away. So we went back to Matilda's and my bedroom, which also had a desk. Matilda found a cooking pot in the kitchen to approximate what we thought the orchids flower pot would look like for size and shape. She placed the pot at the center of the desk. There was enough room so we could stand about ten feet away and tried throwing the bot into the pot. With their legs folded away, the bot was similar in size and shape to a small pebble, and after a few tries we were both able to get our bots into the center of the pot. It was child's play. Matilda would have been better at it because she has a natural, unerring eye and aim for that sort of thing. But we assured ourselves that getting the bots onto the plant was doable, provided we were not caught in the act of throwing them. We relaxed and plugged in the little machines to make sure they were fully charged. The next morning we would head for Chiang Rai, so we completed most of the luggage packing before turning in for the night.

Chapter 21 – Chiang Rai

We drove northeast, along Route 118 from Chiang Mai to Chiang Rai, in a van that Kani had organized for us. We were really beholden to the man and I expected that both Great-aunt Bertha and Paul Tylo would be doing nice things for him. The distance between the two cities is less than two hundred kilometers and the road is excellent, but we were in no hurry. Great-aunt Bertha and Wie Wee were to fly in directly to Chiang Rai and they would probably be settled in at the hotel before we arrived. Kani and Charlotte were driving separately with a truck laden with orchids and the properties needed for their display. They had left before us. We offered to help put in their display but were told in no uncertain terms that this was purely a Thai exercise and they demanded that we must go and play tourist instead, while they worked. Apparently they had also hired a designer to help with their display.

Along the way we stopped at a little modern coffee shop for drinks and pastries. I must admit that the coffee was excellent, although to William's disappointment, *kopi luwak* was not on the menu.

"These custard filled sponge bars look awfully yummy," Matilda said, eyeing the small oblong cake on her plate. "I think I can make something similar when we get home."

"If you do, please remember to invite us over," William begged. He had managed to inhale several of the little cakes before I had finished the first of mine, but I had to agree that they were really good. There was a hint of nutmeg in the custard filling.

"You know, north of Chiang Rai is Doi Tung. It has a botanic garden that is famous for its slipper orchid collection. I wonder if they will have a display at the orchid show," Matilda mused.

"Didn't that wonderful pink species, *Paphiopedilum charlesworthii*, come from that region originally? I suppose it has all been collected out by now," William sighed.

"Probably, but I bet it still occurs in neighboring Myanmar."

"Don't you guys talk about anything else?" Jake grumbled, "Orchids this and orchids that, all the time."

"Okay. What do you want to talk about?" William demanded to know.

"Sorry, I am just getting up-tight about our project. Don't know how we can pull it off." That was so unlike Jake that I was worried. But I also glared at him and pointed at our driver's back. Who knew where bin Osman might have insinuated an informant.

Jake apologized with his eyes.

We drove past small villages and stopped at a small resort at the outskirts of Chiang Rai for a leisurely lunch. I figured we would have enough time to visit the White Temple before arriving at the hotel.

The White Temple, or Wat Rong Kuhn as it is formally known, is one of the more famous of the modern Thai temples. We had been told about it before planning to come to Chiang Rai and it was definitely on our list of things to do if we ever got the chance. The main temple building is an elaborate confection of spires and curlicues as only the Siamese can do. It is spectacular. The outer walls are a blinding white with little inlays of mirror and glass in the stucco, so that it scintillates when the sunlight is right. The white color is said to represent the purity of the Buddha and the glass epitomizes the *Dharma* or philosophy of the Buddha's teachings. Chalermchai Kositpipat is an accomplished artist of whom the country is very proud and the White Temple is his vision of a perfect spiritual place. In his art, he takes the modern frantic world and shows how the Buddha's teachings can lead to tranquility. The temple is a work in progress and will take many decades to finish, but it already attracts hundreds of thousands of tourists.

The White Temple is south of Chiang Rai and it was on our route into the city. As it was still early afternoon when we drove by, I asked our driver if he would not mind dropping us off at the temple for an hour. We joined the lines of tourists, each paying fifty baht (about one dollar fifty each), to walk through the temple and enjoy the grounds. I must say it is everything that one expected even if there was a slight Disneyland allure to the whole experience. It tempered my experience when I noted several devout Buddhists praying quietly at various stops in the temple and on the grounds itself.

Back in the van, we enthused about our visit to the driver who said to us, "If you found the Wat Rong Kuhn interesting then you must also visit Wat Sida, the Black Temple, for the contrast."

I had never heard of it and asked. "What is that? I have never read anything about a Black Temple."

"If the White Temple celebrates all about what is good in the world, then the Black Temple, Wat Sida, is its exact opposite. It considers those things that are bad about this world. There are rumors that its monks worship the dark forces; the fiends of the underworld. Some even believe that the monks make blood sacrifices to Mara." He said it with such disgust that an involuntary shiver ran down Matilda's spine."

I saw William's eyes widen. "Who is Mara? Are there evil spirits in the Buddhist religion?" He asked.

Matilda knew the answer. "Mara is the embodiment of the devil. He tried to tempt the Buddha away from his path of celibacy by using his own daughters."

"There are some who believe," our driver said, "that when the daughters failed to tempt the Buddha that Mara killed them all. He was vexed with them for failing to seduce the Holy One. Now it is said that the evil monks try to propitiate Mara by sacrificing beautiful women to replace his daughters. And they do this in the Black Temple."

"Why don't the authorities stop this barbarism?" Matilda wanted to know.

"The monks are very sly. They pretend that the Wat is only a place to display art. But that art is very dark and gloomy. There is an aura of evil that permeates the atmosphere. Even the forest there, around the Wat, seems sick. Many of the trees are stunted."

"Is this Black Temple also in Chiang Rai?" William always gravitated towards supernatural explanations. It must have come from playing Dungeons and Dragons as a kid. How he managed to justify those interests while being a competent scientist always amazed me.

"We believe that there are demons, both good and bad. Unless both types are honored they can bring down calamities upon the world. And yes, Wat Sida is also in Chiang Rai" And he left it at that.

The Golden Lotus Hotel was indeed a luxury, five star establishment. The building was obviously very new and I was told that it had only been completed a year previously. The hotel must have been erected to cater to all the tourists now visiting Chiang Rai to see the White Temple. But the local community was also taking advantage of the hotel as a meeting place for important events such as our charity orchid show.

When I handed over my credit card to cover expenses at the Golden Lotus, I casually looked at our room rates and almost choked. Thankfully, this was all on Tylo's tab. Room costs rivaled those of other five star hotels in the world's major metropolitan cities. But Chiang Rai was hardly one of those luxury watering holes. However, I thought the SCORE members, with their pretentious lifestyles, would appreciate the costs of their stays. They could boast of it afterwards. The hotel advertised that it went all out to ensure that its guests had a worthwhile experience. So I was not surprised when the concierge welcomed us with complimentary glasses of champagne. Unfortunately, none of our party favored alcohol in the mid-afternoon, but that did not faze the concierge who smoothly suggested a fruit juice, such as either passion fruit or guava, instead. He said, proudly, that those drinks had been specially prepared by the staff from fresh fruit and did not come out of any bottle. The concierge asked what had brought us to Chiang Rai. Was it simply as tourists or were we involved with the big orchid show that was now being set up in the main ballroom? I nodded at the latter suggestion and after paging for bellhops, the concierge took his leave of us, hoping we would enjoy our stay.

While uniformed bellhops gathered our luggage and took them up to our two rooms with William and Jake following, Matilda went across to the registration desk and enquired if Great-aunt and Mr. Wee had arrived yet, and if so could she speak to one of them? Unfortunately they had not yet registered. She then asked about other members of SCORE. Yes, Charles Guildenhuis and his wife had checked in earlier in the morning. No, Hillary Herschel had not arrived and they have no record of her booking a room in advance. Were Mr. and Mrs. Quicker, part of the group? They had already checked in. Matilda remembered that Morris Quicker was the Hedge Fund Manager we had met in Julian. The Hotel was expecting three or more attendees from overseas, as well as a number of local enthusiasts who might stay overnight following the charity function, so that they could indulge without worrying about driving home afterwards. They must all be using this as an excuse for a rather expensive outing. But then only people with bulging pocketbooks would be invited for the first night.

Our rooms were as luxurious as the prices that we were paying demanded. Although our rooms were reserved for the entire weekend, I planned on us leaving as soon as we had secured the pollen. Until then Matilda and I needed to keep a low profile. We agreed to have our evening meals sent up to our rooms.

We had been warned by Great-aunt Bertha that the first night of the show was a dress-up affair and the men had to wear suits and ties. Matilda had found a very chic new gown for the occasion and was anxious that all our clothing was hanging up and wrinkle free. Of course there was a hair salon in the hotel and Matilda made an appointment for the following morning. She was going to change her hair back to her natural blonde so she would be sure of catching bin Osman's attention during the show. She could not wait to get rid of the wig but did need to get her hair styled properly.

When we had gone up to our rooms, I had banged on the guys' door and William opened it to admit me.
"Yes, what gives?"
"I want to tell Jake that the Guildenhuises have checked in to the hotel."
"Good," Jake said coming to the door. "This is a chance to, at least, find out how you, George, stand with SCORE, and if any of them are involved with the contract taken out on you."
"Do you want me to come with you?" I asked.
"Good heavens, no. It will be better done as a one-on-one interaction. I will phone him and invite him down for a drink in one of the hotel's bars and have a little tête-à-tête with him."
"Will he take you up on that?"
"I'm sure the casual mention of Hillary Herschel's name will bring him eagerly to my beck and call."
"Well, please report to me when you are finished with Guildenhuis."

"Sure, but I need to report to Tylo first before I tackle the SCORE president."

"Okay. I want to know Tylo's take on everything also."

In the early evening Matilda received a call on her cell. Great-aunt Bertha was ensconced at last in the Golden Lotus and wanted to reassure Matilda that all was well. She and Wie had enjoyed a pleasant week in Kuala Lumpur and she was now geared to go on the project. No, she had not been in the show room, but had spoken to Happy Forrester who had been allowed briefly into the show room before being sent out. No, she had not seen the plant herself but had been assured that it was indeed a most magnificent, albino, *Paphiopedilum rothschildianum*. Matilda asked if she had seen the table on which the orchid was to be displayed and where it was positioned. She had asked Happy, but Happy was not sure.

Chapter 22 – Jake Interrogates Guildenhuis

It must have been close to ten that evening when there was a rap on our bedroom door and I opened it to admit both Jake and William. As both Matilda and I had been expecting the visit we had not yet changed into sleeping attire; for her that was usually a skimpy night gown and for me, occasionally bikini underwear but more usually nothing.

"Glad you are still decent," William observed. We had had to share rooms in the past and he knew of my preferred sleeping attire.

"We are always decent and you should respect your elders better," I replied.

He merely snorted.

"Come and sit down." Matilda led everyone over to a small sofa and a couple of armchairs that filled one corner of our suite. We took our seats.

"You consulted with Tylo first?" I asked.

"Oh yes, and he had some good suggestions."

"Such as?"

"I will get to those in a little while."

"So tell us what happened."

Jake related the events of his evening. First he had phoned Paul Tylo. It was mid morning in Denver and Tylo was anxious for a complete account. Jake has a good memory and can often relay conversations word for word. He brought Tylo up to date with our activities as well as all of our major concerns. It seemed that Tylo was aware that Soh Fat had ties to bin Osman but had not realized that Singapore had assigned Fat to babysit us. That decision had not been cleared with Denver. He had thought he was using Fat as a conduit to funnel disinformation to bin Osman. He now realized that was not the case. Other agents would be assigned to locate Soh Fat and 'neutralize' him. I really did not know what that meant and did not want to know. Jake had told Tylo that it was too late to deal with Soh Fat at this point. Hopefully, we would have completed our part of the

263

bargain in less than the upcoming twenty-four hours. He did not see that Soh Fat could be located and dealt with in that short a time period. Tylo had said to leave that problem to him.

At this point I thought that taking care of Soh Fat would be meaningless and apparently Jake agreed with me, but knew from experience that one did not contradict his boss. It sounded as if Tylo wanted to make an example of Soh Fat.

Tylo wanted to know if we had been into the show room yet to confirm the existence of the albino *Paph. rothschildianum*. Jake had to admit that according to our sources, the plant would not arrive in the hall until early afternoon, and that only exhibitors and judges would have access to the show room before it was opened for the charity event. No one we had talked to could confirm a hundred percent that this plant was an albino roth, but that was the way people in the 'know' were thinking. Paul Tylo was curious as to who the judges might be. Jake had told him that it was Charles Guildenhuis and probably at least two other senior SCORE members. Tylo suggested it might be helpful if Bertha was on the judging team. Jake had told him that there might be a way to persuade Guildenhuis despite knowing that the SCORE President hated her.

Jake had relayed the reasons why only he and I would drive the microbots and with the problem in retrieving them. Paul made a suggestion for retrieval that might work. He suggested guiding the bots to the edge of the table and letting them fall to the carpet. Then having William and or Matilda present, to push or kick the bots under the cloth of the adjacent display table, once they fell onto the floor. Of course we would have to make sure that the bots were turned off as they fell onto the floor. Because the special plant was to be removed at the end of the charity event, there should be no trouble getting the hotel to open the room later after the show closed so that Matilda could look for a valuable earring that might have been lost near that table. With William and Jake helping her, it should be possible to retrieve the bots surreptitiously. It sounded feasible.

"So tell us what you found out from Guildenhuis," I wanted to know.

"Actually quite a lot," Jake grinned."I phoned him up and introduced myself as a Mr. Summerhays. He was rather rude at first but then I mentioned seeing him at the Sky Park in Singapore and he became more amenable. When I invited him down to the bar for a drink to discuss a video someone had made of him at Sky Park, he seemed almost eager to meet with me."

"How will I recognize you, Mr. Summerhays?" He asked.

"Don't worry. I will recognize you."

The bar had very subdued lighting and Jake selected a table in the corner away from the counter where the few customers sat nursing their drinks. From there he could see the brightly lit hall outside the doorway and would be sure to see Guildenhuis when he entered. A waitress had come up to him and asked what he preferred to drink.

"Only a glass of Perrier with a twist of lime, thank you."

The drink was now on the table before him together with a small bowl of rice crackers and he slowly nibbled on them while waiting for his prey to arrive.

Charles Guildenhuis hesitated in the doorway while his eyes adjusted to the dimmer light. He squinted as he looked around the room and then seeing Jake alone and beckoning from the far corner walked uncertainly towards him.

"Mr. Summerhays?"

"Take a seat Mr. Guildenhuis," Jake gestured to the empty seat facing him across the table. The waitress seeing a potential new customer swiftly approached as Guildenhuis sat down.

"What would you like to drink?" Jake offered.

Guildenhuis glanced up at the waitress. "Glenmorangie, on the ice with a splash of club soda."

"Who are you?" Guildenhuis demanded of Jake.

"As far as you are concerned, it does not matter."

"And what do you want?"

"Oh, a little cooperation will do."

"What do you mean?"

"I need some information and I think that you have it."

"What sort of information?"

"I will ask you in a short while."

"And why should I cooperate with you?"

"Because it is in your interests to do so."

"Are you threatening me?"

"Yes."

"I don't take threats easily," Guildenhuis argued forcefully.

"Perhaps, but this time you will have little choice," Jake kept his voice low and calm.

"How do you know this?"

The waitress arrived with the single malt scotch in a cut crystal glass and placed it in front of Guildenhuis and then she slipped away.

"Let me play a scenario for you. Imagine how the tabloids will react to a story about the CEO of Swansdown, tongue wrestling with the wife of one of the biggest automaker CEOs from Detroit. What do you think that story is worth?"

"This is ridiculous. I do not have time for this sort of nonsense."

"Oh but you do. Not only were there credible witnesses, but there is video of the event too. You and Mrs. Herschel left abruptly once you realized that other members of SCORE were also in the Sky Park. You hoped that you had not been noticed but in fact you had been."

"Are you aware that blackmail is a serious crime, even here in Thailand."

"I think both your wife and Mr. Herschel will be very interested in your little escapade."

"Okay. How much money do you want?"

"You mistake me Mr. Guildenhuis. I am not after money."

"Then what is this all about?"

"First, I have some questions. Depending on how frankly you answer them and your cooperation afterwards – I may be persuaded to forget about your little romp in Singapore. And I can assure you that your unanticipated audience at the Sky Park will also be very forgetful."

"Let us start with this one. Professor George has been followed and threatened since being admitted to your membership. There were attempts on his life in Julian. We know that he was only admitted to membership by the thinnest of margins. What is it about him that you are so against? What role has SCORE played in the attempts on his life."

"Attempts on his life? What nonsense."

"You have forgotten the sniper incident at Whispering Oaks. That was not an attempt on anyone's life?"

"Oh that. But there is no evidence that SCORE had anything to do with that."

"True, although at the hotel the professor's wife, Matilda, received a warning delivered to the hotel. Some yellow roses with a card. I remember what it said. A little doggerel that ran … 'trouble is spawning, this is fair warning, be gone before morning or else, and take that damn professor with you.' Only the SCORE members knew we were at the hotel. It must have been one of them.

The card was not given to the police at Julian, but we kept it for forensic analysis and could give it to the police at any time. The card has sentiments that match those of Harriet Herschel."

Guildenhuis was silent.

Jake continued, "Why was Mrs. Herschel so against the Professor? I was told she created a scene during his talk."

"He was talking about sex. She found it extremely distasteful."

"You expect me to believe this? He was talking about sex in flowers, for God's sake, not discussing human sex, in any pornographic manner. Orchid sex is not salacious."

"She has a reputation to uphold. Harriet is a lay minister in a sect known for its strict puritanical ethics. She thought the professor's attitude towards sex was frivolous."

"And yet she is prepared to hump you, outside her marriage. I think adultery is more serious than orchid sex. I can see the headlines now. 'What the prudish minister was doing behind the scenes with the famous cosmetics CEO!' It will make enticing gossip for the tabloids if they learn that she is having an affair with you. And her husband will surely find that very intriguing, don't you think?"

Gulidenhuis took a deep breath and began. "First let me make clear that SCORE was not directly involved in the attempts on the professor and his wife. Let me explain. Small as it is, SCORE has devolved into two factions, there are those like myself, Harriet and others who want to keep SCORE small and very exclusive. The other faction, that includes Paul Tylo and his followers would like to open it up and expand the membership. SCORE was never intended to be anything other than a small private club for the very wealthy. The

Professor does not fit into this group. We knew that once one non-elite member was admitted, our special club would be ruined."

"But the professor was admitted," Jake pointed out.

"Well Harriet hoped, and rather foolishly one must admit, that she could reverse the damage by persuading the professor to resign. She sent the yellow roses and I told her it was a mistake. She did not see it that way. She also hates what the professor stands for, his insistence that the natural world reflects Darwinian evolution and that he rejects the ideas of a special creation. But she would never condone the use of force and violence against another person. She believes that would condemn one to an eternity of suffering in hell."

"And what about you?" Jake enquired.

"I am more of an agnostic," Guldenhuis admitted.

"Does the name di Sorrento mean anything to you?"

"No, sorry. Who is that?"

"What about Soh Fat?"

"No, never heard of that person."

Jake stared at Guildenhuis for a moment until the other man, getting increasingly uncomfortable, turned away. He guessed Guildenhuis would get up and leave. The man started to get up but then thought better of it and sat back in his chair.

"Have you any more questions?"

"Just a few more. What is the relationship between you and bin Osman?"

Guildenhuis thought for a moment before answering. "Mr. bin Osman is a corresponding member. He has never been to a SCORE meeting. Boris Prokov nominated him for membership on the death of Mrs. Menzes and he supplied a detailed résumé. His bio was so good that his acceptance to membership was almost automatic. There were no other candidates at that time. He received almost unanimous approval. Later, Bertha said she had some misgivings, but by then it was too late. The vote had already been taken."

"Did bin Osman vote against George?"

"Yes, he was vehemently opposed to admitting the professor."

Jake changed tack. "What does Prokov do for a living?"

"He is an immensely successful entrepreneur. A self-made multimillionaire. Works out of St. Petersburg. He is a very active

268

SCORE member who normally does not miss a meeting. He was adamant that we could not admit a mere professor to our ranks."

So assuming that Harriet was no longer an important suspect, that left us with two other possible candidates for our villains.

"Mr. Guildenhuis, we will for the time being keep a lid on your indiscretion with Mrs. Herschel, but I suggest that you warn her that the professor will expect fair and even handed treatment from now on."

"Thank you. I appreciate your discretion, Mr. Summerhays. Good night."

"Oh, one last thing."

"What?"

"I have heard, through the grapevine of course, that Bertha would love to judge the slippers tomorrow. It would be really nice if you could accommodate the old lady's wishes. After all, she is a senior member of your organization. I am sure that you can arrange that. The professor's wife would obviously appreciate that too. She is very fond of her Great-aunt and would want her to enjoy the show. I have been told that the old dame is actually a very good orchid judge." The tone in Jake's voice and one raised eyebrow insinuated that Guildenhuis had better follow the request or else.

"I will certainly see what I can do to accommodate the old lady."

Jake felt he had done his best. He had narrowed down the possible perps and eliminated some others.

Chapter 23 – The Emerald Orchid

Vicknes bin Osman could best be described as a human ovoid. The man seemed to have no neck and his hairless head was crowned by a towering and almost pointed pate. He had no eyebrows over his dark brown, almost black eyes, with irises so dark that it looked as if he only had wide pupils, holes in the centers of his eyes. Later Matilda described them as the eyes of a snake but snakes do have irises. I figured he must have weighed somewhat over three hundred pounds and an inch or two over six feet. Because of his peculiar body shape, his clothing must have all been hand-tailored. Tonight he was dressed in loose, black, silk trousers that nevertheless, still revealed enormous thighs and over which was draped a white, open collared, heavy silk brocade, nehru-type shirt, with its Mandarin style erect collar. It was the traditional Thai *suea phraratchathan* or royal shirt with two front pockets. Running up the length of the left side of the shirt were five large, embroidered, white silk slipper orchid flowers, with just enough gold thread to give the impression of wealth but without too much ostentation. Shoes with sharply pointed toes of shiny, black patent leather completed the picture. He was physically unlike any other man I had ever seen and I believe he knew this and relished it.

Mr. bin Osman stood near the entrance to the display room with a small group of sharp eyed men. I assumed they were bodyguards. A sloe-eyed woman of remarkable beauty clung to his arm. He was showing her off as much as his orchid shirt. Her body language, tenseness of the bare shoulders, and demure avoidance of meeting each newcomers eyes, suggested either reluctance or a wish to avoid being on display. I could not help thinking that this timid woman was merely another of his trophies. I wondered how long she would last before he discarded her for an even better and newer model.

Paul Tylo and Vicknes bin Osman were as different as any two men might be, but they both shared an aura that evoked instant distrust in me. Tylo was suave and elegant, used to getting his own way, cold and calculating, a very cerebral man. I respected him even if I disliked him and what he stood for. As far as I could tell bin Osman was flamboyant, in a way like a king cobra, displaying its flared hood, warning any competition not to even think about messing with him. Like another snake, his motto was, 'Don't tread on me.' Both men could be very dangerous.

Matilda and I entered the room and were introduced to bin Osman. As I expected, he knew who we were. He extended a pudgy hand. "Ah, the famous orchid professor and his lovely wife. Matilda, isn't it?"

Matilda nodded looking up at bin Osman through long lashes. She had really dolled herself up for the evening. No longer wearing the wig, Matilda's hair was blonde once more, glistened with the richness of spun gold and flowed in gentle waves down to her shoulders. The hair salon in the hotel had done a great job. She was wearing a new gown, a bias-cut crepe de chine that not only displayed her magnificent bosom to perfection, but clung to her narrow waist and then draped over her hips in an alluring way. I noticed bin Osman's eyes quickly scanning her cleavage while his hand was still outstretched towards me. I felt a surprising flash of jealousy, fought it back down, telling myself that Matilda's allure was all part of our plan. And I reached for bin Osman's extended hand to shake it. His hand was soft and also limp, as if he did not want to contaminate it by contact with mine. I resisted the impulse to squeeze it as hard as I could to crush the bones together and inflict pain.

"So good of you both to come to pay homage to our humble show," he intoned.

"I suspect it is not at all humble. Those all look like the highest quality orchids." I gestured towards the plants on the tables ringing the walls of the hall. It was an incredible array of flowers. Plants were arranged in landscaped settings. But I could not see the one plant we had come all this way to plunder. A crowd, clustered in front of part of the display in the center of the wall opposite from the entrance way, presumably blocked our view of the anticipated *rothchildianum*. Our host noticed me looking around the room. "You are looking for the special plant, no?"

"Yes," I admitted. "There has been much excitement and speculation on the internet."

"Soon the food and wine will be served and people will be too busy gorging themselves to pay much attention to the flowers. They will move away and then you will have a chance to examine my specimen. But of course only from a distance."

"Of course," I smiled back at him.

"The judges from SCORE were very pleased with what they saw. They awarded my plant a Gold Medal. This is the first time SCORE has ever given a Gold Medal to any orchid anywhere in the world," he said smugly.

"Congratulations. I cannot wait to examine your flower."

"I must greet the rest of the guests." He dismissed us, but not before squeezing Matilda's arm and whispering something to her as I turned away. He was very sly and I almost did not catch the act. But in fact I did and even saw Matilda inhale deeply to bring her breasts more into view. I swear bin Osman was salivating. Later I realized that he had not even bothered to introduce the little vamp standing beside him.

Further back in the line waiting to be introduced to bin Osman were Great-aunt and Wie. She was smartly dressed in a long suit of Thai silk with an embroidered trim in which seed pearls had been worked into the fabric. It suited her figure and unblemished supple skin. I wondered again, what cosmetics her wealth had bought. I doubted that it was Swansdown. That evening she wore a simple string of large and perfect pearls around her neck. On one shoulder she displayed a brooch. It contained a green oval stone surrounded by other precious gems, all looking as if it had been carved from some special nephrite or a darker jade, perhaps of Chinese origin. I had never seen it before. It must have been something that she had bought in Singapore or Kuala Lumpur. Her hair was now fashioned into a neat urchin cut. She had lost the bun she often wore at the back of her head. Wie was dressed in a black suit with a red bowtie. Jake and William were further down the line, also wearing smart suits. Kani had warned Great-aunt Bertha before we left the States that we needed to bring evening wear with us. We had decided to enter separately and pretend we were not part of a single group. If anything went awry we did not want the others to be considered associates. However, I suspected we did not deceive bin Osman.

"What did Osman want with you?" I asked Matilda.

"He suggested that I come and talk to him while you were looking at the orchids."

"And?"

"I smiled and, thanks to my mascara, was able to flutter my eyelashes a little. He liked that."

We walked around the room looking at the various exhibits. They were indeed excellent. Lady Luck was smiling down on us, for all the tables were draped with a rich emerald green velvet cloth that dropped down close to the carpeted floor. The green color of the bots would blend in with the green background very nicely. But still the crowd in front of the special plant was so dense that I could not even catch a glimpse of the orchid. I saw people holding their phones and cameras above the heads of the onlookers. A few flashes of light from their devices illuminated the tops of heads. The table that supported that plant was not against the wall but brought forward a few feet into the room. It would accentuate the special nature of the plant. An armed guard in a military style uniform stood at attention on the left side of the table. He kept an eagle eye on the people clustered around, oohing and aahing over the special orchid in front of them.

The crowd was extremely well dressed. While a few sported traditional Thai garb, for the most part the men wore suits and a few wore tuxedos. Our suits blended in. Most of the women wore sophisticated evening dresses, but a few did display traditional garb with long slim tubular skirts that flared from the knees down. The skirt is called *sin* in Thai and is comprised of three parts. These women also tended to favor the *sabai*, a long narrow shawl that ran from the waist, diagonally across to and over the shoulder, draping down behind. They displayed their wealth by the richness of the brocade in the fabric. Here we had the crème de la crème of Thai society as well as the few members of SCORE. Guildenhuis was there with his wife. I nodded to him and he inclined his head, albeit reluctantly. Of Hillary Herschel there was no sign. Later on I saw Happy Forrester together with Phillipa Madison conversing with Bertha and Wie. They all seemed quite happy.

"I guess Phillipa Madison will incorporate the *sabai* into her fashions next year," Matilda predicted and I grunted in response.

The other SCORE member we had been told might be present was Boris Prokov, the Russian entrepreneur. I did not see him at first but then when I saw a bearded, slim and very pale blond middle-aged man addressing one of bin Osman's bodyguards I figured this could only have been Boris. I thought he was looking at Matilda and me. When he saw me looking in his direction he turned away abruptly. He obviously knew who I was too.

Waiters entered the room carrying large circular trays on which were balanced not only flutes of champagne but also glasses of white and red wine. Others offered a selection of hors d'oeuvres.

Kani had brought Charlotte to the event. He walked up to us with a grin on his face. "Well what do you think of the orchid? Is it not amazing? Well worth the Gold Medal I think."

"Actually, I have not seen it yet. The crowd in front of the table is too dense to let us through to see anything."

"I will take care of that," he said and grabbing both Matilda and me by an arm, said loudly, "Make way for the Professor. He has come from half way around the world to marvel at this wondrous plant!" Like Moses parting the Red Sea, the crowd stepped aside to let him pull us through until we stood in front of a green velvet rope. Two feet away was a circular table some eight feet wide. It was draped with a rich green, velvety fabric that dropped down to, but not touching the floor. In the center of the table was an elegant black ceramic vase decorated with two dragons covered in gold leaf encircling the rim. The container was about fifteen inches wide and of similar height. Sunk into this vase stood the pot containing the orchid. The base of the plant and surface of the orchid pot itself was covered with green tree moss, that also filled the space between the two pots. I was pleased to see this, because it meant that our robots should be able to crawl to the edge of the ceramic vase and then maybe fall off the edge, down onto the table cloth behind the plant. Hopefully no one would witness their escape.

It was truly both an emerald orchid and also a true albino *Paphiopedilum rothschildianum*. The plant took my breath away. It was imposing with its three large fans of rigid belt-shaped leaves coming out at a forty-five degree angle and with two mature spikes of flowers. Each inflorescence was at least three feet tall, with a stout stem emerging from the center of the vee formed by the inner two leaves of each of the two largest fans. Each stem held five magnificent flowers in prime condition. Each flower's dorsal sepal was a vertical sail of clean white background edged and striped with maybe as many as twenty evenly spaced longitudinal stripes of dark, but clear, emerald green. The sepal at its widest must have been at least three inches and it then it arched up to a rounded peak with the stripes converging at the tip. The petals, one on each side, emerging from the base of the dorsal sepal were spread horizontally to give a natural spread for the flower of well over a foot. It was like a narrow rigid mustache, but again, clear white with much finer dark green stripes running along the length of the petals. A rather angular deep green pouch, the slipper shaped petal, hung in the front of yet another snow white part, again with equidistant brilliant green emerald veins. This latter was the synsepalum made from two fused sepals. The pouch was what the pollinator would normally have to crawl through. Emerging from the center of the flower was a structure shaped like a green grasshopper's leg. This was the staminode, a sterile stamen used to attract the pollinator. The staminode itself was fused to a column of tissue bearing the fertile stamens that held the pollen masses. We would have to guide the tiny robots to these stamens to harvest the pollen. With luck, at least one of our two machines would be successful. I looked to see if the pollen masses were visible close to the emergent holes, at the base of the pouch, but was unable to see the stamens. I could not get close enough to any individual bloom. Hopefully the bots would soon find a way.

Even people who did not understand orchids must, nevertheless, have been impressed by the grandeur of the flowers. The crowd clustered in front of the table certainly did. I put my hand in my pocket to reassure myself that my bot was still there. It was motionless, not turned on, but waiting for its assigned role.

"This *roth* is gorgeous," Matilda cooed. "Worth the trip simply to see it."

275

"Indeed," Kani beamed and then excused himself. "I must go and look after Charlotte. She still has not altogether forgiven me for the incident with the flying snakes."

"Blame us. After all, you had us crazy biologists begging to see those reptiles. You were just being a good host."

He smiled good naturedly and hurried off.

Soon we must set to our task, but first we should move away and not attract any attention to our behavior.

Most of the crowd, by now having paid homage to the plant, drifted off to admire other exhibits or hunt down refreshments and food. Or they were chatting with one another, making the most to be seen socializing and hobnobbing with other members of Thai high society. Matilda and I walked off, away from the plant and towards the center of the hall. Here Great-aunt Bertha gave us a meaningful nod before she turned to Wie and dragged him away to talk to some gentleman we did not recognize.

"Let us go and talk to Happy Forrester. She is still over there with Phillipa. Both liked us in Julian and we can get reacquainted. People will not think that we are single-mindedly besotted with this damn magnificent plant."

As we strolled over to them near the center of the room, we passed William, talking animatedly as usual, with Jake. We ignored them but as we passed, Jake murmured quietly, "Soon?"

I nodded as if to myself, without acknowledging him directly, and we passed them by.

Both Happy and Phillipa were indeed glad to see us. They enthused about what they had already experienced. This was their first visit to Thailand and they loved the food and the idea that people should have fun. They had also visited many different wats and were intrigued with the design, artistry, and embellishments displayed on and around the temples.

"Wasn't the White Temple splendid?" Happy asked.

"Wonderful," Phillipa agreed.

The small talk went on for about ten minutes. Having positioned myself so that I could see the roth, I was only listening with half an ear while looking casually around the room. Then I noticed that none of the other guests were at the table that held the *rothschildianum*. The guard of course was still there but nobody else.

I excused myself from the ladies and walked over to the exhibit to the right of the emerald orchid. There I examined the various flowers. There were some lovely hard cane dendrobiums and I took several pictures of them. They are also statuesque plants with simple sprays of geometrically flat and almost round flowers, quite similar to the ubiquitous phalaenopsis found everywhere in the world these days. But these orchids are subtly different and I have always liked them. The Thai horticulturists are the world leaders in breeding this sort of orchid. I worked my way slowly towards the table with the *rothschildianum*. Jake had left William and he appeared to be looking at a collection of vanda orchids on the other side of the central table. He too was working his way towards the albino orchid.

We met in front of the *rothschildianum*, both admiring it for a while. The guard looked at us enquiringly. Jake turned to me, saying hello and introduced himself as if we had never met before. I shook his hand and then returned my own hand to my pants pocket but withdrew it quickly. Now I had my bot hidden in the palm of my hand. Jake held his hand closed, cupping his little robot as well. We were looking at the emerald orchid. Then Jake signaled to William who was stationed strategically away in a far corner. Jake pulled on his ear with his free hand. It was the signal to William. William managed to stumble against a waitress carrying a tray full of champagne glasses. He knocked the tray onto the floor, yelling at the top of his voice in alarm as the glasses crashed to the floor. "Oh, I am so sorry. I don't know how I could have done this. Oh! Let me help you." But he stumbled backwards instead, slamming into a second waiter upsetting a tray of canapés down some woman's bosom. She gave an equally loud shriek and now the entire hall had turned looking at the source of the noise. This included the guard. Only Jake and I paid no attention to the brouhaha. Later I was told that William managed to prolong the incident by brushing the canapés off the woman's breast. She indignantly slapped him in the face and stormed out of the room. He followed her, still trying to apologize, but once she left the room the people turned their attention back to their conversations.

277

While the disturbance was going on, and hoping that the guard as well as the rest of the people in the hall were suitably distracted, both Jake and I quickly lobbed our spyder bots onto the moss at the base of the plant. They both landed where we had intended. Lady Luck was still with us and we then walked away in different directions. I went back to the women and Jake walked over to Kani and Charlotte. William's distraction had given us the opportunity to position our little machines unobserved. Now we had to find the opportunity to pilot them.

Vicknes bin Osman said something to one of his security men who approached William and said in a loud voice. "Sir, I want you to leave the exhibit hall."

"It was an accident."

"That may be, but you have caused a disruption and upset one of our guests. Besides look at the mess on the floor."

"I am sorry about that and I apologized to the lady."

"That may be. But if you don't leave quietly I have been ordered to escort you out of the hall."

William glanced back at us and Jake gave an almost imperceptible nod of his head. "Oh, well," William said, "It's only a bunch of flowers." And he stomped out of the room, glaring at bin Osman as he left.

I heard bin Osman ask one of his henchmen in a loud voice, "Who is that young trouble maker? How did he get a ticket to this event? Make sure he does not come back."

Chapter 24 – Spyders at Work

I thought it was about time to head for the men's room, from where we planned to steer the bots, when I saw bin Osman and Prokov approach the table and the plant. They were speaking volubly, but I could not understand a word of what they were saying, and then I realized they were conversing in Russian and I thought I heard my name. Jake was also watching them. Then I saw Boris point to the ceramic vase and bin Osmin loosened the velvet rope and they both approached the table more closely. Both men were staring fixedly at the pot. They seemed puzzled. I started to think they must have seen the carapaces of the robots. I held my breath. I also saw Jake start to reach for his gun. Boris ran his fingers lightly over one of the embossed golden dragons. Then he turned and said something to bin Osman. It must have been some sort of joke because bin Osman laughed and they both turned back, fixed the rope back in place and strode into the hall away from the plant. Jake dropped his hand down away from his jacket and I managed to avoid a loud sigh of relief. It was time to head for the rest room and activate the robots.

Jake left the exhibition first and after a short pause I followed him. Matilda saw me leave. Her task now was to visit with bin Osman and keep him distracted, and preferably not facing his plant, where he might notice movement as the bots clambered onto the *rothschildianum* and climbed up the flower stalks. We would try to keep the robot activity on the back of the plant away from any audience, but someone with sharp eyes might notice the green bumps moving up to the flowers. No one was in the rest room and we selected two stalls next to each other. It felt peculiar sitting on the commode while still fully clad. I pulled my mobile phone out of my pocket, turned it on and pressed the app. to wake up my spyder bot.

The tiny video camera came on and from the picture on my screen I could tell the bot was lying on its side. So I slid my finger along the left side length of the touch screen as we had been taught and the little machine extended its legs and righted itself. I looked round the pot. There was Jake's bot, still lying on its side.

"Jake," using a loud whisper, "can't you get it up?"

"No. It's not responding. It's limp."

"Have you tried stroking along the length?"

"No, I was using a circular motion."

"Idiot," I thought but then said loudly. "Slide your finger firmly along the left side."

"It's not doing anything."

"Stroke it again, several times. Try the right side too."

"What can you see?"

There was silence for a minute and I was starting to get worried. I heard a few grunts from Jake. And then...

"Ooh, its waking up."

"Is it responding to stroking on the left or right side?"

"Doesn't seem to care as long as it is a long firm stroke."

"Now can you get it up?"

"Yep and it is getting up. Now it is fully erect. Thank God. I thought I would never get a response out of it. This is such a relief."

We were so focused on getting Jake's robot functioning that neither of us had heard somebody walk into the restroom until a very loud and gruff voice said sternly, "You fucking perverts better stop your stuff and get out of this hotel!" He must have been listening to our conversation even though we were whispering. The man's voice had a distinctive Russian accent. It must be Boris Prokov.

I must have blushed in spite of myself. Matilda would never let me live this down.

Jake responded in his harshest voice. "Fuck off, before I come out and wring your fucking neck."

I heard footsteps walking rapidly out of the room and the door shutting. Good thing William was not with us. He would have been laughing hysterically. Now we had to get back to the task at hand, and we had better hurry up in case the interloper Jake had threatened returned with some authority to give us a hard time.

I watched Jake's bot crawl to one of the flower stems at the rear of the orchid plant and start to climb up it. Then I paid attention to my own machine. It was easy to climb over the leaves and get to the stem. Then I moved the bot up the stem to the first flower's sheath. I hoped that Matilda was doing her job and distracting bin Osman. I pushed past the sheath and gripped onto the base of the ovary and hauled the bot up to the top, where there was a gap between the petals and pouch, and pulled my bot to where I could see the column. From here I should be able to see where the stamen on one side hung off the structure. I should be able to touch and rub against the pollen mass from there, transferring the pollen onto the top of the robot's carapace. It came as a shock when I realized that the stamen was not there. I clambered over the staminode to the other side of the flower but there was no pollen there either. Someone else had already taken the pollen.

"Jake, there is no pollen in my flower. I had better climb up to a higher one. Have you reached the first flower on your spike."

"No, not yet."

"Better hurry."

"My stem is quite slippery. The bot is having a hard time making progress."

"Do your best. I am scared that our eavesdropper will return with a security officer. We need to get back to the ballroom as soon as possible."

"If I cannot get to the flower in five more minutes, I will give up and go back to the showroom. You had better see if the next flower on your spike has pollen."

A few minutes later I heard Jake grunt softly, "I am up but it is so hard."

"No more puns. Get to the pollen. Is there any on your flower?"

Another moment went by and he said. "Yes I can see the pollen mass. Looks like a waxy droplet."

"Can you get to it?"

"I'm trying, but the bot keeps slipping."

I was looking for pollen on the second flower but having no luck. That was gone too.

"No pollen on my second flower," I said in exasperation. "I don't know if there is time to get to the next bloom."

"Better try, I don't know that I can get to the pollen."

"Make the attempt," I urged.

A few seconds later Jake groaned. "Goddamit."

"What happened?"

"I was trying to rub the bot's shoulder against the pollen when it slipped and the eye got smeared with pollen. I am blind. Cannot see a thing."

"That what happens when you play with yourself," I almost said. William has too much influence on me.

"Can you jump it off the plant?"

"Yes, but I don't know where it will land."

"Don't jump too far. When I get down, I will look for your spyder and carry it to the edge of the table and drop it off onto the carpet..."

"Okay."

"Jake, I think once your spyder is off the plant you should leave. Prokov will probably come back with security and in case that happens I need to have moved to a different stall. I still do not have any pollen on my bot."

"Done."

Jake left his stall and I heard the restroom door open and shut. I got up and relocated to the farthest stall from where we had been sitting. There I settled down and climbed my device up to the next flower. Here there was some pollen and I rubbed the robot's shoulder against the anther, hoping that some of the pollen was transferred onto the little machine. Then I moved to the other side of the flower and repeated the process again. Visual inspection showed that where there were once globs of sticky pollen, most had been removed. Now all I had to do was climb back down to the flower pot and see if I could find and retrieve Jake's machine and get both to the edge of the table behind the plant without anyone observing any movement. I reckoned that ten minutes had passed since Jake left the room and I was satisfied that the most difficult part of the plan had been completed successfully. We still had to retrieve the bots and scrape the pollen off them.

I had barely reached the moss covering the base of the plant when the rest room door burst open and I could hear several people stomping into the room. From the progression of footsteps they appeared to be parading back and forth in front of the stall doors.

Unlike the restrooms in the United States, here the doors were full length so one could not see the feet of the occupants.

"Everyone in these stalls, you had better come out."

"Who is that?" I called out from the corner stall.

"Security."

"What is the problem?" I asked.

"There are two men engaged in unlawful acts,"

"Well, that is not me and you can wait until I am finished."

"Hurry up then."

I would have to find some additional screen time if I was to get our robots off the flower pot and then get them down from the table. For the time being they would need to remain in the moss at the base of the *rothschildianum*.

"Come on out!"

I deliberately made noise collecting toilet paper, waited so it would seem as if I was cleaning myself and then dropped the paper into the toilet and flushed it. Counted to twenty so it would seem I was adjusting my clothing, and then I cautiously opened the door.

"What is this all about? Is this how the Golden Lotus treats its high paying guests? I want to speak to the manager," I said, directly on the attack.

"We…we…we thought there were two men in here making out. This person…" and he pointed to Boris Prokov, "…heard two men…um…er…masturbating in the stall."

"As you can see, there is only me and I was definitely not playing with myself. And even if I was, that would be none of your goddamn business."

One of the security men turned red in the face and said, "Excuse me. On behalf of the hotel I apologize." And he turned and quickly left the room leaving Boris, another security man and myself standing there glaring at one another.

"I know what I heard," Boris insisted.

"Really? One can hear that? The doors on these stalls are very thick. Was Mr. Prokov eavesdropping, acting like a Peeping Tom? Do you like salacious things, Boris? You frequent men's rooms hoping to uncover some action, do you? Well sorry, nothing going on in here."

"No need to get angry Professor."

"Well I am angry. I was here minding my own business when you come marching in, acting like some sort of informer for the Gestapo."

"I heard two men say they were rubbing their things erect."

"In one stall?"

"I cannot be sure. Maybe next to each other. I do not know exactly, but they were doing things."

I looked at Boris. "When was this? I did not hear any such thing, but I have only been here five minutes or so."

Boris did not seem to know what to say. I pressed my advantage. "Boris, how long ago were you sneaking around in this bathroom?"

"Maybe twenty minutes."

"In that time they probably finished the job and have already left. It was considerate of you to wait so long before stomping into the room."

"I had trouble finding security."

"If I remember correctly, Thailand has a reputation for being a tolerant society. There are no laws here against being gay."

Boris answered. "In Russia we do not tolerate this kind of behavior."

"So I have heard. Modern Russia has a reputation for bigotry and homophobia."

"We must protect the youth."

"Yes," I said sarcastically, "Do you see any young, vulnerable teenage boys skulking around in this bathroom? I do not." I pointed around the room where all the stall doors were open, exposing vacant interiors. The room was empty except for the three of us. And I continued. "Actually I have seen no teenage boys in this hotel. What stuff are you smoking Boris?"

He turned and left the room. Security apologized profusely and followed Boris out of the room.

I still had to get the robots down from the pot and off the table and was about to return to the stall when Jake burst through the door.

"Something has happened to Matilda and William. They have both disappeared!"

Jake looked flustered and I asked him. "What do you mean, Matilda and William have disappeared?"

"They are not in the exhibition hall and neither is answering their cell phone. They just ring and ring and eventually go to voice mail."

"That is odd. They would not leave their phones lying around. Let's go back to the hall."

Just before we got to the hall we saw the doors being shut from the inside and I heard locks snap into place. People were milling around in the anterior lobby to the hall.

"What's going on?" I asked Phillipa who was standing outside with a drink in her hand. She appeared to be uneasy. Happy was still with her.

"I don't know. We were all told to leave the hall. Some emergency or other," she said vaguely. "Could it be a bomb threat?"

"No, in that case we would be told to vacate the building not just the room," Jake supposed.

"Have you seen Matilda and the young man, William?" I asked

"You mean the young man? He was kicked out after he upset those waiters' trays? Security marched him out into the lobby and he was not here when we were told to evacuate the hall. We have not seen him since."

"What about Matilda?" I was starting to become agitated. Had bin Osman figured out what we were doing. I hoped there was an innocent answer to her disappearance, but until I knew that for sure, I feared the worst. I could feel surges of adrenaline flowing through my body. Where were Bertha and Wie. I could not see them in the lobby. Maybe Matilda was with them.

"Last I noticed her, she was talking to Vicknes. They seemed to be getting along super well. I think he was smitten with her. Of course she is very beautiful. I almost thought she was flirting with him. If I were you I would be very careful not to let him get too friendly with her. He has a reputation for having his way with any and every woman that catches his fancy."

I saw Kani and Charlotte and went up to them. "Have you seen Matilda or William since coming out of the hall?"

"In the hall, I saw her talking with bin Osman. Then a waiter delivered a note to her and she said something to him and hurried off

285

out of the hall. I saw bin Osman smiling at her as she left, rather like a satisfied cat playing with a mouse."

"Where is bin Osman now?" I looked around.

"He stayed behind in the show hall to supervise the crating of his *roth* once the rest of us exited the room. I heard him say it was time to put the plant in a secure place."

"Thank you Kani."

He said, "See you later. We are leaving to go home now."

I turned back to Jake who looked stolid and immovable but I knew that inside he was boiling with concern, fretting as much as I was. I said to him in a low voice, "The bots are still in that flower pot, I did not have enough time to climb them out of the pot. What are we going to do?"

He said, "Forget the bots. Matilda and William are more important."

"But what if they are simply sitting and talking in one of our rooms?"

"Get the concierge to phone the rooms for you. Also get hold of Great-aunt and tell her what is going on. While you do that I will try and get into the hall. There have to be back and side doors into the exhibition room. I will get in and retrieve the bots if the plant is still there."

He left and I went to the front desk. What if bin Osman already had her in his clutches and was whisking her away. If that was the case, how would we ever find her? I was scared shitless. My Matilda, what have they done to you? I felt it was entirely my fault. And what on earth had happened to my best friend, William? I wished I had never heard of orchid conservation or Paul Tylo.

Chapter 25 – Great-aunt Bertha Takes Charge

No one answered the phone in either Matilda or William's room. The concierge wanted to know if I needed to leave a voice mail. I demurred. Then I phoned Bertha. She was in her room and she invited me up. Jake had not returned yet. She admitted me into her room, took one look at my face and demanded, "What has happened?"

"It's Matilda, she's gone and William too. They aren't in either room and they are not answering their phones."

Bertha pulled out her phone and punched in Matilda's number. She listened for a moment and then stopped the call.

"Okay, now start at the beginning, don't leave anything out and be concise."

I ran through everything from getting the bots successfully onto the plant, collecting the pollen, leaving the bots on the pot, to Jake informing me that both Matilda and William had not answered their phones. I saw Bertha's eyebrows beetle up and a scowl appeared as I told the story as rapidly as I could. I had just finished when there was a bang on the door and Wie opened it to admit Jake.

He looked at us and said, "The green orchid is no longer in the room."

"And the bots?"

"I looked around on the floor and under the nearest tables. Nothing. What are we going to do. I suppose we had better confront bin Osman and force him to tell us where our people are."

Great-aunt Bertha gave a loud sigh. "I suppose I had better bring in the big guns." She pulled out her phone again, punched in another number, listen to the dial tone and when it was answered merely said. "This is Bertha. Patch me through to Tylo, immediately... I know what time it is... I said immediately. If you want to keep your job you will do as I say."

He must have been contacted right away because now she was saying. "Paul, they have Matilda and probably William as well. No... bin Osman probably has possession of the microbots too. I told you your plan was too iffy to work. Now I have to clean up the mess. I am going to activate Plan Z. I don't care if you think it too dangerous ... we have no choice. Can't leave bot technology in bin Osman's hands. What happens if he sells them to terrorists? We cannot let that happen." She listened for a moment longer and turned her phone off. Squared her shoulders and said to me. "George, you come with me. Wie get a taxi and have it waiting in the front for us. We may need it in a hurry. Jake, you keep looking for Matilda and William. They may be squirreled away somewhere in the hotel."

"Where are we going?" I demanded to know as she marched out of the room and down the passageway towards the elevators.

"The Presidential Suite. Its face-off time with Mr. bin Osman." As we walked she seemed to be searching her phone, gave a satisfactory grunt when she found the app she wanted and punched it active. Then she placed it back in her purse that was suspended around her waist.

It took a special entry card to program the elevator to take us to the penthouse presidential suite. Of course Bertha had such a key. She saw me looking at it and said with a satisfied smirk, "One must always be prepared."

In the penthouse, she marched up to the large double doors and rapped smartly with the knocker.

The door opened a few inches but was blocked by one of bin Osman's bodyguards.

"What you want?" He snarled.

"Let me in," Bertha insisted.

"No one is allowed in tonight. Go away, before I hurt you."

"You would hurt a little old lady? What would your mother say?"

"I mean it. Now scat."

"Hey, Vicknes," Bertha yelled, "Paul Tylo sends his regards."

There was silence. One could almost imagine the cogs turning in someone's skull.

"Let her in," bin Osman relented.

Bertha marched in and I followed as close behind as I could get before the guard tried to push me out again.

"Where she goes, I go," I snarled at him and he looked at his boss who nodded, and the man stood aside.

Great-aunt Bertha is all of four foot ten, even in heels. She was scarcely nipple height to bin Osman but she glared at him defiantly and demanded to know, "What have you done with my ward, Matilda?"

"What a beautiful creature," bin Osman remarked calmly, "Such a shame to have been wasted on a lowlife like this thief." And he pointed at me.

"What do you mean?"

"Come, come Bertha. No need to play games with me. The pollen is missing from my roth and I found these two little green machines nestled in the moss at the base of my plant. They both had pollen smeared on them. My man Soh Fat retrieved one of these machines from the professor's rooms in Singapore. We have been monitoring the professor and his gang in California and even before then."

"You are a member of the Guatemala cartel?"

"No, no. I am the cartel. I run the group."

"You were behind all those attacks on us? You wanted us dead." I was furious.

"Now calm yourself, professor, don't do anything stupid. You are outnumbered here." He pointed to his henchmen standing in a circle around the room. They were looking at Bertha and me. The way a cat watches a goldfish in a bowl. Were they licking their lips too?

"What have you done with my wife?" I wanted to tear that fat bastard limb from limb.

"There is nothing you can do. You are now in my power. Thank you for coming up to my room. This makes it so much easier for me."

"Where is my wife?" I screamed at him. I was seeing red. He sensed this. "Don't try anything foolish Professor. There are several guns trained on you as we speak. I don't want to have to pay to get blood stains cleaned off these beautiful Persian carpets."

I scanned the room. There were three other men and they all brought out snub nosed revolvers with sound suppressors. All of them glared at me, each hoping to be given the command to fire.

"Where is my wife?" I said again through gritted teeth.

"Out of your reach by now." He grinned and continued, full of himself. "I am not stupid you know. Paul Tylo has always underestimated me. I have known of his scheme to steal the pollen and devalue my plant. I could have you all locked in some rotten Thai prison, never to be heard from again, but that would be too easy. It is time to teach all of you a lesson. And you will suffer agonies that you cannot even imagine."

"Matilda..."

"You will never see that pretty morsel again. Of course you might not want to touch her again once you see what we will do to her."

I felt the blood turn to ice in my veins. I wanted to throttle this man even if I could not get my hands around his thick neck. I was shaking with frustration. It was then that Great-aunt Bertha decided to act. First she kicked me sharply on the shin. I gave an involuntary yell and all attention was focused on me as I hopped back a step in pain. Then she jumped and slapped bin Osman's face. Her withdrawn hand left behind her spyder, its legs sunk deep into the flesh of his cheek. Osman screamed repeatedly with pain. The gun men could not fire on us without risking killing their boss.

Acting as if the pain was unbearable, bin Osman sunk to his knees. I grabbed him from behind and pulled him back up against me. It was all I could do to support his weight but now we also had a human shield. Bertha remained close in front of him, almost touching. She turned to his henchmen and said loudly and clearly. "Mr. bin Osman will die shortly if you kill either of us. He has been injected with an extremely fast working and deadly toxin. Only I have the antidote and it is not on me now. You will all cooperate if you want your boss to live. Now put your weapons down on the ground and go and sit quietly in that corner," she pointed to a sofa. The three men looked at their boss. He nodded to them and they complied with Bertha's commands. "George, go and collect those guns. Keep a gun trained on the men at all times. I will deal with this lump of shit."

I let go of bin Osman and he sank to his knees again. By now the one side of bin Osman's face was scarlet and starting to swell like a balloon. The little robot was still attached and blood started to seep down the warlord's cheek, staining his beautiful white shirt. There must have been waves of pain because at regular intervals he groaned and gasped. Tears were pouring out of his eyes.

Great-aunt Bertha squatted down in front of him and grabbed him by the chin so he had to look into her stern face. "Vicknes, let me tell you what I have done to you. You have been injected with a toxin. It is modified after being derived from the Sydney funnel-web spider, *Atrax robustus.* This is the most venomous spider toxin in the world. It is fatal. Now in a few more minutes you will feel your lips go numb and in twenty minutes or so, you will start drooling. This will be followed by double vision and difficulty controlling your eyelids. You should already feel your heart rate start to speed up. It will go faster and faster until you have a massive heart attack and die. As the poison spreads through your body, your muscles will contract and spasm of their own accord. You will evacuate your bowels involuntarily – it will also become increasingly difficult to breathe and without supplemental oxygen you will also suffocate. I do not have oxygen for you. Some people die from a heart attack, others from suffocation. As I said the amount of venom injected is fatal. But I do have the antitoxin. It can save you. The antidote is not with me here. I will have to go and fetch it. So your goons better not touch me. Understand? Nod your head if you understand."

He barely managed to nod his head.

Great-aunt Bertha continued. "If you want the anti-venom, you need to get it as soon as possible. The longer we wait the less likely your possible recovery. I protect my own and am prepared to commit murder if necessary to save them. Now tell me what you have done with Matilda and where she has been taken and also what you have done with young William. Otherwise you will not live to enjoy your green orchid for another day."

Vicknes was already gasping like a fish out of water. He was trying to talk but having great difficulties.

"What is he saying?" Bertha asked me. I bent closer to try and catch what bin Osman was trying to say. But his lips were paralyzed and he was slurring badly. I listened closely.

"I think he said 'whatsa' or something like that."

"You have to do better than that," Bertha said, but bin Osman merely managed to grunt. It was then that I realized that perhaps the dose of venom was too large or bin Osman was more susceptible to

291

the poison than Bertha had expected. Vicknes bin Osman was unable to talk. How were we going to find Matilda?

"Where is she," Bertha demanded again. "Tell me or you will die."

Bin Osman looked at her through heavily lidded eyes. The black holes of his eyes barely visible. Had he been a snake he would have struck at her. Then he shuddered. I thought he had died. He lay still for a minute and I looked at Bertha. Had we lost our chance?

I bent to take his pulse to see if he was dead. Suddenly his legs started to twitch. He was still alive.

Bertha repeated, "Where is Matilda?"

But bin Osman, struggling to answer, could only gurgle. Nothing he tried to say was understandable.

Bertha turned to the men, mesmerized by this small woman who was not only unafraid of their formidable boss but also fiercely determined to get what she had come for from their large boss. Perhaps they had never seen anyone challenge bin Osman before.

"If he dies you are all unemployed," she pointed out to them. I thought to myself if he lived and recovered, he would probably fire them all anyway for being unable to protect their boss from a little old lady. "You can save him if you know where I can find Matilda and William," she continued. "If you save him he will surely reward you handsomely."

One of the men raised a hand like a pupil in class. "I know where the young man is stashed."

"Where?"

"He is in a broom closet on the third floor, near the service elevator."

I was dialing Jake's number. He answered on the first ring. "William is in a broom closet on the third floor. It's near the service elevator."

"Right on. I am on to it."

"Come here when you get him. It's the penthouse floor."

"Doesn't that need a special key." I looked at Bertha and she nodded.

"Take security with you to find William. Persuade security to run the elevator for you."

Bertha turned her attention back to bin Osman. "I am going to release the robot now, but it is not going to help you. You will still die without the antidote. You will not get the antidote until Matilda has been returned to us safe and unharmed. Do you understand?" She pulled her phone out of the purse still attached to her waist and activated it and stabbed at the screen. The bot retracted its limbs and dropped down onto bin Osman's heaving chest. Bertha retrieved it and placed it back onto her broach where it nestled snuggly among the other gems. Until then I had not realized that she had been carrying the murderous device openly all this time.

Bin Osman struggled to reach up to his cheek where the puncture wounds were still weeping slowly. He got his hand half-way up, but then it flopped back down. It was too much effort and he was too weak.

I was getting more and more anxious. Time was passing and we were still no closer to finding out what had happened to Matilda. Maybe she was already dead. Was this to be bin Osman's revenge against Paul Tylo? But why? He had already stolen Tylo's wife, surely that was enough. Why take my Matilda. I did not want to live without her. I felt as if someone had thrust their hand into my chest, was crushing my heart and would rip my heart out. I wanted, no I needed, the release to join with her. If she was no longer alive I was prepared to die as well.

"Buck up George," Great-aunt Bertha said, as if reading my mind. "We can still find Matilda. Perhaps William knows where she is."

I prayed she was correct.

"Should I call hotel security and-or the police?" I asked.

"Goodness no. You want to be an accessory to a murder? If we don't get Matilda, bin Osman dies and I mean it. This thing...," and she gestured towards the man on the floor, "this thing is a big *macher* in this part of the world. We wouldn't even get a fair trial. No, we have to do this without any help."

"I am not going to lose Matilda because I am scared of asking the law for help. We cannot do this on our own. We must get the authorities involved," I insisted.

At this point Jake and William burst into the room. They were followed by the hotel's security agent who had helped them get to the penthouse. They saw me with a gun in my hand pointed at three men on the sofa, and Great-aunt Bertha kneeling on the floor next to a prostrate bin Osman.

Jake had insisted that security accompany him to the third floor utilities closet. The door was locked and security wanted to go down to get the key, but after Jake tried to open the door, they heard William banging his legs against the floor. Jake was not interested in any lock at that point. He had kicked the door open and they found William trussed up on the floor. They untied William as quickly as possible and Jake massaged his limbs. The ties were so tight they had cut off circulation and the returning blood flow caused an agony of pins and needles.

"Who did this to you?" The security man asked.

"One of bin Osman's goons and another man, Soh Fat, who also works for him."

"Soh Fat, he is here?" Jake gasped.

"Yes, where is George?"

"He should be with Great-aunt. They went to confront bin Osman."

"We had better get there too."

The security man led them to an elevator and used his card to clear their admittance to the penthouse level.

Along the way he told them his name. "Bunyarup Sutakuliapoon, but you can call me Buni. I am head of security at the Golden Lotus."

"If bin Osman did this, you are in big trouble. This man is very powerful in Chiang Rai, even I must bow down to him," Buni informed them.

They got to the door of the penthouse and found it was unlocked and pushed it open. There in the middle of the room was Great-aunt Bertha looming over bin Osman writhing on the floor.

"What the fuck!" was William's take.

"Great-aunt, what have you done? Will he die?" Jake wanted to know.

"It's just a little spyder toxin," she said. "If he wants the antidote he needs to tell me what he did with Matilda."

"Not Sydney funnel-web?" William knew his spiders. "Can one really load that into a spyder?"

"Apparently," Jake pointed to bin Osman, struggling for breath.

"So has he told you?" William wanted to know.

"Err...no...seems the dose was too strong. He cannot communicate."

"Oh shit. What do we do now?"

"What is going on here?" Buni demanded. He was already pulling his phone out of his pocket to call the police.

"Wait," George commanded. "This man has kidnapped my wife, Matilda."

"He was responsible for locking William in the closet, too. I must force him to tell me where my Matilda has been taken," Great-aunt explained.

"Is this true?" Buni wanted to know.

"Of course. You saw what he did to me," William insisted.

"So where is Matilda?"

"We don't know what he has done with her."

"I need to get the paramedics here for this man." The security man pointed to bin Osman.

"No point. I mean for him to die unless my ward is returned to me unharmed. Paramedics cannot do anything for him without the antidote." Bertha was adamant. "I have the cure, but he will not get it unless he tells us how to find Matilda."

"How long does he have to live?"

"If no Matilda, he has about five hours left. If we get Matilda back, he gets to live."

"The police will arrest you when they arrive." Security told Great-aunt.

"I don't care. Matilda has always been the most important person in my life. If she dies so does that turd," she pointed at bin Osman. "I don't care about myself."

"Were these men involved with the kidnapping?" Security pointed at the men on the sofa.

"Of course."

"Do they know where Matilda is now?"

"Ask them."

"Okay."

One of the men on the sofa volunteered the following. "We told the lady that her friend Mr. William was in trouble and needed her. We said Mr. William was injured in the street outside the hotel. She rushed out of the hotel."

But none of the men knew what had happened to Matilda after she had left the Golden Lotus. Once she had run out, they lost sight of her. There were lots of people outside and it was dark. It seemed like a dead end.

I turned to William. "So tell us everything that happened to you."

"That ape," he pointed to one of the other men sitting sullenly on the sofa, "marched me out of the room, propelled me into the main lobby, and in front of everyone put handcuffs on me with my arms pinned behind my back. People were watching. He said I was being arrested for being a pervert. He marched me to the service elevator with a gun in my side. I asked him why he was doing this but he just cuffed the side of my head. When the elevator door opened he pushed me inside and as the door closed another man also jumped in. It was Soh Fat. I asked him, 'What are you doing here? Where have you been?' He looked at me and said, 'William I have never left you. Followed you everywhere…even to the flying snakes. Now we need an excuse to get Matilda out of the room to look for you. So you have to disappear. I am so sorry.' The elevator stopped at the third floor and I was marched to a large closet that said 'Staff Only' on the door. I was pushed inside. Then my legs were tied together and I was dumped onto the floor. They gagged me. As he left Soh Fat looked at me. 'You are the lucky one. It should have been you. Unlucky poor Matilda. I liked her but now she must fulfill her destiny.' Then he said something but I don't know what he meant. 'You don't have to worry about *whatsit or...*,' or something that sounded like 'What's it'. Perhaps a Thai or Chinese word? It does not make any sense. I wanted to ask what he meant by it, but I could not speak. He laughed and locked the door. I tried making a noise. Kicking and thumping around the room but no one heard me. I thought I might stay there until I died. Lucky for me, my hero came and released me." He looked at Jake with adoration.

Both bin Osman and Soh Fat had mentioned *what something* or other and then with sudden insight I knew. They were referring to Wat Sida, the Black Temple. Matilda was to be the blood sacrifice for the monks at the Black Temple. Could we get there in time to save her?

Chapter 26 – Wat Sida – the Black Temple

"It is not a good night to visit Wat Sida," Buni told us. "It is much too dangerous. It is the night of the half moon. This is when the sect gathers to celebrate the balance between good and evil, when the moon itself is in balance half light and half dark."

"How do you know this?" I asked.

"There are stories that people tell about this sect. Tales used to frighten off people so they are left alone. No one knows for sure what goes on inside, because the temple is never open to the public. We must be very careful, very quiet," Buni said. He had volunteered to drive us to the temple in one of the hotel's minivans.

"Better to take an unmarked van," he said as he opened the doors for us and we climbed in. Jake sat next to Buni in the front while William and I occupied the middle seat. Jake already had his phone out and was texting away, paying little attention to the road. We had not taken the time to change clothing and were still wearing our suits. It was warm, so I slipped out of my jacket. William did the same but Jake insisted on wearing his. I knew he liked to keep his Beretta under cover.

Buni had told the hotel we were after one of the American guests who had been kidnapped and there was a chance if we could rescue her that we could keep this out of the newspapers. It would look bad for the hotel if the city learned that one of their guests, the Professor's wife, had been abducted. What would it say about the hotel's security? They agreed, and here we were racing through the streets of Chiang Rai. Buni was driving like a madman. He insisted that every minute counted, but the ride to Wat Sida seemed to go on forever. The temple is situated at the southeast corner of the city where it merged into a lightly forested landscape. I was on edge through the entire ride. I tried to keep myself calm by controlling my breathing, keeping it deliberately slow, and ran through the few facts that I knew about weird Southeast Asian Buddhist sects. But the more I recalled, the more I wanted to hyperventilate.

There is some overlap between Hinduism and Buddhism, the latter having evolved from a Hindu base, and its pantheon of gods and goddesses has a large variety of minor spirits and supernatural fiends. Among these was the idea of *yaksha*, usually thought of as spirits in nature who were compassionate and caring. They were often illustrated as being plump dwarves, the custodians of nature. But there are other yaksha, giant demons with cruel fangs, green skins and bulging red eyes, and even cannibals that hunger for human blood, the stuff of nightmares. These yakshas have been added to Buddhist architecture in Thailand, but usually as guardians of the temples. The statues are armed with ferocious long swords. I had heard of Thotsakhirithon, and seen his statue at Wat Phra Kaeo on my first visit to Thailand. This monster not only has the usual set of fangs but also a bulbous nose like an undeveloped elephant's trunk. I was not sure if Thotsakhirithon was the same at Thotsak, a cannibal who tried to eat Rama in Hindu legend. There was a lot I did not know and the main thing I did need to know was what was planned for my beloved at the hands of the Black Temple monks. I needed this information if there was to be any chance of rescuing her.

"Buni, what do you know about the Black Temple and what they worship?" I asked as he sped around a corner narrowly missing a tree in the dark that encroached onto the road.

"Very little, but people do speak."

"Such as?"

"We think that they worship Ravana, king of demons. In Thai he is called Totsakan."

"Is Totsakan the same as Thotsak?" I asked. "Isn't he a cannibal?"

"Maybe, I am not sure. People talk about sacrifices. Both beautiful women and even young men. They say those people are never seen again. Not even their bodies. Some even think they are eaten."

"How far is Wat Sida?"

"We should be getting there soon."

It was dark and we had to rely on our driver's skills to deliver us there at top speed. Fortunately once we had cleared the city there was almost no other traffic. In some places we went through narrow winding lanes, with no street lights. Occasionally, we passed a house with an illuminated window, but most houses were screened by tall hedges.

Jake leaned forward from his seat. "George, I am trying to arrange an escape route. As soon as we get Matilda, we should try and leave the country."

"How?"

"Either a charter plane from the Chiang Rai airport or by car, across the border into Myanmar."

"Why Myanmar?"

"It's only about a 30 minute drive to Tachileik, the city across the border. It is easy to get a one day pass into Myanmar. We can fly out of Tachileik airport. It all depends which airport Tylo can get a chopper or a charter from. He will let me know later."

"We cannot abandon Great-aunt and Wie to the Thai police. Even if she has an excellent motive for her actions, what Bertha has done is not kosher and she is facing real trouble even if she resurrects bin Osman. We have to get them out with us."

"That means Chiang Rei or nothing. It is the closest," William said.

I agreed and Jake texted that to Tylo.

Buni drove past a neon sign advertizing the Great Lanna Elephant Refuge and about a half mile later brought the van to a small turnout on the side of the road. He turned out the lights and turned the engine off.

"Are we here at the Black Temple?"

"No, it is still about a mile away."

"Why not drive," William asked.

"Because the monks in the temple will hear the engine and they might see the lights. It is better to walk quietly up to the temple and surprise them."

There was no sign for the Black Temple but a gothic (in the sense of being dark and gloomy) gate showed the position of an entrance road. The gate was secured by a loop of metallic chain and a rather modest padlock. Jake was able to pick the lock. We opened the gate and slipped inside. The chain went back in position, but we did

300

not snap the lock closed, but merely looped it through part of the chain to look as if it was locked.

"We may need to get out of here fast." Jake reasoned. "Leave it unlocked."

The temple was at the top of a rounded hill, and we followed a dirt road that wound its way between spindly trees and shrubs. The four of us crept stealthily up the road, our ears and eyes straining for the slightest movement, all senses on full alert. At first there was little to see or hear. Then a few night insects started to strum their nocturnal mating calls and a gecko chirped. The half moon provided scant light, but as our eyes adjusted we found the trees assuming threatening postures. Many of the trees had been pollarded, and their stumpy branches, each ending with a crown of short gnarly twigs, seemed to be reaching out towards us. In my fervent imagination I saw evil hands with crooked gnarly fingers twisting out to grab at us. The others must also have felt the malevolent aura that this site evoked. I saw Jake pull his Beretta from its holster and he attached the sound suppressor. Buni also appeared to have a gun in his hand, but his was without a suppressor. William and I were unarmed. I hoped we would be able to persuade the monks to release Matilda without having to resort to gun fire. Casualties would only complicate matters.

Small clearings now appeared in the forest close to the roadside and in the dim moonlight, we could see clusters of ten to twenty erect wooden phalluses in each clearing. In the first clearings they were only a couple of feet tall, but as we neared the temple they were approaching five or six feet in height, each topped with a typical glans shaped helmet. Here they were not erotic. They were threatening. A sudden flap of wings and a squawk from a disturbed forest bird sent the adrenaline coursing through my veins. I saw William jump in surprise. Jake and Buni seemed unperturbed.

In the distance one could hear a slow drone of human voices. The monks were chanting. Then through the trees I could make out the dim and flickering lighting coming from the temple building. The chanting was louder now. I could not make out any words or the language they were using. We came to the edge of the wood. All the trees except for a few spindly examples had been cleared away. The temple loomed in front of us. It was indeed black, with many of the filigree ornamentations typical of Thai temple architecture, but in the darkness and gloom detail was difficult to make out. Smaller buildings were off to the side and behind the main temple. More clusters of wooden phalluses decorated the spaces between the buildings. The eaves and gables of the temple stood out against the starry sky. They had the multiple curves and arcs so common in Thai Buddhist temples. But I knew that Buddha did not smile down upon the men inside who were following their own dark drummer.

On either side of the entrance to the main temple two giant ceramic Yakshas stood guard. In the flickering light they looked creepy enough to scare the timid away.

Doors to the temple hall stood wide open and light spilled out to the yard around the building. There were several open doors some on the side and maybe even at the back. Jake signaled me to go to the front while he and William would approach the rear. Buni motioned that he would take a side door.

We separated and I crept forward towards the entrance door and carefully peered around into the temple from behind one of the doors. What I saw was instantly engraved on my brain and will remain with me for the rest of my life. The flickering light came from torches in sconces on the wall and illuminated a scene out of some bizarre nightmare. The room was decorated with animal skulls hung all over the walls and even a few human skulls suspended from the ceiling. Around the perimeter of the hall against the wall were about fifteen low slung chairs. The legs and arms of the chairs had been constructed from black curved antelope and water buffalo horns. The seats were padded with a variety of animal skins, probably goats and other hoofed animals. The room itself was carpeted by reptile skins from large crocodiles and pythons. They had been polished and glistened in the light. There was no altar but in the center of the room was a low table, its legs also made of black horn and covered with a pile of short black fur, perhaps skins of the Himalayan Sun Bear. I looked around the room. Where was Matilda?

Each chair was occupied by a monk. They wore simple brown gowns tied with a belt at the waist. Their faces and parts of their arms and legs protruding from the robes had been dyed bright green and

302

something applied to their eyes had made the whites blood red. They all stared fixedly at the table in the center of the room as they chanted in unison, their voices rising to a crescendo before falling away again. It was waves of sound. At least fifteen men occupied the chairs. We were outnumbered and two of us were unarmed. I was wondering what to do next and how to find my wife when one of the men arose from his seat and strode into the center of the room. He was enormous, at least six and a half feet tall. Then he walked to a cupboard on one side of the room and pulled aside a curtain and extracted a gold leaf helmet, covered in filigree and rising to a spire at its crown. The chanting sped up and increased in volume as he raised the helmet up in the air above his head and settled it back down on his own head. Then he turned away from me, I saw his hands moving up to his face. He brought them down and glared around the room. I gave a gasp. Here was Thotsakhirithon with fangs and a green bulbous nose. He must have affixed prosthetic teeth and nose while turned away. The monks rose and made the *wai* motion of respect, raising their fingertips to the tops of their foreheads. All the while they murmured, "Thotsak," increasing to a crescendo to, "Thotsak, Thotsak, **Thotsak**."

The monks stayed standing while the giant high priest returned to the cupboard and extracted what looked like a three foot silver tube. It was slightly curved and had been worked with filigree designs. He raised this above his head in both hands and again the chanting sped up and increased in volume. Slowly he pulled his hands apart, slipping a long slender curved Thai sword, a *darb* saber, out from its scabbard. The grip was a solid cylinder of ivory capped on each side with intricate silver. There was enough ivory so that it could be gripped with both hands. There was no hilt below the grip, but instead another band of wrought silver that gave way to the cutting edge itself. Some rusty blotches blade could have been rust or maybe dried blood. Another monk came forward to receive the sheath and placed it aside. Then the high priest slowly circled the central table. The monks lined up behind him still chanting in a monotone Thosak over and over again. They all marched in a single file behind the priest. The monk behind the priest reached up to the priests shoulders and deftly unfastened some stays in the man's robes and they fell, leaving him completely naked except for the spired helmet, but from where I was hiding I could only see his back. His entire body was either painted or tattooed. It was hard to say which and it was covered in swirls and almost paisley-type patterns. Mainly shades of green with a few reds and yellows for contrast. As he marched round in the circle he came to face me. His chest, belly and legs were covered with the same patterns, but from his groin jutted out a giant tumescent penis. It seemed to be covered in green scales and the head had a large white eye tattooed on either side. A piercing through the meatus allowed the insertion of a silver snake's tongue. In the center of each eye on the swollen glans was a large black pupil. No iris, instantly bringing to mind Vicknes bin Osman's eyes; the eyes of a demon.

Now all the other monks casually slipped out of their robes too, until there was a circle of naked men. They were painted various shades of green over their entire bodies and all had engorged erections. They must have taken Viagra or some other medication and perhaps in an overdose to produce those enormous organs, all of which were painted to resemble dragons, snakes or other reptiles. I started to get a very bad feeling. They stopped marching and turned to face the central table. One could feel their excitement in the air. Many were trembling with some sort of anticipation. A few monks, unable to wait any longer reached for fellow monks, turned them around, and started to bugger them while both were still standing up. At first the High Priest grinned at the coupling pairs, but soon turned back to the table, and reaching down, pulled the bear's skin off the table and letting it drop to the floor.

Matilda had been hidden under the pile of skins. Lying on the black wood table-top was my sweet Matilda. She was still partially covered with what looked like another piece of tanned reptile skin, but her beautiful breasts were exposed. She did not move. Her head, leaning back off the table, had half-opened eyes. She was either drugged senseless or she was already dead. I felt my soul sink into a black pit of despair. Then the high priest called out to an acolyte who brought forward a stick of incense and the priest waved it in front of her nose. She stirred and gave a little cough. She was alive. She was, however, still drugged and seemed unaware of what was going on. If she saw the garish priest at all, she must have thought him part of a delirious nightmare.

Now the high priest raised his sword and positioned it high across her neck getting ready to slice through that slender branch. Those monks engaged and lost in thrusting into their fellows did not seem aware of the sacrifice about to be made, but others were grinning and clustered closer to the table. I could take it no longer. I gave a loud wail and yelled at the top of my voice, "That is my wife, you fuckers, leave her alone!"

There was a moment of utter silence as the high priest and the monks looked in my direction. I was striding through the open doorway and started to run. I admit I went berserk, yelling and screaming profanities. At that moment I was unaware of any danger. All I wanted was to protect my soul mate. "Oh my Matilda, I'm coming for you."

The priest merely grinned, ignored me and turned back to Matilda raising his sword once more. He was damned if he was going to let me interfere with his sacrifice.

Several things happened at that point. Jake shot the high Priest in the shoulder. The priest screamed and twisted around, missing Matilda, and then collapsing onto the floor in pain.

"Serve you right you fuck-up," I yelled again as I crashed straight into one copulating couple, knocking them apart and onto the floor. I went down too, but scrambled up from among the slimy bodies and headed for Matilda again.

Buni fired several deafening shots into the ceiling and then yelled in Thai, "Police! You are all under arrest. Surrender! Surrender!" They looked up in his direction but paid him no attention when they noted he was not in police uniform. I rushed on towards Matilda who was trying to sit up on the table. My way was blocked by another couple. A very large man who was jamming himself rapidly, time and again, into a much smaller man. Under the make-up I recognized the smaller monk. It was Soh Fat. I kicked his feet from under him and both men crumpled to the ground. I hoped Soh Fat was seriously hurt. But then another monk stood in my way. I delivered a punch to his stomach that evoked a satisfying, "Oof" and as he double

305

forward I connected with the man's jaw. It was an upper cut that would have satisfied my college boxing coach. (He was so hard to please. Why I remembered that at this instance was unfathomable.) The man went out for the count. Now only one man remained between me and my beloved. It was the giant demon priest. He was standing now but clutching his wounded shoulder and moaning softly. He glared, trying to intimidate me. I was beyond feeling scared. I wanted my wife and nothing was going to stop me. Despite his injury, he crouched down and picked up his sword again, with his good hand. He gripped the hilt tightly and slashed at my head. I ducked down, coming face to face with his still enormous erection, with its tattooed bin Osman eyes staring back at me. The sword missed my head by the proverbial whisker. I swung my hand in a fierce karate chop at his cock and connected half way along its considerable length. Most men do not realize that one can fracture an erect penis with a sharp blow like that, especially if it is to an overly tumescent organ. The priest gave a scream and collapsed writhing on the floor. His pride and joy now had a right angle in the middle of its length. I felt no sympathy for him, jumped over his body and reached out to Matilda.

She was still struggling to sit up. I think she was still trying to figure out if she was dreaming or not. She opened her eyes, "Darling it is you," and then she closed them again. I picked her up and cradled her against my chest. I staggered back with her towards the front entrance. Matilda smelled strange, almost as if she had been bathed in a solution of herbs. I could smell cinnamon, cloves and what might even have been cilantro. Were these culinary preparations? I shuddered.

William rushed over, having picked up one of the monk's robes, and draped it over her. The temple was in chaos. Some of the naked monks sprang apart and scrambled towards the various doorways trying to escape. Others were sprawled on the floor. Some injured, others not. And then there were still irate monks, angry at having their ceremony disturbed, who wanted to do us harm. Jake and William were now in the middle of the temple fighting off individual monks. I saw Jake pick up one of the skull ornaments and smash it into the green face of a man knocking him senseless to the floor.

William tripped another monk that was rushing towards Jake's back, wielding a wicked looking knife in his hand. That monk went crashing down hitting his head against a chair and lay inert. Buni, still standing at a side door, fired at a monk creeping up behind me and the man screamed, going down with a shattered knee. I had been unaware of him, being too preoccupied and concerned with Matilda. The monk had found a spear from somewhere. I owed Buni one.

And then suddenly it was all over, except for all the bruised and naked bodies, moaning and groaning, scattered around on the temple floor. I looked around for Soh Fat. We still had a score to settle but that little rat had vanished. We left the temple and stood in the yard in front of the malevolent looking building. What to do now. I still held Matilda in my arms but she seemed wide awake. William was still panting from excitement but Jake was calm as usual.

Buni, who seemed to be taking everything in stride as if the evening's activities were not at all unusual, tried to give direction. "We must leave this place. It is not safe."

"First, we need to signal Bertha to apply the antidote," Jake said as he fished out his phone. He sent a terse text to Bertha. It simply said:

'Matilda Safe.'

"Do you think the monks will call for reinforcements?" I asked looking anxiously back towards the temple as I started to carry Matilda down the road.

"No. Typically these sects do not have more than fifteen to twenty-five adherents who live at a temple. Often it is less. I think we taught them a good lesson. Those not injured will want to run away before the authorities arrive. We should assume that they will call in more police and medical aid. They are probably confused about who we are too." Buni said and continued, "They will want to clean up first so they can pretend to be innocents wrongly set upon."

"The police are the last people we need to see at this stage," I pointed out. "I am not sure how they will react to us attacking the temple and the monks, even though the monks were going to kill Matilda. It will be too difficult to explain what is going on. It is better if we can simply get away and leave them a mess to puzzle through."

Everyone agreed.

"Let's get out of here."

"George. Why are you carrying me?" Matilda seemed to have woken up out of her trance.

"You were drugged. We rescued you. Now you are safe. I am taking you down to the van. I will fill you in, once we are safe."

"Where are my clothes?"

"No idea."

"Put me down. I can walk."

"You have no shoes."

"Oh. Then you had better carry me, but wouldn't it be easier if you carried me piggy back style."

Yes. That was much better. I could stride down the road and Matilda could hold onto my shoulders and wrap her legs around my waist.

"Put me down first. I need to put this gown on properly and then I will climb onto your back."

She put the robe on and fastened its belt and then I bent down leaning forward so she could climb onto my back. Once she was secure I started trotting down the hill.

"Hold my shoulders. You are throttling me," I warned her.

But we had scarcely walked a hundred yards down the road when I had to stop. The adrenaline had worn off and reaction was setting in. Matilda was getting heavier, but no way was I letting go of her, not even for an instant. However, I needed a rest. The others stopped with me.

"What is wrong? We must hurry," Jake said.

"Suddenly, I feel weak."

"Then let me carry Matilda for a while," Jake volunteered.

"No way." I felt so very possessive.

"I can walk," Matilda insisted.

"Not in bare feet."

William came up to me. "George, I know how you feel, but trying to play the hero is going to jeopardize the whole thing. Let Matilda try walking. She can have my shoes. Our feet are about the same size or at least she can put on my socks. They are very thick."

I leant back against a tree, still waiting for my strength to return and still clutching my wife despite her weight.

"We cannot stay here much longer," Jake said. "George, every moment here puts us in increasing danger. Let me carry Matilda."

"Why are you fighting over me. I can walk on my own," Matilda argued.

While we were arguing I felt a buzz in my pocket. It was my phone and I asked William to retrieve it from my pants pocket. I was partially holding her up with my arms under her thighs and unable to access it without dislodging her. I was still loathe to let her go. I had almost lost her for good.

William pulled out my phone read the text message and showed it to me. It was from Bertha.

Police on their way to Wat Sadai. Bin Osman given antidote and taken to hospital. There is a warrant out for your arrest. Get out of Thailand now. Don't worry about us, we will be okay.

Jake whispered, "We had better move fast."

I gritted my teeth. This was no time to be tired. Somehow I found extra reserves of strength from somewhere and staggered off again down the road. The others followed.

"I love you," Matilda whispered and it was an energy boost.

"Love you too. I almost lost you. That would have been unbearable." I responded.

Were the police racing already on their way to the Black Temple? What now? We must sneak back into the hotel, get Matilda some clothes and shoes. Our passports were in the safe in our bedroom closet. Perhaps we could collect Bertha and Wie too, and then head for the Myanmar border.

"I am going to run ahead," Buni said. "If the police come you will hear them in time, hide in the bushes and let them pass up to the temple. They will be too busy trying to get to the temple to see you. If I see the police turn onto the temple road I will get the van and bring it to the entrance gate. It will save time. I hope you can carry your wife all the way down the hill."

"The professor is very strong. He could carry two people if he had to," William said.

"I don't think so. Professor looks bushed."

"I am okay," I answered. "You go and get the van. Wait. First give someone your phone number." He exchanged numbers with William. Buni set off, sprinting down the hill and leaving us in the dark.

Chapter 27 – Escape

We had scarcely covered a hundred feet around the first bend in the road when I heard someone yelling back at the temple. There were two or three different voices that sounded as if they were coming closer.

"Quick, into the bushes," Jake suggested and we slipped off the road and hid behind a large dense clump of vegetation. I peered out back at the road to see two monks continuing down the path. In the dim moonlight I could just make out that they were carrying traditional priest's knives, held at the ready.

"Probably going down to unlock the gate. We can sneak after them if we are quiet. We need to get as close to our van as possible," Jake whispered.

"What if we meet them on the way up?"

"I still have my Beretta. They only have knives. We can overpower them."

"Not so sure about that. It makes more of a mess, for which we can get into even more trouble. But I suppose we have no choice."

"Well, the only other thing is to leave the road and work our way down the hill through the forest on the other side and see if we can come out onto the road somewhere else," Matilda had recovered enough to make that suggestion.

"In the dark we are probably going to make noise pushing through the bush and stepping on dry twigs, etc.," I countered.

"We go slow," William liked the idea. "When we are far enough away from the road, and the bush is dense enough, maybe we can use the phone's flashlight."

"I don't have my phone," Matilda complained. "Must be with my clothes."

The idea that some man or men must have undressed her, stripped her naked and probably ogled at her beauty, set anger coursing through my body again.

"Did they try to use you…?" I asked through gritted teeth.

"No, I don't think so. I would know if someone did that, I would still be able to feel that," She knew what I was thinking about. It did not calm my anger.

Then in the distance I heard a siren. Was it the police or an ambulance? In either case it would mean trouble for us. Perhaps the monks had phoned in for medical assistance. There was no way to know. If an ambulance, the monks we had just seen had gone down to let the medics in. It seemed that our only option was the forest route and to hope no one fell down or stepped on a snake or other venomous creature. Of course, I had to recollect that Southeast Asia also had giant poisonous centipedes. I had seen the creatures two or three times previously. There are several different species of centipedes in this area, but the nastiest one is *Scolopendra subspinipes*, commonly called the Vietnamese centipede. It is found all over Southeast Asia and even down to Australia. The beast can be over twenty centimeters (eight inches) long and possibly two and a half centimeters (one inch) or more wide across the body and out-splayed legs. Despite its name, this species had no more than eighty legs each capable of delivering a poisonous stab. Imagine thirty or forty simultaneous wasp stings. That is what it would feel like. At the front end, on each side of the head, is a vicious claw tipped with a poison gland. At least one fatality has been reported from its bite. Normally they would not attack a person but if we accidentally stepped on one in the dark it would swing up and sting our ankles. On top of it all, they were nocturnal predators and would be out hunting in the dark.

The siren was getting louder and I had no doubt that it was coming to Wat Sadai. We had to do something. Matilda's suggestion now seemed the best option, despite the possibility of encountering some nasty creature. We hurried back across the road and into the forest on the other side. It was denser here, which was to our benefit. It was impossible to walk through the forest without making noise. Carrying Matilda made it even more difficult. Away from the road the hill became steeper and steeper, and in the dark, I was scared one of us might tumble down. Jake and William were helping each other and they insisted on going ahead of me to find the safest path.

We heard occasional sounds of some unknown creatures scurrying out of our path. We were not alone in that forest. We could not use our phone lights yet, because they might be visible from the road in the darkness. Also, I could still see the lights from the buildings at the top of the hill and, as long as I could see them, someone up there would be able to see our lights as well. Clouds were gathering, and what little moonlight we had to see by kept getting obscured. Several times we had to halt because we simply could not decide where to step, and we had to wait until the moon peeped back out from behind the clouds. The siren was very loud and then suddenly it stopped, to be replaced by a motor's sounds getting louder and louder. Some vehicle, medics or police, was climbing up the road to the temple at the top of the hill. I was sure they would not hear us beating through the brush above their engine's noise and we hurried faster down the slope.

The vehicle continued up the road and must have reached the complex of buildings at the top, because the sound ceased. I suspected the monks had by now washed all the paint off their bodies and would be ready to spin a sympathetic story that the authorities would swallow. I could see the headlines. "Foreign tourists attack peaceful monks at prayer."

Finally we I saw evil hands with crooked gnarly fingers twisting out to grab at us could no longer see any light from the buildings above. It was a combination of trees and how far down the hill we had been able to climb. We turned on our flashlights and that helped immeasurably. At one point, I saw the tail end of a snake disappearing rapidly into the bush. It did not bear thinking how close we had probably come to other denizens of the forest. I reckoned that we had taken half an hour of very cautious walking to make it to the edge of the temple's property without incident. At the bottom of the hill we were confronted by a massive fence. It must have been ten feet high, with very stout vertical posts, between which were strung thick wire cables, so closely spaced that one could not squeeze between them. A five foot wide trail of cleared vegetation made for a clear corridor running in both directions along the fence.

"Don't touch the fence," Jake cautioned, "It may be electrified."

I played my light over the poles and cables but could not see any insulators, so I decided the fence was not electrified and tentatively touch a wire. There was no charge. Maybe we could climb over it if needed.

Matilda complained from my back, "If it was electrified I would also have gotten a shock."

"Naw, I knew it was not live."

Now we must get to the road and hope to find Buni and the hotel's van. But which way to the main road? The road up the hill to the temple twisted on its way to the top. We had come down the side of the hill to what we thought was the opposite side and in fact had not climbed straight down. We had to follow inclines and contours on our way down. Where were we in relation to the main road and the van? And how were we to get to it? Which direction to go?

"Follow the fence," Matilda said. "That would be easiest."

"To the left or the right?"

"Not sure."

"Let's go to the left," Jake suggested. "I'm pretty sure that will come out to the road."

"Maybe it doesn't matter, the temple is on a rounded hill, and it's like a dome. Either way we should come out to the road," was William's contribution.

"Before we set off, please put me down," Matilda insisted. "My legs will start cramping after clutching you all the way down the hill. And William, give me your socks. You too, Jake. I can walk if I have on two pairs of socks. You don't need socks and you can still wear your shoes. George do you have your notebook with you?"

I always carried a small moleskin book for notes and observations.

"Yes."

"Tear out several pages. I will put them between the two layers of socks for added insulation.

"What if you step on a thorn?" I wanted to know.

"If it pierces the papers, then you will carry me again."

I must admit that it was a relief to set her down and I stretched my back. It was aching, but of course I could never admit that. We set

314

off down the trail, walking towards the left. On the other side of the fence was dense forest.

"Luckily this trail is very level and cleared of stumps and broken branches. I can walk without any problems on it," Matilda remarked as we moved along.

"This is a very strong fence. Reminds me of Jurassic Park. I wonder what sort of dinosaurs they keep in there?" William never lacked imagination. "I suppose a Tyrannosaurus could easily burst through."

"William you have too much imagination!"

It was then that I heard an ominous low rumble from deep in the forest. Something large was moving in the trees on the other side of the fence. There was a sharp crackling sound as if an entire branch was being torn from a tree. It was accompanied by creaking and groaning, perhaps trees were being bent or pushed aside. We picked up our pace. The sound seemed to be following us. I tried to see what it might be but the trees were simply too dense and the light too dim.

"There is a dinosaur in there," William squeaked in alarm.

"Don't be ridiculous."

I could pick up other noises in the distance as well. Several vehicles with sirens were shrilly screaming ahead of us. We must be getting closer to the main road and I presumed that the first vehicle, now at the temple, had called for back-up assistance and additional help. These must be answering that call.

In the dark, hearing was almost as important as vision and we were all keenly aware of the night sounds of the forest. Somewhere in the forest I heard a large hurrumph, while to our right up the hill the piping of frogs filled the air. I could pick out the strum of katydids. But there was also a circle of silence around us. The forest animals were aware of us and quieted as we approached them, only to resume the forest chorus once we had passed. There was a curious gurgling sound ahead of us that slowly got louder and louder as we approached it.

"What is making that sound?" Matilda wanted to know.

Our easy walk along the fence came to an abrupt halt when I almost stepped into a gorge that sliced through the path and went under the fence. I was leading the group when I was playing my flashlight on the path in front when the trail disappeared, leaving a large black hole in front of me. It was so unexpected that I almost stepped into it.

Matilda grabbed my arm and pulled me back just in time to avoid a nasty tumble. It looked like bad soil erosion. The walls seemed as if they might crumble at any moment and we stepped back.

"What now?" William asked shining his flashlight down to the bottom of the trench. It must have been at least fifteen feet deep. Running along the bottom of the trench was a rapid stream of water. It cut off our access to the road. This was indeed an unwelcome barrier.

"We either go back or we climb over the fence and see if we can get out through the adjacent property," I offered the two alternatives.

"What is on the other side of the fence?" Matilda asked.

"It's an elephant park."

"Is that what we heard crashing through the forest?"

"Yep. Elephant's have to forage about eighteen to twenty hours a day to get enough fodder to feed their bulk."

"How dangerous will they be?"

"I cannot say for sure. Most of the elephants here are rescued animals. If they are treated kindly and used to exposure to tourists they should be tame enough. They have very long memories and if they were treated cruelly by their former owners, then they might see our presence as an opportunity to seek revenge."

"That is not very reassuring."

"Sorry, it is not, but I think it unlikely they will deliberately harm us. Also we can try and keep out of their way."

"I can see myself a shish-ka-bob pierced by the tusk of a marauding bull elephant. What an ignominious and sorry way to go out," William opined.

"Better than a *T. rex* snack," I could not help adding.

"We need to get out of here," Jake said. "Is there razor wire on the top of the fence?"

We shone our lights up at it.

"No, just another strand of the same cable. Well, no time to waste. Let's get going. Climb next to a post. The cable will be firmer there and it will be easier to get over the top if you grip onto the post as you clamber over."

We started climbing up the fence. Fortunately the cables were all firmly stretched between the posts and with little give, so we were all able to climb over and down the other side.

"How are the socks holding up?" I asked Matilda. "Do you want me to carry you again?"

"No thank you, I can manage."

"Before we get started, William, you have Buni's cell number," Jake said. "We need to tell him where we are and to meet us as near the entrance to the elephant park."

"Hopefully he heard the other sirens and has hidden the van somewhere out of sight."

The walk through the large park that night was something out of a dreamscape. It was not really as dense as it appeared from the outside. If the temple had been a nightmare, the elephant park was a surreal, calm journey, with merely the hint of danger in the background. There were clearings surrounded by trees, dark pools at the edge of darker forest glades, where presumably during the day elephants could swim and bathe and play. We did have to ford a wide muddy stream. I carried Matilda so she could keep her socks dry. We, of course, were still wearing suit trousers and those got wet and muddy.

The elephants themselves had established their own trails that we could follow. From time to time one or several behemoths loomed out of the darkness. They were enormous. They looked at us curiously, perhaps wondering why we were in their territory during the night, but for the most part they seemed to accept our presence. Certainly we were no threat to them and they were unperturbed by us, four small pale skinned creatures, wandering through their territory. Elephants have excellent memories and they would not associate us with their individual *phajaan* torturers.

Once a mother came to stand between us and her new born and trumpeted a warning but when we skirted away from her she went back to her own business.

At length, we came to the entrance gate. It was, as might be expected, locked, but we were able to find a portion of the fence we could climb over and there we were; standing in the main parking lot alongside the road we had driven on earlier in the evening on our way to rescue Matilda. Now where was Buni? He was supposed to meet us near the park gate. I glanced at my watch – two-thirty in the morning. So much had happened this evening. I did not need this sort of excitement anymore. But we must retrieve our passports from the hotel and then escape from Thailand. In the distance, near the edge of the parking lot, we heard an engine turn over and we headed for that sound. We found the van parked behind some large shrubs.

"Thank God you are here!" I could have kissed Buni.

We scrambled into the car. He drove us out of the parking lot and nosed the van onto the main road back towards Chiang Rai before turning on his headlights. Even at this hour of the night there was some traffic on the road. The Thai often like to party late. We ducked down as each approaching car drove by. We passed two police vehicles rushing back towards the Black temple.

I noticed that Jake was busy on his phone texting all the way back to the city. He dismissed William, who wanted to know what he was doing.

"Shush, I'm busy."

At the Golden Lotus, Buni drove round to a service dock in the rear and brought us into the hotel through a staff doorway.

"You have no more than twenty minutes in your room," Jake said. "Enough time for a very quick shower, change into some jeans and pack your backpacks. Leave everything else. Our ride for home needs to be met in about three hours and we have a long drive ahead. Hopefully we can also avoid the authorities. They will expect us to head for the Myanmar border. Instead we are going to a place outside of Chiang Mai."

"What about the hotel bill?"

"Tylo will take care of that."

"Who is going to drive us?"

"Buni. He will be rewarded quite handsomely. I showed him the amount and he is delighted, even though it may be risky for him. Tylo has guaranteed a job if he gets fired from the hotel."

We slipped into our rooms and Matilda stepped out from the monk's robes and jumped into the shower. Meanwhile, I grabbed a change of underwear for both of us and pushed it into my backpack.

Then I headed for the safe and punched in the password. The door clicked open and I looked for our passports. They were still there and I extracted them with our extra money and those credit cards that we had stashed in the safe. After making sure it was empty I closed the door again. I was about to turn away when I noticed, laying on top of the safe a small package, wrapped in brown paper. Matilda's name was scrawled on it and I recognized Great-aunt Bertha's handwriting. I put that into my backpack too, wondering why Matilda had not mentioned it.

Matilda came out of the bathroom, walked over to her suitcase and extracted some clothes that she hurriedly shrugged into. It was then I noticed the red rope marks bruising her wrists and ankles where she had been tied up.

She saw me looking at the marks and shrugged. "They will heal." And she continued getting dressed. She had barely finished fastening her sneakers when there was a knock on the door. I opened it. Buni stood outside, behind him were Jake and William.

"Are you ready?" He asked.

"Another minute," Matilda asked. She also had a back-pack and stuffed it with a sweater and an extra pair of jeans.

"Passports?" She asked me.

"I have them."

"Okay, let's go."

Buni drove us out of town.

"Where are we going?" I asked Jake.

"Route 108, the road to Chiang Mai. We will take a side road to a private airfield there. Tylo has arranged for us to get out of the country. This is the best he can do. I hope it works."

"How long to get there?" I asked Buni.

"Usually about three hours between the two cities but we are only going part of the way."

"Are there any security stops that we have to deal with along the way?"

"Yes, but this time of the night there is minimum staff, so should be no delays."

"Do you think the police may have issued an alert for us? They may have to search the van at the security stops."

"Possible, but there is only one security stop, and I am well known there. I think I can get us through. You will have to gamble I can pull it off. When we get close you must crouch down on the floor and hide," Buni said. "There are blankets in the back. You will have to cover yourselves and not move. It may take five to ten minutes before I can get us cleared.

We drove on. I looked at my watch. It was now nearly four-thirty in the morning. We must get to the checkpoint before sunrise. Darkness would help hide us. The road twisted through the hills and we came to the check point. All cars slowed down. There was a single official next to the stop sign.

"On the floor now," Buni commanded, and l lay down with Matilda on top of me. She pulled the cover over us, head and all, and we tried to keep still. I heard Buni roll the window down and he answered in Thai. We could not understand what was being said. The conversation back and forth seemed to go on interminably.

Matilda's head was nestled against my shoulder. I had her safe and maybe we could escape and leave the country, but I also felt a great weariness and despair. Our project had been a complete disaster. We had failed in our mission, a chance of building that prime orchid reserve in South America was lost and if we managed to escape we could never visit Thailand again. Our wanted status was probably already in the government computers. We would be *persona non grata* from now on. This hurt, because I was fond of Thailand and its people. On top of that we had also lost the spyders. If that technology ended up in the wrong hands, such as terrorists or countries that wished us harm, they would be able to wreak havoc. What a debacle, and I resented Paul Tylo who forced us into this mess.

Through a small hole in the blanket I saw a flashlight play through the car. Then it was withdrawn, something sharp was barked at Buni. I held my breath. Then Buni laughed cheerfully and said "*Khap khun maak*" to the officer. I remembered the phrase meant, 'thank you very much,' in Thai. Buni closed the window and the car rolled forward and was on its way.

"What was that conversation all about?" I asked as we climbed back into our seats.

"I asked him if he had heard about the ruckus in Chiang Rai. He said yes, he was on the lookout for some Americans who had created havoc at a temple. He was not sure which one. He wanted to know where I was going. Said to my girlfriend in Chiang Mai. Why so late? I said I was too horny to wait any longer. He laughed and I laughed as well. Then I told him to keep an eye open for the Americans, but it would make more sense if they went over the border to Myanmar. He agreed. Then he said he hoped my banana would get the care it deserved. He flashed the light briefly through the window. We both laughed and he waved me on."

We drove for a while and then, at a certain place, turned off from the main road going towards the city and drove back into the hills, before coming across what appeared to be a large flat open field surrounded by dense, tall hedges. Buni brought the van to a halt in front of a gate.

"We get out here," Jake informed us. He looked at his watch. "Our next ride will be arriving in about thirty minutes."

We climbed out and thanked Buni profusely for all his help. He was going on to Chiang Mai where he had a girlfriend. Jake offered him an envelope, which was received eagerly and with many thanks. We waved him goodbye. The gate was unlocked and we walked into the field.

"What are we waiting for?" I asked Jake.

"Our ride is coming from Hanoi. It's the closest major airport to where we are now. From there we will be put on planes to take us back to the States."

"There is no runway on this field," I pointed out.

"No need, we are getting a chopper."

"One with enough range to get us to Hanoi? There is only one craft that can make that distance. Most helicopters cannot fly more than three hundred miles."

"True, and Grace Mposa is supposed to be piloting this one."

"Oh, it will be nice to see Grace again," Matilda added.

Matilda asked me to try and get Great-aunt Bertha on the phone. She wanted some assurances that the old lady was safe.

"No reply," I said to Matilda. "And voice mail box is full."

"Send her a text. Ask if everything is alright. And say we are okay and hope to be home soon."

I did that and asked William to try as well. His phone could not get through either and he also ended up sending a message.

In the distance we head the dull sounds of the rotors of the approaching craft. It was a gigantic Airbus Helicopter EC 175. It touched down in the middle of the field and we ran up to it. The rotors were still moving and we automatically ducked as we approached the door. It opened and beautiful Grace leaned out.

"Only four of you? I was told six. Where are the other two?"

"We don't know," I said. "We just hope they are safe and away from here already."

"Well, don't waste time. Come on board," she gestured up the small stair ladder that had popped down to the ground.

"Grace, how wonderful to see you," The two women hugged and chatted as they climbed into the cabin. Grace took the pilot's seat and motioned to Matilda to sit next to her. They had a lot to catch up on since Matilda had last seen her in Africa.

"I thought we were getting an Osprey," William complained as we settled down for the trip to Hanoi.

Grace handed out a pair of earphones to each of us. "It's to deaden the rotor sounds while we are flying and so that we can still talk to each other during the flight." A small microphone positioned to one side of our mouths was attached to the phones to pick up and relay our speech. We could hear everyone in the cabin.

"We had heard that you were assigned to this part of the world," I said to Grace.

"Yes, I was brought to Malaysia to be trained to fly an Osprey. Tylo wants to use the bigger bird for moving men and equipment for some of their mining operations. That is my usual craft, but it would not have worked for this operation. It is too big. Sorry William."

322

"Do we have enough fuel to get back to Hanoi?" I asked. Most of the machines I knew only had a limited range.

"We have only the five of us so the chopper is more than half empty, you have almost no luggage and so we are light. Tylo had an additional gas tank installed in this machine. We should make it all the way back to Hanoi and still have a few gallons to spare. We will make it, so relax and enjoy the flight."

And the rotors started thrumming.

Chapter 28 – Great-aunt Bertha Saves the Day

I leaned back in the helicopter seat, fastened the safety harness, and closed my eyes. What had we achieved? Nothing! This was all one big fucking waste of time. We had been placed in jeopardy many times. It was a miracle that no one had died, and to what end? To try and satisfy one man, Mr. Paul Tylo's hunger for revenge. Well we had been thwarted trying to do that. I had had enough of Mr. Tylo. I would be damned if we ever did anything for him again. There would be no bright new orchid preserve and no accomplishment for any of our efforts. This was depressing. I was so not used to failure, and this was a failure if there ever was one. I could not wait to get home and bury myself in my work at the university. I needed to do something very different to get my mind off our current disappointment. Maybe even change the direction of my research and move away from orchid biology.

"Was your project a success?" Grace had asked.

"Not exactly," Matilda answered. "But we are lucky to be alive and that is what counts."

Perhaps, she was correct. We needed to take comfort in what we had achieved, and what we had achieved was staying alive. Beyond that everything was secondary. But I could not shake the cloud of negativity that loomed over my head or the devil sitting on my shoulder whispering insinuations into my ear of failure, failure, failure…

We landed in Hanoi at the Noi Bai International Airport. Grace handed over business class tickets for the four of us to get back to Los Angeles and we said goodbye to her. Told her that if she ever came to the Los Angeles area to look us up. There were spare bedrooms and she would be welcome to visit as long as she wanted. She was flying back to Penang.

Being transit passengers, we were taken to Terminal Two, after clearance for the trip back to Los Angeles. They examined our passports carefully and did not seem at all interested in the fact we had been chartered in by private helicopter from Chiang Mai. Perhaps the Thai authorities were not interested in other countries learning about our escapades. Perhaps they had no extradition treaties with Vietnam. I did not know and I did not care, as long as we were on our way home.

"I'm hungry," William sounded his usual compliant.

"Perhaps we can find a bowl of *Pho ga* or *Pho bo* somewhere?"

"Won't our business class tickets admit us to the airline lounge. There could be free food in there," William was always happy to get free food.

"I know what *Pho* is, isn't it broth with rice noodles and some garnish? But what is *ga* and *bo*?"

"*Ga* is chicken and *bo* is beef," Matilda explained.

"Either or both sounds good," William said. "Let us find that lounge."

There was a *pho* bar in the lounge and we all enjoyed a bowl of soup. After that we settled down in a cluster of easy chairs to wait for the call to board our flight.

"Why are you looking so glum, George?" Jake asked. "You should be happy that we are all safe and sound and on our way home."

"Well, we failed in our mission. We have nothing to show for all our planning. Vicknes bin Osman will still be wandering about Northern Thailand casting his net wherever he wants. He even got a Gold Medal for that damn plant of his. I bet every slipper facebook page has shared the picture of his fabulous plant. Now he will be world famous with every orchid fancier envying his ill gotten gains. Was there any lesson he learned? Great-aunt Bertha should have let him die. Soh Fat is free and can still perform mischief for his boss. Do you really think those horrible monks at the Black Temple learned any lesson. I doubt it. Maybe they will lock the doors next time. That's all. More young people will disappear. What is there to be happy about?"

The bitterness poured out from me in a torrent and the others looked at me aghast.

"Everything you say is true, but look at it from another angle," Matilda said. "We beat the odds. We survived. We are still a family all together," she held her arms open to include William and Jake. "There is still love in the world. You rescued me from a horrible fate. We support each other. No one person can save the entire world. There have always been horrible people and there always will be, but there are good and wonderful people in the world too. Kani and Charlotte were a delight. Buni was worth his weight in gold. And flying snakes are really cool, even if they mistook William's arms for a branch. Nature is wonderful, even the nasty creatures. Unfortunately, some of the most nasty are human. But one mustn't let them get you down. You are, we are all so much finer than those miscreants." She looked around at us. "And I am not just being a Pollyanna," she said adamantly.

"Matilda, my dearest, you have always seen the world more clearly than anyone else. I love you for it," I said feeling somewhat chagrinned.

"Hear, hear," added William and Jake.

"But," I continued, "there is no way that anyone can describe our mission in any way other than as a disaster. We failed in what we set out to do and as a result we lost the chance to create a wonderful conservation project that I had hoped would be a model and an example for others."

We looked at each other.

"Sorry. I shouldn't be a downer, but I can't help it. I feel so disappointed."

Matilda came and put her arms around my shoulders. "Whatever has happened, just remember this: it does nothing to affect how much I respect you and how much I love you. We all feel the disappointment. But we will live through this and there will be other opportunities to do good deeds." She kissed me on the forehead.

"I hope you are right."

But I was not so sure. The world does not mandate happy endings. I was prepared to bet that bin Osman would not even get a slap on the wrist. He was probably in his castle or where-ever warlords hideout, enjoying his emerald orchid, drinking the finest libations and dangling his latest girl on his lap. And what about Soh Fat? I had hoped he was injured when he and the large monk he was being serviced by had been knocked over. Maybe it would hurt him to crap for a while. Would our paths cross again? I owed him a lesson for putting my family in jeopardy but would I ever get the chance to repay his malevolence?

What had happened to Great-aunt Bertha and Wie? I had faith in her resiliency and ability to survive against fierce odds. Had they both escaped? Wie had not been with us when Bertha attacked bin Osman. Perhaps he was free. Would Bertha have been able to bargain their freedom for the antidote to save bin Osman's life or was she now confined to some cell in a Thai prison? When would we ever know? I knew that Matilda must be brooding about that.

As if in answer to my thoughts, Matilda said. "William, check your phone again. Any messages from Great-aunt?"

William fished out his phone, logged onto the WiFi in the lounge and looked at his messages. "Yes, there is another one from Great-aunt."

"What does she say?"

He read out aloud. "Tell Matilda we are safe and in Kota Kinabalu. Staying at the Royal Hotel, if you need to contact us. In a few days we plan to climb the mountain and look for the wild *rothschildianum*. Have found a good guide."

"That's good. I can relax now. Thank God, she is safe."

"Text her that I love her."

"Okay."

So there we were, sitting dejected in the business class lounge when William's phone buzzed again.

"It's another message from Great-aunt Bertha."

"What does she say this time?"

"Ask Matilda what she thought of my little present. The one by the safe."

"What present?" Matilda asked, "George, did you find a present for me from Great-aunt?"

327

At first I could not recall what she was referring to and then I remembered the small package in brown paper. I had put it in my back pack.

"Oh. I forgot. It was sitting on top of the safe in our hotel closet."

"Where is it now?"

"In my backpack," and I dug into it, bringing out the small package and handed it over to Matilda.

"Sorry, I forgot all about it in the rush."

"Wonder what this is? I remember Great-aunt muttering that my birthday was coming up soon and she had found something special she was sure I would like. Must be my birthday present. But that is not until next month."

She tore open the brown paper wrapper and inside was a small wooden box. She opened that. "Look, here are all five of the missing spyder-bots. Great-aunt must have found William's and the two from the flower pot in bin Osman's room. I had left mine with Great-aunt earlier. Hers is here too."

At least we would not be blamed for loosing that technology. It was a partial relief.

"Here, let me see," I said eagerly, perhaps there was still some pollen on my or Jake's bot.

She handed them over, but they had been cleaned. Not a trace of pollen on either of them. The momentary hope was rapidly followed by another downer.

Inside the box was a black velvet jewel case. This must be Matilda's present. She opened it carefully and gave a gasp. Inside was a gold chain and a pendant in the shape of a carved heart. I did not recognize the stone. It looked like a bright green jade, almost emerald in tone but opaque. Running around the perimeter of the heart was fine gold lacing. Matilda placed the pendant around her neck.

"Isn't it beautiful," she purred.

"Yes, lovely," I agreed and fingered it, lifting it up and turning it over in my hand. I felt a groove running around the circumference and I peered more closely. The heart was suspended from the chain by a thick knot of metal. I don't know how I recognized what it was but I tried depressing the knot and the heart came loose in my hand.

"You broke it," Matilda cried.

"No, no, it is a kind of locket. Look there is a tiny hinge on one side and a little clasp on the other." Those were hidden within the gold filigree work and could easily have been overlooked. I held the heart in my open palm and pressed down on the clasp and it opened like a little book. It was hollow on the inside and cradled in one half was what looked like the scarlet false fingernail that would fit on someone with small fingers. Great-aunt had little fingers. She had worn false nails. I tapped it out onto my hand and turned it over. There, cradled under the rim of the nail, were several small honey colored waxy blobs.

"Look at this!" I said excitedly.

"Ear wax?" William said.

"No William. *Rothschildianum* pollen. Great-aunt Bertha must have used her nail to scoop up pollen when she was judging or measuring the flowers, after they had been awarded. It would have been easy for her to do. I wondered why the pollen was missing when my bot was on the plant looking for it."

I closed the nail back inside the locket, attached it to the chain, and hung it back on Matilda's neck.

"Look after that carefully, dear. You have the weight of an entire orchid reserve hanging around your neck!" And I kissed her.

POST SCRIPT

I am often asked who my characters are based on or if I see myself in a certain character. The answer is that I am all of the characters and none of them are based on anyone else in particular. This does not mean that I endorse or agree with everything that my characters say and do. Sometimes they end up doing things that I would never dare.

In an argument with a colleague, who once tried to get me to resign from a conservation advisory panel because he hated one of the other members of that panel, and could not understand why I continued to serve on it, I said to him that I would sleep with the devil if it prevented the extinction of a single orchid species and I stayed on that panel. Years later my statement started me thinking if I really meant it. What one might do if a certain illegal activity resulted in a very much greater good like saving an entire ecosystem filled with orchids. How would I react? And this led to the current story about George and the emerald orchid.

For much of my career I was a university professor in Southern California who taught biology and, I suppose, thus emerges the need I have for explaining about things. Please forgive me for being somewhat pedantic, but it is in my nature and I cannot help it. I hope you enjoy reading this adventure as much as I enjoyed writing it. For me. stories come to life as I write them. I am often forced to sit down and compose (write) so I can find out what is going to happen. Weird, huh?

Just the facts:

All of the biology related in this story is factual, with the exception of the existence of an albino *Paphiopedilum rothschidlianum*. Albino forms, which are unable to make red pigments, are known for many other species in this genus. Albino slipper orchid species always commanded much higher prices than normally colored forms of the species. Among the slipper orchids, *Paphiopedilum rothschildianum* has always been the most prestigious, with enthusiasts prepared to pay astounding prices for better clones. No albino roths are known but such an orchid, if it existed, would command a large fortune, especially if there was only one such plant. All the other orchids mentioned in the story do exist.

Julian is a pleasant little town in the mountains of southern California, known for its apple pie. Whispering Oaks does not exist, but is based on another lovely little inn on the edge of the town.

Flying snakes and little gliding dragons actually occur in Southeast Asia. Whether or not one could get a cloud of them all at once remains to be tested. Unfortunately, the *phajaan* method of training elephants, or crushing their will, still exists in Thailand. With rising tourist expectations for ethical treatment of animals, one hopes that one day *phajaan* will be relegated to the dust heap of history where it belongs. This is also the reason why one no longer sees trained elephants in circuses in civilized countries.

The White Temple, Wat Rong Kuhn, is real and must rank among the most interesting of modern Buddhist temples. The Black Temple, Wat Sida, does not exist, but is based very loosely on the Black Museum, also in Chiang Rai. The Black Museum is filled with skulls, dried skins and furniture made from animal horns and is worth a visit. The monks at the Black Temple in this book, however, are purely a figment of my fevered imagination and have nothing in common with the Black Museum. Such a sect does not exist outside of fiction.

Atrax robustus is the Sydney Funnel-web Spider and exists. It is one of the most venomous of all spiders. Males are particularly toxic and thought to be responsible for at least thirteen recorded deaths. The

331

venom can kill within fifteen minutes but can take longer. An antitoxin is available.

I have used the following formula for dealing with Great-aunt Bertha. When referring directly to Bertha, 'G' is always capitalized. When simply referring to a great-aunt, the 'g' is lower case. I use lower case 'a' in aunt despite my friends who want to see the 'a" in upper case.

The descriptions of cities mentioned here, and their streets, were researched from satellite images, maps, web pages and accounts by other travelers.

Support the Orchid Conservation Alliance

The Orchid Conservation Alliance is a worthy group that deserves your attention. It actually does buy up land in tropical countries for orchid conservation and they have helped to set up a Dracula Preserve in Ecuador, among other projects. They gave George the idea in the first place. Please join them, become a member. Plant species need all the help they can get in this era of forest conversion and global climate change. They can be reached at http://www.orchidconservationalliance.org

Acknowledgements:

A large number of people have encouraged my writing and let me bounce ideas off of them. Others pointed to sources of information.

1. The following are good friends and family members; importantly they are also friendly proof readers, Simone Friend, Stephen Hampson, Lynn Hillman, Karen Muir, and Hendrik van der Hoven who do not hesitate to point out errors and inconsistencies, but also encourage me along the way. I must mention Agi Lovasz separately because she always knows the correct preposition to use and comes up with appropriate words whenever I have trouble getting them to materialize. Carol Beule, who dresses the stars, took me to task for my lack of fashion design sense and made several excellent suggestions about what my characters should wear and I followed her suggestions most of the time.

I appreciate the above friends wading their way through various drafts of this story and making suggestions and pointing out errors and problems. I must admit that I have not always followed their advice. Of course, all errors and inconsistencies are my responsibility.

2. Janyaporn (Katai) Thawornsatisukul was a wonderful host in Thailand who went out of her way to show us a good time in her country, while unbeknownst to her, I was gathering background information for this book. She taught me that in Thailand, fun is an important concept. The Thai people have an intense interest in all plants but I was amazed how orchid growers have great reverence for their native slipper orchids.

3. My thanks to Joanna Vose for preparing the manuscript for publication. She understands the mechanics of getting the manuscript into shape for print and I would be lost without her help. She has worked on *Orchid Digest* projects for many years.

4. My gratitude also goes to Debrah Shaw for her patience in teaching me some of the magic of Adobe® Photoshop®, and her

enthusiastic help in conjuring Steve Hampson's *Paph. rothschildianum* into an emerald orchid for the book cover.

5. Steve Gollis worked on both the cover art and layout. He is the Executive Director of *The Orchid Digest* and also a very good friend.

6. I am indebted to both Google and Wikipedia for the way they were able to facilitate my search for information on the web. It makes one appreciate all the work that must have gone into researching through libraries in the days before we had computers and the World Wide Web for reference.

7. The Orchid Digest Corporation is a not for profit 501(c)3 organization. All profits from the sale of this book go to support publication of the *Orchid Digest Magazine* as well as other books. You can help too, by making donations, giving memberships and *Orchid Digest* books as gifts to your friends. Visit the *Orchid Digest* at http://orchiddigest.org

8. If you enjoyed reading about these characters, you might also enjoy *Orchid Tales; the Adventures of George and Matilda.* This is a collection of short stories. *Diamonds and Disas* is George and Matilda's first full length adventure. Both are available as either an ebook or a paperback on Amazon.com. Again all profits go to the *Orchid Digest* for their publication fund.

9. Keep an eye open for George's next adventure.

About the Author

Harold Koopowitz grew up in the Eastern Cape of South Africa where he spent most of his childhood exploring the plants and animals of the veldt. He has a M.Sc. degree from Rhodes University in South Africa and a Ph.D. from UCLA. Harold lives in Orange County, Southern California where he is Professor Emeritus in Biology at the University of California at Irvine. He has written a number of non-fiction books on conservation and gardening topics as well as over a hundred papers and chapters on scientific topics. His hobbies include breeding orchid and daffodil hybrids and writing. He shares a modest home and very large greenhouse with his husband Stephen Hampson who is horticulturist and proofreader supreme. Harold has been honored with the Herbert Medal from the International Plant Life Society; the Westonbirt Orchid Medal as well as the Ralph B. White Medal for innovation in daffodil breeding both from the Royal Horticultural Society. He has been recognized with the Orchid Digest Medal for meritorious work on orchids as well as Gold Medals from the American Orchid Society and the American Daffodil Society for his contributions to both orchid and daffodil worlds.

www.ingramcontent.com/pod-product-compliance
Lightning Source LLC
Chambersburg PA
CBHW030641260626
47157CB00007B/2432